TO REJECT A MATE

POPPY IRELAND

To Team Poppy: Thank you for not saying we'd lost our minds when we decided to start a new pen name. You may have been thinking it, but we appreciate the fact that you kept that shit to yourselves. 😉

We're forever grateful for all of your help and enthusiastic cheerleading along the way.

CHAPTER

ONE

Nicole

MY FUTURE STARED BACK at me from outside of my father's Honda Civic. Redwood University was situated between two mountain ranges, like a secret tucked away amongst tall trees, sloping hills, and shadows. A blanket of clouds blocked out the sun, giving the landscape a gloomy appearance, and my cell phone lost service about an hour ago, shortly before we passed through the last major town. My last text message to my best friend was "If you don't hear from me, send a search and rescue team."

"What do you think, Nicole?" Dad's voice cracked through my thoughts like a whip as he rolled down his window and took a deep breath of pine-scented air. "It's pretty impressive, right?"

It was... *something*. Redwood University did not offer the sprawling city and skyscrapers I had envisioned, nor did it have the same frenetic pace as New York City, where I had originally intended to study.

I couldn't put my finger on it, but there was something *off* about this place. Don't get me wrong; the campus was beautiful from what I had seen so far—some might even say picturesque in a Gothic sort of way—but it was the exact opposite of anything I had imagined as a child whenever I had thought about going to college. It was too clean. Too quiet.

Too remote.

Truthfully, I was creeped out.

I didn't want Dad to feel bad about bringing me along for the ride. I had plans to attend college at the Parsons School of Design, but he was offered a research position here—his dream job. The free tuition they offered me was too good to pass up, and I didn't want to be across the country from a man whose idea of cooking an elaborate dinner was tossing frozen chicken nuggets in the air fryer. Dad needed me, and I was willing to follow him to the literal middle of nowhere.

"It'll be great," I lied. "Are you excited?"

I shifted the focus onto him, gave him an opportunity to babble about the grant he'd received to continue his studies as a geneticist. He'd been presenting some of his research at a conference when the university approached him. The team here was eager for his talents, and I couldn't blame them. Dad was one of the smartest men in the world.

"Nine Nobel Prize winners, Nicole. Nine! All from this university. Their contemporary approach to genetics just makes me giddy."

I grinned as he took the opening to discuss his work. Dad got excited when it came to science.

"The lab is state of the art, too," he continued. "They already said I had free rein of the PCR machine. I get to play with a piece of equipment that costs ninety-thousand dollars—and get paid to do it, Nicole! I'm just shocked. Not only that, they're giving me a top-of-the-line furnished apartment, and the benefits are out of this world. I'm officially the highest paid researcher in the country. Not to mention, free tuition for you. It feels too good to be true."

"I'm really excited for you, Dad." I *was* excited but couldn't hide the disappointment in my tone as I looked out the window at our new home.

His brown eyes—that bore far too much wisdom for his forty-five years—assessed me carefully. "Are *you* excited about your first year at college? Don't think I didn't notice you tried to change the subject, young lady."

I swallowed, buying myself time to choose my words carefully. Barring a few hormonal teenage exceptions, my dad was my favorite person in the world. The last thing I'd ever want to do was hurt him. Not only was he a lovable teddy bear, but he was a single dad who learned how to do pigtails while splicing DNA. I couldn't imagine how shocking it was for him to check into the hospital so his wife could give birth to their daughter, only to check out as a widower with a newborn in tow. Amid his profound grief, my dad had to navigate life as a working, single father. And with his... quirks, I was sure it was even more challenging. The man was a literal scientific genius, but peopling and nurturing were not his strong suits. Despite this, I'd never doubted his love for me. I knew he was doing the best he could under the circumstances.

"It's not exactly the fashion design capital of the world," I mumbled. "But I'm excited to get started. The course catalog and their internship opportunities are impressive. It's weird how connected the university is, considering it's out in the middle of nowhere."

I picked at my thrifted, upcycled Gucci skirt. The

black silk hit mid-calf, and the studs I added to the seam gave it an edgy look. I'd been buying designer pieces and putting my own spin on them since Dad got me a sewing machine for my seventh birthday. It made sense that I would go to school for design. It was a competitive industry with plenty of dreamers and not enough winners, but if I was getting a free degree at some nowhere university, it would be in something I loved.

"You're going to do great." I could see the pride reflected in his gaze from where I sat. "And you're rushing Mom's old sorority. She would be so proud."

As I brushed my fingers along the gold locket that once belonged to my mother, I smiled. Even though she was gone long before I had the opportunity to know her, I still inherited a lot from the woman. My long brown hair. My curves. My piercing blue eyes. But most importantly, I inherited her love for Beta Phi —the sorority that made her the woman she was. Her sisters lived all over the globe but stepped in as surrogate mother figures in my life. Every birthday, I got a minimum of sixty postcards from successful, thriving women who loved her. I'd always admired the sisterhood and their commitment to Mom, even in death. I craved that sense of community.

She was the president at Beta Phi's Cambridge

University chapter, and I felt closer to her by rushing the one here at Redwood. Dad attended MIT, and they met at a local coffee shop while studying for finals. It was the perfect meet cute.

"Do you want to check out your place first? Or maybe hit the dining hall? I'd scope out pizza delivery, but since I can't seem to get any service, that option's out."

Dad chuckled, glancing at his phone screen. "The chancellor said each apartment is equipped with a landline, but I should probably invest in a signal booster, anyway. Maybe I'll get a second one for your room."

I frowned, feeling itchy at the thought of not having cell phone service. Growing up in Baltimore, that definitely wasn't a problem. Maybe it was just our service provider? I couldn't imagine an entire university full of eighteen- to twenty-two-year-olds would be cool with not having access to their lifelines.

"That would be great, Dad. Thank you. If I didn't check in with Bee, she'd probably send her father after us."

Dad scowled. "That man terrifies me."

His response made me giggle. Beatrice had been my best friend since kindergarten. Her father's job in the army had them moving all over the world, but we kept in contact over the years. We'd perfected the art of long-distance friendship.

"General Minifred is rough around the edges, but he's actually a total softie. Remember that time I lost my blanket at the airport? He had it found and hand-delivered by some guy named *Mr. Smith* in a blacked-out town car."

Dad nodded. "I suppose you're right. He just has such a firm handshake. It's like he enjoys crushing my bones in his fist."

I laughed as we pulled into a parking space. Dad cut off the car, and I let out a sigh. This was it. A strong sense of anticipation took root in my gut. It wasn't that I was excited to be here, but the anxious ball of flutters in my belly was uncontrollable. It was like I suddenly felt the need to explore this place.

"Why don't you get settled while I go scope out my sweet new pad? I'll check in with you soon."

I smiled at his poor attempt to sound cool. That was Dad for you, though. Always trying to be hip, as he called it, but invariably landing somewhere in the vicinity of painfully awkward.

"Sounds good." I took a fortifying breath as I unfastened my seat belt.

The students and faculty of Redwood University lived on campus because it was so remote. However, according to the welcome packet Dad received before our move, the staff housing was at the far end of the thirty-acre forest behind the dormitories. Luckily, I'd already memorized the campus bus schedule so I could make sure he wasn't eating ice cream every night for dinner. Having such a vast divide between students and staff was the university's attempt at creating better work-life balance, I supposed.

Not that my father would know anything about that.

I opened the back door, yanking out my two suitcases with a grunt.

Dad's bushy brows lifted. "You need some help there, kiddo?"

I extended the handles on my bags and gave them a twirl. "Nope. I've got this. Thank God for wheels, right?"

"Right." His eyes sparkled with amusement. "I'll see you later. I feel like I'm supposed to cry while dropping off my only daughter at college, but I'll see you at dinner."

I laughed. Not every kid brought their dad to school, but I was thankful that we could be together. "Love you, old man."

"Love you, too."

I grabbed the email I had printed out from Gretta, the Resident Advisor at my new dorm, and headed toward the building. The instructions had stated she would be waiting for all the arriving freshmen in the front lobby at the welcome station. As I pulled open the heavy door to Cypress Hall, a flurry of activity surrounded me. At least a dozen other students—some eager-looking, while others looked downright terrified—were lined up in front of a folding table that I was guessing was the aforementioned welcome station. A woman, probably a few years older than me, sat behind the table, with a bright smile on her face and colorful braids piled on top of her head. She was talking to the boy at the head of the line. I watched as she handed him a thick manila folder and sent him on his way.

I spotted what looked to be the designated space to park our bags while we checked in, so after dropping my luggage, I took my place in line. That nervous flutter in my chest made me sick. I was naturally an extrovert—I enjoyed being the life of the party and meeting new people. But something about this campus felt instinctively wrong. Perhaps it was the gloomy trees shadowing the grounds, or maybe it was the fact that I didn't originally want to come here. Either way, I couldn't help but feel like a stampede of horses was barreling through my body. My pulse was racing so hard that it almost made me dizzy.

As I stood in line, I eavesdropped on the surrounding people. A beautiful girl with long caramel hair was chatting with her friend behind me. "I can't wait to see him!" She clapped her hands together excitedly. "I heard he's going to be at the party tonight. I picked my best bikini top."

"Get in line, Britt," her equally gorgeous friend replied with a laugh. "*Every* girl—and some boys—at Redwood U can't wait to see him." The black-haired beauty extended her arm, cell phone in hand. "We need to document this on Wolfebytes. Now, smile and say, 'Tenshi is my bestie!'"

"Tenshi is my bestie!" the first girl repeated with a wide grin.

I suppressed a sigh. Man, what I wouldn't give to have Bee here right now. My own best friend decided to take a year off from school to work on a photography series in Italy.

Wait a minute...

"Hey, you have reception up here?" I turned fully toward the pair, waving my phone screen to show them its zero connectivity bars. "Mine completely disappeared about an hour outside of campus." When two sets of carefully sculpted brows pinched together, I realized how abrupt my interruption was. "Oh, I'm sorry. I should probably back up. I'm Nicole Fairweather. Nice to meet you. Are you guys freshmen, too?"

"Um... this *is* freshman move-in day." The black-haired girl—Tenshi, I was guessing—gave me her best *duh* look.

I laughed nervously. "Right. Sorry, I overheard your conversation—not that I was purposely eavesdropping or anything—and you seemed really familiar with this place."

"That's because we *are*." The other one's expression—Britt—mirrored her friend's. "Our sisters are in Beta Phi—that's, like, a sorority, if you didn't know. We hung out here quite a bit last year."

"Oh." I nodded. "That's awesome! I'm rushing, too. I've tried finding information about open rush activities, but nothing is listed on their website. Do you know anything about that?"

A pregnant pause lingered in the air. God, why was I being so awkward? Was there an obvious answer and I was sounding like a total idiot? I was usually much better at meeting new people. It must be the weird vibe this campus had that was throwing me off.

"Um… no," Tenshi answered in a strange tone. "Maybe check the school's announcement board or something." She gave her friend a look, and they both giggled conspiratorially.

I chewed on the inside of my cheek. What was that about? Maybe they considered me competition for rush?

I remembered my original question and gave my phone a little shake to get back on topic. "So... phone reception? Do you have service here?"

"Yes..." Britt's tone couldn't possibly sound more disinterested in this conversation. "But we're from Ridgeview." The *duh* was implied in her tone.

Ridgeview was the closest suburb to Redwood University, about thirty minutes out. As Dad and I were passing through, we marveled over the abundance of gated mansions in such a small, otherwise remote area. It also had a quaint town square with interesting looking shops and cafes. I made a mental note to visit as soon as possible.

"Ah." I nodded in understanding, even though I didn't really understand why being from the same town would affect their reception.

Maybe they both had a local provider? I desperately wanted to ask, but Britt and Tenshi had resumed their selfie session, seemingly over this conversation. "Did you see the Beta Phi update on Wolfebytes? Mara shared a photo of their renovated lounge, and I squealed."

"It's perfection!"

I couldn't help interrupting again. "I'm sorry, what is Wolfebytes?" If there was information about Beta Phi somewhere, maybe it could clue me in on the open rush activities.

The girls glanced at one another again and rolled their eyes in unison.

"You have to receive an *invitation* for Wolfebytes." Tenshi looked me up and down and sniffed the air before continuing. "I wouldn't hold your breath."

What the hell was with these bitches?

I was about to tell them to suck my spiritual dick, but a voice interrupted me.

"Next!" the woman behind the table called.

I took a deep breath and smiled as I approached her. "Hi. I'm Nicole Fairweather. I'm here to check in."

Her full lips curved into a smile. "Hey, Nicole. I'm Gretta, your official Resident Advisor. Welcome to Redwood U and Cypress Hall."

"Thank you." I took the large packet she was offering.

"So..." Gretta nodded to the envelope. "Your room key and a hard-copy map of the campus are in there, plus all of your login information. Your university-issued laptop should be in your room on the desk, so be sure to log on and select a new password ASAP. Protect that password with your life since the student portal will be your go-to place to access your assignments and the campus messaging system. If you click on the home page, you'll find links to dining times and a ton of information about the university's history. If you're interested in athletics or clubs, the list of our available options is in that same section. Tomorrow is our official freshman orientation day, so there'll be tables set up in the student union where you can talk to representatives from each. We will also offer tours of the campus so you can find your classes on Monday. The bookstore will be open all weekend if you still need to purchase any textbooks. While it's not required, I highly recommend you attend orientation so you're prepared for the first day. If you're rushing a sorority, the first event for open rush starts tonight, so if you want to get a feel for Greek life, there'll be plenty of parties all over campus."

Wow. I didn't think she took a breath throughout that entire spiel.

I gave the envelope a little shake. "Thanks. Do you know where the open rush events will be?"

"Did you have a particular sorority in mind?"

"I'll be rushing Beta Phi this year. I'm a legacy." Saying that out loud had me preening with pride.

She sniffed the air and frowned. Why did people keep sniffing me? The last leg of our trip to Redwood U had me feeling greasy, but I'd put deodorant on.

"Well, I'll mark you down as staying in the dorms all year, and if that somehow changes, let me know." She winked as if she had some secret I wasn't in on.

Did she think I wasn't Beta Phi material or something?

Straightening my spine, I responded with a little arrogance, mostly because I was tired of letting this weird place make me uncomfortable. "I'm sure I won't be here for long. It was nice meeting you, though." I winked right back at her and spun on my heels, almost instantly regretting not asking her where the elevator was. According to my packet, I was on the top floor, and it was going to be hell dragging my luggage up six flights of stairs.

I was sifting through my packet, looking for the map, when I hit a hard wall of muscle that nearly knocked the air out of me. My heart started racing as I looked up, and up, and *up*. A tall man with bulging muscles stared down at me in awe, as if I hadn't just rudely bumped into him. His brown eyes were soft as he took in every inch of my face. In a moment of such tenderness, his lips parted and the sharp lines of his face appeared delicate as he stared at me.

"Sorry," I mumbled. "Wasn't watching where I was going."

I felt awkward in his presence. Something about him made my pulse thud and my cheeks turn warm. The guy was attractive, but my body's reaction felt foreign to me. He smelled like freshly cut grass and warmth, which was suddenly the best scent on earth.

His large hand reached up and twisted a lock of my hair. That move would have normally made me slap a man. I didn't like strangers up in my space, but all I could do was stand there like an idiot and gape at him. "Please... tell me your name."

I swallowed. "Nicole."

The strange guy leaned in, and it was then that I realized everyone was staring at us. The girls I had chatted with earlier were shooting daggers my way with their angry glares.

He brushed his lips to my ear and breathed me in. I took a step back, suddenly realizing this was insane. Something about the distance between us seemed to anger him, and he took a step closer.

I backed up some more. "What's *your* name?"

His eyes narrowed, and he looked at me with more clarity than before. "I'm Alexei. Where are you from?"

"Baltimore," I choked out. "Uh... as in *Maryland*. You know, that state on the other side of the country?" *Why was I acting like such an idiot?* "And you?"

Alexei frowned as I retreated once more when he reached for me again. "Something is wrong."

I twisted the fabric of my skirt between my fingers. "I'm sorry? What does that mean?"

Alexei's nostrils flared as his chest rose with a deep inhalation, espresso eyes widening in alarm before he whispered, "*Impossible.*"

My nose scrunched in confusion as he spat out the last word. He spoke in such a low tone. I doubted anyone else had heard him, but there was no way I could miss the harshness behind his statement.

"What's impossible?"

Alexei took a step back and looked around the room, seemingly realizing the audience he'd gathered with his weird behavior. I debated on running from this guy as his chest heaved.

"Are you okay?" I asked him. "Do you need a doctor or something?"

"*Fuck*," he muttered in disbelief while putting more space between us. I watched in confusion as he started pacing back and forth, raking a hand through his dark hair. "This can't be right. My senses must be off. That's the only explanation."

I flattened my body against the opposing wall. "Look, buddy, I don't know what your problem is, but I think you need to chill." I gestured to our gathered audience. Every single person had dropped jaws and rounded eyes.

The psycho stood taller, assessing the crowd with a strange sort of detachment.

"Alexei!" I watched as a guy with dark blond hair sped over to us, looking fresh from an afternoon at the country club. Preppy Boy wrapped an arm around Alexei and gave me a disdainful glance. "Is this freshman bothering you, dude? Been here five minutes and the coeds are already throwing themselves at the school's hottest alpha, huh?"

My eyes narrowed at the newcomer. "I was *not* throwing myself at him."

The asshole chuckled, his expression brimming with arrogance. He looked at the crowd with a smirk. "Sure you weren't. Be careful, darling. You wouldn't want to get eaten by the *big bad wolf.*"

Some people laughed, others had blank expressions on their faces. His insult made no sense, but the tone of his voice made me feel small. I didn't like this guy and the way he was talking to me.

"I do not know what the hell that is supposed to mean. Is this some weird-ass hazing?"

He ignored me. "This chick isn't worth your time, Alexei. She's crazy. Come on, we have a pack meeting to plan for, and if I don't go for a run soon, my wolf is going to chew my ass out."

I gave him a look dripping with indignation. "*I'm* crazy?! You're over here talking about your pet wolf chewing your ass."

My words seemed to stun him. The popped-collar jerk gave me an incredulous look while sniffing the air. *Seriously, what the hell was up with all the sniffing?*

"Interesting. Lemme test this out: Wolf. Alpha. Shifter. Doggy Style."

He stared at me, waiting for a reaction. Around us,

a large group of freshmen had dazed expressions. "If you're asking if I'm down for doggy style, you're insane," I spat.

He turned to Alexei. "We'll need to get that glitch fixed ASAP." His whisper was almost too low for me to comprehend, but the next words out of his mouth were loud enough for the entire lobby to hear. "I don't know what you're talking about. My buddy here isn't interested in someone like *you*, so stop throwing yourself at him." He then looked around, pumping up the crowd with his taunting. "Can you believe this chick?" Something about the way he spoke hinted he was demanding they all agree with him.

The crowd laughed, all of their attention now on my humiliation.

"I just bumped into the guy!" I argued. "It was an accident!"

Alexei was breathing so hard I thought he was going to pass out. His dark eyes were practically feral as he glared at me.

"Unbelievable," Alexei muttered. He pulled away from his annoying friend, then kicked a trash can, sending it flying. Britt and her bestie both screamed as the metal bucket narrowly missed their heads. "Let's go, Corbin."

Corbin pinched the bridge of his nose and mumbled, "I don't get paid enough for this."

My fellow freshmen and I stood frozen as the two men marched out the door. I was surprised the glass didn't shatter from the forceful way Alexei pushed it open. I didn't dare take my eyes off of him until he was completely out of sight. Then, and only then, did I finally allow myself to take a deep breath of relief.

What in the hell had just happened?

CHAPTER
TWO

Alexei

My wolf scratched at my soul as I stormed through the quad, putting as much distance as possible between me and Nicole. My skin itched with the urge to shift, and it was taking every ounce of alpha power I had to contain myself.

What the fuck just happened?

I squeezed my eyes shut for a moment to drown out the thudding in my skull. My senses were going haywire, and every instinct in my body was telling me to go back to her. But it was impossible. There was no way that tiny, helpless human was my mate. There was no way fate was that cruel.

I sensed my beta, Corbin, stalking behind me. He

probably had just as many questions racing through his mind as I had running through mine. "Alexei, what just happened? You know you have to be on your best behavior because Pack Daddy is watching your every move. You had a full audience of freshmen that will gossip for weeks about you freaking out like that."

"Do *not* call my father Pack Daddy. It seriously grosses me out."

Corbin had this uncanny ability to irritate the fuck out of me while simultaneously being the only person I could trust in our pack.

"The containment spell wasn't working on that girl. Should we call your father?" Corbin was out of breath from keeping up with me.

Now that he mentioned it, how *did* she hear Corbin's statement about wolves? When my grandfather founded this university fifty years ago, he paid big bucks to a high witch to cast a containment spell over the campus. I could literally shift in front of a human and they wouldn't see it. Whenever I talked about supernatural affairs, humans thought I was asking for directions. The spell allowed us to coexist while keeping our secret safe.

"Don't call him." Dad didn't like it when I bothered him with shit unless I had all the information and a solution already prepared.

"Let me test it." Corbin stopped in front of a frantic-looking freshman lugging a suitcase half his size up the hill. He reeked of that human stench. "Yo, kid. I was thinking about shifting into a big hairy wolf and humping a fire hydrant later. How does that sound?"

The freshman's eyes glazed over, and he blinked twice before responding. "Oh, yeah, man. I just passed a coffee shop about a block that way." He pointed down the road.

It was a good thing we weren't actually looking for directions, because this idiot was completely wrong. *Freshmen.*

"Yep. Looks like it still works." Corbin rolled his eyes. "Maybe she wasn't human? I didn't get a close enough sniff. I was too busy trying to keep you from creating a PR nightmare. I told you to listen to that meditation podcast I sent you. You can't go off on every human that thinks you're hot. You'll spend all semester pissed off."

"No." I shook my head. "She was *definitely* a human." It was a shock to the system. When I breathed her in, I'd expected to smell that distinct scent of a shifter—of my mate. But the unmistakable aroma a human gave off was most definitely present beneath her lilac perfume. "And that meditation podcast was audio erotica. I don't need some whispering man to tell me to gently stick my hand down my pants, Corbin."

"You're missing out. Getting off works wonders for my mood. Something about his calm, reassuring voice just makes me feel safe during my *me time*."

I rolled my eyes. I didn't want to tell Corbin why I had reacted so strangely. Admitting that I mated a human was not only embarrassing, it was downright shameful. "My senses are off. It's all these damn humans roaming the campus. My wolf is itching to get out and run, but I don't have time for that. My father wants me to attend meetings back to back, and I still need to finalize preparations for open rush activities."

I heard him sigh at my back—I wasn't sure if it was exasperation or relief. "I know you're stressed. Your father always gets extra grumpy and demanding when the humans come back for the fall semester. He doesn't share your grandfather's appreciation for them, that's for sure."

My best friend made a great beta. He was a lot smaller than me, so my wolf never felt threatened by him. Corbin drew his power from his fat bank account and his parents' status within the community, but even as wealthy as they were, they were still no match for my family's holdings.

"After your meetings, we can have a fun night at the house," he suggested. "I've got open rush covered, and Damien is grilling steaks tonight. I bet if you asked him real nice, he'll make yours extra rare."

My inner wolf howled at the thought of devouring a juicy T-bone. And Damien, one of our pack members, was an exceptional cook. His family's personal chef came from a three-star Michelin restaurant and taught him everything she knew. That skill definitely came in handy when you were living in a house full of wolves who were known for their over-the-top appetites.

"Also, we have a photoshoot for *Wolf Weekly* scheduled tomorrow morning, and your pores are in dire need of a facial."

I was used to living in the public eye as the future alpha for our community, but living under a microscope was getting old. I could never mess up, never relax. Someone was always watching, always holding me to a higher standard because I was born to lead our pack.

"Fine," I groaned. "But for the hundredth time, I don't need a damn facial."

"Agree to disagree, dude." Corbin was an impressive multi-tasker. Even while handling me, he was typing away on his phone, probably checking his crypto account for the fifteenth time today and trading stocks like a gambling addict in Vegas. "I've emailed you a list of interview questions and responses. I left the questions about your love life blank, so you'll need to prep some responses for those. Evidently, readers want to know if you're looking for a mate. Everyone is curious who the future luna will be."

Fuck.

How in the hell was I going to keep this from everyone? I knew how I felt. The moment I saw Nicole, it was like my soul was lit on fire. Mating a human was unheard of. But as much as I'd like to deny it... I couldn't forget the feeling that washed over me the moment I spotted her. Gazing into her impossibly blue eyes felt like coming home.

I felt torn. But none of it mattered. Even if she *was* my mate, there was nothing I could do about it. She was a human, and I would be the next alpha of our pack. Not only were there laws against it, but no one would take me seriously if I entertained the idea of being with a human beyond a casual fuck. Whatever just happened couldn't ever happen again. I would just have to keep as far away from her as possible.

My wolf fucking hated that idea. If he was in charge, I'd already be begging for her forgiveness for acting like such a dick. If she were a shifter, I'd get my ass handed to me for behaving in such a volatile way around my mate. It was disrespectful. Luckily, no one cared about an insignificant human.

"I'm going to change into my suit, then meet my father for an investors' meeting. Tell Damien I'll have my steak when I get back." I had to force my feet to move toward our frat house. Corbin started rattling off about pack politics and his latest ventures, but I was consumed with concern for Nicole.

Did she have to move into her dorm by herself? Did she have a roommate? What if she got tired? Or hungry? What if she ran into another dude and he wanted to—

I halted and growled. I couldn't fucking focus if I was worried about her.

"Uh, Alexei?" Corbin frowned. "What's going on with you?"

I clenched my fist.

"Call your sister," I grunted.

"Okay. But why?"

I spun around to face him, my chest rising and falling with each labored breath. Fuck. I needed to sort my shit out, but I couldn't do that if my wolf was freaking the fuck out about Nicole. "Tell her to monitor the girl we had a problem with in Cypress Hall. Have Mara pump her for information and send me updates. I want to know *everything*. Why she's here. Where exactly she came from. *What* she is. And if she *is* human, we need to double-check that the containment spell isn't glitching."

Mara wasn't the most trustworthy, but I didn't have many options. Not if I wanted to keep this a secret. My wolf howled within me, angry that I was letting Mara anywhere near our mate. It needed to fuck off and get in line. I couldn't be with a human. I just had to figure out what the hell was happening to me, and this was a good way to manage how I was feeling while doing a little research.

Corbin stared incredulously at me. "You want *my sister* to follow that chick around? What's going on? Is there something you're not telling me?" I was acting like a new mate, but it hadn't even occurred to Corbin that Nicole was fated to me.

Good.

"Yes. I think she could be trouble if the containment spell isn't working on her, and your sister is the only person who can erase her memory if she sees something she shouldn't."

"I'll text her now." His thumbs flew across his phone screen and, within seconds, it pinged with an incoming message. "Done. Mara is on the job. Although, don't be surprised if she tries to get a date out of it."

Corbin's sister was a useful member of the pack. She was one of the strongest influencers—wolves who were gifted with the power of persuasion—on the West Coast. Those psychic abilities were becoming rarer with each new generation, but the power itself was somehow becoming more concentrated. Having an influencer in your pack made getting information and forging connections considerably easier than threatening or torturing ever could.

But as valuable as Mara was, she was also a notorious clout-chaser. Because I was alpha, she'd had her sights set on me for years, and that girl was determined to elevate her rank. She went through a phase where she thought dating lesser members of the pack would make me jealous, but all it did was make me want her less. Thankfully, as an alpha, I was blessed with immunity from her gift, but the rest of the human and shifter population were not. And since humans were inherently weaker in every respect, they were the most vulnerable of all. I knew Nicole would call Mara a friend within the next twenty-four hours, divulging all of her deepest, darkest secrets.

I scoffed. "Mara needs to stop thinking that will *ever* happen."

Especially now that I'd found my mate. Not that I could *be* with my mate.

Pack politics were complicated.

We walked to the frat house, and every step had me growing more agitated. I wished I had a pledge so I could punch my frustrations out, but I had to be on my best behavior. Every shifter who was worth a damn was in our frat, Alpha Nu. If you were accepted, then you were guaranteed a spot in pack leadership. My position as future alpha was highly coveted, which meant the house was full of shifters spying on me and looking for any opportunity to rip me from my throne. This year, since I was president, there was a certain expectation to be the best. We needed the strongest pledge class, and I was determined to show everyone how capable I was.

They're still telling stories about my father, Alpha Jones. There was a photo of him in the lounge at our frat house, and I had to greet his smug face before class every morning. My father was an incredible alpha, but I was sick of being compared to him.

Alexei isn't as strong as Jones.

Alexei is more hotheaded.

Alexei is falling behind in school.

Maybe Alexei isn't the man for the job.

Being Alpha Nu's president was like a test run for the real thing. Everyone was watching to see how I'd handle leadership. Many were hoping I'd fail. Weakness wasn't an option.

Being mated to a fucking human wasn't an option, either.

They already doubted me. This could be the nail in my coffin. If word got out, wolves from all over our territory would challenge me to the death for my birthright. A strong mate was a good indicator of a powerful alpha, so what did mating a human say about me?

Corbin hooked an arm over my shoulder, pulling me into his side. "Yeah, well, in case you haven't noticed, Mara is tenacious, if nothing else. And *you*, my friend, are the biggest, juiciest bone she could possibly sink her teeth into." He laughed. "I'm pretty sure she won't be backing off until you meet your mate. And between you and me, accepting defeat would be purely out of self-preservation. She knows she's not formidable enough to challenge an alpha bitch."

No, but Mara *was* strong enough in her wolf form to snap a human's neck in half within seconds.

A growl rumbled from deep within my chest. "If she fucking tries, I'll kill her."

"Whoa, man." Corbin held his hands up in the universal gesture for *calm the fuck down*. "I'm sure that would *never* happen. When the fates choose your mate, she's going to be the baddest bitch around. I'm sure all she'll need to do is give Mara one stern look, and she'll go running with her tail between her legs." He took a deep breath, inhaling the aroma of red meat being seared over the grates. "Now, loosen up. After your meeting, we've got the party, where there'll be plenty of women begging to put a smile on your face.

And I'll be right by your side, waiting to console the ones you turn away."

I gave him a wry look. "So, just your average night, then?"

He wagged his brows as his lips quirked. "Exactly. Beta Perks 101, bro."

"This year needs to be perfect." I clenched my fist. "Dad is watching me. If I fuck up..."

Corbin softened a bit, the playful arrogance leaving his expression. "I know you're under a lot of pressure, but you got me, dude. I won't let you fuck this up. My future job is also on the line." He shoved me with a laugh, and my frown deepened. It wasn't like I needed the added pressure of my best friend's future on my shoulders, too. "You got this. *We* got this. No stress. Maybe you need to get laid, find some nice lady to rub the stress outta your dick."

I rolled my eyes. Corbin thought any ailment could be cured if he stuck his cock in a willing female.

"Yeah. You're right. I need to work through some of my stress." My mind instantly went back to that tight little skirt Nicole was wearing and the way it clung to her long legs. I wanted nothing more than to pry her legs apart and—

Corbin punched me in the shoulder. "You're thinking about it now, right? Yes, you need to get laid.

STAT. As your beta, I'm making it my mission tonight."

My wolf whined at the idea of being with anyone but Nicole. I just hoped I could quiet the animal inside of me long enough to fuck her out of my system for good.

THREE

Nicole

TODAY WAS WEIRD. I was still reeling from that strange run-in with the angry-ass roids dude and his asshole friend downstairs in the lobby. Everywhere I went, people stared at me and whispered. Apparently, they were both a big deal on campus, and everyone saw how they accused me of throwing myself at Alexei. I literally couldn't have started my year off any worse.

And for what? They were so odd, trying to make everyone think it was *me* hitting on *him*. He was the one practically begging for my name and crowding my space. And what the hell was that part about being eaten by a big bad wolf? Maybe the guy was high out of his mind. Maybe by tomorrow all of this would blow over. *Maybe* I would have been better off attending Parsons.

"Knock, knock!" a sultry voice said before opening my door. I was literally in the middle of changing into some yoga pants and a crop top when a complete stranger just waltzed into my room. "Oh, look how cute you are!"

I quickly pulled my pants up. "Hi, um, hello? Can I help you?"

I was forcing myself to be polite despite the gross invasion of privacy, if only to turn this day around.

"Nicole, right?" She spun her blonde hair around her finger and smiled. "My name is Mara, and we're going to be best friends."

Well, she just jumped right into it, didn't she?

"Oh? How did you know my name anyway?"

"I asked your RA." She waltzed over to my closet and started sifting through my clothes.

I used all my anxious energy earlier to set up my single bedroom. My mauve comforter was begging me to go to bed and read something to get my mind off the day, but now this Mara was picking up my framed photos and inspecting them.

What was with this girl? "What were you saying about friends?"

"After today, you could really use someone in your corner. Alexei was acting so strange, don't you think?"

I sighed in relief. Either she was fishing for information to bring back to others or she was genuinely taking pity on me for earlier. Either way, beggars couldn't be choosers. "It was weird for sure. I accidentally bumped into him, and he got super pissed off about it."

She looked me up and down while pulling out my favorite mini bodycon dress. It was a light nude color that looked pretty against my bronze skin. "Alexei doesn't normally associate with... What are you, anyway?"

I frowned in confusion. "A freshman? Is that what you're asking?"

The nostrils on her pert nose flared as she considered that. "Right... a *freshman*. Alexei rarely associates with freshmen. I think it would be best to just stay away from him."

I laughed. "You don't have to tell me twice."

Mara threw the dress at me. *"You'll wear this tonight."*

I shook my head as her voice ricocheted through my skull. I nearly ripped off my clothes and put on the dress right then and there at her command. "Um... why would I do that?"

"Because the welcome back party is tonight. You want to look hot, don't you? All the Greek houses are co-hosting, so everyone who's anyone will be there."

"Okay…" I already knew about the party since it was all anybody seemed to talk about in the halls, but I wasn't planning on going. I was still feeling unsettled about what had happened earlier and needed time to process and gain some confidence. "But considering I wasn't planning to attend, I think my current outfit will work just fine."

Mara's green eyes widened. "*Not going?!*" Her tone implied my statement was the most ridiculous thing she'd ever heard. "*Of course* you're going. How else am I supposed to introduce you to some of the most delectable single guys Redwood U has to offer?"

"I'm not really looking for—"

"C'mon, Nicole," she tsked. "You don't need to be coy with me. *Everyone* hooks up. This is college! It's, like, a rite of passage or whatever. And lucky for you, since I've decided we're going to be the best of friends, I shall pass my knowledge of all the dos and do nots of the male student body onto you." She tilted her head to the side, as if something had just occurred to her. "Unless you're already seeing someone? *Tell me if you're seeing someone.*"

"I'm not seeing anyone." I stretched my jaw, surprised by how quickly I'd answered.

"Oh! Are you into girls? Because if that's the case, just say the word. I can still point you in the right direction. Or warn you off from the scary bitches around campus."

I shook my head. "Boys are fine, but I really wasn't looking to party tonight."

What I really wanted to do was check on Dad and figure out dinner, but he got the number to the landline in my room from the student directory and called a while back, saying he was tied up. Unsurprisingly, while I was getting settled in my new room, he was checking out his new lab. Knowing my dad, I bet he took one look at the place, and his brain instantly kicked into gear, demanding he get to work on his research.

"Is this about Alexei?" Her tone was a smidge condescending. "You can't let him scare you off. By tonight, no one will remember what happened earlier. You should go out and have fun."

"I'm not scared of him." It was important to me that she understood I wasn't the type to cower. "I'm just tired. Dad and I drove all day, and he wants to meet tomorrow for an early breakfast."

"Aw, that's sweet. Your dad stayed to make sure you got settled. We can go meet him if you'd like?" Wow. She already wanted to meet my dad? She was really asserting herself in my life.

I scratched the back of my neck. "He's busy getting

set up at the lab tonight. He's working at the university."

Her brow arched, and I swore I saw a flare of interest in her eyes. "Oh? How interesting." She pulled out her cell and typed something before sticking it in her back pocket.

"Yeah. Sure." Something about this girl wasn't right. "So, anyway. I'm just tired. I'm going to curl up with a book and get some rest."

"*No.*" Her voice washed over me like ice. My muscles tensed at the tone. "*You're coming with me to the party.*"

"I'm coming with you to the party," I repeated, my voice dazed as I spoke.

"*We're going to be best friends.*"

"The best," I echoed. My gut was swirling with anxiety, but she seemed so nice and welcoming. She just wanted me to make friends and have the full college experience, right? How nice of her to take me under her wing. And gosh, up close, she was even more beautiful.

"*You love me, don't you? Everyone loves me. Everyone wants to be me.*"

"I can't believe you're spending time with me," I gushed. "I mean, you're... you."

She nodded enthusiastically, and a sour taste flooded my tongue. What was I just saying? "Go ahead and take a shower, love. I'll curl your hair. We're going to have a great time."

I still didn't want to go but couldn't find it in me to argue with her. "Okay." I grabbed my toiletries and robe. "I'll just go, uh, shower."

She plopped on my soft bed, and I stared at it with longing. Pulling out her phone, she dialed a number and smiled as I walked out. The last thing I heard was her speaking to someone on the other line.

"She's coming."

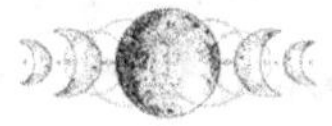

THE PARTY WAS in full swing by the time Mara and I arrived. She spent thirty minutes explaining the importance of showing up late and making an *entrance*, and boy, did she make one. Evidently, she had planned on getting ready in my room and had a change of clothes stashed in her bag just for the occasion. Now, she was wearing a silver bathing suit top and black booty shorts that left little to the imagination. Her long blonde hair was in large curls all the way down her back. She had on tasteful makeup and glossy lips that shimmered in the moon's light.

I did *not* wear the bodycon dress. When I'd put it

on, Mara scowled, saying that it wasn't the right vibe for the night and that I needed to wear something less dressy. She settled on shorts that were slightly big on me and a black, high-neck tank. I looked a little sloppy compared to her, but the way she beamed when I got dressed made me feel beautiful. Mara had this way about her I couldn't put my finger on.

"Go get me a drink, Nicole." She scanned the crowd as if she were looking for someone in particular.

"Yeah, okay!" I hesitated a little. I didn't want to go by myself but also didn't want to upset her. She grinned like a Cheshire cat before swaying through the crowd of coeds toward a tall man whose back was to us. Something about the gleam in her eye made my stomach twist, but I chalked it up to nerves.

A bunch of guys stood at the cooler, towering over me in an intimidating way. They all had bright smiles, bulging muscles, and matching shirts with a fraternity symbol I didn't recognize.

"Um, hello? May I grab a beer?"

Was I supposed to ask? Was anyone allowed to grab one? What if it was a BYOB situation? I'd never been to a college party and didn't exactly know how this worked. Whenever I partied at Jimmy's house in high school, we all contributed ten bucks to the keg his older brother bought for us.

One of them had bright blue eyes and a dimple on

his cheek that looked both rugged and adorable. In the shadow of night, I noticed some scruff on his jawline. "You can have whatever you'd like, gorgeous." He shoved one of his friends in the chest and took a step closer to me. I breathed in, the smell of cologne on his skin mixed with a musk that was both sexy and manly.

I nervously tucked my hair behind my ear. I'd decided not to wear makeup today at Mara's request, but kind of wished I would have. This guy was seriously hot.

"A beer, please." I smiled. "And a White Claw." I wasn't sure what Mara liked, so I figured having options would be best. "I'm Nicole, by the way." I jutted my hand out to shake his like a fucking idiot.

"Cristian." He winked before grabbing my hand and kissing the top of it. "Nice to meet you. Freshman? I haven't seen you around before."

"Yep," I replied, popping the *p*.

He lowered his voice and leaned in. "What are you? Belong to any clubs?"

I cleared my throat. *What am I?* I'd already told him I was a freshman. Maybe he wanted to know about my major. "I'm a fashion major?" I answered, feeling dumb. "And not yet. I'm going to rush my mom's old sorority, Beta Phi."

He nodded, like that answer held more meaning

than I intended it to. "Shame. I'm in Rho Eta Theta." One of the nearby guys laughed. "We rarely mingle with the shifters of Beta Phi, but some ladies like to take a walk on the wild side occasionally."

I frowned. Shifters? Was that some derogatory term? Corbin had said that word too. Maybe it was meant to be an insult. I tried to salvage the conversation, though I was slightly embarrassed. "Are you from around here? Seems like everyone I've met so far is from Ridgeview."

He smiled. "My friends and I are actually from Canada. We're a part of the exchange program the university started up a few years ago." Wow! I wasn't expecting that. I briefly wondered if they had other programs available. I'd kill to spend a semester in Paris. Maybe I could attend fashion week.

Not that I'd ever leave Dad here. But maybe after he'd had a few semesters to settle. I could make a bunch of freezer meals... set up a housekeeper... Yeah. Maybe...

"How long are you here for?" I asked.

"I'll go back to my clan after graduation."

Clan? The only people I knew who used that word to refer to their family were between the pages of a Highlander romance novel.

"Cool." Cristian's gaze honed in on my bottom lip as I pressed my teeth into it.

"So, Nicole, who's the second drink for?" He handed me a can of Coors and a hard seltzer.

"Oh... um, this girl, Mara. I came with her."

"Really, now?" His head tilted as he took another step closer. We were practically chest to chest, and I had to crane my neck to look up at him. "You're with Mara's crew, then? A Beta Phi girl that hangs out with Mara but smells just like a *human*. How curious."

I sucked in a deep breath as he reached out and traced my jawline with his index finger. I was positive he could feel the frantic beating of my heart as that finger slid down the slope of my neck, pausing over my pulse point. It was strange; this guy moved his body with unnatural grace. He had this... presence about him that was larger than life. And disturbingly sexual. What was it about this university? Were all the guys exceptionally attractive and touchy-feely?

I blinked and the next thing I knew, Cristian's hot breath was wafting over my neck. "A shame, really. We could've had so much fun." I stiffened as his tongue peeked out and wet my skin. "Maybe we still can. You certainly don't smell like a mutt."

What did he just say?!

I reared back. "Excuse me?"

Cristian smiled, his white teeth glinting in the moonlight. Man, he had some serious canines. Ironic, considering he just referred to *me* as a dog. My eyes must've been playing tricks on me, because in the next breath, they seemed normal again.

"There you are!" Mara's voice called from behind me.

The living god before me stood to his full height as she came to my side. "Mara."

"Cristian," she purred. "I see you've met my friend, Nicole."

His full lips stretched into a wicked grin. "I have. And what a lovely *friend* she is. Have you known her for long?"

"Long enough to know she's too good for *a vampire*," Mara spat.

Why were they talking about me like I wasn't right here? And what the hell did she just call him?

He laughed. "Aw, Mar, jealousy looks hot on you. It's been a while. Wanna go somewhere and *catch up*?"

Any idiot could decode the double meaning behind that phrase. Mara looked around as if worried someone had heard them. "That was a one-time thing. You know I'm not supposed to fuck vamps."

That was the second time Mara had referred to him as a vampire. It made me snort, the sound unattractive and drawing their attention. "Vampire? Did he suck the orgasms out of your soul?"

They both raised their eyebrows in shock before

Mara muttered, "I guess that answers the question about the containment spell."

"Spell?" I shook my head. "*What* spell? And why did you call him a vampire?"

"*I didn't say a word about spells or call him a vampire,*" Mara denied. "*We're having a normal conversation. I called him a dick.*"

That same strange sensation of feeling drawn to Mara's words washed over me. I shook my head and turned to Cristian. "You're a massive dick."

He preened. "I do *have* a massive dick. Mara knows all about it."

"Rules!" Mara yelled.

"I'm not a big fan of silly things like *rules*. In fact, I feel like breaking a few of them right now with your friend Nicole," Cristian purred.

Yeah, no. Something about him was definitely off. And I didn't want to piss Mara off by messing around with someone she obviously had been with.

Mara looked over her shoulder for a moment before turning her attention back to us. "She's not one of us, Cristian. Which means she's fair game, though I doubt she'd lower her standards for someone with your particular *tastes*."

"Does your alpha know the containment spell isn't working on *this* human? Because I know it's working just fine on the others."

A million thoughts raced through my mind, and Mara groaned before glaring at me. Her words rattled my brain and made me dizzy. *"There are no such things as spells."*

I echoed her, my mind in a daze. "No such thing as spells."

Cristian's eyes widened for a moment, pleasure dripping from his expression. "I didn't think you were the type to venture outside of your friend group, Mara, but I'm glad you did. I haven't claimed a feeder yet, and she smells delicious."

My heart started racing, and I stared at him in shock. The truth felt like it was just within grasp, but Mara kept yanking me back down to reality.

"Cristian!" she cursed before speaking once more to me. *"You have nothing to be afraid of, Nicole."*

"I'm not afraid," I whispered.

Mara turned back to Cristian, scowling at him. "I was... compelled to meet her and show her the ropes. Stop fucking with her. I want to have fun tonight, not babysit."

"Interesting." His grin was devious. *"Very* interesting."

Meanwhile, I was losing *interest* with every word that left his perfect mouth. "Well, it was... nice... meeting you, Cristian. I suppose."

I spun on my heels, prepared to leave and try to

salvage the rest of the night in the company of someone less weird and offensive, when a hand wrapped around my wrist, and I was pulled into a hard chest. "I'm sorry, gorgeous. I was just feeling you out. This school is full of cliques, and people can be pretty territorial of their friends."

I struggled against his hold as Mara watched us with annoyance.

"If you think flirting with someone in front of me is going to win me back, you're severely mistaken, Cristian," she grumbled.

"I'm not doing this for *you*, Mara." He leaned in to brush his lips along my neck, and a shiver of lust traveled through me. My eyes were fuzzy and Mara's words played on repeat in my mind. But Cristian smelled good. *Really* good. He splayed his hands across my stomach and pulled me tighter against him. The pressure in his fingertips guided me in a seductive way that had my chest heaving up and down. What the hell was wrong with me? I was embarrassing myself in front of my new friend, but it was like I couldn't tear myself away. "Do you feel that, Nicole? Your pulse is racing from my touch. Oh, yes. We could have a *lot* of fun."

Mara had this disgusted look on her face. "Aren't you bored, Cristian? It's hardly a challenge."

I frowned and shook my head. *What the hell was she implying?*

Cristian chuckled. "Sometimes it's nice to have someone obedient. I enjoy submission. Perhaps you could try being a little more agreeable to your alpha and he'll give you a chance."

At that, Mara scowled. "Fuck you, Cristian." She ripped the White Claw from my hand and stalked away, leaving me with this manhandling stranger without a second glance. Once she was gone, Cristian turned me around to face him, our mouths barely an inch away.

Why the fuck couldn't I escape him?

"Now," he rasped. "Where were we?"

My hooded eyes were heavy with desire as I tilted my chin up. "I-I don't..." I couldn't finish my sentence. I felt like someone had drugged me. He leaned closer, the sharp tips of his teeth delicately scraping my neck.

A low growl boomed through the party, and Cristian snapped his head up. Eyes wide, he dropped his hold on me immediately.

I blinked rapidly as the fog lifted, trying to figure out where that noise came from. Was there an animal nearby? Shouldn't we all be running?

"Luca, care to explain what. The. Fuck. You think you're doing?"

I'd know that deep voice anywhere. Which was

strange, considering I didn't really know *anyone* at this party. *Who the hell was Luca?*

The crowd of onlookers parted as Alexei stalked toward me, wearing a fitted T-shirt and a pair of distressed jeans. His chest was heaving, his nostrils flaring. But the fury in his gaze wasn't directed at me. He was looking over my shoulder.

I stepped to the side, creating as much distance as possible between me, Cristian, and the hothead. I didn't know what was happening, but I knew I didn't want to be in the middle of it. Before I could get too far, though, another hand clamped around my wrist. When I looked up, I was shocked to find Mara holding on to me. Her grip was surprisingly strong for someone with such a delicate frame.

"Mara! Let me go!" I whisper-shouted, not wanting to draw too much attention to myself.

"Stay," she commanded, releasing me from her grasp.

Although many warning bells were going off in my head, I couldn't seem to gather the will to leave.

I was startled as Alexei and Cristian stood toe-to-toe, practically snarling in each other's faces.

"Who's Luca?" I found myself asking her.

Mara pointed one perfectly manicured nail toward the two men. "Cristian *Luca*. He's the president of Rho Eta Theta. And Alexei is the president of Alpha Nu."

Ah, Cristian's reference to an alpha earlier now made sense. Sorta.

"So, this is about some weird frat rivalry?"

"Something like that. Look, I don't know why Alexei has such a sudden interest in someone like *you*," Mara huffed in annoyance. "But clearly, he *does*, which means you need to heel."

Heel? What was she talking about?

"What's that supposed to mean?"

"I asked you a question, Luca." My head whipped up at the venom in Alexei's voice.

Cristian schooled his expression and smirked. "I was just having a little fun and getting to know Nicole here. She's lovely."

Once again, everyone was watching a showdown involving Alexei and me. Part of me was thankful that he interrupted whatever was happening with Cristian, but I didn't get what he was after.

"Stay away from her," Alexei growled.

Then Corbin appeared. He scrambled up to Alexei and grabbed his arm insistently while muttering something in his ear, likely trying to talk his friend off the edge.

Cristian walked up to me and wrapped his hand around my waist. Once again, that intoxicating smell wafted over me, and I felt my eyes grow heavy. "Is she one of yours?" Cristian looked around the growing crowd. "Because if she's available, I'm in the market for a feeder, and I think she's the *perfect* candidate."

Alexei opened his mouth to respond but snapped it shut when Corbin tugged on his arm. My mind was nothing but a dizzy echo. Alexei looked at his friend, then back at me, seemingly deciding something in an instant.

"Corbin claimed her. She's off-limits."

A few gasps came from the students. Even Mara dropped her mouth open in shock. My gaze turned to look at Corbin, who had to quickly school his expression into something that looked like a mixture of confusion and sincerity.

I snorted. "*Claimed* me? Is this a joke? This asshole was making fun of me a few hours ago."

"It's true." Corbin looked around and shrugged. "I, um, called dibs. Yep. She's mine, ha ha ha..." Then, he winked at me.

That statement was enough to clear the remaining fog in my mind. *Dibs?* Was this guy serious? I shrugged out of Cristian's grip, marching over to the preppy douche.

I poked Corbin in the chest and scowled. He was cute, but I did a full stop at misogynist. "First of all, women aren't a piece of pie you can call dibs on. I wouldn't date you if you were the last *big bad wolf* on campus." I was referencing his weird-ass comment from earlier.

Apparently, enough people had heard about our brief argument at the dorm, because the crowd started roaring with laughter, Cristian included. I ignored them. "Second of all," I began while whirling around to face Cristian. "I'm not sure what your deal is, but you need to learn the meaning of personal space."

Cristian shrugged as if he knew this but wouldn't be changing his behavior anytime soon.

"And *you*." I moved in front of Alexei, who stiffened as I got closer. "You keep showing up and..." I paused to lower my voice. "*Embarrassing me*. I'm sorry for running into you earlier, but it was an *accident*. Please just leave me alone."

Alexei's face twisted into a flash of pain that was so quick I wouldn't have noticed it had I not been paying attention. He leaned down, our faces close together. "I'm sure I'll be seeing you a lot this year. Expect a text from Corbin soon."

What the shit?

I stood there, dumbfounded, as Alexei and Corbin turned their backs to me and walked away. I didn't like that he had the last word, so in a last-ditch effort to save face, I shouted, "Good luck! My phone doesn't even work in this stupid-ass town."

Mara swung an arm around my shoulders. "I can't say I've ever seen that happen before. My brother isn't the type to claim any girl, let alone a... erm, a brunette." She laughed. "He usually goes after blondes."

I was still terribly confused, rolling the last ten minutes around in my head.

Wait a second...

I turned to Mara. "Brother?"

Mara's bright smile sent a calming wave of energy through me. "Yes, my brother. Corbin. The one who called 'dibs.' I'm sure he has an excellent reason for staking a claim like that. It looks like I'll have to investigate. Those two are up to something."

I frowned. "What do you mean?"

"Oh, it doesn't matter. It's nothing you need to worry your pretty little head about."

I didn't like her condescending tone. "Mara, what's going on? I feel like I'm missing a *really* big chunk of information, but for the life of me, I can't figure out what that is."

Her stunning grin was back in place. "What's there to know? My new bestie is dating my brother! I'm so excited for you! Aren't *you* excited? *You must be really excited.*"

Her words washed over me, but my mind felt

foggy. I wanted to be excited with Mara but couldn't quite force myself to think this was okay.

"Your brother *didn't* ask me out," I corrected. "He said *dibs*. In order for us to be dating, he has to actually, like, be a decent person, introduce himself, and ask me on a date. Not call dibs. Please tell him thanks but no thanks." I crossed my arms over my chest.

Mara's eyes turned cruel, an angry expression crossing her features. "Are you saying my brother isn't good enough for you?"

Yes. That was *exactly* what I was saying, but I didn't want to piss her off.

"I don't know him," I countered. "I'm sure your brother is nice, but I prefer a man who gets to know me first. It was a little too caveman for my tastes."

Mara furrowed her brow. "Damn, I shouldn't have chugged that White Claw. I'm a little off. I don't think you heard me, Nicole. *You must be very, very excited. My brother is a catch. He's going to make you incredibly happy.*" She stared at me, her eyes boring into mine. She paused to gag. "*Corbin is so... hot.*"

Now that she mentioned it, Corbin *was* pretty hot. And the fact that he claimed me in front of everyone? I was *honored*. "You're right. He's great."

Mara nodded. "*Corbin is the best. You're going to treat him very well, Nicole. Think about him all the time, and when he contacts you, be sure to do whatever he says.*"

I blinked twice. "Whatever he says. I can't stop thinking about him."

"Perfect. I'm so glad you agree! *It's going to be great, babe.*" Mara gave me a blinding smile.

Mara was so awesome. I couldn't believe how lucky I was to have her helping me. "Great," I echoed.

I waited for Mara to tell me more about her *amazing* brother, but she was staring off at the crowd, her eyes locked on Alexei and her lips pressed into a fine line. I wanted to ask her what she was thinking about, but I was too busy obsessing over *Corbin.*

Alexei

"FATED MATES, Alexei?! Don't you think I deserved a heads-up?! I was supposed to be chasing pussy this year, not locking myself down with a *human*." Corbin spat out that word like it was a curse, and my wolf wanted to rip him to shreds. The mere thought of him spending time with Nicole made me rage, but this was the only way. I wasn't about to stand by while fucking *Cristian Luca* claimed her as one of his blood whores. Anyone in the pack was off-limits to the vampires, so I did it to keep her safe. I wanted to be close to her, but I couldn't let my pack know that my fated mate wasn't a wolf.

We were sitting in my room at the frat house. I'd

spent the last hour pacing the floors and updating Corbin on everything. I knew I could trust him with the truth, but his reaction still frustrated me.

"I'm sorry," I groaned. "I was trying to figure shit out. I was just so mad when I saw fucking Luca with his hands all over her. Goddamn bloodsucker."

"What exactly is your plan here?" Corbin questioned. "I can't actually claim her. For starters, you look like you're about to rip my throat out. But also, you're not the only one with family obligations. My dad would *kill* me. Mara is probably calling him right now."

"I just need you to pretend. It's an easy way to keep her close. You don't even have to really talk to her. I'll be the one texting her. In fact, if you could just never speak to her, that would be ideal."

Corbin grinned. "Worried I'll steal your girl because I'm the better-looking one?"

My wolf growled, making him laugh.

He held up his hands. "Calm down, I'm not interested, and I don't want to piss off the future alpha. You seriously need to figure out how to break this bond, though. You'll never be alpha with a human mate."

Corbin was right. Maybe it was wrong to do this, because I was just prolonging the inevitable. I hated being in this position.

I sighed. "I'll figure it out. But I need to talk to her. I'm wired. I can't even fucking function."

"That sucks, dude. I couldn't even imagine mating a human. They're so weak and vulnerable."

Another thing he was correct about. It felt like every single person on this campus was a threat to Nicole. She was already on the vampire's radar. What if she befriended a witch—or worse, a fae? The university was meant to build alliances between each supernatural faction, but sometimes it did more harm than good. I'd start a fucking war if any of them hurt her.

"Knock knock," Mara's voice rang as she pried open my door and let herself in.

I glared at her in response. She was always invading my personal space, and now that I was a mated man, her presence infuriated me even more.

Mara continued as if I wasn't trying to murder her with my eyes. "Are we talking about the human? I want in on whatever prank you're planning. She's *so* annoying. You seriously need to call your father's team of witches about the containment spell over the university, Alexei. I had to keep compelling her to forget shit she saw. It was *exhausting*. I kind of wish Cristian would have used her as a blood bag. Maybe I could have actually enjoyed the party."

I had to fight the urge to grab her by the neck and

toss her out of here for threatening my mate. "I'm working on the containment spell problem."

"So what's the deal with her, anyway?" Mara asked.

"We just want to monitor her." Corbin scratched his chin, a visible sign the wheels in his brain were turning.

"Why?" Mara's lips twisted. "She's nothing special."

Corbin looked at me. We had to play this carefully. If Mara knew the truth, she'd use it to blackmail me.

He shrugged. "She challenged Alexei, and the containment spell isn't working on her. You know we can't let a human walk around knowing what we are."

"Does this mean I have to keep babysitting her? You know I can't compel people when I drink. I don't want to spend my semester sober, Corbin," Mara whined. "She's a dumb-ass human. Let's just get rid of her and be done with it."

I swallowed my anger, the venom I wanted to spew swirling in my gut.

"Mara," Corbin warned while eyeing me. He knew I was on the edge of losing it. "You know how important this year is to Alexei. We need to prove to Alpha Jones that we can handle this. Are you saying you don't want to help the future alpha of our pack?"

Corbin was hitting her where she was most insecure. Mara wanted to be useful so she could get close to me. I didn't like where this was going. Mara was reckless, jealous, and careless. Involving her any more than necessary was a risk, but we had no other choice. There were only a few circumstances when a human would be allowed to know about us. Witches and vampires had loopholes, but the rules were very clear in the shifter community. Putting Nicole at risk by forcing Mara to follow her around went against the very nature of our mate bond. I didn't like the idea of her being in danger.

"I'd love to help." Mara did not disguise the bite in her tone.

Corbin rolled his eyes. "Just keep her out of trouble, learn about who she is, and make sure none of the other supes fuck with her."

Mara started bouncing on her heels. "This is going to be the worst semester ever. That dumb little virgin was attracting all kinds of attention. I even caught a few of those creepy-ass fae dudes eyeing her."

I frowned. My blood was boiling at the idea of anyone looking at what was *mine*. Something stuck out about her statement, though. "Why do you think she's a virgin?"

Mara shrugged. "She was being really weird when I was talking about hooking up with some guys. Major prude vibes on that one." A devious grin stretched across her face. "But not for long. Right, Corbin? Apparently with you *claiming* her and shit. Are you going to fuck the human to teach her a lesson? I don't normally want to hear about my brother's sex life, but I'll make an exception for this."

I fought the growl rising in my throat. The thought of Nicole being with *any* other guy made me rage, especially my best friend. *Why was I doing this again?*

Oh, right. My birthright. Pack politics. The fact that they'd never accept a human as my mate.

Fucking hell.

Corbin looked at me nervously. "Uh... I'm not going to screw her, Mar. I just was trying to keep her away from the vampires until we figured out what was going on. You know how her father works for the university? It would be a PR nightmare if one of those idiots drained his daughter dry, don't you think?"

"Pft." She waved him off. "That's not even fun. If I have to babysit her, then the least you can do is make it enjoyable for me. Just fuck her and then break her heart. Maybe she'll get so sad that she won't leave the dorm. Problem solved!"

I needed to shift this conversation to something much safer before I did something like, oh, I don't know, go on a murder spree, starting with the bitch in front of me.

"Tell me more about her father's job."

My tone left no room for argument. With a whimper, Mara immediately heeled, taking a seat in my desk chair.

"I didn't get much from her while we were getting ready. But so far, I know that he's some scientific genius or whatever. The university is paying him to conduct research on something or another. Maybe he's teaching, too? It was all very boring, and to be honest, I tuned that part out."

"Your job was to get *information*, and this is the best you could do?" I shot up from my bed and stomped across the room. My nostrils flared as I towered over Mara with clenched fists. "Do I need to find someone else to do it for me? Are you no longer interested in pulling your weight for the pack?"

She blanched. "What?! No, Alexei! Of course not!" She pulled on my pant leg. "I'd do anything for you! *Anything!*"

I stepped back, giving her a disgusted look. "Don't fucking touch me."

"Dude," Corbin interrupted. "Let's all just chill, okay?"

"If your sister wasn't so fucking useless, we wouldn't need to chill!" I tossed another glare in Mara's direction. "Get. Out. I'll contact you when I need something from you. In the meantime, *do not* fuck with Nicole. Your job is to get information, not to subject her to your petty, mean-girl bullshit. Mara, *I am the future alpha. I make the rules. I make the plans.* You'd do well to remember that."

She scrambled up from the chair, holding her hands up in a placating gesture. "I understand. I swear. I just want to make you happy. In *all ways.*"

Yeah. I knew what she meant. If I gave her the green light, she'd be on her knees, ready to suck my cock.

"Go!" I jerked my head toward the door.

Once she was out of sight, I relaxed some. Mara knew exactly how to get under my skin.

I turned to Corbin. "This claiming bullshit is just a temporary solution, got it? And don't let your cock forget, she's *off-limits.* If you even *attempt* to fuck her, I'll throw your dick in a wood chipper, got it?" I infused every shred of alpha power I had into my threat.

"Of course," he stammered. "My dick won't go near any part of her."

Good.

Corbin was my best friend and the only person I could trust here with my secret. But there was nothing that would stop me from destroying him if he made a move on my mate.

He cleared his throat. "So. You going to text her?"

I felt like a fucking junior high punk going through puberty. Just the thought of messaging her made me… giddy. I was a future fucking alpha. Giddy shouldn't even be in my vocabulary.

"She needs a phone. Get her on Ridgeview's wireless plan." Blocking reception from all other carriers was one way we locked down the university. We couldn't have some asshole accidentally posting anything supernatural on social media. Even if the humans on campus couldn't see it, thanks to the containment spell, anyone located outside of Redwood University could. Ridgeview's wireless plan had sophisticated filters, allowing them to screen for anything supe related. We still gave everyone their privacy, but if something triggered the bots, it'd automatically send it to a team in charge of reviewing it.

"I can handle that. I'll have it delivered to her dorm first thing in the morning. Want me to throw in a rose? Bitches love roses."

"Don't call her that."

Corbin looked as shocked as I was by the malice in my tone. I hadn't meant for it to come out that way, but the thought of anyone degrading my mate made me furious.

"I meant nothing by it," Corbin swore. "It's just that, you know, the technical term for a female wolf *is* bitch."

"She's not a wolf," I reminded him.

"Right. I knew that." Corbin shifted around uncomfortably. "But can I be frank, Alexei? Without risking bodily harm?"

I made a hurry-up motion with my hand. "Get on with it, then."

He took a deep breath. "Well, like you said... she's not a wolf. And even worse, she's a human, dude. You *are* planning to somehow break the bond, right?"

I ground my teeth. "I said I'd figure it out."

Too bad there wasn't any kind of precedent for this. I didn't even know if it was possible. If I wanted to remain alpha, though, I didn't have any other option. Fated or not, Nicole couldn't be mine.

My inner wolf howled in protest.

I just hoped I wouldn't spend a lifetime pining for a woman I had no hope of ever having.

"I have this... *friend*, Juniper," Corbin continued. "She's a pretty powerful witch and honestly the hottest woman I've ever seen. We're... close."

I pinched the bridge of my nose. "Fucking a witch, Corbin? You're an idiot. If she finds out how much of a whore you are, she'll spell your dick."

He scoffed. "It's casual. I casually eat her out, and she casually rides my dick."

Corbin was way too comfortable talking about his sexcapades. I'd never really been a kiss-and-tell sort of guy, so I didn't get the appeal. "Why are you bringing this up? Get to the point."

He shrugged. "Well, like I said, she's powerful. Her whole family is. Juniper stole a lust potion from her mom once, and I came, like, fourteen times. Highly recommend trying some if you ever get the chance. Anyhow, I suppose if you wanted to break the bond, June would be a good contact. And she knows how to keep her mouth shut."

I scratched my chin. It was a risk to trust a witch with something like this, but I didn't have a lot of options.

"Fine," I spat. "Call her. Let's get a meeting."

"As you wish, Alpha. Just don't stare at her pet raven. She gets pissy about that."

I frowned. Of course she had a pet raven. Witches were weird as hell.

I was probably going to regret asking this, but I had to know. "When you and this witch are getting down... do you ever feel like you're being watched? Ravens have those all-knowing eyes, ya know? They creep me out."

Corbin's eyes widened. "Yes! I swear that little winged asshole studies us fucking, taking notes and shit for all his raven friends. One time, Juniper and I were getting extra freaky. I had her bent over, grabbing onto her ankles while I railed her, and she was screaming for more. Begging for it, telling me what a god I was in the sack. The best she ever had. Then, thirty seconds later, the damn raven started cawing wildly right before it flew across the room and started attacking me. I swear, it tried to peck my eyes out! I ran the hell out of there when it went after my nuts."

I shook my head. This idiot's dick was definitely going to get him into trouble one day. And my bet was on sooner rather than later. I started laughing when another thought occurred to me. The more I thought about it, the funnier it became, until I was practically hysterical, my eyes filling with tears.

"What, bro? Why are you laughing like that?"

I rubbed a hand across my mouth, trying to smother my smirk. "Did it ever cross your mind that maybe this raven of hers could be something else?"

Corbin's brows drew together. "What do you mean?"

I gave him a look that said, *use your brain, moron.*

His jaw dropped. "Oh, shit. You think?"

I lifted a brow. "Do I think it's possible her *pet* is really a shifter? Perhaps another lover who didn't appreciate watching her declare some other dude the best she ever had? Yeah, I think it's possible."

"Bruh, that makes so much sense." Corbin scrubbed a hand down his face. "*So* much sense. Holy shit. I'm in the middle of a cuckold relationship, aren't I?"

I barked out a laugh. "*Relationship?* I thought it was casual?"

"It is," he insisted. "I think. Now, I'm questioning every interaction we've ever had."

"Question it all you want." I pinched the bridge of my nose again. "Just don't let your sex life fuck up the only hope I may have of fixing this mess I'm in." At Corbin's horrified, contemplative look, I laughed.

CHAPTER
FIVE

Alexei

"Iꜰ ʏᴏᴜ ᴘᴜᴛ makeup on my face, I will break every finger on your hand," I growled at Corbin. He was sneaking closer with some brush in his hand and an evil grin on his face.

"Oh, don't be scared, little puppy. Daddy's just going to get rid of those nasty circles under your eyes," he cooed before pouncing on top of me. Corbin straddled my lap, and I felt my alpha wolf rise to the surface as he swiped the tan shit under both my eyes with a stealthy quickness that surprised me. The motherfucker had probably been planning his attack all morning.

"Enough." I shoved at his chest. He got off my lap

and straightened his tie with a smirk. It was too damn early for this shit. I had to get up at four in the morning to answer some bullshit questions for a magazine.

"You look so handsome. I'll have to put the photos from this shoot on my nightstand."

I rolled my eyes. Corbin was just doing his job as my beta, but he was annoying the fuck out of me. I didn't really want to come here today, especially not at the crack of dawn. I was feeling on edge, like there was a big-ass sign above my head flashing *mated to a human.*

"The journalist just walked in. Please try to smile and compliment her. We want her to paint you in the best light. Strong but approachable. A good leader, a gentle lover—"

"I get it, Corbin," I gritted as a woman wearing a pantsuit sauntered over to us.

We'd set up at the School of Business by a large window. Corbin said the lighting was *ideal* or some shit.

"Mr. Koenig." The woman extended her hand. "It's so nice to meet the future leader of the Ridgeview pack. Thank you for making time to meet with me. I'm Quinn Mathers."

I stood up and put on a brave face. My father taught me how to act. What to say. How to be the most powerful man in the room. Thrusting out my hand, I shook hers, her fingers lingering against my skin for a moment, which made my insides crawl.

I couldn't help but think of Nicole. I felt like I was betraying my mate by noticing how attractive this lady was. I wasn't sexually attracted to her, but there was no denying her beauty.

Fucking hell.

Would it always be like this?

"It's nice to meet you, Ms. Mathers." I pulled my hand back, resisting the urge to wipe it against my pants.

She beamed. She couldn't have been but a few years older than I was, and when her eyes swept over my fitted suit and broad shoulders, I knew this interview would be a piece of cake. "I'm so excited to interview you today. I hope you don't mind, but I wanted to ask a few additional questions that weren't on the preliminary round I sent your beta."

I didn't let her see me panic. Had word about Nicole gotten out? No. Impossible. Only Corbin knew.

"Of course, but we will have final say on anything put in the article." My beta offered his hand in greeting. "Corbin Sullivan. We spoke on the phone."

Quinn shook his hand and smiled. "Nice to meet you. And of course. The photographer is running late, so we'll go ahead and get started with the interview if you don't mind."

"Not at all." I gestured toward the chair across from mine. "Please have a seat."

We both got comfortable in the leather lounge chairs Corbin had set up, and my beta positioned himself at her back so he could coach me from behind the scenes. He smiled big and pointed at his teeth, wordlessly reminding me to appear approachable.

I forced a grin while Quinn set up her recording device.

"Mr. Koenig, since this is your senior year, I'm sure you're thinking about officially working alongside your father, Alpha Jones Koenig, after graduation. How are you preparing for your new role, and what are you doing now to leave a legacy at Redwood University?"

Easy question. I could answer it in my sleep.

"I think, in many ways, I've been preparing my entire life. My father always pushed me to take extra classes and sit in with him at meetings. This is just the next step in years of preparation, and I feel ready to show the pack everything I've learned while studying to lead under my father." I smiled at her. Corbin nodded encouragingly. "As for my legacy at Redwood, I'm president of Alpha Nu, and this year, we've already made plans to have the best pledge class since my father was president, and we're on track to raise three million dollars for the charity our philanthropy division is focused on."

"That's incredible. Your father must be so proud." Quinn scribbled a note on her pad of paper.

I swallowed. Nothing I ever did would be good enough for my father. "He's always pushed me to be the best alpha I can be. I take this job seriously and hope to not only make him proud, but also serve our community with strength and integrity."

Quinn nodded before continuing. "You've already established your team. I've had the privilege of working closely with your chosen beta, and I know you're working hard at Alpha Nu to find the next generation of advisors and pack leaders. But what about your future luna? Everyone knows an alpha is only as strong as his mate. You've seen firsthand what a powerful partner can do for an alpha's career. Everyone loves your mother."

Her question made my heart race, but I kept my face stoic. "My mother is the perfect example of what a strong luna should be." I forced my voice to be even. "She's smart, ambitious, and compassionate. I'd be lucky to have a woman with half her accolades."

Quinn leaned forward. "Readers want to know. What *are* you looking for in a luna? Specifically, has anyone caught your eye?"

Corbin had a look of terror on his face. I wasn't exactly in the right frame of mind for this question, but I had to power through. "I'd like someone who is a good leader and—"

Quinn cut me off. "Yes. Of course. You want a great leader, someone who comes from a powerful family. We know what the job description requires." She laughed before continuing. "But what are you *specifically* looking for?"

Corbin widened his eyes, willing me not to lose my shit.

I smiled, telling myself I could handle this. "If you're asking if I prefer blondes or brunettes, then I'm afraid your readers will find me to be terribly boring." I chuckled, knowing that Quinn was hanging onto every word. "I want a partner. Someone I can share my life with." I leaned forward while forcing myself not to think of Nicole. "I want a friend. A confidant. Someone genuine and authentic. I don't need a pretty face who'll simply hang on my arm at events. I want a mate who helps me shed the weight of my responsibilities. Someone who supports the man that leads our pack but also loves the man that comes home to her."

I barely knew Nicole, but something told me she would fit that description. Why else would the fates choose her as my mate?

Quinn gave me a longing look. Her mouth parted as her eyes misted. "That's... that's beautiful."

"I didn't realize this was an article on eligible bachelors." My father's rude voice cut through the tender moment like a knife. He adjusted his cufflinks while strolling toward us. "Sorry I'm late."

Quinn's spine straightened. "Oh! Alpha Jones. Welcome. It's an honor. I wasn't expecting you for at least another thirty minutes."

He chuckled darkly. "Clearly, or you wouldn't be bombarding my son with questions about his love life. I thought this was an interview about the university's new research grant and how well suited my heir is to lead the pack after I retire."

Her painted lips formed into an O. "I didn't mean any harm. I promise. It was just a little fluff piece for the she-wolves' enjoyment." She winked. "Since you're not available, Alexei here is the most eligible bachelor around. Every single lady in Ridgeview is dreaming of a chance to rule by his side."

"Unless you're willing to get on your knees right now and suck my cock, flirt on your own dime, Ms. Mathers." My father's upper lip curled in disdain. "Ever hear the expression *time is money*? I don't give *one flying fuck* what the single ladies of Ridgeview dream about."

She straightened her shoulders, green eyes

growing brighter as they filled with tears. "Of course, sir. My apologies."

I clenched my jaw as my father slapped me on the back. "Father. It's nice to see you."

"Alexei." My father squeezed my shoulder in a bruising grip. "You don't mind if I let the sexy little journalist interview me first, do you? I really need to be on my way. You can finish up with her after. Hell, if you're feeling generous, you can let her have the pleasure of sucking *you* off as an apology for the last-minute schedule change."

Fuck, he was *such* a misogynistic, inconsiderate asshole. Never mind the fact that I had already started my portion of the interview, nor that I had a ton of shit on my plate as well. Jones Koenig may have been a good alpha, but he wasn't a good *man*. I really did not know how my mother put up with him.

"The blowjob won't be necessary," I grumbled.

"Eh. You're not missing out on much. *Trust me.*" My father eyed my chair pointedly and cleared his throat. I got up without a word and took a place standing against the wall next to Corbin.

"Such a delightful peach, that one," my beta muttered under his breath.

The poor journalist looked like she was about to bawl as she sorted through her notes, looking for my father's interview questions.

"Here they are!" She held up some papers. "I'm sorry it took me so long to find them."

My dad folded his arms over his chest. "Well, are you going to ask me a question, or am I supposed to just sit here and look pretty?"

"Questions..." She cleared her throat nervously. "Of course. First question. According to the memo your secretary sent me, you recently brought a brilliant geneticist on board to Redwood University. Dr. David Fairweather is his name. You have tasked him with finding a cure for the mutation that's causing some full-blooded shifters to be born without a wolf counterpart. Tell me more about that."

My ears instantly perked up as she mentioned Nicole's father's name. So, that's why he was hired. The question was... why didn't I know that before now?

"Well, you see, Ms. Mathers..." My father gave her a perfectly practiced grin. "This genetic mutation that's plaguing our people must be rectified as soon as possible. It's become one of my top priorities. Did you know that, twenty years ago, the odds of a full-blooded shifter being born without their wolf counterpart was only one in a hundred thousand? As of last year, those odds have spiked to one in *one* thousand! It's a travesty! Could you imagine the shame someone born from pure bloodlines must feel when they learn they cannot shift? That they do not possess an inner wolf? You're part of the pack yet *not really* part of the pack."

"Oh, yes," she agreed. "It must be *terribly* shameful."

"Not to mention, it's *horribly* uncomfortable for those who *do* have a wolf counterpart," he added. "Why should we feel guilty for our abilities over others less fortunate? But we *do*, because we *care*."

I held back a scoff, appalled by the lies he was spewing. My father didn't feel the *slightest* bit of guilt for having the ability to shift over someone born with faulty DNA who couldn't. He felt *superior* because of it.

"There are some individuals criticizing you for outsourcing this job. Hiring a *human* to research shifter genes is unprecedented."

My father clenched his jaw. He *hated* humans. I knew for a fact it was a swift kick to his massive ego that he had to hire one to help with a shifter problem. "I suppose to some extent, I'd have to agree with those who have concerns. Hiring a human was not my first choice. We have a team with members of every super-natural faction working hard to find a solution. Dr. Fairweather has plenty of experience, and his research complements the work my team has already accom-plished. The lead on the project, Dr. Viden, assured me that our new hire is more than capable of making vast contributions to the study. Surprisingly, Dr. Fairweather's limitations as a human have not hindered his intellect. I trust Dr. Viden's judgment on this and will defer to her should he fail."

Quinn nodded. "What do you have to say to those who think it's unwise to tell a human about our world? Especially one so well known in the scientific community?"

Once again, my father's eyes flashed with anger. It thrilled me to see him so agitated. "I still firmly believe it is in the best interest of the pack to keep our world a secret from the humans, and I assure you, we have proper precautions in place." My stomach dropped. Nicole was immune to the spell that protected Redwood. I needed to figure out why and what to do about it without him finding out.

Dad continued. "My father was an idealist who founded this very university as proof that we could thrive alongside the humans without them knowing what we are—while also monetizing our cohabitation. Humans pay double the tuition of their supernatural classmates, and their contributions have allowed us to offer more scholarships and have more top-of-the-line laboratories. I recognize their purchasing power and use it to the pack's advantage." *I'll say.* Dad's latest venture was to buy up commercial property and rent it to humans at a premium. "We invest millions into tech and spells that allow us to maintain our way of life without the fear of exploitation. In fact, I'm working with a startup that wants to commercialize memory spells in an easy-to-use powder, so shifters won't have to hire a witch for any unintended encounters. I'd love to keep everything within the pack, but as you know, influencers are rare, so many of us have no choice but to rely on witchcraft."

"What a rather large undertaking," Ms. Mathers stated. "It must be especially challenging when you're not getting the full support of other supernatural factions."

No shit.

Witches made certain accommodations for humans they deemed fit to join their society. Vampires regularly acquired humans as blood sources, and don't even get me started on how careless fae could be with humans.

My father scowled. "Although *they* are comfortable in exposing our world, I am not."

Something he and I actually agreed on.

"Didn't you vote in favor of an exposure ban at the last Supernatural Summit?" Quinn asked.

"I was one of the few brave individuals that put our people first." Dad flashed her a political smile. "Unfortunately, others didn't share my vision. I believe witches shouldn't hold a monopoly on magic, and all factions of our delicate society need more government oversight on who they allow into their communities. I'm in the process of writing a bill that requires all witches, fae, and vampires to submit formal requests before revealing themselves to a human. Also, the spells that protect us should have stricter guidelines. Shifters should not have to pay a premium for safety."

Quinn cleared her throat. "Many people support your views. What do you say to your constituents that question this new hire? It contradicts the policies you've worked so hard to implement."

He looked directly at her, pure alpha power simmering under his evil grin. "I say to them, I hear you, and I agree with you. Humans are weak. They're *unworthy*. The bottom of our pyramid in almost every way. They only supersede us in population—for now. If we want to grow our numbers, we have to solve this missing wolf crisis."

Dad was all about increasing our population. He encouraged families to have as many children as possible, stating it was for the good of the pack. It was a slap in the face when his own wife could only bear one child.

"When wielded by a competent leader, humans can be somewhat useful creatures. Or at the very least, a means to an end. Dr. Fairweather has earned a spot on our team because he's proven to have valuable information we need to save the future of our pack. It's a sacrifice I'm willing to make for the good of our people."

Ms. Mathers gave my father a tight smile. "Well, thank you for your time, Alpha Jones. This was quite informative." She gestured to the photographer standing off to the side. "Do you have a few extra moments to pose for a few photos with your son?"

He buttoned his suit jacket as he stood and looked at the Audemars Piguet on his wrist. "I'll allow exactly five minutes."

Quinn nodded submissively. "Thank you, sir."

My father and I stood side by side in front of the camera, flashing our most campaign-worthy smiles. The entire time, I was practically vibrating with worry for my mate. I knew, once this went to print, David Fairweather was going to be a shifter household name. And nothing good usually came from a human being on a shifter's radar like that. Like the journalist said, some people didn't agree that bringing a human on board was smart. They felt the risk for exposure was too great. What if someone decided to take care of the *problem* themselves?

"What kind of security do you have on Dr. Fairweather?" I whispered under my breath.

"Don't worry about it, son," my father assured me. "I have a team of supes watching his *every* move. It works as protection for our investment and... *insurance.*"

Insurance? Insurance for *what*?

Fuck.

I didn't like this one bit.

CHAPTER

SIX

Nicole

I TURNED my phone off and on again, praying that somehow it would work. I'd woken up early, still confused about the night before. I just wanted to call my best friend and tell her all the crazy shit that had been going on here, but I had zero cell service. Even better, there was a problem with my user ID and password, which meant I couldn't access the school's Wi-Fi. I'd asked my RA for help about a dozen times, but apparently, I had to call the tech office for that, and they weren't open on the weekends. And to make matters worse, my land line only let me call people at Redwood.

I needed internet. Now.

A knocking sound on the door drew my attention, and I got up from my bed to answer it.

It was a delivery man wearing brown shorts and a button-down shirt. "Nicole?"

"Yeah?"

He didn't spare me a glance as he shoved a box in my face. "Here you go."

My brows rose as I looked down at the package. I squealed when I saw the Ridgeview Wireless logo printed on the box, which I assumed was a local cell service provider.

"Oh, thank goodness." Dad must have gotten us a new plan with coverage here. He knew how important it was for me to call my best friend.

I quickly ripped open the box and powered on the phone. It had a full battery and was ready for me to use it. I was just about to dial Dad to thank him when a text message came through. I scowled at the name programmed in the caller ID.

Corbin.

I had this weird flutter in my chest that didn't feel right. Mara kept reminding me how lucky I was that Corbin *claimed* me in front of everyone. She made it feel like an honor. But when I was alone with my thoughts, I started to doubt what she was saying. The whole situation was strange.

I opened the text and read it.

Corbin: You're welcome.

I stared at the screen for a long moment. What a fucking pretentious message. You're welcome for what, exactly? Claiming me in public? That was fucking weird.

Nicole: I don't know how you got this number, but you can go ahead and delete it. I'm not interested.

Corbin: I bought you the phone.

He bought it?! What the hell?

Corbin: You mentioned you had no service here, and my sister mentioned you were bummed about not being able to call your friend.

Well. That was... thoughtful. I felt like an ass for telling him to delete my number.

Nicole: Wow. Thanks, I guess. You didn't have to do this. My dad and I were talking about getting on the local plan.

Corbin: I was happy to. I had an ulterior motive. I want to get to know you.

I squinted at the screen. Mara had told me to give him a chance. She'd insisted on it, actually. I'd never been much of a texter. I liked to see a person's face when we spoke and hear their words. You could read too much into texts. If Corbin was genuine in his feelings, then I wanted to experience it so I could understand what all this craziness actually meant.

I hit the video call button and waited for him to answer, my heart thudding as it rang.

"Uh, hello?" Corbin looked flustered, as if he'd just run to the phone. His eyes darted past the camera, wide and insistent at something or someone in the background. "Sorry, I wasn't expecting your call."

"What's your deal?" I wasn't planning on this being an interrogation, but it seemed better than wasting both of our time.

"Deal?"

I nodded while getting comfortable on the bed. "The first time we met, you were a complete asshat, yet a few hours later, you decided to call *dibs* on me. Now you're giving me an expensive cell phone. You seem a bit unhinged, and I don't want to end up in a ditch somewhere." A growl in the background made me pause. "Is someone with you?"

Corbin cleared his throat. "Alexei is here, but don't mind him."

My stomach sank. Alexei hated me. I didn't under-stand his animosity, but it was all so strange.

"Your sister thinks I should give you a chance."

Corbin grinned, and I noted that he had a pleasant smile, both mischievous and playful at the same time. "My sister is a pain in the ass, but I agree. You *should* give me a chance."

I giggled. "She can be a bit pushy, I suppose." I chewed on my lip, and Corbin squirmed uncomfort-ably, once again looking up at who I now knew was Alexei. I got the sinking feeling that he was nervous about talking to me. Did Alexei not approve? What was the point of this?

"I get the feeling you don't really want to talk to me."

Panic scattered across his features. "No. Uh, I'm just... uh—"

"Thank you for the phone, but I'm going to have to return it."

"No!" Corbin snapped. "I'm fucking this up. I'm glad you called, okay? Really glad. I want to get to know you. I wanted to apologize for being a dick when we first met. Look, I think you're really pretty and—" Another growl.

I scowled. "Sounds like Alexei doesn't want you talking to me."

"Alexei is... protective."

I arched a brow. "Protective? Is he... in love with you or something?"

Corbin busted out laughing, clutching his stomach as he curled over in a fit of humor. "Alexei *absolutely* loves me."

"Give me the fucking phone," a rough voice barked.

I sighed as the screen was jerked around, and Alexei's hard face filled the screen. His eyes widened at the sight of me. I looked down at my pajamas and shrugged when I saw the silk tank top and short shorts. I didn't really care what he thought of me.

"Hello, Alexei." I gave him a tight grin.

He was shirtless, and the scruff on his jaw looked... hot, as much as I hated to admit it. He closed his eyes and inhaled, like my voice bothered him. "I'm fine with you talking to Corbin."

"I didn't realize I needed your permission." I cocked my head to the side.

He huffed. "Corbin and I come from... influential families. They have standards about who we date. I'm just looking out for him."

I pressed my lips into a firm line before responding. "We're not dating. I don't even know him. Again, this is weird."

"So go on a date with me!" Corbin exclaimed while popping his head over Alexei's shoulder. "I'd love to take you out. We can start over and pretend all this crazy, psycho behavior never happened." He said that last part while glaring at Alexei. "*Of course* it's weird that I called dibs in front of everyone. And having my *best friend* intrude on our *first call* is obnoxious. You're probably *really fucking confused* about all of this and need nothing else to fuck it up." Corbin shoved Alexei in the ribs with his elbow, then stole the phone back before continuing.

"Let me tell you about myself, okay? I'm in Alpha Nu. V.P. this year, actually. I like rare steaks and camping. I grew up not too far from here, in Ridgeview. I'm double-majoring in Finance and Computer Science. Your turn." A grin stretched across his face.

Damn, he was awfully chipper in the morning.

I, however, was not an early bird. Especially considering I spent half the night tossing and turning, thinking about everything that happened last night. It was way too early, and I was way too under-caffeinated for this conversation, but he seemed so eager to get to know me that I felt like I should try.

I tapped my index finger on my lips. "Well, let's see. I'm a freshman, but I suspect you already know that."

Corbin nodded. "I did. My sister told me."

"What else did your sister tell you?" I lifted a brow.

He briefly looked away before answering. "Uh... I think she mentioned something about your dad working at the university, but that's it. So... does he? Work for the university?"

"He does," I confirmed. "That's why I'm here, actually. I was accepted into Parsons—I'm a fashion major—but when my dad was offered the job of a lifetime, along with free tuition for me, I came here instead. It's easier that way. Financially, it made sense. I followed him so that I don't have to worry about him from the other side of the country. He gets so involved in his research he forgets about important things like eating and sleeping, unless I remind him."

He laughed. "So, you two are close, then? And here I thought college was about getting *away* from the parentals. Man, I've been doing it wrong."

My lips curved into a smile. "We *are* close. My mom... she, uh, died in childbirth, so it's been just us my whole life. We're a team."

Corbin's eyes softened as he cleared his throat, seemingly caught off guard. "I'm sorry, Nicole. About your mom. That sucks."

I shrugged like I always did when someone said that after learning about my mother's death. No matter what, people always seemed to have the exact same response. There was a moment of awkward silence, followed by pity and some kind of apology. Corbin was evidently no different.

"It's all good. I never got to know her, so I don't really know what I'm missing, you know?" My fingers fiddled with the gold chain around my neck as I gave him the same scripted response I'd given everyone else in my life. The funny thing was, nobody ever seemed to question it, no matter how disingenuous my tone may have been. Well, nobody but Bee, that is. She called bullshit on it right away, and we were only eight at the time. That's how I knew she was someone special.

I could hear a deep voice speaking in the background—presumably Alexei's—but I couldn't make out what he was saying. Whoever it was definitely had split Corbin's attention.

"She was in Beta Phi, though. I'll be rushing this year. Kind of makes me feel closer to her."

"Uh... huh." Corbin's focus was still on whatever the other person was saying. It kind of bothered me that he wasn't really paying attention, especially since I was talking about Mom.

"Obviously, this is boring you."

His eyes snapped back to me. "No! No. I'm so sorry, Nicole. What were you saying?"

I slumped my shoulders. I couldn't do it. "Corbin, I'm sure you're really nice, but I don't think this is going to work. I'll leave your phone at the frat house, okay?"

"No, no, Nicole. I'm sorry. Alexei is being a major pain in the ass right now."

I nodded. "Because he's worried your *influential* family won't approve."

Corbin sighed. "Yeah."

"Well, nothing to worry about. I'm not interested, so you can date someone more their style." I hung up the phone just as Corbin started sputtering off another explanation. I gave it a good try, but I had higher standards for myself than that.

He immediately called me back, but I sent it to voicemail. I decided I would get dressed and return the phone as soon as possible. There was no use holding onto it and prolonging the inevitable. I wasn't about to accept an expensive gift from a guy I wasn't even talking to. Mara was sweet, but there was no way in hell I'd give her brother a chance. This was all too weird.

I was going to put on a pair of leggings and a slouchy shirt, but dressed up in the end. Rush was coming soon, and I wanted to get a bid. Looking nice and standing out as a candidate was half the battle. I picked out a short white tennis skirt that flared when I walked and a hot pink Chanel crop top. It looked great against my tan skin and highlighted my white sneakers. Once my hair was up in a high ponytail, I gathered up the cellphone and the box it came in so I could drop it off.

When I walked outside, the air was warm and comfortable. My dorm was a short distance from Greek Row, so I enjoyed the brisk walk. It gave me an opportunity to look at some of the school's buildings and appreciate the architecture. Everything about the university was beautiful. The picturesque mountains and greenery molded around each building, giving the illusion that each brick was part of nature instead of taking over it. The paved sidewalks had wildflowers growing beside them, and bees flew happily between each petal.

I wanted to go to the city for school. The busy hustle and bustle called to me, but there was something pleasant about Redwood University. Despite my initial impression of it, I could see why so many people were drawn to this place.

I even noted a cute cafe to stop at on my way back for coffee. I'd need caffeine if I was going to survive the day. Maybe I'd grab Dad a coffee cake. He had a sweet tooth and probably hadn't eaten yet. My priority was to ensure he had enough groceries for the week in his new apartment. Because I'd be rushing, I should probably make him a couple of frozen meals, too.

Greek Row had seven mansions lining the streets. It was impossible not to gawk at the large white houses with towering columns and gold Greek letters bolted to the side. Few students were up this early, but there were a few girls walking out a front door in workout gear and headphones in their ears. I waved politely at them, but they tilted their noses up dismissively before giggling to one another.

Maybe rush would be harder than I thought.

The Alpha Nu house was the most impressive building on the block, yet it was also intimidating. It was tall and sprawling, with manicured lawns surrounding it. There was a huge wraparound porch with wicker furniture. A fountain in the front yard boasted two wolves fighting, which felt oddly aggressive for a college campus.

I walked up to the front door, prepared to leave the box on the front step, when something caught my eye.

There was a shiny golden plaque on the heavy wooden door right below the iron knocker. I traced my finger over the engraving as I read the words.

"'Where there are sheep, the wolves are never very far away.' –Plautus."

This quote, combined with the fountain statues engaged in combat, was rather strange, wasn't it? I couldn't help thinking it was a warning of some sort. Although, considering Redwood U's mascot was a wolf, maybe I was reading too much into it. Maybe my imagination was getting the best of me. This was a highly accredited university, for shit's sake.

I really needed to talk to Bee. She was a pro at acclimating to new places. She would likely tell me my unease since stepping foot on this campus was perfectly normal. It was human nature to resist change. Especially a change so drastic to everything I'd ever known. I took a deep breath, feeling relieved after my mini pep talk. Until I heard an unmistakable growl.

"Oh, shit." The box slipped out of my hand onto the porch as I first spotted the large dog approaching me with a snarl. As it got closer, I amended my previous thought. This wasn't someone's pet. It was too large. Too wild. Its lips pulled back as it released another growl, sharp teeth fully on display. In any other situation, I'd probably note how beautiful the animal's brown coat was. But considering this predator had me locked in its sights, and it seemed the opposite of friendly, my mind was too busy trying to think of a way out of this situation without getting mauled to death.

I took a step back but hit the front door to the frat house.

"Easy there, puppy," I said, even though this wild animal in front of me was far from being an adorable little pup. It had paws the size of discs and long teeth that would rip out my throat if given half a chance. My heart rate spiked and adrenaline coursed through me.

With trembling hands, I reached for the door handle behind my back and prayed it was unlocked. If I could just get inside...

My movement made the animal's growl deepen. The hair on its back stood on edge as if preparing to lunge for me. It was almost like this crazed creature was protecting the frat house. But that was insane, right? Alpha Nu wouldn't have wild wolves roaming their property and killing coeds.

I twisted the knob.

I took a deep breath.

Oh, thank God. It was unlocked!

Once the door was open, I shoved myself inside and slammed it shut, just as the wolf launched itself at me. The front door rattled as the furious animal on the other side threw its body against it. A sharp scream escaped my lips, and I didn't care if I wasn't supposed to be here or if I woke up everyone in this damn house.

"Fuck!"

A dozen or so guys wearing nothing but boxers started running down a grand double staircase in the foyer.

"What are you doing here?" one of them yelled,

fists clenched at his side as he approached me. "You're not allowed here."

I stammered. "I-I was just bringing Corbin a cell phone, and a wolf was there—he tried to attack me and—and—" My vision was blurry as I was breathing so hard.

Holy crap, I could've been killed just now.

I took several deep breaths, telling myself not to cry. I was safe. I wasn't currently getting my jugular ripped out by a wild beast. As I surveyed the room, I realized this option maybe wasn't much better. I was locked in a house with a bunch of giant, nearly naked dudes, all glaring at me. There was no mistaking the hostility in their gazes nor the strength each one possessed. There was so much testosterone in the air it was stifling.

"Are you going to answer me?" the same guy asked. "What. The. Fuck. Do you think you're doing?"

"I was..." I swallowed, trying to ease the lump in my throat. "Corbin. I'm here for Corbin."

Their posture relaxed marginally as I mentioned their frat brother's name again. I wasn't an idiot, though; I knew they were still on edge. Every one of these dudes had major junkyard guard dog vibes. One wrong move, and I'd be screwed. Ironic, considering what led me into inviting myself into their home in the first place.

"Where's Corbin?" one of them asked another.

"In the meeting room with Alexei," he answered. "They've been down there since they got back from that interview. Probably didn't hear all the commotion over the music they're blasting."

Now that he mentioned it, there was a steady thrum of bass coming from somewhere in the house. Why would they blast music during a meeting?

"Go get 'em, Damien."

Damien hurried down the rest of the stairs, toward the back end of the house.

Fuck. I wasn't in the mood to talk to Corbin or Alexei again, but I guess it was preferable to the angry dog outside.

I raised my hand to get their attention, but pulled it down when I realized how dumb I must've looked. "Isn't someone going to do something about the wolf?"

One guy laughed. Fucking *laughed.* As if me almost dying was humorous. Fuck these guys.

"Corbin's coming," that Damien guy said as he popped back into the room, catching his breath. "Alexei looks pissed."

I was about to take my chances with the wolf, but both guys came charging into the room before I could take off, heading right toward me.

Alexei spoke first. "Everyone leave. Now."

The guys scattered like his word was law. I was about to find a bathroom to hide in until I knew the wolf was gone, but Alexei grabbed my arm and pulled me close. His dark eyes carefully cataloged each one of my facial features. "Are you okay?"

The care in his tone caught me off guard. Corbin cleared his throat.

"Not really. Did you know you have a wolf in your front yard right now? It was about to attack me!"

"Shit," Alexei cursed. "I'll call someone about that. Why are you here?"

"I was just trying to drop off the phone Corbin got me."

"Ah." Corbin scratched the back of his neck. "You didn't have to do that. It was a gift."

"Yeah." Alexei's jaw clenched. "I would prefer you kept the phone."

I stared at both of them. Why did Alexei care if I kept it? "It's fine. Probably broke when I dropped it out there. Sorry." Standing this close to Alexei was intense. I looked down at where he was still grabbing me, and with a huff, he let go.

"Nicole, can we talk?" Corbin asked. "Away from this grumpy asshole?"

Alexei looked murderous, so I slipped away and walked over to Corbin. His hair was messy, and he wore black sweat pants low on his hips. After grabbing my hand, he led me to a sitting area. Trying not to think of all the scandalous things that had probably happened on a frat house couch, I sat down. "I'm so sorry. About everything. Alexei is my best friend. I kind of can't do anything without him in my business."

"I can tell." My brow arched.

"This is usually second-date information, but I didn't exactly have the best family growing up. They put a lot of pressure on me. It was pretty lonely, and Alexei was, like, my only friend. Sometimes he forgets that I'm *more than capable of doing shit on my own.*" He eyed the doorway. Sure enough, Alexei was standing there, arms crossed over his chest.

"I have a friend like that. She's not as grumpy or invasive, but I get it."

"I'm sorry the wolf scared you. Are you okay?"

I nodded. It felt like I'd just taken a massive stress test, but ultimately, I was fine.

"Next time, I'll call before coming over," I joked. "That way, you can make sure no crazy wolves attack me on my way inside."

Corbin's face brightened. "You'll come over again?"

I looked him over. Corbin was nice enough, and if we hadn't had such a weird introduction, I probably would have gone on a date with him with no reservations. "Yeah. Maybe. Just stop being so..."

"Stalkerish?" he finished for me. "Psycho? Lame? I could go on for days." He looked up at Alexei once more.

"How about you walk me back to my dorm?" I offered. "I'm still a little freaked out by the wolf."

"I want to, Nicole, but I have a meeting with my advisor in thirty minutes. Alexei could take you, though. Give you a chance to get to know one another better so you understand what I have to put up with." Corbin laughed.

"I'll take you," Alexei said at my back.

I absolutely did *not* want to walk with Alexei. Not even a little bit.

I blinked a few times, trying to think of a way out of this, before turning toward him. "Uh... shouldn't we wait for Animal Control to clear the area first? That wolf looked crazy. Maybe it has rabies or something."

Corbin straight up guffawed at that.

What in the hell was so funny about a rabid animal?

"I think I can handle it." Alexei's full lips curved into a smirk.

My eyes widened. "What?! No way. I will not be responsible if you get eaten by that thing!"

Alexei took a few steps toward me and extended his arm. "C'mon, Nicole. You'll just need to trust me on this. Whatever is out there, I *guarantee* it won't mess with me."

"Trust you?" I balked, resisting the urge to roll my eyes at the absurdity of his statement. "Why would I trust you? I don't *know* you well enough to trust you."

His nostrils flared. "But you know Corbin well enough to trust *him*?"

"Well, technically, I *do* know him better than I know you," I sassed, thinking about my brief, but informative, conversation with his best friend earlier. "All I know about you is that you're a macho guy with a pretty face and muscles for days, who's far too cocky for his own good. Nobody in their right mind would willingly head outside right now after I told them an apex predator almost attacked me! There's a fine line between confidence and stupidity, and in my opinion, you, sir, are on the wrong side."

"Oh, shit." Corbin coughed into his fist, but I was pretty sure he was covering up another laugh. This guy sure did amuse easily.

Alexei's brown eyes slid to his friend in annoyance before focusing back on me. "Is this a good time to remind you that *you* were the one who suggested leaving the house in the first place? Or was that some other beautiful brunette who requested an escort back to her dorm?"

I narrowed my eyes, telling myself to ignore the

fact that he just called me beautiful, because it was totally irrelevant, regardless of how tingly it made me feel inside.

"Fine. But if some feral wolf chases us, I'm tripping you and running for my life."

At my words, something unexpected happened.

Alexei smiled.

CHAPTER
SEVEN

Alexei

Nicole looked beautiful. The tight little skirt she wore swished when she walked, showing off the curve of her ass in a way that had me clenching my teeth. I noticed a few joggers eyeing her as we walked, and I had to convince myself not to beat the ever-living shit out of them.

This morning was a disaster of epic proportions. My plan was already falling apart, and we hadn't even started yet. Nicole was *supposed* to text me, and we were *supposed* to get to know one another behind the safety of the screen. Instead, she video called me and tried returning the phone I got her. When I saw her name pop up with a video chat, I ran like a bat out of hell to Corbin's room and forced him to answer the phone. We'd just gotten back from the early morning interview, and he was getting ready for a nap.

It pissed me off but also made me respect her more. She didn't want some bullshit texts or flashy gifts. She wanted to understand things.

There were plenty of wolves in our pack that would have gladly let me spoil them with gifts. But Nicole wasn't in my pack. She didn't know that I was a future alpha or that my family had more money than God. She just seemed to think Corbin and I were a pair of creeps. It made my wolf whine to know how I was failing at courting our mate.

I wanted to give her flowers and take her on luxurious dates. If I didn't have to worry about what anyone thought, I'd send her a fucking lot more than a cell phone.

"So you care for Corbin, huh?" Nicole asked.

I fucking hated that our conversation had to revolve around my best friend, but this was the bed I made, and now I had to lie in it.

"He's like a brother to me. He's probably the only person who understands what kind of pressure I'm under." I wanted to stick to the truth as much as possible. It was important to my wolf that she knew us. The real us. But I had to be careful about some of the details.

"Your family, right?"

I cleared my throat as our hands brushed. My dick was hard enough to crack concrete. "Yeah. My dad owns a pretty big, uh, corporation. I'm set to take over one day."

"Do you want to?"

The question caught me off guard. I didn't think anyone had ever asked me that before. There was never any doubt *if* I'd be the next person to lead our pack, provided no one challenged me. I had been groomed for the job my entire life. It was decided before I was even born. The only variable was *when*, and that was after my father retired. Part of an alpha's job was to provide for their pack. I wasn't lying about my dad's corporation. My father ran an incredibly successful tech company that employed our entire pack in some capacity, along with thousands of other shifters across the globe. The more success you had as a legitimate business owner, the more respected you were in the supernatural community. And with great success came great influence in political matters. Humans weren't the only ones who understood the power that wealth held. Hell, they'd probably be shocked to learn how many members of the world's wealthiest one percent weren't even human.

"Alexei?" Nicole touched my arm, sending a jolt of electricity straight through me. "Did you hear me?"

"Failure isn't an option."

Two lines appeared between her brows as she frowned. "That wasn't exactly an answer."

Ah, but it was. I tried to think of some way to explain it without revealing my true nature.

I cleared my throat. "It's what's expected of me. It's been that way since the day I was born. I don't really have a choice in the matter."

"Everyone has a choice," she argued. "That's the beauty of being human. You have this nifty thing called free will."

And therein lies the problem. I *wasn't* human. My family and I lived by an entirely different code, and that was something Nicole would never understand.

"I overheard you talking about your dad to Corbin. You wanted to go to school in New York. Major in fashion, yeah?"

She frowned a bit. "Dad needed me here, though. I feel responsible for him."

I nodded. "I'm responsible for my family's legacy and all the people employed by my father's corporation. If I don't step up, I'm not sure I could trust anyone else to properly care for them."

Nicole nodded as if that made sense. "I could hire Dad a housekeeper. Have every meal delivered and talk to him every day, but..."

"But you feel better knowing he's taken care of because you're the one in control," I finished for her.

Her steps slowed. We were only a few minutes away from her dorm, but I wasn't ready to say goodbye yet. Part of me wanted to take her out for breakfast or show her some of my favorite spots on campus, but too many people would question why I was walking with a human. Luckily, it was still early enough that we didn't have that problem yet.

Nicole eyed one of my favorite cafes. "I'm gonna grab some coffee. I'll need the fuel for freshman orientation, and I don't think any wolves are going to jump out to eat me now, so..."

Did she want me to join her? Did she want me to leave? This was so fucking complicated.

"I'll join you," I blurted out.

Her eyes widened in surprise, but I didn't care. I just craved more time with her.

"Okay," she replied reluctantly.

We walked up to the cafe doors and let ourselves inside. I immediately scanned the room, worried a shifter would see us, but thankfully no one from my pack was there. A warlock was working behind the counter. He had electric blue hair and sweeping eyes that took in the sight of Nicole. He cleared his throat and straightened his spine when she walked up to the counter to order.

"What can I get you, beautiful?" he purred.

Hell. No.

I positioned myself at her side and gave him a *don't you fucking even think about it* look. He didn't even seem fazed.

"Small Flat White, please. Also, two coffee cakes and whatever this grumpy asshole wants." She then turned to me. "My treat since you escorted me back."

"No. I'm buying." I didn't mean to snap, but my wolf was insulted that she wanted to pay. I should be taking care of her. It was my job as her *mate.* "I'll take a black coffee. Large."

The warlock gleamed at her. "Would you like anything *special* in your coffee?"

This particular cafe sometimes put hits of spells on their brew for an additional cost. Mara once brought me lust coffee, and I was so horny I had to jack off until my dick was raw. She was hoping I'd take out my *frustrations* on her, but instead I banned her from any Alpha Nu parties for a semester.

She thought about it for a moment. "Maybe a little honey."

"Just honey?"

"Yes, please."

The warlock looked at both of us, seemingly realizing that she was human. "Whatever you'd like, gorgeous."

Nicole gave me a dirty look as I practically threw my card at the magical prick behind the counter to pay. As we stood off to the side waiting for our coffee, I kept a close eye on the barista, ensuring he wasn't murmuring any spells over my mate's drink. I was beginning to think I must've done something terrible to the fates in a previous life. It was bad enough I was mated to a human, but being mated to this particular human, who seemed to attract the attention of every supe in her vicinity, was going to be the death of my sanity. She was so fucking vulnerable on this campus I couldn't help but worry. I needed to find a way to work through my anxiety. Usually, I ran under the moon or I fucked, but neither of those things was an option while I was with Nicole.

The bell over the door dinged as a new customer entered the cafe, and I gritted my teeth when I saw who it was.

Mara sauntered over to us, swinging her hips. "Hey, you two. Funny seeing you here. *Together.*"

Nicole rocked back on the heels of her sneakers, fidgeting. "Um... Mara. Hi. Alexei was just walking me back to my dorm. I had a bit of a scare with a wild animal earlier, and he, uh..."

"A wild animal," Mara interrupted, a devious twinkle in her eye. "You don't say. What kind of wild animal?"

My mate swallowed nervously. "A wolf, I think. At first I thought it was a German shepherd because it had the same coloring, but when I got a good look at it, I really don't think that's the case. It was *way* too big. It tried to attack me."

A muscle in my cheek jumped when Nicole described the animal's coat. There was only one member in my entire pack with those shades of brown in her fur, and I was currently looking right at her. Based on the panicked look in her eye, I'd say she just realized I was on to her.

Mara cleared her throat. "Well. Guess it's a good thing I'm here, then. You should have called me, Alexei." She reached for my arm and gave it a squeeze. I wanted to toss her out of this coffee shop.

"Why would we call you?" Nicole asked. "Are you going to fight off a wolf?" At that statement, Nicole started cackling. Apparently, the idea of Mara fighting anything was humorous to her. I had to agree. Mara didn't fight. She just controlled people—made them bend to her will with her words.

"Because of this," Mara hissed before placing both hands on Nicole's shoulders and looking her in the eye. "*A wolf did not attack you this morning. You went on a pleasant walk and ran into Corbin.*"

"Corbin..." Nicole mumbled.

"This isn't necessary, Mara," I gritted.

Mara stopped talking to Nicole to glare at me. "Of course it's necessary. I'm just following orders, Alpha." She turned back to Nicole. *"You and Corbin had a romantic walk."*

"I really like Corbin," Nicole singsonged.

"Corbin asked you on a date," Mara continued with her bullshit, seemingly unbothered by my obvious rage. *"To the Alpha Nu party tomorrow night after class."*

"But what will I wear?" Nicole questioned in a daze.

"Enough, Mara," I growled.

Mara snapped her attention to me. "This is what *you* wanted, Alexei." She turned back to Nicole one last time. *"You better go find a cute outfit. But not too cute. And nothing slutty while we're on the topic; never wear that skirt again."*

"Mara!" I yelled, making everyone in the cafe turn to look at me, including Nicole.

"What are you doing here?" Nicole asked me. "Where did Corbin go? He's so romantic."

The most frustrating part about all of this was that Nicole wouldn't remember our conversation while walking here. It felt like Mara had stolen one of the few moments I was allowed to have with Nicole. Rage burned through me like an inferno.

"Corbin had to leave." I didn't even try to disguise the bitterness in my tone.

Her teeth scored her lower lip as she thought about that. "Huh. Weird. Why don't I remember that?"

I exhaled harshly, knowing Mara was right, as much as it killed me to admit that. The less Nicole knew, the better. I needed to think about my pack and not my selfish desire to bond with my mate. I supposed it was easier this way. If Corbin's witch friend did have some way of changing fate, any bonding efforts I made with Nicole would be one giant waste of time, anyway.

I gave Mara a *help me out here* look.

She smiled, loving the fact that I needed an assist. *"Nicole, he* did *tell you. Remember? Right before he left, he said he'd pick you up at eight, and he was really looking forward to your date tomorrow tonight. Now, run along. Alexei and I will see you at the party."*

"Okay," Nicole agreed.

"Flat White for Nicole!" the blue-haired barista called.

Nicole turned on her heels. "Oh! I almost forgot my coffee!"

Mara and I watched as Nicole went up to the counter, grabbing her coffee cup. The barista leaned closer, whispering something to her as he handed her the pastry bags. My ears perked up, but I couldn't make out what he was saying because Mara decided to speak at the same time.

"They'd make a cute couple, don't you think?"

"You're pushing it, Mara," I snapped.

"How so?" Her eyes narrowed. "I'm simply trying to please my alpha." She licked her lips. "You know I'd do *anything* to please you, Alexei. And I really do mean *any*thing."

"So you keep telling me," I mumbled. "You know what would make me happy right now? Keep your fucking mouth shut."

Mara huffed, but she was smart enough not to say another word as we watched Nicole head toward the door. Right before Nicole exited the cafe, she gave Mara a little finger wave.

Mara waved right back with a fake smile plastered across her face. "Bye, Nicole! See you at the party!"

"No, you won't." I told her. "You will *not* be at that party."

"What are you talking about? It's a pack party! Of course, I'll be there."

"No. You *won't*. After that stunt you pulled earlier, you are banned from all frat parties until further notice."

Mara's jaw dropped. "What?! Please, Alexei. Don't do that. It was a harmless joke. I wasn't going to actually hurt her. How am I supposed to keep an eye on her and compel her if I can't come?"

I knew her disappointment wasn't because she gave two shits about Nicole. Mara couldn't stand being excluded from anything, especially an Alpha Nu party. We were known for throwing the best parties. Invitations were only extended to the elite, and anyone who attended was guaranteed to have a night they wouldn't forget.

"Actions have consequences, Mara. And *you* are officially on probation for your little *joke*. Doesn't seem so harmless now, does it?"

She let out a scream of frustration before storming out of the cafe. I watched through the window as she headed back toward campus.

With that, I grabbed my coffee from the bar and left the cafe without another word.

EIGHT

Nicole

"A*RM YOURSELF WITH THE TRUTH.*"

That's what the barista told me when he handed me my coffee. I felt a tingling sensation down my spine as a result of his strange words.

Truth felt like a fuzzy concept I was close to but could never fully grasp. Whenever I got closer to an answer, Mara was right there, reassuring me it would all be okay.

I was thankful to have her as a friend. I knew she was just looking out for me, and I was so *honored* to have such an amazing guy like Corbin wanting to date me. Life was perfect. Everything was magical. How lucky was I that Mara even talked to me? I laughed at how insane it was. She was *the best*. The most popular. I was literally nothing but dirt beneath her shoe.

As I thought these things, my own sense of self-worth was screaming at me, but it felt like there was a thick wall between reality and the utter joy I felt at being in Mara's presence.

When I got on the sidewalk, ready to dedicate my day to finding a cute but not *too* cute outfit to please Mara, I took a tentative sip of the hot drink while mulling over the barista's words.

Arm yourself with the truth.

The moment the creamy coffee hit my tongue, it felt like my brain was being torn wide open. The coffee smashed against the rough concrete as my mind was bombarded with information. I found it difficult to sort through the onslaught of data being poured into my head. The history of the school. The creatures that roamed the grounds. My stomach churned from the intensity of it, and electric blue smoke poured out of my mouth and nostrils. With blurry eyes, I reached my hands out, searching for a wall or something to hold on to. A shrill scream escaped my mouth, and then I clenched my jaw so hard that I thought my teeth would crack.

Arms wrapped around my middle, and a towering figure tugged me toward the side of the building. "Nicole! Nicole!" Alexei shouted. His voice was urgent and drenched in concern. I reached for him, tangling my fingers in his shirt while I clung to my sanity. It was all too much. Too quick. It was like getting waterboarded with knowledge. I didn't even have a chance to gasp for air.

More visions assaulted me. Vampires. Fae. Shifters. Witches. I knew them all by name, knew their lore, their history, their *danger*. The details weighed heavily on my mind, and after a few more seconds of pain, my body went limp as I collapsed in his arms.

Arm yourself with the truth.

The barista's words taunted me as the last of the knowledge wove its way through my consciousness.

"Corbin. Come quick. Bring that witch you were talking about." He was screaming. I was too lost. I knew it was a spell cast on me. The warlock was trying to open my eyes to this strange world. "I don't know —I think that fucking warlock spelled her. She's weak, Corbin."

My body convulsed from the shock. The magic wreaked havoc on my body. I was too weak for such a powerful spell.

"Stay with me, Nicole. Hold on." Alexei whispering to me was the last thing I heard before everything went dark.

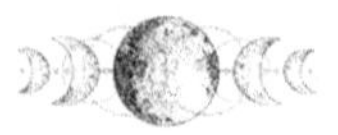

A PRIM, high-pitched voice dragged me out of my deep sleep. "Wow, that's a doozy of a spell for a human. Normally, we'd take more precautions before performing one on someone. Did she consent? Consent is very important in witch culture."

Where was I? I was stretched out on something soft, a mattress, I believed. And the room was warm. It smelled like some sort of heady spice.

"I did *not* consent to this," I choked out while forcing one eye open. The lighting was extremely bright, but I made out three people standing around me. Someone was holding my hand, and another was hovering over me, brushing something soft across my forehead.

Someone tsked. "I'm going to have to have a conversation with Antonio."

"He's a dead man," Alexei promised.

"I'd ask what the fuck happened to me, but I already know. It feels like I know *everything*." I rubbed my temples and groaned. "Cristian is a real life vampire. He was going to suck my fucking blood, and I made a joke about him sucking the orgasms out of people."

My embarrassment made me slam my eyes shut once more and cover my face with my hands. I'd received a lot of information today, but that seemed to stick out in my mind. And Mara? Just let it happen.

No, she didn't just *let it happen.* She did her little hypno bullshit and made me think it was all okay.

"What the hell is she talking about?" Alexei asked Corbin, anger in his tone. "Orgasms? Why would she be talking about orgasms with him?"

I removed my hands to give him an incredulous look. "*That's* what you're focused on? You're a shifter. Like, you can turn into a cute little wolf. Why am I not screaming right now? I should be having a full-on breakdown."

"My wolf isn't *cute.* It's powerful and dangerous."

I rolled my eyes. "Wanna tell me your dick is ten inches long while you're at it?"

A woman cleared her throat to get my attention. "I'm sure you're very confused, Nicole."

"No shit." I scoffed.

It wasn't this lady's fault that I was having a no good, very bad day, but come on. This was crazy. CRAZY.

She didn't seem fazed by my attitude. "This sort of spell is normally intended for vampires that get turned and have no clue why they suddenly want to go on a murdering spree, or for when a changeling fae discovers they aren't exactly *of this world.*" She paused to let out a tiny giggle. "It expedites the process of telling them what they are and the community they're joining. But this, *this* was unnecessary. Antonio abused his privilege. If he had gotten even a single measurement wrong, she could have had permanent brain damage!"

"Can we reverse it?" Corbin asked.

I popped open my other eye and glowered at him. "No more messing with my brain, *Wolf-boy.*"

He side-eyed Alexei. "She's kind of sexy when she gets all growly like that."

The woman with deep purple corkscrew curls grinned at me. She had a slight gap between her front teeth and curious yellow eyes. "On the bright side, the spell makes it easier to cope with the information. Think of it as magical Xanax. I've seen many humans struggle to deal with the realities of our world, so she's lucky she has that."

"Lucky?! I just learned the entire world as I know it is a complete lie! How is that anything close to lucky?!" I didn't even care that my tone was shrill and manic, maybe even a little petulant. Under the circumstances, I thought it was perfectly justified.

The woman smiled indulgently. "Well, that's not *entirely* accurate."

"How do you figure?"

She shrugged. "People have been telling stories for thousands of years, whether it be word of mouth or, in the last few hundred years, with books. And once Hollywood jumped on the bandwagon, it got really out of control. It's supposedly a big secret, but really, we've been hiding in plain sight all along." She pointed a finger at me. "Don't even try pretending you haven't binge-watched a vampire drama or two in your life. Especially that one with the delicious love triangle."

I was sure my deep blush confirmed I *had*, in fact, watched that show, among several others. I focused on the dark wooden posts of the bed I was lying on, willing the blood to drain from my cheeks. "You're talking about fiction, not real life."

"Again, not entirely accurate," she argued. "While those storytellers may have taken their own liberties, letting their imaginations run wild, each one is steeped in truth."

"I don't particularly want to have a philosophical conversation right now. Regardless of what you think, my world has just been turned upside down, and it's a little stressful for me."

Alexei huffed. "Stressful for *you*? I walked out of the cafe and saw smoke pouring out of your mouth. You collapsed in my arms, Nicole. It seriously freaked me out."

I stared incredulously at him. "Why do you even care?"

He groaned. "That's not important."

"I think it's very important," the witchy woman interrupted. "Your bond should be celebrated—"

Corbin lunged at her, slapping a hand over her mouth. "Juniper, don't."

I gaped at him for a full ten seconds. Did he seriously just cut her off?

"Okay. Tell me what's going on," I insisted.

All three of their mouths pressed into a firm line.

"Seriously?!" I used my arms to prop myself up. The grouchy jerkface beside me tried to help me, but my stink-eye caused him to reconsider. I took a moment to breathe through the dizziness before speaking again. "Somebody better tell me what the fuck is going on before I lose my shit."

"Haven't you *already* lost your shit?" Corbin asked. "Maybe she needs more of that magical Xanax."

I swear, an honest-to-God growl ripped from my throat. "You are so high up on my shit list right now, buddy. It's not even funny. This is *not* the time for your cutesy jokes."

"Awww, she thinks I'm cute." Corbin smacked the back of his hand on Alexei's bicep.

"Shut the fuck up, Corbin! Not everything is a goddamn joke!" Alexei shoved Corbin away.

I flinched. The information overload gave me a lot to think about. I knew wolf shifters were incredibly strong and could outrun a car if they had to. I also knew they were short-tempered when their furry counterpart was feeling agitated.

Alexei's expression sobered. "Nicole, I don't know how to say this—"

"Just spit it out," I pressed.

"You're my mate," he stated with all the bravado of a pimply faced teen working the drive-through window at a fast-food restaurant.

My mind instantly recalled everything I knew about mates, the knowledge flooding my mind as if I had access to a supernatural encyclopedia. It would have been cool if the spell didn't feel like a total hard and fast mind-fuck.

"Mates?" I asked.

"Yep." He popped the *p*.

"You sound overjoyed by this," I replied sarcastically. "Truly."

"It's nothing personal, but I could never seriously date a *human*." He spat the last word out like it was a curse.

"And I could never date an asshole. Seems we're at a stalemate," I fired back.

Corbin clapped his hands together. "Oh, I really like her."

"Not helping!" Alexei and I exclaimed in unison.

"Holy shit," Corbin laughed. "That was adorable!"

"Corbin, don't be a child," Purple Hair chastised.

My gaze flicked to the pretty witch. "Who *are* you, anyway?"

Her golden eyes sliced to Corbin. "You wanna take this, or shall I?"

He rubbed the back of his neck nervously. "Uh... Juniper is my... uh... I mean, one of my..."

"Don't strain yourself, babe." Juniper shook her head, patting his cheek condescendingly, before looking at me. "Corbin is my third on occasion."

"Third?" I repeated. "Your third *what*?"

"June, baby," Corbin whispered. "We don't need to talk about that right now."

"The fuck we don't," Alexei interjected. "I wanna hear more about this shit. I thought you didn't know whether or not he was a shifter."

I was so confused. "Didn't know *who* is a shifter? What are we even talking about right now?"

"My fiancé, Ivan," Juniper answered. "Corbin is my lover, and my fiancé likes to watch while we fuck. He has a jealousy kink—which can be really hot—but he'll only participate while he's in his feathered form. He's a raven shifter, which Corbin was *well aware* of from the start."

"Um..." I swallowed, having no idea how to

respond to that bit of information. I was no prude, but I had never been around anyone who had discussed their sexual proclivities so openly before, either. "So, wait. You and Corbin are sleeping together? And your fiancé joins you during sex while he's a bird? Like, you're actually doing the dirty with a *bird*?"

"Fuck no!" Corbin shouted. "What kind of sicko do you think I am?"

The poor guy looked mortified.

Wait a second… Why was I suddenly so concerned about Corbin's embarrassment? This idiot deceived me on an epic level!

Corbin looked at me, then pointed at Alexei. "He's the one who sent Mara after you to gain intel. He also wanted to send dick pics to your new cell phone."

I dropped my mouth open in shock.

Alexei threw his hands up and shook his head. "I said nothing about dick pics!" he roared.

"So you just wanted to sext me?" This was all getting way out of hand. "And yeah. I know all about Mara now. What the fuck is wrong with her? She had me thinking she was God's gift to man."

Juniper scowled. "That she-wolf is an opportunistic bitch. I had to wear *truth earrings* so she'd stop compelling me to give her free potions."

"Can I have a pair?" I didn't want to be compelled ever again. That shit was weird.

Juniper took one of her many pairs of earrings out and handed it to me. "Free of charge. That bitch is crazy."

I held the silver jewelry in my hand, admiring it. They were simple infinity knot studs with a clear gemstone in the middle. It amazed me how something so unassuming could contain power, but I could feel it buzzing through my palm where they rested. "Thank you."

"No prob." Juniper shrugged. "I have a matching necklace, too, back at my place if you want it."

"Mara has always been a brat about that shit," Corbin pouted. "When we were kids, she'd compel me to give her all my desserts. It was awful."

Juniper gave him a look full of pity. "My poor little wolfy-poo."

"Wolfy-poo?" My brow rose.

"Babe, I told you not to call me that in front of anyone." Corbin looked terribly embarrassed.

"Can we please fucking focus?" Alexei begged.

I seconded that. I wanted to point out that the only reason Mara compelled me in the first place was because Alexei *ordered* her to, but I needed to move this conversation along, so I tabled it for now.

"Your toxic masculinity is showing, Corbin," Juniper chastised, completely ignoring Alexei. "You've got to embrace your sensitive side."

Corbin scoffed. "Toxic masculinity, my ass. I literally let you peg me while—"

"Enough!" Alexei said to Juniper and Corbin. "Get out!" The two of them held their hands up in mock surrender and backed away like Alexei was about to detonate a bomb.

"Oh." Corbin dug through his pocket. "Found that phone. You can use it until you figure your cell situation out." He placed the cell on the dresser and continued to back away slowly.

"Thanks." Now that I knew there were a bunch of monsters that went bump in the night roaming the campus, I needed to at least have it for emergency situations. I wasn't about to go without a way to check on Dad. I watched them leave the room and then turned my attention back to the infuriating wolf shifter that was now red in the face.

"I just wanted to get to know you," he admitted quietly. "My wolf is eager to be near you, okay? But logically, I know we can't ever be together like *that*. The mere idea of a wolf mating with a human is ludicrous."

"So you were just planning on using your friend to lead me on?" I asked.

I couldn't tell how I felt about this. Part of me was hurt that this man was so disgusted by his desire for me that he wanted to make me his dirty little secret. The other part was just over it all.

"I was just trying to find a way to have you in my life without the rest of the world finding out. It's not... allowed. Nothing could ever come from this. I'm an alpha, Nicole." A few hours ago, the word *alpha* would have meant nothing to me. This fucking spell warped my mind, and all the reasons we couldn't and *shouldn't* be together rushed through my consciousness. "I'd be a joke in my own pack."

Ouch. Well, that was harsh.

"Tell me how you really feel, Alexei," I mumbled.

"I'm just trying to explain everything. I can't ever be with someone so weak—"

"Weak, huh?"

"You know what I mean." Alexei's tone was full of exasperation. "You're *human*. Every time you turn a corner at this damn university, I have to worry if another supe is going to spell you, suck your blood, or—"

"I might like to meet a succubus. I hear they feed off sexual energy," I interrupted him once more. "Could be kind of fun."

"Absolutely not," Alexei replied.

I watched him struggle with the idea of me being with someone else for a moment before continuing.

"So you can't have me, but no one else can either? That seems unfair."

"This bond makes me insanely jealous and possessive. I can't help it. Believe me, if I could make it go away, I would."

I knew he felt this way, but hearing him say these things still stung. Although, considering I didn't know him, I didn't know *why* it stung so badly. Today was a lot to process, and I needed time away from all the craziness to cope with it all. A man I just met was claiming to be my mate—which was the human equivalent of a husband. And despite the *magical Xanax*, I was not coping with all this new information as well as Juniper had thought.

"Okay," I mumbled. "Then we won't be together. Easy enough."

He snapped his attention to me and clutched his chest as if I'd wounded him. "What?"

I shrugged and placed my feet on the floor, the soft carpet grounding me as I spoke. "You said it yourself. We can't be together. You don't *want* to be together. I don't even know you. This is literally very easy to fix. Stay the hell away from me, and I'll do the same."

"You'll *reject* me?" He was incredulous, as if it just occurred to him that was even an option. "You'll reject our mate bond?"

"Well… yeah? Why not?" He blanched, leaning back as if I'd slapped him, and from what I knew about mate bonds, it probably had felt exactly like that. It was a deeply physical and emotional pain to be torn from your mate, but I refused to be with someone who was embarrassed or ashamed of me.

"I guess I thought…" His voice trailed off.

"Is this, or is this not, what you wanted?" I pressed.

"It *is*. I just didn't think you'd take it so… easily."

I grabbed my purse from the nightstand and slung it over my shoulder. "It's like you said. I'm human. This shifter shit doesn't affect me. You're the one missing out. I'm just missing…" I glanced at my watch. "*Shit*. I missed orientation." Alexei stared at me as I fixed my ponytail. I looked around the cozy space, wondering whose bedroom I was in. "Where are we, anyway?"

"My place. This is my bedroom."

Of course it was. If I had been thinking clearly, instead of recovering from a magical mind-fuck, I would've instantly known that. Alexei's delicious scent permeated the air. The furniture was sturdy and masculine, and clearly expensive. It was a room fit for a king, or I supposed, in this case, an alpha.

"Right." I nodded. "Well, this has been fun and all, but I've gotta jet. Evidently, I need to walk myself around campus to scope out all my classes for tomorrow."

He stood up with panicked eyes. "Wait. I think we should talk about this some more. This is a really serious decision. We should weigh all the pros and cons before acting on anything."

I held my hand up. "Hard pass. There's really nothing to talk about or think about, dude. You already made up your mind about me when we first met. Remember?"

His mocha eyes narrowed into slits. "I'm still figuring shit out. And don't call me dude. I am *not* your dude."

"No, you're just my mate, right?" I laughed breezily, despite knowing how serious that title was in his world. Because I *wasn't* a part of his world. And I had no desire to throw myself into the wolves' den, literally or figuratively. A quick extraction was the most pragmatic solution for everyone involved.

"Nicole—" he started as I turned the handle to the door.

"Nuh-uh. As far as I'm concerned, this discussion is over. Problem solved. I'm just going to go back to my dorm and pretend I never met any of you and this whole day never happened. Later, dude." I held up a finger. "Or, you know, *never*. Because you no longer exist to me."

He gave me a long look, and a small part of me wanted him to protest just a little more. Was it wrong to be wanted, even if I knew it was just a magical bond pushing him to choose me, a bond he didn't even want?

"Fine," he croaked, though he sounded like he was in pain. "But now that you know about our society, you're required to follow our guidelines. Rule number one, you can't tell anyone about what you learned today."

"Considering they'd all think I'm crazy, you won't have to worry about that."

Alexei nodded, and silence stretched between us, the tension so thick you could sink a needle through it. "Corbin can give you a tour of the campus. I had him grab the orientation packet for you while you were resting."

"No thanks." I scoffed. "I'll take the packet, but I can manage finding my classes without him."

Alexei pulled a phone out of his back pocket and started typing something. "We'll figure this out, Nicole. I don't want to make things more difficult for you."

I paused at the door, a million thoughts still racing through my mind. "My dad is safe here, right? I mean, with all these supernaturals walking around?"

"You both are safe. At the very least, I can promise you that."

Alexei's word didn't mean much. I barely knew him, and we hadn't gotten off to a great start. It wasn't like I could tell Dad about everything I'd learned today. He was logical. Clinical. He'd think I was losing my mind. I'd need to find a way to protect him.

"Okay. Well, see you around, dude."

The absolute devastation on Alexei's face gave me pause, but I promptly reminded myself why this was the most sensible way to solve the issue at hand. And as I walked back to my dorm, haunted by his forlorn expression, I had to remind myself why I was doing this at least a dozen more times.

Maybe if I repeated it enough, I'd actually believe it.

Nicole

Since I'd missed the freshman orientation, I decided to at least visit the buildings where my classes would be so that I didn't get lost on the first day of school. I had Intro to Fashion Design, Intermediate Business, and Statistics tomorrow. My schedule was fully booked, and even though my mind was still reeling from what happened earlier, I knew I couldn't just leave.

The witches had a packet full of rules waiting in my dorm room when I got back. It was titled, *So Now You Know About Witches. It's Okay!*

Some quirky guidance counselor with a sense of humor had definitely written that. There were quite a few rules I had to follow, but there was one under-lying theme spelled out painfully clear:

Don't tell any humans about the supernatural community.

There was a long list of punishments for any humans brought into the fold who spoke about the supernatural world. Imprisonment. Fines. And in extreme cases, *death*. It spelled out a nasty future where everyone I loved would be spelled to forget about me. It even detailed how my bones would be ground and used for spells.

It was... intense. Terrifying.

All I wanted to do was call my father and tell him to pack a suitcase and get the fuck out of here. But until he learned about what was really going on at Redwood, I couldn't tell him. He'd think I was crazy if I made us both leave in the middle of the night like a couple of thieves. This job was *too* good of an opportunity. He'd be concerned if I was giving up free tuition and his lifelong goal of receiving a Nobel Prize for his work.

I had to stay here and learn. I had to figure out a way to protect both of us without letting him know the truth.

"Knock knock." Corbin strolled into my dorm like he owned the place.

I snapped my attention to him and frowned. "The

purpose of a knock is to wait for someone to invite you in."

Dammit. I needed to remember to lock that thing.

"You literally have a welcome mat in front of your door. It's basically an open invitation. Speaking of which, you might want to remove it before any vampires see it. Cristian would happily crawl into bed with you while you sleep."

I couldn't tell if he was joking or not, but the new encyclopedia in my brain rushed through facts about vampires, supporting his claim.

"Shit," I cursed before running past him to remove the mat. I thought it was cute, but I definitely didn't want any vampires thinking they had free rein in my dorm room. Dad also had one of these that I'd need to ditch as well. "Thanks for the tip, but what are you doing here?"

Corbin grinned. "I'm your tour guide. Plus, everyone thinks I've claimed you now, so I thought I'd give the gossip mill something to chomp on. I can almost hear it now *'Corbin was with that beautiful human today. I bet his gigantic, monster-sized cock broke her in half.'*"

"You're disgusting." I grabbed my purse and slung it over my shoulder. "I don't need a tour, and I definitely don't want to associate with a shifter. Alexei made it very clear how unwelcomed humans are."

His brow arched playfully as he looked me up and down. "It's true. I'm slumming it with you. But you're hot, so I'll make an exception."

"Gee, thanks."

"You're welcome. Come on. I already printed off your new schedule and—"

"*New* schedule?"

Corbin gave me an apologetic look. "Since you're in the know now, supernatural law requires you to take a course on the rules. Basically, they'll show you a bunch of videos of humans getting tortured for trying to tell people about us."

I clenched my jaw. "Excuse me?"

"It's a required core course. You can thank Antonio for that one."

I let out a sigh and squeezed my eyes shut in frustration. This was all way too fucking much. "Why did Antonio do this to me? I don't get it."

Corbin shrugged. "Witches are weird. No one really knows why they do the things they do. But if you'd like, we can make a pit stop on our tour and go chat with him."

I wasn't really thrilled about the idea of spending a late afternoon with Corbin, but getting information out of Antonio and kicking his ass sounded fun. Knowledge was power. At least this way, I knew I could keep Dad safe. But it was still intrusive and dangerous. I didn't like that I had no say in any of this.

"Deal," I snapped. "But no coffee, Wolf-boy."

Corbin chuckled and followed me out of my room. As we traveled down the hall, some of the students stared at us. I could hear their barely contained whispers, even though I tried to ignore it.

Why is she with Beta Corbin?

She's a human, right? What's so special about her?

She's not even pretty.

"Hey, gorgeous," Corbin called loudly to me so that the entire hall could hear him. "I love the way your ass looks in that skirt. Makes me want to take a bite. *Rawr.*"

I blushed, ignoring him as I fast-walked out of the dorm building and took a deep breath once I was outside, away from all the prying eyes.

"Antonio will be in the art building where all your design classes are, so we can start there. He's studying sculpting." Corbin nodded toward the quad. "After you."

"So you can stare at my ass as I walk? No thank you."

Corbin tilted his head back and laughed, the sound playful and full of joy. I was kind of getting the vibe that Corbin lived by the motto: Work Hard, Play Harder. "Fair enough."

As we walked down the quad toward the art building, Corbin gave me information that I was certain I wouldn't get at the human freshman orientation.

"The fae run the agriculture garden. Humans walking through it only see normal earthly plants and crops, but there are actually a lot of plants native to their lands there. Some are creepy looking. Some deadly. They spelled the ones that can kill you with barriers so no idiot humans find themselves in the belly of a Corpse Flower." Corbin shivered.

"I'll avoid the fuck out of that, thank you very much."

I was creeped out and curious all at once. I'd have to make sure Dad didn't take his lunch breaks there. He loved the outdoors and gardening, even though he could barely keep a fake fern alive.

"Over there is the history building. The witches have a summoning room for ghosts. Grad students get to interview people from the past for the most accurate thesis. It's actually pretty cool."

I froze in my tracks. "Could they summon my mother?"

Corbin turned to face me, his expression solemn. "Ghosts are usually people with unfinished business. It's always possible that your mother stayed behind, but more likely than not, she's already crossed.

Usually, you have bitter world leaders or people that died from traumatic world events who stay."

I nodded. "Could we try? I mean, maybe she's here?"

Corbin placed a comforting hand on my shoulder. "Believe me, it would be better if she crossed. Ghosts have... for lack of a better term... haunting experiences."

He was right. I wouldn't want my mother to suffer for almost nineteen years. "Right. Okay." I chewed on the inside of my cheek and cleared my throat. "Shall we continue?"

Corbin nodded at another building. "Chemistry lab is there. Most witches are chem majors for obvious reasons. The biology lab is there, where your father works."

"You know where he works?"

"I know a lot about him. The university is very excited to have him."

I looked at Corbin, trying to understand if there was a bitterness in his tone. "Is there something I need to know about my dad, Corbin?"

He looked around, as if trying to see if anyone was listening in on our conversation. "Let's just say Alexei and I will keep an eye on him to make sure he's safe. Some of the applications for his research have super-natural benefits. I'm not sure if he'll be given a reveal spell or not. They might let him continue to conduct his research without letting him know they're applying it to our genetics."

I swallowed, my throat feeling dry. "What kind of benefits?"

"Nothing sinister. It'll actually help a lot of shifters with a mutation in their genes. Your father is very important here—probably more than he even realizes. It's a good thing, actually, because that means Alpha Jones—Alexei's father—will protect him."

That did sound like a good thing. But what if his research didn't pan out? Would he still be safe then?

"Thank you for telling me that. Despite everything I've learned today, I'm mostly just worried about him."

"Alexei is watching him right now, actually. No vampires can get into the lab. The witches won't bother him. And shifters that are loyal to Alpha Jones will do anything to keep him safe. He could be the answer to our prayers."

"What about shifters that aren't loyal to Alpha Jones?" I had a sinking feeling in my stomach.

Corbin gave me an amiable smile. "Well, I suppose Alexei will tear out their throats." My eyes widened. Fuck. "Let's go see Antonio."

And with that ominous statement, Corbin started

whistling and strutted down the quad. Not a care in the world.

My eyes lingered on the biology lab, trepidation making my spine tense. I'd keep my father safe, supernaturals be damned.

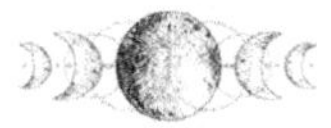

ANTONIO WAS IN AN ART ROOM, humming to himself and working on a sculpture of a gigantic cock. He covered part of it in plastic, but there was no denying its phallic shape.

"Wow! It looks just like mine," Corbin said in greeting the moment he walked through the door. "You even got the freckle on my shaft right."

Antonio didn't look bothered by Corbin's crude statement. "What do you want, shifter? If you're trying to get on my good side to get closer to my womb mate, you're wasting your time. I may be into dick, but I wouldn't touch *your* dick with a fifty-foot Fleshlight."

"As if I'd need your help to get Juniper to like me." Corbin scoffed. "And my dick is rather occupied with your sister, anyway."

Antonio made a fake gagging sound.

My brows crinkled when Corbin mentioned his witchy friend. "Wait... Juniper is related to this guy?!"

Antonio's golden eyes flicked to me in surprise as if he just noticed I was in the room. "Oh, hey there, gorgeous. I didn't see you there." He gave me a good once over. There was no mistaking the interest in his gaze. "And yes, June is my twin sister. Can't you see the resemblance?"

Now that he mentioned it, they definitely had similar features, especially the unique eye color.

"How are you feeling?" he asked.

I folded my arms over my chest. "Oh, I'm super! It's not every day someone has their brain magically rearranged."

He winked. "You're welcome."

"I wasn't thanking you." I glared. "Ever hear of a thing called sarcasm?"

Glops of wet clay clung to the ends of his electric blue hair as he brushed it away from his face. He grabbed some kind of wooden tool from the table beside him and began molding the clay to resemble veins. The way his hands moved over the erotic art oddly transfixed me.

"Sure, I have," Antonio replied. "Your boy here is an expert at it."

"Corbin's not my boy. I *have* no boy."

"Hmm... funny, because I heard differently.

Classes haven't even started yet, and the whole campus is already abuzz with the beta's sudden interest in a human."

"Awesome," I grumbled.

Antonio's lips twitched. "But it's good to know you're unattached. We should go out sometime. Are you by chance into DVP? Because I've been seeing this guy who really wants to try it. It's harder than you'd think to find a willing girl."

"What the hell is DVP?"

Corbin coughed and muttered, "Oh shit." He swung a heavy arm around my shoulders. "You're adorable, Nicole. Has anyone ever told you that before? You see, our pal Antonio here, was propositioning you for a three-way. Specifically, *two peens in your V.* Now, there's something I've never tried, and I've tried most things. I've gotta admit I'm intrigued. What do you say, Nicole? Are you interested?"

My jaw dropped as I took a giant step back. "What the hell is wrong with you two?!"

Both men laughed, making me scowl.

"I'm so glad I could amuse you, assholes." I flipped them off to punctuate my statement.

Corbin held his hands up. "Hey, I was just joking. I have no desire to get my ass kicked by my best friend. I can't say the same for Antonio, but that fucker gets off on risky behavior. He's always breaking the rules."

I snorted. "Like slipping *a potentially fatal spell* to an unsuspecting human?"

"Hey!" Antonio shouted. "You were perfectly safe! I know my measurements! But this particular situation had nothing to do with my impulses. When the fates give me an order, I follow. I've learned not to question the visions. When I saw you walk into that shop—the girl I've been dreaming about for weeks—I knew I had to act while I had the chance."

"Visions?" I questioned. "*What* visions? About me?"

He mimed sealing his lips. "Can't say. When it's time for you to learn, they'll let you know."

"So you're telling me that you had some sort of vision that no one else can see, and I'm just supposed to be like, *oh cool, no problem, bro!*" I hissed. "That's pretty damn convenient."

Antonio shrugged. "You don't have to believe me. But witches are allowed to reveal our world to humans in extenuating circumstances. My visions once stopped an entire island of people from dying from an exploding volcano."

I looked to Corbin to see if he was bullshitting me. "It's true. Antonio brags about it at parties to get laid."

"Being clairvoyant isn't easy, you know. I have dead people in my head all the time telling me to *save that squirrel* or *don't let that girl go to that party.* And my personal favorite—*make sure to wear a condom, or your child will take over the world.*"

I cringed. "Okay. Point made."

"Is he complaining about his evil, non-existent child again?" Juniper asked while waltzing into the room. She smiled at us and waved her fingers flirtatiously at Corbin.

"Antonio Junior is a menace. He keeps me up all night with his plans for world domination. I had to break up with my last girlfriend because the monthly scares were too much." The warlock shivered.

Juniper rolled her eyes. "I'd hardly call that vampire she-devil a girlfriend."

"Okay. Friend with benefits."

"Friend?" Juniper scoffed.

"Fine. Booty call."

Juniper wrinkled her nose playfully. "Much better. Visions or not, you should have discussed it with poor Nicole before giving her the spell. What if she'd fallen on the concrete and cracked her head open?" I could see now that they were most definitely siblings. The way they ribbed one another was proof of that.

"Believe me." Antonio laughed. "She would have been fine. Promise. In fact, she's *more* than fine."

I narrowed my eyes on him. "What the hell is that supposed to mean?"

"You'll learn soon enough. Nice necklace, by the

way." His lips formed into a knowing smile that I wanted to pick apart with a blade.

I brushed my hand over the gold chain around my neck.

"I was thinking maybe you could hang out with Ivan and me this week? I've got room on my calendar for a little fun." Juniper was giving Corbin some major *fuck me* eyes.

"I was thinking..." Corbin shifted on his feet. "Maybe just you and I could—"

"I'd prefer the *three* of us," Juniper interrupted. "It's so much more fun."

Corbin's expression flashed with disappointment for a moment, but he slipped back into his easygoing persona. Something about their interaction made me feel... believe it or not... *sorry* for the asshole. "Of course, I'd love to. I've been dying to eat your pussy—"

"Disgusting. All of you. Out of my space! I can't let my sister's sex life ruin my creative process." Antonio shuddered and gestured to his giant sculpture of a pocket rocket.

Juniper gave her brother an incredulous look. "You're literally creating a sculpture of Corbin's dick with the photo I sent you. I think the lines have already been blurred."

"Wait. What? I thought... oh... I was kidding,

but..." Corbin tilted his head to the side. "Yep. That's my cock."

It was all I could do not to laugh.

"You told me I could share that photo." Juniper grabbed his arm, pressing her chest against his lean muscles.

Corbin looked up at the sculpture with fresh, wide eyes. "I was thinking you'd send it to your hot witch friends. Not your twin brother."

"I'm calling this piece *A Massive Disappointment*," Antonio said with glee. "What do you think? Pretty catchy title, right?"

"Sure..." Corbin agreed. "If by '*massive disappointment*' you mean '*sex so great you'll be dickmatized for life.*'" Corbin lifted his chin toward Juniper. "Tell him, baby. I'm the best you've ever had, right?"

"You know how much I love riding your monster cock, Corbin." June rolled her eyes. "But I didn't think you were the type of guy who needed an ego stroke."

"I've got something you can stroke." Corbin wagged his brows.

I threw my hands up. "Oh, my God, you guys! Have you ever heard of something called TMI?"

I swore everyone I'd met at this university so far was sex-crazed.

Not everyone, my brain taunted. *Alexei seemed genuinely interested in getting to know you.*

I scoffed to myself because even if that were true, it didn't matter. Alexei made his position on our supposed *fated mates* status clear. And no matter how curious I was, I couldn't entertain the idea of being with him.

CHAPTER

TEN

Nicole

INSTEAD OF THE nine a.m. statistics class I had planned to attend, I was walking into Introduction to Supernatural Laws and Regulations. I couldn't say I was going to miss doing math so early in the morning—why any school would schedule math before noon was beyond me—but I wasn't exactly thrilled about my new class, either. My unease grew as I stepped into the small classroom, which was about the size of a shoe box, and saw only two other people.

So much for my plan to blend in with the crowd.

I took the only empty seat, next to a girl with wild auburn curls and gold bangles stretching to her elbows on both arms. "Hey. I'm Nicole."

"Hi! I'm Isla!" My new classmate had a thick brogue and a big smile.

"So…" I looked around, wondering where the professor was. "You know about supes, too, huh?"

"Oh, yeah." Isla nodded, gesturing to the boy beside her. "Angus and I accidentally happened upon an old Druid circle one day back home and had *quite* the eye-opening experience. Our Ma and Da had been tellin' us stories for years, but we never gave it much thought. It was folklore, ya know? Lots of that back home."

Angus, who I presumed was Isla's brother, gave me a little wave, pushing his black-rimmed glasses up his nose.

"A Druid circle?" My eyes widened. "Where are you from?"

"A little lochside village in the Highlands. You've probably never heard of it."

"What happened? Did you… travel through a portal?"

"You could say that." Angus's face drained of color as his sister spoke. "But we don't talk about it. We may have been forced into this exchange program, but as far as my brother and I are concerned, we want *nothing* to do with *them* ever again. We're out of here as soon as this term is over."

"*Them?*" I could tell the topic was disturbing the

siblings, but my curiosity got the better of me. "What kind of *them*?"

"The fae," she whispered, while her brother looked like he was about to puke.

"What *about* fae?" All three of us startled as the musical voice spoke.

"Uh…" Oh, man, poor Angus looked like he was going to piss himself now.

When I followed his gaze, I found the most beautiful creature I had ever seen in my life. I instinctively knew this woman was fae, which explained Angus's trepidation. The pair sitting next to me obviously had a terrible encounter with her brethren. *This* fae, however, wasn't giving off evil vibes. In fact, she was… dare I say, friendly? Elegant and classy, too. Dressed in a smart pantsuit that hugged her hourglass figure—Chanel if I wasn't mistaken—and a pair of killer red-soled heels. She stood tall at the front of the class with a warm smile stretched across her face. Her pale blonde hair was loose, falling to her waist in beachy waves. It was so shiny; I had a sudden urge to touch it, to feel if it was as soft as it looked. Her emerald green eyes were round, framed by thick, inky black lashes. I fixed my gaze on her pouty red lips as she introduced herself.

"Hello, everyone. Welcome to Intro to Supernatural Law and Regs. I'm Dr. Cammie Viden, your guide into the Wonderful World of Weird."

"Hi," Isla and I mumbled in unison.

"Why don't we start with introductions? Just the basics. Tell me who you are, where you're from, and why you were enrolled in this class. As you can see, our group is small, so we'll have *plenty* of opportunities to get to know one another better throughout the semester." She clapped her hands together. "I'll start. Most of my colleagues call me Dr. Viden, but that's much too stuffy for me, so you can call me Cammie. I'm a fae, but don't worry about giving me your name in return because, *A*, I already have your names on my student roster. And *B*, as a professor at this university, I can't use it against you. We're magically bound. In fact, that applies to *everything* said in this room. Nothing you tell me—or each other—within these four walls can be used to harm you or expose any secrets."

Well, that was good to know. Giving a fae your full name was giving them power over you. After the bullshit with Mara, that was the last thing I wanted.

Cammie gave us a moment to process that before continuing. "I like to think of myself as more of a… *progressive*, which is why I volunteered to teach this class. For thousands of years, many of my kind have treated humans rather poorly, so we don't have the best rep. I feel it's my responsibility to help change that perception. Not all fae are bad, just like not all humans are good. I grew up as a member of the light court but left my royal post about twenty years ago to live on earth and help improve human-fae relations." She pointed to Isla. "Now, you go."

"Uh..." Isla blushed, visibly uncomfortable with being put on the spot. "I'm Isla McMillan. This is my brother Angus." She inclined her head toward her brother. "He hasn't talked much since... well, *since*, so if ya don't mind, I'll be doin' the introductions for both of us. Anyway, we grew up in a small Scottish village about thirty kilometers outside of Inverness. We're here because we... uh... accidentally traveled beyond the veil through some standing stones."

"Oh, my!" Cammie gasped, placing her palm against her ample chest. "That must've been quite harrowing! Passing through the stones is one of the most barbaric methods to travel between dimensions. You never know where those things are going to dump you. My deepest apologies! I'm so relieved you made it back safely. How many earth years were you gone?"

"Um... thank you?" Isla and her brother looked thoroughly confused, and I was guessing I did, too. "We were gone for just over twenty-two earth years, but it really only felt like a few days. It's weird. One late summer day, we were getting ready to go back to university with our friends, and the next, most of those same friends were our parents' age. Or... our parents' age when we... uh, disappeared. They're much older now."

Holy shit.

I knew time passed differently in Faerie, the land of the fae, but I didn't realize it was that extreme.

"It's nice to meet you both." Cammie's ethereal eyes briefly shifted to Angus before slicing over to me. "And our last-minute addition, go ahead and introduce yourself."

I cleared my throat. "I'm Nicole Fairweather. I was born and raised in Baltimore. I was originally planning to attend Parsons, but when my dad was offered a research grant here, I decided to attend Redwood U instead."

"Yes, I've met your father." Cammie smiled fondly. "He's quite charming."

My eyes widened. "You met my dad?"

She nodded. "I did. I'm actually the lead geneticist at the university, so I suppose that technically makes me his boss. Hopefully, he doesn't think I'm too bossy." God, even her laugh was pretty. "So, Nicole. I know why you're at Redwood. But I do *not* know why you're in *this class*."

Crap.

How was I supposed to explain this? Was it okay

to tell her? She said she was magically bound not to say anything, but what if that wasn't true?

"Go on, Nicole," Cammie prompted. "I promise on my life, this is a safe space."

"Um..." I really hoped I didn't regret trusting this woman. I supposed I could give her the basics, without revealing anything I learned about Antonio's supposed visions or the fates. "A warlock slipped me a reveal spell, which gave me an instant crash course in all things supernatural. As you can probably imagine, it's been a weird couple of days."

Her perfectly sculpted brows lifted in surprise. "Wow. That's... did you consent to this spell?"

I shook my head. "Nope."

Her lips curved into a sad smile. "I'm sorry."

I shrugged. "What's done is done, right?"

"It still doesn't make spelling you without your consent right," she insisted. "But I'm glad to meet you."

"Same."

As Dr. Viden, er, *Cammie,* launched into her overview of the syllabus, I listened to the course requirements, feeling a bit relieved that there wouldn't be too much work involved. "I take a different approach to this class than what my superiors deem appropriate. I think it's important to provide emotional stability and support during this tumultuous time in your life. I understand that all of this can be very confusing, and the sudden shift in reality can make you question what's real and what's not." Cammie's voice was solemn as she spoke. "I'd like to take turns and discuss some of the things you're struggling with."

Everyone turned to look at me, as if they expected me to kick off this little trauma dump. I cleared my throat. "Guess I'll go first." I tapped my pencil on the top of our shared table and stared at the tile floor as I spoke. "I suppose learning about everything isn't as hard for me as I thought it would be. The witches explained that a component of the spell would make it easier for me to accept all of these changes. But the hard part is not telling the people I care about. I've been somewhat avoiding my father because I don't know what to say to him."

When I looked up at Cammie, she gave me another sad smile. "Many people in your position feel that way. It can also create tension in your relationships when you're burdened with such a powerful secret."

"I guess I'm just worried about his safety more than anything. Now I know about all these dangers lurking around every corner, and it feels like we can't escape it. And even if I were to pack our bags and demand that we leave, he wouldn't understand. My dad is the most important person in the world to me, and I can't even look him in the eye."

Cammie grabbed a box of tissues and walked it over to me. I hadn't even realized that I was crying. If my first class on the first day of school was any indication of how my year would go, then my time at Redwood University was going to be total shit.

"I can assure you that your father is very safe. I know we haven't established a foundation of trust yet, but he is on my team, and I take the safety of my colleagues very seriously. Your father is a brilliant man, and his research is important to a lot of people. The shifters might run this school, but there is a reason everyone fears the fae." She winked and Angus whimpered.

I shrugged. "Everyone keeps reassuring me that he's safe. It's just hard to trust in that, and I still feel like I'm keeping this massive secret from him."

Cammie averted her eyes, and an expression crossed her features that I couldn't place. Was it regret? Concern? "Perhaps you won't have to keep that secret for long. Like I said, your father is very important to the university."

I sat up in my seat. "Are you saying you're going to give him a reveal spell, too?"

She looked around the room and cleared her throat. "I'm not at liberty to discuss that. However, I *can* tell you that sometimes a person can feel more grounded in their reality if they find common ground and things that tie them to the life they knew before learning about all of this. Maybe you should focus on what your father does know. Find ways to include him in your life without telling him everything."

I nodded. I could still tell Dad about my classes and maybe even about my boy troubles. I could still take care of him—in my own way.

Cammie then turned her attention to my other classmates, but I tuned them out while thinking of all the ways I could still protect my father. This class would allow me to arm myself with knowledge. And although I was still wary of Cammie, she was another resource—another pair of eyes to watch Dad when I couldn't. Perhaps this class wasn't such a bad thing after all.

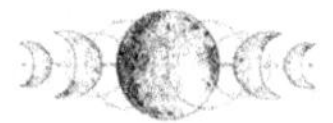

After the heaviness of my morning class, I was absolutely thrilled to go to my Intro to Fashion Design course. The moment I stepped through the classroom door and saw an entire wall of fabric, I squealed. A few of my classmates turned to stare at me, their noses pointed high in the air, but I didn't give a single fuck. Fashion was in my blood. And right now, it would be something that kept me sane.

I scanned the room, my spelled mind cataloging every supe in attendance. We had quite a few vampires chatting in the corner and eyeing me with hunger, and a couple of fae were whispering to themselves at a desk. I spotted a lonely human sitting down and immediately decided that they would be my friend this semester. I didn't care if they turned out to be a nose-picking bitch. I needed someone of the human variety to sit with.

I sucked in a deep breath and moved to go sit with the blonde girl biting her nails in the front row, but a firm hand wrapped around my bicep, stopping me. I spun around and tipped my head up, my mouth dropping open as I glared at the infuriating vampire who tried to suck my blood the night of my first college party.

"*Cristian*," I gritted before trying to jerk out of his grip. He was incredibly strong.

"Nicole," he purred. "I'm so happy to have run into you again. I'm afraid I didn't make the best first impression."

"You mean when you tried to pull your vampire voodoo bullshit and take a bite out of me?"

He flashed a smile, the pointed tips of his teeth

sending a shiver down my spine. "You caught me! Guilty. I want to lick, suck, and bite that creamy skin of yours."

My breath hitched as I fought the urge to knee him in the balls. My mental encyclopedia ran me through everything I needed to know about vampires. They used lust and pheromones to trap their prey. Everything about them was supposed to draw in weak-minded humans. Their venom made the experience pleasurable for humans, and their saliva healed wounds. A vampire could be born, but for some reason, the encyclopedia halted mid-stream of thought with how they could be turned.

"I heard you got a reveal spell, little human." Cristian grinned. "If you're wanting to join the club, I'm afraid that handy spell won't tell you our little secret. The world doesn't want a bunch of bloodthirsty immortals walking around."

He licked his lips, and I frowned at him. "I have no desire to become one of you."

He leaned even closer, his lips mere millimeters away from mine. "Shame. We could have had so much fun. Vampires have impeccable stamina."

I blushed. I wasn't sure if it was his vampire powers or the heated way he stared at me, but there was a bit of a flutter in my belly from his words. I didn't understand it.

"Just keep your hands to yourself. I'm not interested."

He took a step back and a deep breath. "Please forgive me. Your blood calls to me. I can't explain it. I can barely control myself."

I looked over at the group of vampires that were talking earlier. All of them wore equal expressions of desire. "What do you mean?"

He leaned in and took a deep breath. "You smell so sweet. Like a decadent treat."

Swallowing nervously, I took a step back. "Well, why don't you sit on the other side of the room so that I'm not a temptation for you, yeah? I'd hate for you to lose control. Also, I'm supposed to be on my period in three weeks, so you should probably just skip class then."

His eyes first widened in shock, then he roared with laughter, his chest shaking with every chuckle. "Oh, I like you. I'll have you know, orgasms are great for menstrual cramps. A thoughtful vampire lover is way more effective than ibuprofen, little human."

I cringed. "That's disgusting."

"Don't knock it till you try it."

"I... I'm literally speechless because I'm now visualizing something that is making my asshole clench."

"I wasn't talking about your asshole, but I'm always game if you're into that." Cristian laughed some more and walked around me to place his hand at the small of my back, guiding me to a seat. I would have swatted him away, but I wasn't quite sure what he was capable of. It really freaked me out, and I hated that once again the supernatural world was stealing my slice of normal pie. "Let's sit together."

"I was thinking of sitting with that human girl over there, actually, so if you don't mind—"

A booming voice cut me off. "Take your seats. Become acquainted with your tablemate because the seat you chose is yours for the semester."

It came from a woman wearing green... pajamas? It looked like the silk pajamas I wore on Christmas Eve. She had cropped red hair and wore purple glasses. My mind-fuck wasn't going off, so I assumed my new professor was human.

"Hello." She plopped a large leather portfolio on the podium. "Welcome to Intro to Fashion Design. My name is Professor Hankey, and I'll be teaching this course." She rolled her neck and gave the classroom a bored once-over.

"I-I thought this was art history." The blonde girl that was sitting in the front stood up, her eyes wide. "I need to go find the right class."

Professor Hankey looked annoyed. "This isn't an airport, darling. You don't have to announce your departure."

The class laughed. Beside me, Cristian leaned over to whisper in my ear. "Guess you're stuck with me."

Lovely.

Professor Hankey started writing on the board.

"Why are you even in this class?" I hissed.

"Easy elective. Plus, I'm a damn good model."

"I can assure you this *won't* be an easy grade." The professor stopped writing and spun around to glare at Cristian. "Mr. Luca, is it? I looked at your transcripts. Last semester, you took Intro to Sculpting. The semester before, you took Intro to Dance. I'm curious why this is your fifth year at Redwood. One might say you're avoiding graduation by constantly switching your major."

How did she know who he was? I supposed if this were his fifth year, he'd have plenty of time to build a reputation. Although, it didn't sound like Cristian had a *good* reputation. Not that I was surprised.

Cristian returned her frosty expression. "One might say that's *none of your concern*."

The tension in the room was palpable as our professor and the vampire engaged in a standoff. I had to give the woman credit. If she were human, as I suspected, she had some serious lady balls.

A catty grin stretched across her face as she broke the silence. "Well, one might say this is *my* class, so *everything* is *my* concern. But as long as you apply yourself and don't waste my time, we won't have a problem. Understood?"

A muscle in Cristian's cheek jumped. I had a feeling he wasn't used to being challenged. "Understood."

"Good. Let's begin, shall we?" The professor nodded. "As I mentioned, this is *not* an easy class. I do *not* grade on a curve. Redwood University's fashion design program has been compared to the Parsons School of Design, and I have every intention of maintaining that accreditation. I expect you to show up, follow directions, and I want to see ingenuity, people! If you don't have a creative bone in your body, get the fuck out of my class *right now*."

My jaw dropped as three other people left the classroom. I didn't think I'd ever heard a teacher curse before. Was this normal in college, or did Professor Hankey just not give a damn? I had a feeling it was the latter.

She waited until the last student ran out the door. "This class gives you a purposeful perspective into the world of fashion. It'll give you the framework for success, introducing you to several relevant art and design concepts, tools, and methods. We'll examine traditional disciplines as well as more progressive paths. We'll explore form, silhouette, material, and process. By the end of the semester, you should have a firm grasp on design-thinking and creative problem-solving strategies. All that said, if it doesn't sound like this is the right class for you, *get the fuck out.*" The professor stared pointedly at the vampire by my side, but he didn't take the bait. There were, however, two more students who left. Now, there were only ten of us left.

Sheesh, Hankey obviously had a *tough love* approach to teaching.

I wasn't sure if I should be terrified for what's coming or excited because she takes it so seriously. I really hoped I could live up to her expectations with everything else going on.

I supposed time would tell.

ELEVEN

Nicole

"Dad. You can't keep eating this crap. Your teeth are going to rot out." I pinched the bridge of my nose.

His new apartment was covered in Twinkie wrappers, and he hadn't unpacked a single box. I'd had every intention of going back to my dorm to try and sort through my thoughts, but the idea of being alone and coping with the knowledge that shifters, vamps, fae, and who knew what other creatures were prowling this campus made me want to avoid reality for a little bit longer.

"But they're so delicious," Dad pouted like a toddler that wanted dessert for dinner.

"I'm putting you on a diet. You can't spend twelve

hours in the lab and come home and have a Twinkie. You need protein and healthy fats."

He shrugged before flipping through a textbook.

I sighed. "Dad. I'm serious. Those things have a seven-year shelf life. Do you know how many preservatives need to be in one to make that possible? It's disgusting. Forget about your teeth for a moment. Think about what your diet is doing to your arteries and your heart."

He jotted down some notes on a pad of paper before speaking again. "Honey, I appreciate your concern, but I'll be just fine. Why don't you tell me about you? How was your first day of class? Have you made any new friends?"

"My room is great," I hedged, not willing to touch the friends topic with a ten-foot pole. "I'm glad I got a single, even if living in a dorm is only temporary."

"That's wonderful, sweetheart," he mumbled distractedly, scratching more notes onto the paper.

I laughed to myself. Whenever he'd get in the zone, I liked to mess with him. "I also wrecked your car."

"Hmmm."

"And I met a guy having a threesome with a bird," I added.

"How interesting."

"I put that picture of Mom on my nightstand."

That had to work. Anytime I brought her up, he tuned in completely.

"Oh, honey." He finally looked up from his work. "She would be so proud of you for rushing Beta Phi."

I held back a sob when my built-in supernatural reference guide produced some upsetting information. The moment I thought about pledging, it just popped into my brain like a Google search result. Although fraternities and sororities all belonged to national chapters, they were run a bit differently at Redwood U. At this university, each house was assigned a different supernatural faction. Sure, anyone could pledge, because they couldn't risk exposing themselves to humans, but unless you were a proud card-carrying member of the wolf shifter community, you'd never get into Beta Phi. I was a legacy; it was my mother's sorority from her days at Harvard. That should have given me a leg up over other pledges. But since I was a lowly human in their eyes, I had zero chance of being accepted.

In a nutshell, shifters were making my life hell.

"Are you okay?" Dad asked, jolting me out of my thoughts. This whole mind-fuck thing was super useful, but also overwhelming.

"I'm actually wondering if I should just focus on school, though. A sorority is a big, um, time commitment and—"

Dad whirled around and stared at me. "What? You've literally been talking about this for years, Nicole. Is everything okay?"

I swallowed. "I just... it's really competitive. Now that I've met some of the girls here, I'm not sure being a legacy is enough to get in."

Dad wordlessly pulled out his laptop and started mumbling to himself. I was hoping for maybe a few words of encouragement, but this was typical of him. He wasn't good at pep talks or knowing the right thing to say sometimes. It wasn't until I heard the sound of his video chat dialing that I realized what he was doing. Evidently, he didn't have the same problem with his login info.

"Dad?"

He looked down at his kitchen table and smiled a little. "You deserve to see how great you are, Nicole."

I smiled back at him. Even though he didn't meet my gaze, I knew he was subtly showing me in his own way how much he loved me. This wasn't the first time he called on the girl gang to give me a pep talk. When I started my period, all of mom's old sorority sisters threw me a virtual party to celebrate my womanhood, while dad went out to buy red velvet cake.

"Hey, hey, hey!" a chipper voice sounded.

I rounded the table, and Dad got up so I could sit down. Mom's sorority sister Jade was in the frame with Chanel sunglasses on her face and the wind whipping at her black hair. I could see the beach in the background and knew she was on another one of her lavish vacations.

"Hi, Jade!" I gave her a little wave.

"Hey there, beautiful. Love your outfit. It's super chic."

Another person joined the video chat. She was yelling at someone behind the screen. "I told you, Bridget. When the Fairweathers call, you cancel my plans." Hannah Oakley, CEO of one of the largest book subscription boxes in the country, then smiled at me from her home office in New York. "Hello there, Nicole baby. Jade! You look fabulous, as always."

"Back at you, darling." Jade winked. "Love the bangs. They're super trendy right now."

Hannah ruffled her blunt blonde hair with a smile, then turned the conversation back to me. "Last time your father called, he wanted us to give you the sex talk before college. You're wrapping it up, right?"

If I was eating something, I would have choked on it. I surreptitiously glanced at my father and saw his ears reddening.

Awkward much?

"Nothing to report."

Jade pouted. "Well, that's not fun. You need to

remember to loosen up while at that middle of nowhere school."

I giggled. Jade was *very* against me going to Redwood—and Hannah was too for that matter—but they understood why I did. They both loved Dad like a brother and also helped him whenever they could. They were Mom's best friends and surrogate mothers to me throughout my life. We were so close, I often referred to them as my aunts. I got my sense of adventure, drive, and fashion from both of them.

"Where is Bee? She's usually on these calls," Hannah asked, and as if summoned by her, my best friend in the entire world came on the screen.

"Oh my God, Nicole!" she shrieked the moment the line connected. "I almost sent a search party. You haven't answered a single one of my texts!" I smiled at my best friend. She had on a cozy knit sweater and wide-rimmed glasses. Her wavy black hair was piled up in a messy bun on top of her head.

"Sorry, Bee. This place has terrible cell service. I'm borrowing a guy's phone in case of emergencies, but I'm trying not to use it otherwise."

Dad ordered the signal boosters online, but they would take about two weeks to get here. According to him, two-day delivery wasn't an option this far out from civilization.

"Seriously?" Jade scowled. "I don't like that one

bit, though I'm not surprised, considering where you are. And what *guy*? Is he a sexy guy? A friend with benefits, perhaps?"

"Just a friend," I stated. "*No* benefits." I didn't really want to get into a conversation about Alexei *or* Corbin.

"This is unacceptable," Hannah agreed. "Once you have your phone working, I'll be asking about this *friend*. Don't think you can avoid our question, missy!"

Bee sighed in relief. "Tell Pops thank you for calling us."

"You're welcome," Dad chimed in from beside me. He didn't like to be on screen. He said he didn't know where to look or what to do with his hands while video chatting.

"So what's the emergency?" Jade swatted at a mosquito. "You only call all of us when something is wrong."

"Nicole is thinking about not rushing this year," Dad explained.

My stomach tightened. I wasn't necessarily ready to discuss this with everyone. I'd only just learned about the sorority being *shifters only*.

"What?!" all three women exclaimed at once.

I ducked my head but quickly reminded myself I had nothing to be ashamed of. I didn't ask for this, and I certainly didn't need to wear a mask in front of these women. I mean, I couldn't exactly give them *all* the details, but I could talk this out with them.

"Nic." Bee smiled softly. "Tell us what's going through your head."

"*So* many things," I answered honestly. "It's just… this place… the people… they're not what I was expecting. I don't know if I'm what this branch of Beta Phi is looking for."

"Oh, honey, it's natural to have doubts," Hannah assured me. All four of us chuckled when Hannah's twenty-pound cat, Mr. Whiskers, jumped onto her desk and aimed his kitty butt right at the camera. "Quit showing off, Mr. Whiskers!" Mr. Whiskers let out a whine that sounded suspiciously like *meow-maaaa* as she picked him up and set him on the floor.

"It's okay if you don't want to rush because you have other interests," Jade assured me. "Please don't feel like you have to do this because your mom did. She would want you to be happy—"

"And we will support whatever direction you decide to go in," Hannah interrupted.

"But if you're backing out because you don't think you're good enough, then I'm hopping on a plane to slap some sense into you," Bee finished.

Jade and Hannah nodded their heads in agreement. After clearing my throat, I spoke. "I just don't think I'm what they're looking for. I've been… learning a lot about this particular chapter, and they only pick... locals."

I swore Jade and Hannah exchanged loaded glances.

Jade pushed her sunglasses onto the top of her head. "I'm going to call my friend Becky. She's an alumnus at your school and was in Beta Phi. Her family has... influence in the area. Trust me. I'll get her to write you a letter of recommendation, okay? She owes me one."

My eyes widened. I wondered if Jade knew her friend Becky sometimes turned into a fucking wolf.

I wasn't sure that was going to help my situation, but I was thankful she was willing to use her connections to help, so I gave her a polite smile. "Thanks, Jade."

"And I'm going to proof your application," Hannah offered. "Make sure it puts you in the best light. My personal stylist already sent you to school with the best rush outfits, so you know you're good there. And be sure to look super hot at all the open rush events. Ooh! Make sure you wear the extra-risqué lingerie." She wiggled her eyebrows. "You know the sets I'm talking about. It'll help with your confidence, even if no one sees it."

My dad groaned and mumbled, "Why, God? Why?"

"What if I don't get in?" I choked out, tears now flowing down my cheeks.

"Rush isn't just about the sorority choosing you." Jade's tone was warm. Motherly. "You have to choose them back and find something that's a good fit for you. Be open to all the houses there, and if nothing feels right, then that's okay. We will find you an awesome club that's a good fit so you still get to be involved at the school. At the end of the day, we want you to be happy. That's all that matters."

"And don't forget, you already have a sisterhood," Bee added. "Us."

I nodded as Dad handed me a tissue.

"Thanks, you guys. I love you."

"Love you, too," they said together.

I ended the video call and took a moment to blow my nose.

"Why didn't you tell me you were having a hard time?" Dad gave me a sad smile. "I feel like this is my fault. If I hadn't accepted this position, you would be at Parsons right now."

"No, Dad, it's not." I wiped the remaining tears away. "I *wanted* to come here with you. That was *my* decision."

"A decision made out of some warped sense of obligation." He gave me a knowing look, running a hand through his thick head of hair. "*I'm* the parent in this relationship, Nicole. I feel like you forget that sometimes, and maybe that's because I've allowed you to take on too many responsibilities."

"We're always there for each other, Dad. It's what we do."

"And I'm thankful for that. I really am. You've always been so nurturing. But I want you to really enjoy your college experience without worrying about me. I'm a grown man and even though I have a sweet tooth and may not be the most organized person in the world, I still know how to take care of myself. Why don't you run off and get ready for rush so I can unpack, okay?"

"Dad. You don't have to—"

"Go, Nicole. I'm fine. I love you for wanting to take care of me, but you have to let me take care of you. Go get your nails done or something." He started digging in his wallet and pulled out some cash.

"I don't even know *where* I'd get my nails done around here," I sputtered as he handed me a wad of bills.

He smiled sheepishly. "Sorry, habit. I suppose my citified self needs to remember we're living in a more... remote environment now."

I laughed. "I'll say."

"But seriously, Nicole, go pamper yourself some-how. I know you have all the girly things somewhere in your dorm room. I'm sure there's some kind of party happening tonight. Get dressed up. Meet new people. Go out and have *fun*."

My brows lifted. "Dad, are you aware of what goes down at a college party? Are you actually *encouraging* some debauchery?"

He shook his head. "Well, I wouldn't go that far, but I do want you to enjoy yourself, honey. You've got a good head on your shoulders. I trust you make sound decisions."

"What about that one time in high school when I drank trash-can punch and you had to hold my hair back while I puked?" I shuddered at the memory.

I had no idea what I was doing and called Dad when I started to feel sick. He stormed into the party with a determined look on his face and carried me out of there like a toddler.

"And you called me," he reminded me. "I knew I could always trust that you'd call me if you were in trouble. You still can, kiddo. Be safe, but if shit ever hits the fan, I'm here for you. Now, do you need a ride back to your dorm?"

I glanced at the time on his microwave. "No. The campus shuttle should actually be out front in a few minutes."

He pulled me into a tight hug. "Then, get out

there. Have fun. *Be an eighteen-year-old college freshman.* Don't worry about me."

I found myself feeling teary-eyed again at his words. "Love you, old man."

"Love you too."

CHAPTER
TWELVE

Alexei

MY FUCKED-UP soul felt like someone had tossed it in a wood chipper. I was all kinds of twisted up inside about Nicole. Getting rejected by my fated mate was necessary, but my wolf was protesting hard. He desperately wanted to run to her. I couldn't focus in any of my classes—I knew my professors would give my father an ear full—and ever since I got back to the frat house, I'd been hiding up in my room.

Nicole had gotten under my skin like a deep cut, and I wasn't sure there was anything that would make the sting of her rejection go away.

I thought this was what I wanted. Though I knew this was necessary to become the alpha my father always wanted me to be, it still hurt. I couldn't blame her for not taking the mate bond seriously, not when I'd been fucking it up, too. She didn't know what it felt like for a wolf to be away from his mate. She didn't know that rejection was like splitting my soul in half. That was the problem with being fated to a human—she would never experience the same intense obsession I did. The balance of power was off, and as an alpha, it made my chest burn. How was I fucking supposed to focus on open rush when I couldn't even convince myself to go downstairs?

"Time's up," Corbin sang while waltzing through my door. He had two cups of coffee in his fists, and I prayed he had the foresight to add a splash of whiskey to mine. "Got you coffee so you'll be energized for our party tonight. I let you wallow in here all afternoon while I set everything up. I checked in with Nicole, too, after her last class let out. She really is a lovely girl. It's a shame she's human."

His words made me want to vomit. "How was she doing?" The selfish part of me wanted her to be as miserable as I was.

"Do you want me to tell you what you *want* to hear or what you *need* to hear, bestie?" Corbin asked.

"Want. Definitely want. My head's not in the right place for a pep talk."

Corbin nodded, then slipped dramatically into an

Oscar-winning role. "She was sobbing. Kept telling me how incomplete she felt without you and how the only thing that would make it better was deep throating your monster cock."

I rolled my eyes. "At least try to make it believable."

"She wants to hate fuck you?" Corbin tried, his voice tentative.

I laughed bitterly. This was all so messed up. I wasn't against a good old-fashioned hate fuck, but that wasn't what a mate bond was. It was pure intimacy and compatibility. Raw passion I'd evidently never get to experience.

I cleared my throat. "Though that might actually be true, I need to focus on rush since that'll never happen."

"Atta boy." Corbin formed his hands into finger guns, shooting off a couple of imaginary rounds. "Open rush will be over before you know it, and we want to go out with a bang before formal recruitment starts. Make all the sorry fuckers that can't be in Alpha Nu hella jealous when they don't get an invitation."

I dragged my hands over my face and groaned before sitting up and taking the coffee from him. I'd probably never be able to drink the bitter beverage without thinking of Nicole. It didn't help that my bedding smelled like her from when she was here yesterday—crisp lilacs and a hint of spice—and now that sweet scent was faintly wafting from my skin. It made me hard and fucking depressed, which was very confusing.

Being rejected by your mate was no joke. Somehow, I needed to convince my wolf that it was *us* doing the rejecting. She was a human. My father would disown me. Everything I'd ever worked for would vanish into thin air.

I hummed in appreciation as I took a sip, confirming the presence of top-shelf whiskey. My beta knew me well. The spiked drink didn't pull me from my morose thoughts, but it did help numb the pain. Maybe I should invest in a distillery. I had a feeling there would be a lot more liquor in my future.

I held my cup up. "Thanks, man."

"Anytime, bro. That's what second-in-commands are for, right?" Corbin started digging through my dresser, pulling out a pair of jeans, socks, and under-wear, throwing them in my direction. "Go shower and make yourself all pretty. The Beta Phi girls will be here soon." With that, Corbin practically pranced out of the room.

Normally, the presence of our favorite sorority would excite me. Beta Phis were eager to please a fellow wolf, especially their future alpha. But my wolf —and okay, maybe the man, too—only had eyes for one sassy brunette, and knowing she wouldn't be at this party tonight made me question why I was even bothering. No one compared. No one even came close. I wanted *her*.

I got up and set my drink down on the nightstand before going to my ensuite bathroom. I turned on the steamy water and thought of how good Nicole looked in her tight little skirt yesterday. That swishing fabric would haunt my daydreams for the rest of my life. She was so stunning it hurt. So fucking perfect that if it weren't for my responsibilities standing in the way, I'd worship every damn inch of her creamy skin and luscious curves. I was hard as a rock just thinking about it.

Stepping into the shower, I let the hot water run down my body and braced a hand against the tile. Part of me didn't want to wash her scent off of me, but I knew I'd be miserable all night if I didn't. I couldn't stand the tease of knowing what she'd smell like on my skin without ever having the pleasure of tasting her. I pumped soap into my palm and massaged the suds over my abs. My eyes were heavy with thoughts of my mate as I had this ache in my core. That hot pink crop top. The way her long eyelashes fluttered when she looked up at me, or the mischievous curve of her plump lips when she was telling me off.

I groaned and fisted my cock.

My mind pictured Nicole kneeling before me, offering me a challenge with her impossibly blue eyes as she took me into her mouth. She'd suck me in deep, gagging on my length as it hit the back of her throat. I moaned at the thought of my dick in the veritable heaven of her mouth until I couldn't wait another second to sink inside of her sweet cunt. I'd pull her into a standing position, bracing her hands against the marble tiles before pressing my hand on the small of her back, encouraging her to present her round, luscious ass to me. Sucking me off would've made her so hot her pussy would be dripping as I lined myself up against her entrance, thrusting inside of her in one smooth motion until I was buried balls deep, groaning as I nibbled on the soft skin where her neck met her shoulder.

My mate would scream as I fucked her with wild abandon, pleas of "More!" and "Harder!" falling from her parted lips in between breathless pants. She'd take everything I had to give with the utmost enthusiasm. With one hand braced on her hip, and the other wrapped around her front, rubbing her swollen clit until she shuddered through her release, I'd make her come at least a few times just like that before I couldn't hold back any longer, my baser instincts taking over.

My balls tightened as a familiar tingle rolled down

my spine. Thick ropes of cum spurted against the shower wall, but in my head, I was filling Nicole's tight little body with my seed. I was owning her in the most primal way, marking her as my mate. The future mother of my children. She'd moan as she milked me dry, my hands kneading her full tits, twisting her peaked nipples until she was balancing on the precipice of pleasure and pain. We'd be absolutely spent, yet our need for one another was so insatiable, we'd be ready for round two within seconds. I'd drop to my knees, burying my face in her pussy, groaning as I tasted our combined arousal as I licked and sucked and nibbled her hot flesh until she was once again screaming my name.

I rested my forehead against my folded arm for a few moments, catching my breath as the fantasy faded.

I had no doubt Nicole Fairweather would be my perfect match sexually, but she'd also challenge me on an intellectual level like I'd never known before, which only made me want her more. She was the ideal mate in almost every way.

Except in the most important way.

Well, that thought was certainly a boner killer.

I turned the tap to the coldest setting, hissing as the icy spray pelted my body. But I needed the harsh contrast of the cold water against my scorching skin to jolt me back into reality. It was a solid representation of the chaos running through my veins. The dichotomy of being a hot-blooded wolf who'd found his mate but was shackled to his responsibilities, facing a lifetime of freezing cold winters without her.

My wolf whimpered as I poured more body wash into my palm, scrubbing my skin and rinsing the suds as fast as possible. I turned off the shower, hastily drying myself off before pulling my boxers and pants on. The last thing I wanted right now was to attend a stupid party. But as president of Alpha Nu, I knew my absence wouldn't go unnoticed, so hiding in my room, pouting like a little bitch all night, wasn't an option. I simply had to wolf the fuck up and take care of business.

I was an alpha, and I refused to let some human who didn't even want me screw up my chances of claiming my birthright.

With that decided, I pulled a shirt over my head, combed my fingers through my hair, and headed downstairs to get this party started.

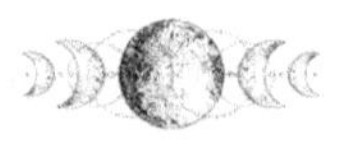

"My dad works for your dad's company," the bratty shifter hanging on my arm screamed in my ear. It was hard to have a legitimate conversation in this loud-ass house, but she was determined to deliver her pitch to be my girlfriend.

"Cool," I yelled back.

The party was perfect; the drinks were flowing, and I had a hot girl on my arm.

But I wasn't feeling it. It was near impossible not to be a moody bitch. I couldn't help but compare every girl in here to Nicole. The sophomore that had a vise grip on my bicep had a nasally voice, not smooth and confident like Nicole's. It also smelled like she bathed in a pool of expensive perfume. I couldn't stop fucking sneezing every time a breeze wafted the scent around.

I'm sure she was nice, but I didn't really care about *nice*. I was here to throw a rager and possibly get my dick sucked. Blow jobs were the perfect remedy for a broken heart. Too bad my dick was currently passed out from boredom.

"Yeah. I saw you a few times at the company's family picnic," she added.

I nodded, mostly because I was tired of shouting over the music.

I was about to extract myself and find a bottle of whiskey to drown in, but a brunette with bright eyes caught my attention from across the room.

What the fuck was Nicole doing here?

And more importantly, what the fuck was she wearing? I was going to have to beat the shit out of anyone who looked at her. She had on some thigh-high brown leather boots and a silky, baby blue minidress with thin straps I'd probably dream about slipping off her shoulders later. There was a green jacket wrapped around her waist, and I prayed it was a trench coat, because she needed to cover up before I went absolutely feral.

I was about to march over there and drag her up to my bedroom when Mara slid between the girl who was talking to me and myself, shoving her out of the way so she could latch onto my arm like a leech. "Cool party."

"I specifically told you not to come," I growled. "I ordered the guys at the door not to let you in."

"You and I both know that you want me here, babe." Mara purred her words like she took notes on how to seduce a man from a porn star. Dragging her manicured nail down my chest, I shuddered in disgust before jerking away from her.

"You didn't follow my order, Mara. Disobeying the alpha has consequences."

"*Future* alpha. You're not in charge yet."

The music changed to a softer slow song, the DJ mixing it up so a few couples could dance. I was thankful I didn't have to shout my threat at Mara. "You are treading on thin ice. When I give you a command, you fucking listen."

She pouted, her glossy lips looking absolutely ridiculous as she whined. "Alexei, I just wanted to spend time with you. I think we could be so great together if you'd give me a chance."

"It's never going to happen."

"Why not?" Mara straightened her shoulders, which pushed her tits out. "I'm hot. I'm in Beta Phi. Our families get along. My brother is your best friend and future second-in-command. We would literally be perfect together. I could make you *very* happy, in all ways." She reached for the waistband of my jeans and tugged me closer. I was feeling heartbroken and rejected, and Mara wanted nothing more than to ride my dick. If I didn't think she was a fucking terrible person and if I wasn't obsessed with a certain human, I'd probably take her up on that offer.

Against my will, my eyes slid over to Nicole. She stood against the wall, laughing at something Corbin said. It bugged me that he made her smile. *I* wanted to be the reason for her happiness. *I* wanted to make her comfortable with me.

I turned back to Mara. "It's never going to happen. Drop it."

She raised a brow. "What's the deal with the

human, Alexei? I thought we were fucking with her. I heard a rumor today that concerns me."

My eyes widened, and I tugged her away from the crowd, out the kitchen door that led to the backyard. What the fuck kind of rumor did she hear? If Mara knew I mated a human, then... FUCK!

I backed her up against the siding with my bulky body, and she grinned like it was *me* that was in trouble. "What did you hear?"

"I heard Antonio Hale gave the human a little *knowledge*." Her tone was full of excitement, which was no surprise considering Mara loved to gossip.

"And?" I pressed.

"And that's bad?" She tilted her head to the side in question.

I sighed in relief. She didn't know.

"You know I don't have jurisdiction over the witches. If they told her, then she's allowed to know."

Mara's face twisted into a scowl. "I don't like that filthy human knowing our business, Alexei. What if she tells someone?"

"I'm figuring it out."

"She has to pay," she insisted.

I reached out and wrapped my hands around her throat, snarling as I did. No one would ever fucking threaten my mate. "I said I have it handled, Mara." Her eyes widened, and she reached for my wrist, but I kept my grip firm. It was an alpha's job to discipline disobedient wolves, and Mara was in a lot of trouble for coming here and questioning my authority. "Mind your fucking business. If and when I need you, I'll call. Otherwise, stay out of my way."

She moaned as I tightened my grip even further.

Fucking crazy bitch was getting off on this.

With a look of disgust, I released her, the sound of her gasping for air music to my ears. I had to tread carefully, moving forward. Mara was getting too curious, too rebellious and disrespectful. If I had to give up Nicole, then I'd be the best fucking alpha there was, and God help any wolves that got in my way.

Nicole

"So, what would you do if you were in my situation?" Corbin grinned, tugging on my arm. "C'mon, Nicole. You came to the party. I know you wanna forget everything you learned yesterday, but the fact that you're here is very telling. At least do me a solid and give me some female perspective. You spent enough time with me and Juniper yesterday afternoon to have *some* opinion, don't you think?" He leaned his head on my shoulder, giving me the biggest puppy-dog eyes ever. Now that I knew he could actually turn into a canine, the expression held an entirely different meaning, but it *was* adorable nonetheless. "*Pleeeeeeeeease.* I can't trust anyone else with this information."

Damn charming mutt. Now that he wasn't being a total creep trying to fake date me, he was significantly more likable.

I smiled, despite my best attempt to remain stoic. "I find it rather odd that I'm the *only* one you can trust. Corbin, I hardly know you, but you definitely don't seem like someone who would avoid talking about his sex life. In fact, you kinda seem like a douchey dudebro who would *boast* about it."

He winced. "Ouch."

I shrugged. "Just calling it like I see it."

"Don't be like that, boo."

I gave him a wry look. "I am *not* your boo."

"Oh, trust me. I know exactly who you belong to, and I'd prefer to keep my dick attached to my body, thank you very much. I'm quite fond of it. As is June." He waggled his eyebrows. "She's very, *very* fond of it."

I laughed. "Okay, fine, playboy. Give me the deets. And for the record, I don't *belong* to anyone."

"Uh-huh. Sure, you don't." He pulled me to the side, looking around to ensure we didn't have any eavesdroppers. Thankfully, the DJ had just switched to a slow, quieter song, so we were no longer yelling to be heard over the music. "Okay, so you know about the... uh, arrangement we have, yeah?"

"Your little 'party of three' arrangement? Yes. What specifically is causing you so much strife?"

I had a feeling I was going to regret asking, but for some reason, I was softening to this idiot.

"I like her, Nicole. Like, *really* dig her. But she's engaged, which totally blows, ya know?"

I frowned. "Okay, so she's engaged, but her feathered fiancé obviously has no issue with you *being* with Juniper."

"He has no issue with me *screwing* her," he corrected. "And lately... I don't even know if that's true anymore. He's been *super* territorial the last few times he's... uh... watched us."

"Why do you think that is?"

Corbin's shoulders lifted in a shrug. "Dunno for sure. But I'm thinking maybe because he can sense June and I really vibe, ya know? Like, I wanna take her out on dates and shit. I think she's into me, too. But she's *engaged*. And, you know, a witch, which poses its own problem."

"Why would *that* be a problem? She clearly has no qualms about being in a relationship with a shifter."

He scoffed. "A *raven* shifter. *Big* diff. That feathery fucker doesn't have the same kind of expectations a wolf would have. We're supposed to keep our bloodlines pure. Fucking another supe—or even a human for that matter—is totally fine as long as you wrap it up and keep it casual. But *producing heirs* with someone who isn't a wolf? *No way.*"

"Are you thinking about *having babies* with her? I thought you were more the noncommittal type."

He nervously scratched the back of his neck, and the most adorable blush turned his cheeks pink. "I don't know. I kind of want to see where this thing goes. I tried to keep cool, but—"

"You can't help it because you like her so much?"

He nodded. "Yeah."

"I get it. While we're on the subject, can I ask you something?"

"Sure," he replied.

I'd be lying if I said I wasn't curious about Alexei. If he wasn't a total asshole the first time we met, I probably would have flirted with him. He was handsome and I wouldn't mind seeing if there was any merit to this whole mate thing. But it wasn't really worth getting attached if we had no possibility of a future.

"If it's such a bad thing to date a non-shifter, then why were you willing to fake date me? Wouldn't that ruin your reputation as much as it would Alexei's?"

Corbin leaned closer to me, and I could smell the whiskey on his breath. "I'd do anything for Alexei," he admitted tenderly. "He's like a brother to me. And, yes, it would be social suicide to date a human—no offense—but it would be even worse for him. His father is... intense."

"How so?"

Corbin cleared his throat. "He was teaching him how to fight when he was just a kid. Alexei would show up at my house covered in bruises and shrug it off like it was no big deal. He didn't have a real childhood. He was born with the expectation of being brutal enough and strong enough to lead our pack."

"That's terrible," I whispered.

I mulled over that information, my heart squeezing a bit at the thought of Alexei getting beat up at such a young age. I couldn't imagine what that sort of training did to a person.

The sound of giggles around us made me look up, and a pair of girls pointed at Corbin and made a gagging gesture.

"Uh-oh," I murmured. "It looks like your fake *claiming* scheme is already hurting your reputation. Want to loudly break up with me in front of everyone so you can save face?"

Corbin gave me a curious look, like he couldn't quite figure me out. "You know, pretending to date me could help your chances of getting into Beta Phi. If they think you have *some* connections to the shifter world, they just might consider you."

I contemplated his offer for a brief moment before deciding against it. "You're not nearly as bad as I initially thought you were, Corbin." I took a step back.

"And I appreciate you wanting to help." The condensation from the cup of ice water in my hand dripped onto my fingers, giving me an idea.

"Dating you would hardly be a hardship, darling." He dragged his eyes up and down my body, wagging his brows.

I shook my head. "I *was* feeling bad for what I'm about to do, but you had to go and say something douchey again."

He gave me a broad smile and leaned closer. "Give me your worst, beautiful."

I lifted my drink and poured it on top of his head, smiling as he tensed up from the cold, icy water. Oh, yeah. I was going to have a ton of fun with this.

Sucking in a deep breath, I made sure to yell loud enough for everyone to hear. "YOU ASSHOLE! I CAN'T BELIEVE YOU!"

Corbin wiped his forehead and tried his best to glare at me. "What's the problem, darling? Are you not adventurous enough?"

"Was I just a joke to you?!" I bellowed.

He gave me a condescending smirk. "Come on, you didn't think I'd want anything more than a fuck, did you?"

We had an audience now. A few shifters gaped at us. Most of them laughed at Corbin's words. "I can't *believe* you wanted me to dress up like a raven and suck you off! Do you have some sort of bird fetish?!"

He coughed, then spoke under his breath. "Good one. Way to kick me in the balls, Nicky."

"You're disgusting! The answer is *no*! Absolutely not!"

Damn, I deserved an award for my acting skills.

"Your loss!" he countered.

I spun on my heels and marched away, grinning like an idiot when he yelled, "Call me!"

I lifted my finger, giving him a different kind of bird as I made my way toward the back of the house.

As I entered the kitchen, where a group of clearly intoxicated frat boys were doing keg stands, I spotted something out the window that gave me pause. Alexei had Mara pressed against the side of the house, a proprietary hand around her throat. I couldn't hear what they were saying, but she looked like she was on the verge of having an orgasm. In the next moment, Alexei released her from his grasp, stomping away. He ripped open the door leading into the kitchen with so much force everyone present jumped, including me. He stood in the frame, chest heaving and nostrils flaring as our eyes met. At that moment, I could plainly see Alexei for the predator he was. I should've been terrified, but strangely, I wasn't. Like, *at all*. If I were being honest with myself, the most prominent feeling I had was... arousal.

Oh, hell.

"You!" He pointed a stern finger at me. "Do not even *think* of running."

I smirked, because running was the *last* thing on my mind right now. I was filled with adrenaline from my fake fight with Corbin, ready to meet this pissed off shifter's challenge head-on. My amusement seemed to confuse the growly caveman, which caused my lips to curve into a full-on grin.

I cocked my head to the side. "I'm not a runner, Alexei."

"You could have fooled me," he grunted before surging forward and grabbing the arm of the green jacket tied around my waist.

"Cold?" I grinned playfully. "If you wanted to borrow my jacket, you could've just asked."

"Put this on." He yanked the material for emphasis.

I scowled at him before glancing down at my outfit. "Why?"

A muscle jumped in his cheek. "Just... do it." He looked flustered, and something about the way his chest heaved sent flutters throughout my belly. Though what I just saw with Mara quickly put out whatever flame was building within me.

"Why don't you go worry about what Mara is wearing instead, hmm?"

I realized my mistake when Alexei's head perked up and his mouth curved upward.

Dammit.

"Jealous, Nicole?" His words came out in a low rumble that had my body paying attention.

"Nope. I just thought alphas weren't supposed to fall victim to a smooth talker."

His mouth popped open, and I had the sudden urge to kiss him. Nope. Bad idea.

"You think she was trying to *compel* me? You think she'd defy her alpha like that?"

I snorted. "I *think* Mara will do whatever suits Mara."

Mara's pre-mind-fuck attempt telling me not to dress *too* cute tonight was part of the reason I made sure to wear this outfit. It was stylish but also one of the sexiest things I owned. I even took Hannah's advice and wore the racy lingerie underneath. She was right. It *did* help boost my confidence. The other reason why I decided to attend this party almost immediately after I had sworn to pretend supes didn't exist was that I refused to back down after learning about Mara's manipulations. The more I thought about it, the more I wanted answers, and I wasn't going to get them by sticking my head in the sand.

"Why did you ask her to be my friend? The *real* answer."

"To get information about you and compel you if you saw anything supernatural. The containment spell wasn't working. I had no choice." Alexei's forehead wrinkled. "I already told you that."

"You trusted that psychopath around me?"

His brown eyes scanned the room, making me realize we were drawing attention. Normally, I wouldn't give a damn about some drunken frat boys, but after talking to Corbin, I knew the simplest interactions between me and their alpha were suspect, and I didn't want to cause Alexei any more problems. This wasn't a situation either of us asked for.

I sighed in resignation. "Forget it. I'll go."

I spun around and was about to leave when I felt his chest at my back. Every muscle in my body froze as his hot breath feathered over my ear.

"Meet me in my room in five minutes. We'll talk."

"I don't know if that's such a good idea," I murmured under my breath. The freshly-installed Wolfipedia in my brain said that shifters had enhanced hearing, so I didn't need to raise my voice nearly as much as someone would need to do for me to hear them.

"I *know* it's not," his deep voice rumbled against

my ear. "But I don't care. We need to talk, and we need privacy to do that."

"That's the problem, Alexei. You want to hide me away like a dirty secret. It doesn't matter how much we talk. The end result will always be the same."

"Nicole." A shiver ran down my spine as he exhaled. "*Please.*"

I couldn't see his face, but I could tell that one word took extreme effort. I had the feeling Alexei wasn't a man who was used to asking nicely for anything. He was more the type to bark demands—no pun intended—and have his every wish instantly fulfilled. For that reason alone, I decided to indulge his request. But I would do it on *my* terms.

"Fine. I'll meet you in five minutes, but you only *get* five minutes. Then, I'm out of here."

"*Fine,*" he gritted, and in the next moment, my skin cooled from the absence of his colossal body.

It took me a while to navigate the rowdy crowd of drunk coeds, and when I got to the staircase, a bulky shifter that looked like he wanted to be anywhere *but* on security detail stopped me. "No humans upstairs."

"But, um, I'm meeting someone up there."

I tried to move around him, but he wouldn't budge. *Crap.* Was I supposed to tell him Alexei wanted to speak with me? I wasn't great about sneaking around, even if this was totally innocent.

Well, not *totally* innocent.

I still kind of was a *little* curious about those broad shoulders and sculpted arms.

"Let her through, Gabriel," Corbin commanded behind my back, prompting me to look over my shoulder. "Have *lots* of fun." He winked before taking a shot of clear liquid and rejoining the party.

I took my time walking up the massive staircase and long hallway leading to Alexei's bedroom. There was a couple in one of the rooms, half dressed, locked in a passionate embrace on the bed with the door wide open. *Whoa.* Was that supposed to be some kind of open invite? I had to force myself to move along and not to stare at the fervent way they kissed each other.

Once at the right door, I raised my fist to knock, feeling awkward as doubt settled in.

The wooden door swung open just enough to allow me to slip inside. I held my breath when Alexei crowded me against it as he closed it, turning the lock with an ominous click.

Real smart, Nicole. You just locked yourself in a room with a dude who could snap your body in half like a twig.

Although... when I lifted my chin, my baby blues locking on his mocha irises, I realized personal safety wasn't the problem at hand. No... the *problem* was the fact that Alexei was staring at me like I was the answer to every prayer he had ever had. And when his large hand reached out, tracing the curve of my jaw, we both groaned at the heat sizzling between us.

My attraction to him confused me. I should have been running for the hills, but there was something about him that drew me in.

"Explain something," I breathed before biting my lip. "I know what a mate bond is between shifters. But am I supposed to feel so... so..."

He leaned closer and breathed me in. "Tell me." His gruff voice practically made my skin vibrate with need. I longed to feel his lips on my neck.

"I ache," I whispered. "When we're close like this."

He moved a hand to my waist and squeezed. I gasped when he pulled my hips forward until there was no space between us. Alexei's hard cock strained against his jeans, and it was driving me crazy.

"Do you feel what you do to me, Nicole?" he rasped. I didn't know what to say. I wasn't even sure what to *think*. I'd come up here for answers but was sucked into his orbit. "Every time I see you. Think about you. Dream about you. *This* is what happens." He pressed into me further. "It's maddening. Nothing will extinguish this need burning inside of me."

"You've known me for *three days*," I pointed out, really hoping my voice wasn't as breathy as I thought it was. "How bad could it really be?"

"Mmm," he hummed into my ear. "But it certainly doesn't *feel* like it's only been three days, does it?"

No, it didn't.

"But... why?" I whimpered as he pressed his lips against the slope of my neck. "If this is a wolf thing, why am I feeling it, too?"

"We're compatible in every way." His tone was matter-of-fact, as if that simple sentence somehow answered all of my questions. "We attract each other in every way. It's how the mate bond works."

"I've been attracted to plenty of people—" He cut me off with a possessive growl, but I continued. "But it's never been like *this*."

He smirked, the cocky expression full of power. He was obviously getting off on my honesty, but I genuinely wanted to understand, so I let it go.

"Some people think that mates emit certain pheromones that make the attraction seem more intense." Alexei trailed his fingers down the length of my dress, stopping below the hem so he could brush against my skin. My breath hitched as he teased me more, sliding those fingers over my leg and gently touching between my thighs. I squeezed my legs together and heaved in air. Every rise and fall of my chest had his eyes dipping to my cleavage.

"So by that theory, you should probably back up," I croaked.

"I probably should." He moved his hand up ever so slightly. Alexei was so close to touching the part of me that ached the most.

"Maybe you should do that now," I whispered.

"Maybe..." His fingers brushed over my barely-there lace panties. My legs shook at the intimate contact, parting automatically to allow him better access.

"Fuck," Alexei muttered as he discovered how wet I was for him.

His fingertips flirted with the edge of my panties. It would be so easy to slide them aside, touching me skin to skin. I wanted that more than I could even comprehend. My body was acting as if we were long-lost lovers. His touch was familiar. Electrifying. Damn near irresistible. But warning bells were ringing in my head, telling me this was crazy. This was too much. Too fast. This wasn't what I came here for. I came to the Alpha Nu house tonight to make a stand. To demand answers. Yet, here I was, acting like a bitch in heat—*pun definitely intended*—and I needed to put a stop to it.

I pressed both palms to his chest and shoved. To my surprise, Alexei moved easily, though there was heated longing in his gaze. "Go stand on the other side of the room. I can't think straight when you're hovering over me like that."

Alexei smirked but did as I asked, obviously not wanting to push me too far. We both knew I was seconds away from bolting out of this bedroom.

I released a breathy exhale and cleared my head. The further he got, the easier it was to think straight, even though I still wanted to wrap my thighs around his waist and grind against him. It was ridiculous.

"So," I began, clearing my throat. "Pheromones. I guess we need to keep at least ten feet between us at all times." I laughed, trying to lighten the mood, but my suggestion seemed to anger Alexei.

"I can assure you no amount of distance will make this go away."

"Maybe not," I replied, "but I'm less likely to jump your bones if you're not within reach."

He playfully took a step closer. "How about now?"

I huffed. "I'm trying to be serious here, Alexei. We have to figure this out. We're not going to work, and not just because you're a wolf, but also because you really went about this in a shitty way. I'm still upset about Mara. Why would you have her control my mind like that, knowing what kind of person she is?"

His expression sobered some, and the bravado slipped from his posture. "Involving Mara was a mistake. I know that now. I just wanted control of the situation. In case you haven't noticed, I get a little... antsy... when I'm not in charge."

"You don't say."

He gave me a wry look. "You don't need to be so snarky about it."

I laughed a full-on belly laugh. "Holy shit, I think my *snark* is the least of your worries right now, dude."

He legit growled. "Don't call me dude."

I propped a hand on my hip. "What *should* I call you then? Baby? Sweetheart? Sugar pie? Honeybuns? Any of those work for you?"

He frowned, as if my question genuinely stumped him. "I... don't know. None of those. Christ, especially not *dude*. That's reserved for friends, and I'm *not* your friend, Nicole. I will *never* be your friend."

"Wow." I nodded in mock understanding. "Okie-dokie then. Good chat."

"I'm not trying to be cruel," he countered. "You just have to understand how serious this is. We're *always* going to be drawn to one another. It literally feels like someone's stabbing me in the chest when you're away. *Normal* mates in my world become a couple immediately upon learning they're bonded. There's no questioning it. If they're already adults when they meet, they move in together right away. If they're younger... their families ensure they never have to stay apart for too long at a time. If it's possible, they move next door to one another. That's why there are so many shifter-only communities like Ridgeview."

I cringed. "I'm not necessarily a commitment-phobe, but the idea of settling down at such a young age sounds terrible."

My supernatural encyclopedia told me shifters wouldn't recognize their mate until after puberty, but in my opinion, you were not mentally prepared in your tween or early teenage years to make such a monumental commitment. This wasn't the fifteenth century.

"That's another problem. You'll never understand this mate bond and what it means to a shifter. When you rejected me, it hurt me a lot more than you'll ever know."

I tossed my hands up in frustration. "You rejected me *first*. *You* were trying all this shady shit to push me away, and I didn't even know what was going on."

"I'm still trying to figure everything out, okay?" Alexei's volume was rising as his anger grew. "This isn't what I had planned for myself. I was supposed to find a strong partner to support me as I lead my pack. Not some fucking *human* who doesn't even under-stand how lucky she is to be mated to me."

Wow. Just wow. I was completely stunned by his words and thoroughly pissed off.

I held up a hand. "I guess it's a good thing this *human* wants nothing to do with you, then."

"Shit. Nicole, I shouldn't have said that." Alexei softened once he realized how cruel his words were.

"I didn't ask for this," I continued. "I didn't ask for *any* of this. And for the record, I was ready to walk away earlier today. It's *you* who wanted to talk. *You* called me up here. Maybe you need to figure out what it is you actually want so you can stop kidding yourself." I jabbed an index finger at him. "Because whether or not you realize it, *dude*, that's *exactly* what you're doing."

I unlocked the door, twisting the handle. "When you're ready to have an honest conversation—not some macho alpha bullshit spew session—*maybe* I'll be willing to listen. But until you're willing to do that, do me a favor and leave me the hell alone."

I turned on my heels and practically ran out of the house without another word.

FOURTEEN

Alexei

EACH MORNING THIS WEEK, I woke up hard as a rock, and no amount of jacking off would satisfy me. It didn't matter how much I drank the night before. It didn't matter that I spent the majority of the evening in my wolf form, hunting, running, and sparring with Corbin. I was wired. On edge. Every sound made a tic in my jaw pulse, and my soft sheets against my skin simply agitated me more. My very existence was burdened with discomfort. Having Nicole away from me for such long periods felt like the most unnatural thing in the world. My wolf was clawing at my soul, begging me to go to her. It was the most intense desire I had ever felt.

My thudding pulse served as a painful reminder that I was on the verge of losing control. I didn't feel comfortable in my own skin, and it was taking every ounce of alpha power I possessed to keep myself from shifting and running to her. It didn't help that I knew exactly where she was. I knew how many steps it would take to walk to her dorm. How I would greet her in the morning with a kiss. How I would take her. I was so tuned in to her existence that it made my stomach clench. Walking around campus was like dodging bombs. Every time I got a hint of lilac, my bones ached. When I walked past the art building, it was like every cell in my body was struck with lightning. I was alive, and it was an excruciatingly painful existence.

Being close to Nicole and then having her ripped away was torture.

It had been three days since the Alpha Nu party. Nicole was under my skin like a live wire just as much now as she was while I was touching her heated flesh through the thin barrier she wore. Buzzing through my veins like the most powerful drug. Giving me a rush of euphoria one moment, only to be doused in ice water the next. Nothing would make this itch subside. I knew Nicole was the only one who could settle my wolf, so I didn't even think about trying to replace her with any willing female, but she was also the primary cause of my vexation.

I could not mate with a human.

I could never have her.

As I got dressed for the day, Corbin sent me my schedule. Dad wanted to meet between my finance and ethics classes. He insisted that I take twenty-one credit hours this semester. Double majoring wasn't for the faint of heart, but it was even harder when my father wanted me to attend all of his publicity events and pack council meetings on top of it. The school year had just started, but I already felt overwhelmed by the constant wave of tasks and responsibilities. I was thankful to be busy, because it kept my mind off of my doomed mate situation. But every minute of my day had been consumed by longing. I couldn't focus.

After grabbing a quick breakfast and walking toward the quad, I scrolled through my emails. Pack updates. Business acquisitions. Social events. I wasn't sure how my beta managed to keep my life so organized, but I was grateful. As I was approaching the business building, my phone rang.

I braced myself as I saw my father's name on the caller ID. "Hello."

"Alexei. You missed the conference call this morning with the Belfast pack. It took me weeks to get on their schedule to negotiate our trade deal, and it was embarrassing that you couldn't roll out of bed and be present. How am I supposed to prove that we are a valuable partner if I can't even convince my son to attend our meetings?"

I cursed under my breath. Corbin had set fifteen alarms for me this morning. I must have turned them all off in my sleep. He had to get up extra early to prepare for an Alpha Nu rush event before class, so he wasn't there to make sure I woke up in time. It wasn't his fault, but I was embarrassed that the one thing I was supposed to do on my own today, I failed at.

I'd been doing that a lot lately—failing.

"I'm sorry, father." Even though he was over the phone, muscle memory made me slump my shoulders, dipping my body as if preparing for an attack. If he were here, he'd shift and grab me by the throat with his powerful jaws just to prove a point. Disobedience was a sin. Embarrassing him was unforgivable. I represented him in every way. My father took my failures as a personal attack.

"You're such a disappointment!" he shouted into the phone. "Do you have any idea how easy you have it? I've practically handed you the keys to my kingdom, and you can't stop partying for five minutes for a goddamn phone call!"

I wanted to tell Dad that I was up late working on my speech for the Fae Alliance event next week, wrote a paper for my senior English course, and also spent four hours sparring to prepare for my alpha trials, but I kept my mouth shut.

"What do you even do all day, Alexei? Get your fucking head in the game, or I'll find an heir that can actually get shit done."

"I promise to do better, Alpha." My tone was dull as I delivered the same line I'd been rehearsing since before I could walk.

"You better, because if it's not our enemies challenging you for this pack, then it'll be me! I'll come back from the fucking grave before I let my worthless heir take over!" Dad cursed before disconnecting the line.

I shoved my phone in my pocket, the urge to punch something coursing through me.

But people were watching.

Everyone was waiting for me to fail.

I had to fucking control myself.

I had to be fucking perfect.

I clenched my fists, rage rolling over my skin and sinking into my bones like venom.

"Alexei?"

I closed my eyes at the sound of the soft voice, savoring the way she said my name before turning around. Nicole had on high-waisted shorts and a flowery crop top that showed off her toned stomach. I briefly daydreamed about running my tongue along her skin before scanning the rest of her. Her long legs were accentuated by the high-heeled sandals she wore. I wondered how she would look wearing nothing but those fucking heels, bent at the waist as I claimed her from behind. I wanted to fuck my frustrations out and couldn't help but imagine what she'd look like wrapped around me, her soft curves against my hard muscle. Her lips parted as I—

"Alexei?" she tried again, her beautiful blue eyes looking up at me with concern. "Are you okay?"

I slipped into my familiar mask of duty. I hated that she could see me like this.

Angry.

Hurting.

Unworthy.

"I'm fine." The bite in my tone made her jump.

For a moment, Nicole looked surprised by my anger, but then her expression changed to annoyance. "I was just trying to be nice." She crossed her arms over her chest. "No need to bite my fucking head off."

Oh, I wanted to bite her, alright. I wanted to sink my teeth into the round globes of her ass and watch her squirm in my bed. "I'm just having a rough morning."

"Obviously. You look pissed."

"That's none of your concern." I hated feeling

weak. I hated that I couldn't be what my mate needed. "Just because we're..." I paused to look around, wondering if anyone was eavesdropping. "Just because we *know each other* does not mean you have a right to just come up and talk to me. People could see."

She laughed. "I don't care what people say. I was just checking on you, not getting on my knees to suck you off."

Oh God, what that visual did to me. I shifted my weight from foot to foot, my cock straining against my jeans. "Don't say shit like that. And don't worry about me. I'm fine."

"I was just trying to be nice," she whispered. "Why can't we be cordial?"

I looked around, finding a hidden spot on the side of the building. Reaching out, I wrapped my hand around her arm and tugged her toward it.

"I *can't* be cordial with you. I can't be nice. I can't be *near* you."

"Why?" If she was angry about me manhandling her, she didn't say it. "I'm not saying we have to start hanging out or anything, but if I see you in the quad looking upset, am I just supposed to walk the other way?"

I looked deep into her eyes, my heart racing from

being so close. "That's exactly what you're supposed to do."

She rolled her eyes. "Fine. No problem, Alpha Asshole. You just looked like you needed a friend. Sorry that I forgot. I'm not even good enough for that."

The fact that she still cared about me after all the shit I'd put her through made my soul ache. It wasn't fair. "I've got too many people waiting for me to fail." I suddenly felt desperate to make her understand.

"Is that what I am to you, Alexei?" Nicole's shaky voice exposed her pain. "A failure?"

I wanted to tell her no, but my father's voice was still ringing in my mind. His disappointment made me feel sick to my stomach. "Yes."

Her hurt instantly morphed to annoyance. "Wow. Okay, then. Silly me for thinking we could handle this like adults."

"People can't see us together."

"And yet we keep gravitating toward one another." Her tone was sad again. Dejected. "But I get it. I don't have time for this, anyway. I'm off to meet with Cristian to go over our project. Hope whatever has got you in this pissy mood gets better, stranger. See ya."

I wasn't sure what pissed me off more, the fact that she was going to meet with Cristian or that she'd called me a stranger.

"You do realize Cristian is a vampire, right?"

"Yes," she said dryly. "He's made that *abundantly* clear. He won't stop asking for blood sex, whatever the hell that is."

I raged. *No.* Absolutely fucking not. No way in hell was my mate going to hook up with a damn bloodsucker.

"Cristian is dangerous, Nicole. I can't focus if I know you're hanging out with him."

"Holy whiplash, Wolf-man. One second I'm a failure to you, and the next, you don't want me talking to other guys? Could you please make up your mind? It would make things much easier for the both of us." She licked her lips, annoyance rolling off of her in waves.

"How about *you* make up your mind? You're the one who came over and talked to me."

She rolled her eyes. "Because I was being *nice.* Nice people make sure their friends don't wolf out in the quad and go on a murder spree."

My lip twitched. The fact that she knew I was struggling to contain my wolf made my chest swell with pride. "Stop being nice to me, then. It's confusing."

"Easy enough." She flipped her brown hair over her shoulder and gave me an evil grin. "I'm leaving now. I'll be sure to tell Cristian you said hello. He wants to meet in the fae gardens. It's kind of romantic, don't you think?"

I scanned her expression, knowing damn well she was bullshitting me. Taking one step, and then another, I crowded her space. Her back hit the brick, and her raspy breaths made me ache. "You want a romantic date with Cristian, huh?"

"Yes," she croaked.

Liar.

"You want him to eat your pretty pussy, Nicole? Worship your perfect clit with his tongue?"

She let out a harsh breath, the pink blush on her cheeks giving me all sorts of naughty ideas. "Sure."

"You're a terrible liar. I know that, right now, my words have you fantasizing about riding *someone's* face, and it isn't the fucking vampire's mouth you wish you could grind your cunt on. It's *mine.*"

Her mouth popped open. "God."

Fuck.

I wasn't supposed to be doing this. But I leaned in closer, anyway.

"Just so you know... I'd have you screaming my name, baby. You'd paint my face with your cum, and you'd squeeze my skull with those silky thighs of yours. Go enjoy your meeting with Cristian."

And with those parting words, I pulled away and started walking back to the building.

She yelled at my back, and shockingly, I didn't really care if anyone heard her. "Fuck you, Alexei! You confusing, infuriating asshole!"

Well, look at that. I was starting to feel better already.

FIFTEEN

Nicole

"WHY ARE YOU AVOIDING ME?" Bee asked the moment I answered the call. I told myself I wouldn't use the phone Corbin gave me unless it was an emergency, but the temptation of speaking to my best friend was too hard to resist. As she continued, I sighed. "I understand not having service, and I know things are hectic with the first week of classes, but I *know* you, Nicole. You're avoiding me, and these one word texts aren't going to cut it."

That was the problem. Bee *did* know me. She could practically read my mind. It made it impossible to hide anything from her. She knew when I lost my virginity. She knew before I did when I was going to turn down Parsons to follow Dad here. Bee was my best friend, which meant it was significantly harder to keep secrets from her than my father.

"I'm not avoiding you," I lied.

I *was* avoiding her. How the hell was I going to keep this gigantic secret away from my best friend?

"Stop lying to me and just tell me if I need to book this flight to see you," Bee breezed.

I stopped walking to my next class, my feet practically leaving skid marks on the pavement.

"No," I snapped. "I'm fine. You don't have to come. Everything is great."

Bee let out a humorless laugh. "Yeah right. I'm booking this flight. Something is up and I'm not buying your act for one second."

I didn't want Bee to come here. I wasn't allowed to tell her what I knew, and being here put her at risk. I'd always have this big secret looming between us. I hated it, but there wasn't anything else I could do.

"Bee, I'm just stressed. The people here aren't... welcoming."

She cursed into the phone. "Who's giving you a hard time? Just give me a name, and I can have it handled." I knew my friend was very capable of taking care of business, but that didn't mean I wanted to involve her.

"Everyone. It's just an adjustment. I'm honestly

fine." I forced my feet forward. Class started soon, and I needed to hurry up.

"Purchased," Bee sang. "I'll see you in a few weeks."

Sonofabitch. "Bee, you really don't—"

"Shut up, Nicole. I know you. I *know* you, okay? My best friend senses are tingling, so if I want to use my dad's credit card to buy a ticket to the middle of nowhere to see you, that's what I'm going to do! Speaking of, do they have running water at that school? Electricity?"

There was no use fighting with her. Bee always did what she wanted, consequences be damned.

"Ha. Ha. Hilarious," I replied. "We have all of those things."

"Are there any cute guys?" I pictured her lounging on her bed and staring longingly at her stack of paperbacks. She loved to read romance novels and had a bad habit of thinking every guy she met was like the men in her books. Men written by women were always ten times better than the real thing.

"There's lots, actually," I breathed.

None I'm letting you date, though.

I cringed at the thought of Cristian trying to suck her blood or Corbin inviting her to a threesome with a fucking bird.

Actually, if Corbin wasn't a shifter, he'd probably be perfect for my friend.

But no. That was never, ever happening.

"I'm kind of jealous. I'm glad I took a gap year, but it feels like maybe I'm missing out on the whole college experience. Making friends. Kissing boys."

"Believe me." I couldn't hide the sourness in my tone if I tried. "You're not missing out on anything."

Bee scoffed. "I won't lie, I'm kind of terrified you'll find a new best friend while you're there, but maybe you're looking for friends in the wrong places."

I stopped in front of the business building and sighed. Maybe Bee was right. "And who would you suggest I befriend?"

She hummed to herself for a moment. "Find the weird girl. That's what everyone called me at our elementary school, remember? You shoved Lindsay Lewis into a trash can when she made fun of me. Us weird girls have a good track record of being badass friends."

I giggled. Bee never spent more than two years in one place at a time. She was outgoing but quirky. She didn't care what anyone thought about her because she never stuck around long enough for it to matter.

"I do get along with weird girls," I mused. "My own best friend once dragged me to a rave in an ice cream shop because the *aesthetic would look good in print.* A man wearing a pink thong asked me on a date."

"Hey, I won an award for those photos! And he would have been hot except for the whole *constantly scratching his ass like he had scabies* thing."

"I know, I know. It was epic. Weird, but epic."

"Just don't let the haters get you down, sis. I'll be there soon enough, and we can raise hell together."

Nervousness swirled in my gut. It really wasn't a good idea to let Bee come, but I couldn't explain to her why it wasn't safe. I'd just have to protect her while she's here.

Easy enough, right?

"Okay, girl. I'll chat with you later, okay?"

"Okay. Bye!"

"Love you, bye."

I pocketed my cell phone and made my way up the stairs. I had Intermediate Business today and was somewhat dreading the class. I was more of a creative at heart, but I understood the importance of being business savvy in today's day and age. It's why I took college courses my senior year of high school so I could get ahead. This was one of my larger classes, held in a giant auditorium filled with at least two hundred students. It was clear where each supernatural faction sat. Vampires in the back, hidden by the shadows. Shifters on the right, the loud and rowdy bunch chatting excitedly with one another. The fae sat in the first couple of rows, and the witches were on the left. I didn't know where I fit. Oblivious humans were scattered around them, not realizing the invisible lines they were crossing.

I found Mara surrounded by shifters, all of them hanging on to her every word. "Who does this human think she is, sitting with shifters?" She gestured to a small girl with a nose ring and glazed over eyes. "Hey, girl. At night, I turn into a big, bad, scary wolf."

Mara's companions laughed.

"The coffee shop is down on Main Street," the girl replied in a monotone voice.

Ah, the spell protecting this school was hard at work.

"Sometimes, when I shift, I like to fuck under a full moon in my wolf form." The group howled with laughter as Mara continued.

"The coffee shop is down on Main Street," the girl repeated, blinking a couple of times in confusion.

The shifters were cackling so loudly that even the vampires were starting to watch.

Mara sneered. "You're nothing. Just a weak, pathetic human. A blood bag for vampires. A toy for fae—"

"Th-the c-coffee shop is down... street," the girl

choked out, her head rolling to the side as her eyes fluttered shut.

"That's enough!" I yelled, making everyone turn their attention to me. Some of the laughter died down. The poor girl slumped over in her seat. "You're obviously hurting her." I only knew what my magic encyclopedia told me, but too much mind magic on a human was dangerous. What the fuck kind of person intentionally messed with a person's brain like that?

Mara. Mara did.

"Look who it is." God, I wanted to smack the smirk off her face. "You learn about supes and suddenly think you have a right to tell me what to do." Mara sauntered over to me, navigating the rows with ease. I noticed some of the shifters looking at me with pity. Interesting. *"Bow down, bitch."*

Her words hit me like a bad itch. I scratched my ear, feeling thankful as fuck for the earrings June gave me.

"No." I smiled.

Some of the shifters gasped in response. One guy in the front row grinned.

"You're going to stay away from Alexei. You're not going to attend any more Alpha Nu events. You won't go to the party tonight."

I scratched my chin with my middle finger. "I actually have plans tonight, but I'll be at the rest of the events. Will *you* be there, Mara? I thought Alexei kicked you out at the last party."

Mara looked around, her cheeks flushing with a combination of anger and embarrassment. "Shut up." My ears didn't itch this time. I was thankful for the truth earrings, which she suddenly seemed to notice. "I see you got a little gift from the witches." She nodded at my ear before leaning closer, her expensive perfume hitting me like a hard slap. "But it only lets you hear the truth. Those cheap-ass studs won't protect you from me, Nicole. And I suggest you fall in line before I *make* you."

I'd be lying if I said Mara didn't scare me. I was a human, and she had the ability to shift into an animal that could tear me apart with its teeth. But if I backed down now, then she'd always know she could intimidate me, and I refused to give her that satisfaction. I refused to give *any* of them that satisfaction.

"Then do something, Mara," I taunted in a sickly sweet tone. "Or do you hide behind your words?"

"You little cu—"

"Settle down, now." A man wearing a suit walked into the room, eyeing Mara, who huffed in annoyance. "Damn shifters."

All the humans in the class spoke up in unison. "The coffee shop is down on Main Street."

It was creepy, and I wondered if that would have been me if I hadn't taken a reveal spell.

The man waved his hand. "Yes, yes. The coffee shop is on Main Street. Let's all sit down and focus. I'd hate to have to tell Alpha Jones that his students are causing trouble in my class."

Mara glared at me before turning back to the professor. "Yes, Dr. Gilberts. I apologize. *You're going to forget this happened and give me straight As all semester.*"

A whimsical look crossed his features as he stared at her. "All As this semester."

What the hell? Did Mara do this to everyone? Where was the line?

Mara turned to me, a psychotic smile on her face. "Enjoy the semester, Nicole." Then, her compulsion rang out across the auditorium. *"Nicole is going to fail every assignment in this class. No one wants to sit by her because she smells bad."*

My mouth dropped open, and I looked around the room. Professor Gilberts scowled at me and made a note in his journal. A few kids nearby pinched their noses and leaned as far away from me as possible.

"You might be impossible to compel, but *they* aren't. Have a great semester, Nicole." She returned to her seat, looking far too pleased with herself.

This meant fucking war.

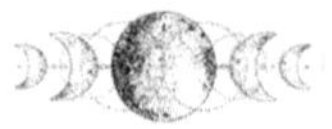

I'D DEBATED on going to Alexei, but after considering my options, I knew that he was the only person who could put Mara in her place. Even though it stung, I didn't care if everyone thought I smelled bad. But compelling my professor to fail me was out of line.

Was it a bit impulsive to go to the Alpha Nu house and barge in like I owned the place? Maybe. Was it a bad idea to storm up the stairs and kick open his door like I was the rapture?

Absolutely.

Did I give a fuck?

Nope.

I was fuming. Raging. Ready to punch something or someone by the time I made it to his bedroom door. When I kicked it open without knocking, I had hoped to disturb an afternoon nap or studying session.

But no.

Instead, I was greeted with the sight of Alexei gripping his cock while biting his sinful lips.

And oh my God, what a sight it was. It would be burned in my brain no matter how much of a fucking asshole he was.

"Shit! Goddammit, Nicole!" he yelled before

releasing his gigantic trouser snake and throwing the comforter over his lap. "What the fuck?!"

I slammed my palm over my eyes and winced. "Sorry! No one was guarding the door or the stairs, and I was so mad—"

"Fucking hell."

I peeked through my fingers at him. His bare chest was heaving as he glared at me, the heat in his gaze unmistakable, and I knew that a million naughty fantasies were running through his mind.

"Get dressed." I crossed my arms over my chest. "I don't want to talk with your dick hanging out."

His face twisted into a scowl, and he shoved the comforter off his lap. When he stood up, I got a full view of his muscular body. My brows rose in appreciation. He was toned, tall, and *huge*. I licked my lips at the sight of his bobbing cock pointed straight at me. "You want me to get dressed? You're in *my* space, baby. You want to talk, let's talk."

The insufferable bastard. I would have stomped my foot if it wouldn't have made me look like a bratty toddler.

"You want to talk while you're like"—I gestured toward him—"*that*?"

He smirked. "Does my cock bother you?"

Quite the opposite, actually. Between the pheromones and his hot body, I was about ready to drop to my knees for the asshole. It's a good thing he was being a total prick, because it was the only thread of sanity I was clinging to. "You need to control your girl Mara."

"She's *not* my girl." His growl caught me off guard, and I felt the urge to swoon.

No. Not happening, Nicole.

"She's a shifter in *your* pack, and she's making my life hell. She compelled my professor to fail me and told an auditorium full of students not to sit by me because I smelled."

Some of the bravado fled from Alexei's shoulders. He stormed back over to his comforter and wrapped it around his waist. "She did what?"

"You need to tell her to back off." I wasn't going to cave on this. I wouldn't let her intimidate me, and I sure as hell wasn't afraid to tell Alexei to make her fall in line. She didn't have to like me, but Mara's bullshit stopped today.

"Okay." Alexei sounded defeated. "I'll make sure she leaves you alone. I'm sorry she did that."

Well, damn. I wasn't expecting Alexei to be so helpful. He was normally so difficult about everything that I'd expected some push back. Scratching the back of his neck while clinging to his comforter, I admired the way his arm flexed.

My throat was dry, so I cleared it. "Thank you."

He nodded. "Um, other than that, did you have a good day?"

His question left a bitter taste in my mouth. Just yesterday, he'd made it clear that we weren't friends. We weren't even acquaintances. I was a failure.

"Don't ask me about my day," I whispered.

"I'm just trying to be nice, Nicole."

"Like I was trying to be nice? What was it you said...'Stop being nice to me. It's confusing.'"

Alexei's shoulders dropped, and for a moment, I thought he was going to lose his grip on the comforter—not that I'd complain. "Nicole. It's complicated, you know?"

"Yeah. I know. Thanks for taking care of the Mara problem. You can go back to—" My abrupt pause made him laugh. I can't believe I was about to tell him to go back to jacking off like it was nothing. "See you around, Alexei."

I turned around and opened his bedroom door. And as I walked out into the hall, I could have sworn I heard him whisper, "I wish it could be different, Nicole."

Alexei

MY HEAD WAS THROBBING. While the rest of my brothers were partying it up, as we did most Friday nights, I ended up letting down my pack and spending most of the evening getting drunk off my ass in my room. The alpha was supposed to be downstairs making sure everything went smoothly, but I didn't have it in me to pretend I was having a good time. After I accepted Nicole wasn't going to show, I grabbed the fullest bottle I could find and ducked out of there without saying a word. I seriously needed to get a handle on my shit, or everything I'd worked hard for would go down the drain.

"You look chipper this morning." Corbin's tone couldn't possibly have been more sarcastic.

I was sitting on the edge of my bed, hunched over and wondering how I was going to get through another day.

I grunted in response and held my hand out, knowing without even looking that he had another spiked cup of coffee waiting for me.

"Is everything ready for today?" I grabbed the to-go cup and took a gulp. The burn traveling down my throat was just what I needed.

"Yep. We're all set for the Alpha Nu slash Beta Phi river float. The charter buses we booked to take us to the float drop are on standby. I had the sophomores inflate all the tubes, and all the ice chests are packed."

I gave him a grateful but weak grin. I was fucking thankful for my best friend. I'd planned a day float for open rush a while ago. As wolves, we loved being in nature. The house parties were fine, but there was something about floating down the river, surrounded by chicks in bikinis, with a beer in your grip, that made people happy.

"Got the first aid kit?"

"Packed and stocked. I also have a few pre-med majors attending." He winked. "They're human, but they're smoke shows. I might pretend to get hurt just so they can nurse me back to health."

I rolled my eyes. There were still a few humans interested in Alpha Nu and Beta Phi. Even though they'd never get a formal invitation, we still wanted to give them a good open rush experience. If only so they could truly understand everything they're missing out on when they didn't get in.

I cleared my throat. "You think Nicole will come?"

Corbin gave me a sympathetic look that had my wolf whining. I hated feeling so goddamn pathetic. "Do you *want* her to come? I thought you said you were giving her space, but if you want, I could drag her out of bed and—"

I cut him off with a growl. I didn't like the idea of him seeing her in bed. The thought of her lying tangled in a fit of sheets in her silky pajamas made my stomach clench. "If I want her to come, *I'll* get her."

Corbin laughed. "I'd love to hear the gossip. *Did you see Alpha Alexei storm into the girls' dorm this morning? I heard moaning from Nicole's room...*" He gave his best impression of a gossipy she-wolf, complete with a high-pitch voice.

"I *don't* want her to come." That was a complete lie. I *did* want to see her—more than anything—but nothing had changed. It wasn't fair to keep stringing Nicole along.

"Are you sure about that?" Corbin asked. "You know, I've been thinking. Maybe we could find a way to make this work. I hate seeing you upset, and I kind of like the idea of you two together. Nicole's good people."

I arched my brow. "She dumped ice water on you in front of a hundred people," I deadpanned.

The footage of their fake breakup was all over Wolfebytes, and it made me swell with pride. Nicole was an enigma, and even though it made me a territorial asshole to see her with Corbin, I really liked that she cared about his image and could mess with him without caring what anyone thought. There were lots of people who thought it was hilarious. I nearly broke my phone when a couple of lower-ranking shifters commented how hot she was. I'd be giving them grunt work today.

"I kind of liked it," Corbin teased. "I wasn't expecting her to want to protect me, you know? In her own way, of course."

I understood. The more I learned about her, the more I felt like she truly would be good at my side. She obviously was very caring, based on what I knew about her relationship with her father. She was sassy and strong-willed. She demanded only the best from herself, something any alpha worth their merit could relate to.

"It'll never work," I croaked. "I need to move on."

"We could always talk to June? Maybe there's a spell or something? I know her mom wasn't able to help magically lift your bond, but maybe we can—"

"There's not a spell to turn a human into a shifter," I interrupted, refusing to feel hope about this hopeless situation. "That's the *only* solution that would make her an acceptable mate."

Corbin sighed in exasperation. "Maybe not. But maybe there's a spell to help people accept it? You shouldn't have to give up your fated mate, Alexei. You've already sacrificed a lot to be alpha. It wouldn't hurt to ask."

I put down my coffee cup as I considered his words. Nicole already knew supes existed. Hell, thanks to the meddling warlock, she knew a helluva lot more than that. She could probably write a goddamn dissertation on the history of every faction. Since we weren't allowed to erase her memory, why shouldn't I consider making it easier for everyone involved? I could feel the air of discomfort around my pack when they learned a human knew our secret. Asking Juniper for a spell would make my pack happier, and as alpha, pack satisfaction was my duty. Plus, it would be considered an apology from the witches. Compensation, if you will, to make up for that idiot's actions. And if I got to spend more time with Nicole as a result, it was simply an added bonus, not my true motivation.

Yeah, you keep telling yourself that, dickhead.

"Yeah." I nodded. "Give her a call."

Corbin preened. "*Happily.*" I really needed to talk to him about his unique relationship with Juniper and her fiancé. I could tell he was getting emotionally invested, and I didn't want to see my best friend get hurt. "And while I'm at it, I'll send Nicole a little invite. She's trying to rush Beta Phi, so I bet she'll wanna come, even if your grumpy ass is going to be there."

"Fine," I gritted. I'd be lying if I said I didn't want to see my mate in a bikini. Even if the sight of her would be fucking torture. I hated how everything had played out. She deserved to be chased—to be courted by an alpha. The push and pull was hurting her, which made everything worse.

Corbin pulled out his cell and hummed to himself before announcing, "Done!"

I scrubbed my hands down my face, then stood up, ready to take on the day and fucking deal with the shit storm that had become my life. "Let's go."

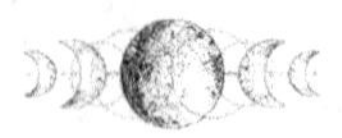

I TOLD myself I wasn't stalling, praying that she'd show up. Everyone was waiting on the buses as I pretended to take a long look at our supplies, meticulously going over the inventory while keeping a look out for Nicole. I knew Corbin told her at the last minute, but I was still hoping that she would show.

"You think she meant it when she said she'd keep the phone this time?"

Corbin nodded. "Yeah. At least until she and her dad can get set up with their own plan. She seems smart enough to know it's good to have in case of another emergency."

"Yeah, you're right," I agreed.

"We have to get going, Alpha," he whispered. "Everyone is waiting."

I gritted my teeth. It was probably better this way. I needed to focus on my pack and not be distracted.

But still...

"Everything looks great. Let's go," I grumbled, and Corbin slapped his hand on my back and waved at the buses.

"You heard him," he bellowed. "Let's party!"

I could hear the yells from everyone on the buses, and Corbin ran up to the doors and started chanting, "Shots! Shots! Shots!"

I was following behind in my truck with all the

tubes and gear, and was suddenly thankful that I volunteered to not ride on the bus. A quiet drive would help me get my head straight. I watched as the two charters pulled down the road and then got into the driver's seat.

Clutching the steering wheel, I let out a shaky breath, then pushed the button for the ignition. I was about to put it in drive when a palm slapped the windshield. Looking out the window, I saw a breathless Nicole giving me a tentative look. I schooled my expression, even though my fucking heart was racing a million miles a minute.

She was dressed in a pair of tiny cutoff jean shorts with a navy half shirt. I could see the strings of her bright blue bikini top tied behind her neck. Her long dark hair was pulled into one of those artfully messy bun-things girls did, exposing the graceful column of her neck. A quick glance down her long, toned legs ended with pink-tipped toes and a pair of flip-flops. Nicole looked effortlessly casual yet gorgeous.

I rolled down my window as she fought to catch her breath. "Hey."

"Hey," she replied, watching a bus's taillights fade in the distance. "I'm too late, huh? I came as fast as I could."

"To catch the bus? Yeah." I swallowed, hitting the

button to unlock my doors. "But I'm heading that way. Hop in."

Her eyes rounded. "Uh... I don't know if that's the best idea, Alexei."

Was she blushing? Or was that the flush of arousal creeping up her neck?

My wolf liked the thought of the latter very much.

"I promise to keep both hands on the steering wheel," I teased. I couldn't help flirting with her.

She once again looked down the road where the buses disappeared, then back at me. "Fine." She rounded the truck and settled in the front seat. Sitting beside Nicole was going to be torture, but I was thankful for the time alone with her. I'd been fucking everything up at every turn, but ultimately, I wanted to know her.

"Thank you. I was with Dad when Corbin texted me. He shoved me out the door when I told him about the float trip, but I was trying to make him breakfast. That man would eat nothing but processed, sugary crap if I let him."

I smiled while pulling onto the road. "You're close with your dad, huh?"

"Very. He's really excited to work here. He'll probably spend every waking moment in his new lab."

"Does he have everything he needs?" I asked. "If

he needs more equipment or anything, I can call my father."

She gave me a curious look. "What would your father do?"

Ah. She didn't know. "Well, my grandfather built this school. We kind of own it, actually."

Her mouth dropped open in surprise. "Oh. Wow." She picked at the fray on her shorts. "Can I clarify something? It's probably best to get it out of the way since we're going to the same place."

My gut clenched, but I gave her a subtle nod in reply.

Nicole blew out a breath. "I meant what I said... about wanting you to stay away from me until you were done with the whole denial thing. But I realize I may be sending you mixed signals, because I keep showing up at Greek events. I'm not trying to be confusing."

I scratched at the scruff on my jaw. "Then what *are* you trying to accomplish, Nicole?"

"I've mentioned it before, but I really want to rush Beta Phi. I know it's a pipedream. The mind-fuck supernatural encyclopedia in my brain made it very clear that they won't allow a human to join. It's just important to me."

I took in her words while trying not to feel selfish. Did I want her to show up today because of me? Absolutely. Despite everything, I had this strong need to be desired by her. It was normal in mate bonds.

"Why is that so important to you? Because of your mom?"

She nodded. "All her sisters from Beta Phi took me in when she died. They acted as surrogate mothers when I had none. Dad did his best, but I saw their success and love for Mom, and it made me feel closer to the woman I never got the chance to know."

My chest constricted with pain. I didn't have the most nurturing parents—they were trying to raise a strong alpha and not coddle a needy son. But at least I *knew* them. They were in my life. I didn't have to ponder countless *what ifs* as I was sure Nicole had done about her mother. I couldn't imagine what it had felt like to live with such a monumental loss from day one.

"So, you're here today because it's a sorority event? There's *no* other reason why you wanted to come?"

"Alexei," she sighed. "Unlike you, I'm not pretending I don't feel some sort of cosmic connection with you. I'd be lying to you and myself if I said otherwise."

I had to fight a smile. "Why do I feel like there's a *but* coming?"

"*But*," she continued, "to answer your question...

yes. The sorority is the *only* reason I am here today. Regardless of how my body responds to you, my brain knows better. I *know* I shouldn't be in this truck right now, but I also know since I have no shot at actually becoming a Beta Phi sister, rush events are my only opportunity to experience what it's like. And I selfishly *want* that experience if it's the only piece I can have. Like I said, it makes me feel close to my mom. If you knew me, you'd know I'm a really sensible person. I had to grow up a lot earlier than most girls my age. My dad is... Parenting and tending to others' needs doesn't come naturally to him. Hell, he can barely tend to his *own* needs. It was something I recognized early in life, and I guess you could say my instincts stepped in. I became *his* caregiver around age ten or so."

Guilt rocked through me. My father started this chapter and was adamant about not including humans. He wanted a safe space for shifters to experience what it meant to work together as a pack. I'd always agreed with him because it was all I knew.

But now, I wasn't so sure.

"What if I could help?" I blurted out, my wolf and the mate bond spurring me to want to fix this.

"Help?"

I passed a semitruck, accelerating while I considered my offer. "Look, I won't lie to you. I feel responsible for you in a way that is outside of my control. Because I'm your mate, my instincts make me want to take care of you. Even though this will never work out, you'll always have whatever you want. I physically can't stomach the idea of you not being provided for. Knowing how important this is to you makes me want to rewrite our bylaws just so I can see you smile."

She turned her head to look at me. "I don't want someone to fix my problems, Alexei. This is something I have to do on my own. I'll apply and let my merits speak for themselves. If and when I don't get in, I'll still move forward, knowing I did everything I possibly could. I can appreciate your feelings of obligation, even if I don't fully experience them myself, but you don't have to take care of me. I've been taking care of myself for a long time, and I'll continue to do that."

I grumbled. Nicole deserved someone who prioritized her and cared for her. If she was taking care of everyone else, who took care of her?

"Corbin was going to talk to Juniper about a spell to make people more accepting of you."

Her eyes thinned into slits. "Would this be for *me* or for *you*, Alexei?"

"There's not a spell on this earth that would make my pack accept a human as their luna. I just think it could make your experience here better. Your newfound knowledge of our world makes my pack uncomfortable. This could benefit both of us equally."

Her jaw dropped. "So it's just common knowledge across campus that I know?"

A growl rumbled in my chest, thinking about how careless that blue-haired fucker had been. "You were spelled in a public place, Nicole. People saw blue smoke coming out of you. There's no way to explain that besides magic. The spell itself has an automatic concealer built in for any humans who may have witnessed the event, but any supe would've known without a doubt what was going down. News travels fast."

I could see her nibbling her lip out of the corner of my eye as she thought about it. "One of those witnesses being my good pal Mara? I'm sure she couldn't wait to spill the tea."

I shook my head. "Mara took off right before it happened, but she did hear about it pretty quickly thereafter, which I'm sure doesn't help one bit."

"Lemme ask you something. According to my reference guide"—she tapped her temple—"alphas make the rules, right? And when you're a member of the pack, your alpha's word is law. You have to do what they say."

"In an ideal world, yes," I admitted. "But that's not always how it works. Alphas are responsible for ensuring *pack* law—which was established long ago —is being followed. We have discretion on how to make that happen, but we're not the be-all and end-all decision makers. There's a high council that steps in when need be. Was that not part of the download?"

"I knew there was a council." She paused for a moment. "But the information in my head is more of the practical, fact-based variety, rather than how things run in real life. I suppose that makes sense, because each pack would be different based on the individual personalities."

"If you're asking if I can change the rules to include you—"

"I'm not," she interrupted. "Not at all. I want to do this on my own, Alexei." Her stubbornness made me grin. Yeah, in another world, she would make a great partner to an alpha. "I'm just curious, I suppose. And the more I know, the better chance I have for rush." I pinned my mouth shut. It didn't matter how much she knew or how involved she was. She'd never get in. "Do you have any siblings?"

Her sudden change of topic surprised me. "Nope. I'm an only child. I'm sure my father would have loved to have a backup heir, but it never happened."

"Tell me about your mother."

I liked that she wanted to get to know me better. It

soothed my raging wolf that we were becoming acquainted with one another.

"She's a great luna. She's always starting charities to benefit whatever cause she learns about. Right now, she's off designing temporary housing for our lone wolf populations in transition to joining a pack."

She smiled to herself. "Loves philanthropy. Let me guess, she was a Beta Phi?"

I smiled back. "President, actually. And my dad was the president of Alpha Nu."

"Were they fated mates?"

"No. They weren't. My mom... she was, uh... actually mated to another future alpha. They were high school sweethearts, but he was killed in a motorcycle accident right before their graduation."

She clapped a hand over her mouth and mumbled, "Oh, my God, that's so sad."

"She hasn't told me much, but yeah... I know it cut deep. But when she came to Redwood U and met my dad, he recognized the luna qualities in her right away and thought she would make a suitable partner. Evidently, he was relentless in his pursuit and can be quite charming when he wants to be." I laughed. "It's really hard to imagine, because my dad has been so damn serious my whole life, but I do think he made her loneliness a bit more bearable at first. Nowadays... their relationship seems like more of a business arrangement, but unless my dad suddenly met *his* fated mate, walking away isn't an option for her. You don't leave an alpha."

"Whoa." Nicole's hands formed into a timeout position. "Hold up. You're telling me after they've been together all these years, if he met the woman he was supposedly fated to be with, he'd drop your mom like a bad habit? Just like that?"

"That's how it works." I shrugged.

"That's complete and utter bullshit." She scoffed, folding her arms over her chest. "Your mom can't divorce him—or whatever the wolfy equivalent is—but he can toss her aside *no problemo* if someone better comes along?"

"She understood what she was getting into when she agreed to be with my father. It's just the way it is."

"The word you were looking for is misogyny," she grumbled.

Nicole's flippant dismissal was a glaring reminder of why we could never work out. She just didn't get it, and she never would unless she were a wolf.

"I guess we'll have to agree to disagree."

"Guess so." She huffed, leaning into the door, as if she were trying to get as far away from me as physically possible. "How 'bout we just stop talking altogether? That'll make this drive a heck of a lot more pleasant."

"Fine by me." I clenched my jaw, wondering once again what I did to the fates in a past life to deserve a human for a mate.

Whatever it was, I must've pissed them off *big time.*

SEVENTEEN

Nicole

So far, my attempts at mingling and making friends hadn't been working. I'd introduced myself to every Beta Phi I saw, and all of them snubbed their noses up at me and giggled with their friends. It was discouraging, and many times I'd asked myself why I was trying so hard to be liked by people who would never accept me, but I was stubborn.

Stubbornly sitting alone in an inner tube while floating down the river. Everyone else had tied their tubes together and had created little islands of partiers. I tried to keep up as I clutched my beer and paddled closer, but they always floated farther away. It was like a stupid game of cat and mouse.

I'd appreciated the fact that Alexei and Corbin weren't interfering. I made it clear that I wanted to do this on my own, but now that I was watching him, I was regretting that. Women flocked to Alexei, and not just because he had the floating cooler with all the beer. They craved his attention—his approval—and it made me sick.

My tube bumped into a guy's, and he laughed. "Looks like we're both stragglers." He had bright red board shorts and messy ash-blond hair. His long legs were slung over the outer rim of the tube as he kicked. "Didn't expect anyone to talk to me, but still annoys the hell out of me. One of the perks of being born without a wolf, I suppose."

My mind raced with information, and I gasped. "Wait... *you know about the wolves?*"

Did this guy get spelled like I did?

He laughed. "Of course. My parents are wolves. So are all of my siblings."

I frowned, rolling that around in my head. "So, you're adopted?"

"I wish. Being human would've probably been less shameful than having wolf-shifter blood running through your veins but not having an inner animal. No offense." He winked with a lopsided smile. "It's a genetic defect. Happens every once in a while, but scientists have never been able to figure out why."

I hadn't realized it was possible to be a shifter without an animal counterpart. I couldn't imagine being in the shifter community but not truly *being* a part of them.

"I'm sorry," I whispered.

"I have a confession to make." He smiled conspiratorially. "I wanted to meet you when I heard you got an information download. None of the shifters here will talk to me because my very existence makes them uncomfortable, and no other human understands pack politics."

"Why would your existence make them uncomfortable?"

He shrugged. "I dunno... because I remind them it's possible for their future children to be just like me, which would bring shame down on them?"

"That's terrible." I frowned.

"Eh, I'm used to it." He shrugged again. "So... what do you say? Wanna be my friend?"

Hell, I wasn't really in a position to turn down friends—or potential allies.

"I'm Nicole." I raised my beer can in the air in greeting.

"I'm Hunter. Nice to meet you."

"Are you rushing?"

He let out a puff of air and took a drink. "Trying to. Probably won't get in, but if I'm going to disappoint my parents, then I might as well do it while drunk. This is my third time at open rush."

Would this be me? Trying every year to be a Beta Phi and failing? I made a mental note to think about that later. I wasn't sure I could handle rejection over and over again.

"Are you in any other clubs? I'm trying to think of my back-up plan."

At that question, a broad grin crossed his features, blinding me with his bright teeth and charming smile. "I'm a business major. We have an entrepreneurs club that is really fun. We get to practice pitching business ideas to investors. I know it sounds lame, but I've made a lot of friends there."

I smiled. "It doesn't sound lame at all. I want to become a fashion designer, so I'm hoping to find something related to that if Beta Phi doesn't work out. It's nice to hear there are other ways to feel involved."

"Absolutely! If you need help finding trouble to get into at Redwood, I can maybe show you around?"

I chewed on my lip for a moment, trying to decide if he was flirting with me or being friendly. "I'd like that."

His grin grew. "And maybe I could take you on a date."

My mind fleetingly went to my supposed mate. I

couldn't help but compare the two of them. Hunter had bright blue eyes and light hair, over Alexei's espresso eyes and nearly black hair. And while Hunter certainly had a great body, he had more of a swimmer's build, like Corbin, over Alexei's massive frame. Both men were incredibly attractive, but I definitely favored darker features and bulk. I always had. Personality-wise, Hunter had a playfulness about him that immediately drew you in, over Alexei's seemingly constant surly disposition, which should've been a plus in Hunter's column, but for some reason, it wasn't. Not to me, anyway. I hated to admit it, but I liked the challenge Alexei's moodiness presented. I had this crazy need inside of me to be the one who made him smile.

Stupid bond.

Maybe I should agree to a date with Hunter if for no other reason than to prove fate did not rule me. That *I* was in control of my destiny.

"I'd like that." I told myself to ignore the strange pang in my chest.

"Oh, you better hold on. We're coming up on some rough water." He nodded in the distance, and I followed his gaze. Sure enough, the water was churning and turned white as it flowed between rocks and down ledges. Some of the shifters ahead of us cheered as they got thrashed around. My heart started to race. I wasn't that great of a swimmer, and it looked intense.

The water flowed quicker, and as my tube picked up speed, my hair whipped around my face. I put my beer between my knees and gripped the rope wrapped around my tube for stability. Hunter went through the rapids and almost flipped over. Another shifter girl was getting pulled through the water, but she seemed strong enough to keep her head above the surface.

I was thrown against a hard rock, causing serious whiplash to my body.

"Be careful, Nicole!" Hunter yelled from the other side of the rough patch.

I had to swallow my scream as my tube hit the ledge and I was thrown through the air and then into the rough water. When I landed on my inner tube, I was pushed out by the water and hurtled into the rapids. Without my tube to cling to, I panicked. Cool water crashed against my face, jostling me, and as I was being carried further and further, my legs scraped against sharp rocks as the current yanked me along. The first attempt to swim up had left me disoriented and in a panic. I quickly realized that I wasn't strong enough to swim through the rushing water.

When my knee hit a rock, a sharp pain raged through me, and I screamed.

Fuck. The feeling of panic was like a vise around my throat. I could feel my lungs burning. It felt as though my whole body was beaten and battered.

You can't fucking die like this.

Strong arms wrapped around my waist, and I went limp as someone pulled me toward the surface. My burning lungs expanded the moment air hit my face, and I choked and coughed, sputtering up river water while clinging for life to the person rescuing me.

"Hold on, Nicole. I've got you."

Hunter.

Thank fuck.

He swam both of us over to the river bank and helped me onto the rocks.

I lay there on the side of the rushing rapids, gulping for air like a fish out of water. Each inhalation was a struggle. My throat was raw from the force of my cough. My top knot had fallen out completely, so wet hair plastered my face.

Hunter gently patted my back as my coughing subsided. "Hey. You're okay. Breathe."

I swiped my long strands away from my face and turned just enough to meet his concerned gaze.

"Thank you," I wheezed.

He gave me a soft smile. "What happened back there?"

I blinked water out of my eyes as my useless limbs flattened against the ground. "I don't know. I'm not the best swimmer, but…"

I hissed as a stinging, painful sensation hit me. Looking down, I noticed a big gash along the top of my knee, coated in tiny pebbles and sand. Blood was dripping steadily down my leg from the wound.

"Shit." Hunter winced. "We need to clean that up and get some bandages."

I looked back at the water, hoping like hell the rest of the group hadn't left us, when I saw something that made my mouth drop open. Alexei was swimming toward us, his impressive muscles working hard against the current.

"What did you do to her?" Droplets of water flowed down his skin as he hit the shallows and stood, stomping toward us with a furious expression. "*Why is she bleeding?!*"

Alexei's nostrils flared as his chest heaved. Hostility radiated from his every pore.

"Uh…" Hunter stuttered. "Nothing, man. She tipped over in the rapids, and I pulled her out of the water. She must've been scraped up by the rocks or something."

"Move," Alexei commanded, shoving Hunter aside.

He dropped to his knees and reached out, trailing his finger over my cheek ever so gently. I shivered as a current of electricity shot through my veins.

"Nicole, you scared the shit out of me."

I would've laughed if I didn't think it'd hurt too much. "Yeah... well. Sorry for almost drowning. Wouldn't want to inconvenience you."

"What are you talking about? I was worried about you. If you..." His dark brows pinched together. "If something were to happen to you. If you were hurt, that would've killed me."

"I'm sure your harem would've consoled you," I grumbled. "By the looks of it, you would've forgotten all about me by the end of the day."

I knew I was being immature and possibly a tad bitchy, but I couldn't seem to help myself.

"Um, Nicole..." Hunter started. "Should I—"

Alexei leveled my rescuer with a murderous glare. "*Leave.* I'll handle this from here."

Hunter's anxious eyes flicked to me. "You okay with that? Uh..."

The poor guy looked like he was about to piss himself, but I appreciated his attempt to stick by my side, regardless of the ocular threats being thrown his way. I decided to put him out of his misery. I didn't exactly want to be left alone with Alexei, but this was getting all kinds of uncomfortable, and I knew Alexei wouldn't harm me. I couldn't say he'd extend the same courtesy to Hunter if he stuck around much longer.

"Hunter, I'm fine. Thank you for the rescue."

He looked back at me, indecision on his face. "I'm just glad you're okay. You sure? I don't mind staying if—"

"Leave!" Alexei roared once more.

Hunter's eyes widened, and he nodded vigorously. He might have had a missing wolf, but he understood the pecking order here. With his hands up in mock surrender, he made his way back to the water. The rest of the group was long gone, floating down with the current way up ahead. I felt bad that Hunter had to catch back up to them on his own, but it was probably better than staying here.

I gave Alexei a look. "Thanks for checking on me, but I'm fine. Hunter had it covered."

Alexei looked murderous at my words. "Oh he did, did he? Why were you even in the water in the first place? If we were floating together, I would have—"

I cut him off. "But we *weren't* floating together! You were off flirting with a bunch of she-wolves while I was drowning."

"Nicole," he breathed. I could see that my words were frustrating him.

"It doesn't matter." I wiped my dirt-covered palms on my thighs. "I don't need you. It's not like you *could* have floated with me or pulled me from the water, anyway. I mean, what would all the other gossipy shifters think? Helping a *human*," I taunted while twisting my face up in disgust. "I don't even know why you're here right now."

"I would have helped you!" he shouted. "You're my..." He looked around as if to make sure no one heard him. "Mate. You're my mate, Nicole."

I tipped my head back and laughed. We were all alone, and he still whispered that four-letter word like it was a curse. This was nothing more than a giant waste of time.

"It doesn't matter. Go ahead and join back up with the group. My tube is gone, so I'll just walk the rest of the way to the buses." I bent my knee and hissed in pain once more.

"I'm not leaving you," Alexei gritted.

I pressed my palm to my chest, giving him a scandalous look. "And risk someone seeing you with me? Oh, Alexei, you really shouldn't." My sarcasm was dripping with venom.

"Don't be like that," Alexei pleaded while I stood up.

The moment I put weight on my injured leg, a spike of pain traveled through me. *Fuck.*

He scrubbed a hand down his face with a groan. "Nicole... don't hurt yourself any more than you already have just for the sake of being stubborn. Look, I can carry you back to—"

Oh, I'll show this asshole stubborn.

"Nuh-uh." I shook my head. "I said I don't need your help. And I certainly don't want to be carried in your arms, listening to whatever lecture you're dying to give me on the way back."

I pressed my toes into the ground, putting a tiny bit more weight on it, telling myself to breathe. "Argh!"

Dammit.

This wasn't going to work. I was exhausted, bleeding, and every muscle in my body felt like Jell-O. But I really didn't think I could handle being held by Alexei, either. I was emotional from my near-drowning, and this stupid bond between us made me want nothing more than to give into it, seeking comfort in his muscular arms.

"What if I..." He rubbed the back of his neck. "Oh, fuck it."

Before I could process the fact that he just dropped his swim trunks right in front of me—and holy beje-sus, his dick seemed even bigger—Alexei's skin started to change. Where there was a glorious golden tan before, icy white fur filled every inch of his body.

His nose elongated into a proud snout, and I gasped at the sharp teeth in his mouth.

Alexei went on all fours, but it was paws that hit the dirt instead of hands and feet. Long tree-trunk legs and a huge muscular chest. Thick fur. Bold black eyes. A swishing tail that brushed along the dirt.

Holy shit. Alexei was a wolf. I mean, I knew he was, but seeing it in the flesh made a hysterical giggle travel up my throat. My rational brain didn't want to believe what I just saw.

"Please don't eat me."

"I'm not going to eat you, mate," a warm voice buzzed in my mind, the sound like melting chocolate on hot concrete. Smooth. Sensual. It stuck to my brain and sent a shiver down my spine.

"I'm hearing voices in my brain," I shrieked before taking a step back. I hadn't truly had a good freak out moment about all the supernatural shit that had happened to me, but seeing Alexei shift and hearing voices was just enough to send me over the edge.

"You can hear me?" the voice asked, excitement brimming over every syllable.

"I can hear *something*." I took another step backward but yelped when I tripped over an exposed root at the edge of the tree line. "But I still haven't figured out if it's real or a hallucination."

I swear, his lips curled into a grin. *"You* can *hear me. That's... unexpected."*

I remained frozen in place as the large animal approached slowly before nudging his snout against my good leg. "Is this, like, a mate thing? Or has the stress from the past week finally made me snap?"

His cold, wet nose switched to my other leg, sniffing my wound. When his rough tongue peeked out, dragging along my skin, I wanted to run like hell from the wild wolf with sharp teeth, but somehow, I managed to stay still. He continued licking until every trace of red was gone.

"Get on, Nicole."

"Get on *what*? And did you just *lick* my owie?! That's kinda crossing a boundary or two, don't you think, buddy? Not to mention gross."

Okay, now I knew he was grinning. *"My* back. *I'll give you a ride. And I was cleaning your cut. There are enzymes in my wolf saliva that'll prevent infection. It was an instinct. This is me taking care of you."*

I eyed him suspiciously. "If I accept your offer... and the only reason I'm even considering it is because I really don't think I can walk however many miles are between us and the buses. Do you promise not to crack any jokes about me riding you afterwards?"

He scoffed. *"Give me a little more credit than that.*

I'm not Corbin, for fuck's sake. Grab my swim shorts and get on."

I giggled. Corbin would *totally* make jokes about that. It took a minute for me to get on his back, partly because of my injury and partly because I couldn't get my damn body to stop trembling. I knew that the massive creature before me was Alexei and that he wouldn't hurt me, but it was hard to force my brain to believe it.

"You're a lot bigger than I expected." I grabbed his white fur in my fist, with his wet swim trunks balled in the other. His coat was a lot softer than I imagined. I debated kicking him in the ribs like a horse and yelling *yeehaw*, but I figured that would probably be a smidge offensive. "How can I hear your voice in my head?"

"*For the record, I'm being very good and not making a 'That's what she said' joke. Just throwing that out there.*" I giggled. "*And it's a mate gift. We can communicate in our wolf forms. I'm honestly surprised you can hear me.*"

"How come my encyclopedia brain didn't tell me about this?" I asked out loud.

"*Probably because it's so rare. Only some of the strongest mate bonds are gifted with mind speak. I personally have only heard of it happening in legends. It's... a great honor.*"

"Or it would be," I began. "If I were a shifter."

I heard Alexei's whine in my mind, and I hated that we never really stood a chance. I was still overwhelmed by this whole new world I was learning about, but if this was truly a bond that fit you with your perfect match, why would Alexei be paired with someone he could never have?

"It's still an honor, Nicole. Even if the rest of the world doesn't see it, I'll treasure knowing we were blessed with this."

His sincerity and vulnerability shocked me. I didn't delude myself into thinking it changed anything, but the reverence in his tone made my heart clench with affection. I cleared my throat. "Your wolf is beautiful. I wasn't expecting you to have white fur."

"You thought about what I looked like when I shifted?" I wobbled as he took a tentative step, keeping a slow pace to allow me to adjust.

"I dunno... maybe? I guess I didn't consciously think about it, but after I saw the brown wolf by your house, I think I assumed your coloring would be the same because your hair is so dark. Guess I was wrong. Speaking of the wolf that tried to bite my face off... one of your guys, I take it?"

He tensed. "She'll be punished. I'm working on it."

"*She?* It was a girl? Who was it? Have I met her?"

When Alexei chose to walk in silence instead of replying, I knew the answer.

"Mara." I gasped. "That's why she's not here today, isn't it?"

I was pleasantly surprised when Mara was nowhere to be found as everyone gathered around Alexei's truck to grab an inner tube. As president of the sorority, I had assumed she'd be present.

"I forbade her from coming," he confirmed. *"Mara is... She likes to party, probably more than anyone I know. Ejecting her from any type of social event is the equivalent of waterboarding to her."*

"But she was at your party last Monday," I pointed out.

"I told her she wasn't allowed to attend before that party even began, but Mara likes to test limits, which is what she did that night. She won't make that mistake again. She's banned from everything involving Alpha Nu until further notice."

"Thank you," I mumbled, not really sure what to say. I was thankful that Alexei was looking out for me where Mara was concerned. "Are you going to get in trouble for missing the rest of the float?" I ducked to avoid a low-hanging tree branch.

"Probably. But I don't really care right now."

It was foolish, and my head kept constantly reminding me that this was useless. I shouldn't be getting to know him when it would never work out. But a tentative smile still graced my lips.

"Thanks for the ride, Alexei," I whispered.

"I'll always take care of you," his mind whispered back.

We traveled the rest of the way in comfortable silence, and I tried not to feel a little more attached to the man I couldn't have.

EIGHTEEN

Nicole

I'D BEEN CONFINED to my room and *ordered* by a certain alpha shifter to rest and recover since I returned from the river float yesterday. Every part of my body hurt. Last night, Dad brought me pizza and put new bandages on my knee, and we had a movie marathon like we used to when I was little.

A couple of anonymous deliveries showed up at my dorm this morning. Flowers. My favorite coffee—minus the magical mind-fuck—and cozy slippers. I knew in my gut Alexei was responsible for sending them, and part of me was flattered, but another part of me wanted to return everything. It bothered me that he wanted to take care of me from afar. It sent mixed messages and made it harder to cut him off entirely. Seeing him so concerned for me at the float trip made the walls I'd built up around me crack just a smidge. It was nice to be cared about, even if the person caring for me would always be at arm's length.

I stared at myself in the full-length mirror, frowning at the purple bruises and scrapes marring my skin, before stepping into my dress. There was a meet and greet for the university staff and their families tonight, and Dad wanted me to accompany him so he could *show me off*. I'd much rather stay in and rest since I had classes in the morning, but I knew he needed me. When my father playfully said he wanted to *show me off*, that really meant he needed me for emotional support.

I was naturally extroverted, so striking up conversations with complete strangers was a breeze for me. For my dad... not so much. More often than not, the poor guy would start mumbling nonsensically or he'd crack horribly cheesy science jokes that almost always went over people's heads. Ironically, since coming to Redwood U, I had had little opportunity to showcase my excellent social skills, because I kept running into complete assholes who thought humans were comparable to dog shit, so maybe this would be good for me. Maybe it'd help me feel a little bit more like myself. Lord knew I'd had trouble with that since I got here.

Fake it until you make it, right?

I'd picked one of my best upcycled outfits, a blush ruched maxi that flowed around my body, but at the same time, it hugged my subtle curves. I wanted something that was concealing, covering my legs so I didn't have to explain my accident to every person I met, but was also stylish in case I ran into any of the design faculty members. I paired the dress with a trendy Coach X Jean Michel Basquiat clutch and some Gucci wedges. I felt high-fashion but ready for cocktail hour.

A knock on my door drew my attention, and when I went to answer it, I found my father standing in the doorway with a fist full of pretty pink and white flowers.

"Aw." I accepted the bouquet with a grin. "Thanks, Dad."

His lips curved into a shy smile as he stared at his feet. "I was thinking about all the times I used to take you on daddy-daughter dates and figured I'd spoil my new college student with a bouquet."

I put the flowers in a plastic tumbler and poured some bottled water into it.

"You look nice." He was wearing the navy blue suit I picked out for him, but his tie was crooked. "Want me to fix that?" I nodded to the silk neckwear.

"Please do. You know I hate wearing suits. Why can't I throw on a lab coat again?"

"Because you need to make a good impression on all of your new colleagues." I adjusted the knot until it was a perfect Half Windsor.

"I'd take microscopes and test slides over this social mumbo-jumbo any day."

I smiled as I straightened the silver tie clip, chuckling at the quirky nod to science. Most people wouldn't know the metal resembled a double helix structure, but I did, because I gave it to him for Christmas a few years ago.

"I know you would, Dad. But this will be good for you. And if you get nervous, I'll be right there with you the whole time."

He smiled softly as I thumbed the locket around my neck. "You remind me of her more and more every day, kiddo."

"I know." I quickly used my wardrobe mirror to freshen my lip gloss. "I'm a spitting image."

"You are," he agreed. "But I was referring to your personality. *Your heart.* You really did get all the best pieces of her."

My eyes watered. "Dad, you're gonna make me cry."

He laughed nervously. "Please don't. You know I don't handle tears very well."

Now *I* laughed. "Definitely not your strong suit, old man."

He took my hand, hooking it in his elbow. "C'mon, smarty pants, let's get this over with."

We walked in comfortable silence to Sequoia Hall, where the reception was being held. I knew Dad was anxious about socializing and needed the quiet to sort through all the conversations we'd both have to endure. Once we got to the front table to check in, we were both handed name tags and walked inside.

My anxiety spiked the moment we entered the banquet room. My brain instantly cataloged all the different types of supernatural creatures in attendance, making me nervous for my father. He already hated navigating the nuances of human interactions, but what about supernatural cultural norms?

"Ooh," he said excitedly. "There's my department lead, Dr. Cammie Viden. Isn't she lovely, Nicole? She's absolutely brilliant, too!" He pointed at the beautiful professor standing in a corner.

How was I going to approach this? I couldn't exactly tell him she was my new Supernatural Law and Regs teacher. According to Cammie, my original statistics class would still show on my college transcripts. What if he introduced us? Should I pretend I didn't know her? Would she do the same? My heart started racing as three of the most important rules when dealing with fae ran through my mind.

Never make a deal with the fae.

Never promise them anything.

Never give them your full name.

I knew I was protected as a student thanks to her magical binding, but were her colleagues protected as well? If not, my dad was screwed. Something told me that the last rule was already ruined. Dad couldn't exactly apply for this job with a pseudonym. He wasn't some erotica author, he was a scientist. Now, I wondered if she had some sort of power over him, and he was completely oblivious.

"Dr. Viden!" Dad lifted his hand in a wave to get her attention. As she joined us, I could feel his nervous energy. "Hi. It's nice to see you again."

Cammie's red lips curled into a smile. "David. It's lovely to see you again. Hopefully, this isn't too forward, but you look quite dashing in that suit."

Was my father *blushing?* "Oh... uh... thank you. You look beautiful, as always." His eyes rounded. "I'm sorry. Was that inappropriate? It *was*, wasn't it? My apologies. I'm so, *so* sorry."

It really was difficult to ignore her beauty. I caught myself staring at her several times during class, entranced by her flawless features. I loved her fashion sense, too. Tonight, she had on an all-white pantsuit, and her blonde hair was tied up in a neat bun on top of her head.

The fae's musical laughter rang through the room. "It's perfectly fine. Thank you." She turned to me and extended her hand. "You must be Nicole. It's lovely to meet you. David's been talking about you all week."

"Hi, it's very nice to meet you." I shook her delicate hand with probably a little too much vigor.

Cammie turned her attention back to Dad. "How are you settling in, David?"

"Great!" Dad smiled proudly. "I'm so excited to be on this project. I know you really championed bringing me on board, and I promise to do my best."

Well, there went two rules, right out the proverbial window.

"By *promise* he means he *intends* to do his best," I added.

Dad gave me an incredulous look. I knew he thought I was being rude. Ugh. This would be so much easier if he knew the truth.

The fae's grin grew even wider as she assessed me. I was pretty sure she was trying not to laugh. "You're quite... *astute*, aren't you, Nicole?"

I nodded. "I am. I've learned *a lot* in my short time at Redwood University."

"Well," she began, while giving me a pointed look. "This is a fantastic school, so that doesn't surprise me one bit." She then turned to my father. "No need to make promises, David. I've read your research. I know without a doubt that you'll be an amazing asset to our team."

The man was *definitely* blushing.

"Thank you, ma'am. So much."

She reached out and touched his forearm. "Please. Call me Cammie. I look forward to working more with you, David. Now, if you'll excuse me, I must move along. Always so much mingling to be had at these things." Dad was beaming like a lovesick fool as she winked.

Dad waited until his colleague was out of earshot before grilling me. "What the heck was that about, Nicole? Why were you acting so strangely? You're supposed to be the non-socially awkward one!"

I sighed. "I'm sorry, Dad. I'm just feeling a little off, I guess."

He frowned before straightening as a middle-aged couple started walking in our direction. "Well, here's your chance to make it up to me. That's the owner of the university. He's the one who approached me at that convention in Palo Alto and invited me to apply for this job."

I studied the pair as they crossed the room, and couldn't help feeling like I knew them somehow. The man was handsome, large in build, with dark brown hair, a strong jaw, and tanned skin. The woman beside him was much smaller in stature, but she held her chin high, as if she had an important place in this world and she knew it. They were impeccably coiffed and dressed to the nines, obvious designer labels from head to toe, but at the same time, they gave off an energy that promised savage violence. My Spidey senses told me they were both shifters, so I supposed that last part made sense.

They were predators, after all. This whole damn university was filled with them. I needed to remember that.

"Dr. Fairweather." The man extended his arm to shake Dad's hand. "It's nice to see you again." Now that he was closer, I could see a little salt-and-pepper effect around his temples. I also couldn't shake the feeling that I'd met this man before. Why did he seem so familiar?

"It's nice to see you as well, Mr. Koenig." Dad nodded, gesturing to me. "This is my daughter, Nicole."

Mr. Koenig's calloused palm swallowed mine as we shook hands. "Nice to meet you, Nicole. Your dad told me you're a legacy in one of our sororities. How is open rush going for you? Are you enjoying your classes so far?"

"It's been... an experience, for sure." I gulped. "My classes are great."

I really meant that, too. Stern professors and annoying classmates aside, I needed the monotony of schoolwork to get my mind off all the other craziness that had been thrust into my life.

He quirked his head to the side. "I'm sorry, but I don't recall which house you were interested in."

"Beta Phi," I supplied.

A cunning smile stretched across his face. "Ah, a fine house indeed. Well, I wish you the best of luck in getting a formal invitation."

It took considerable effort not to glare at my dad's new boss's boss. We both knew how this university felt about humans, but he didn't *know* I knew. At least, I didn't think he did. Who knew with the rumor mill?

"Thank you, sir."

"Forgive me, dear, I haven't introduced you yet." Mr. Koenig smiled at the blonde next to him before looking back at me and Dad. "This is my wife, Anya."

Holy shit.

As the woman made pleasantries with my father, I took a good look at her, and all the pieces clicked into place. Now I knew why these two seemed so familiar! There was a framed picture of Mr. Koenig in the Alpha Nu lounge, listing him as the fraternity's most notable president. It gave me the chills because it felt like his hazel eyes were following my every move from behind the photo. And this gorgeous woman, who was now shaking my hand, had espresso eyes that drilled straight into my soul, because they were identical to her son's.

These people were Alexei's parents! Physically speaking, Alexei was a younger version of his father but with his mom's eyes. Why hadn't I made that connection the moment my dad mentioned this guy owned the school? Alexei had even told me his family founded the university. And if Alexei were my supposed mate, why hadn't I thought to ask for something as simple as his last name before now? I felt so dumb. It must be all the new data taking up space in my brain. Maybe I was approaching informational overload.

Awesome.

"Are you okay, dear?" Her curious eyes roamed over my face. Her voice was lyrical, soothing, but at the same time, it was tinged with an unmistakable authority like her husband's.

I nodded. "Yes, of course. I'm sorry. I was caught off guard for a moment because you have the same eyes as your son."

Now she looked *really* curious. "Oh? You know my son?"

Crap. Why did I even bring him up?

And now I had Mr. Koenig's undivided attention. "Tell me how you met Alexei."

"Uh…" I wrung my hands together. "Open rush… Beta Phi partnered with his fraternity."

That sounded perfectly reasonable, right?

His eyes narrowed. "Hmm."

"Oh, speak of the devil and he shall arrive!" Mrs. Koenig chuckled, raising her hand to get someone's attention from across the room. "Alexei, over here!"

Double crap.

Alexei's eyes widened infinitesimally as he saw who his parents were with, and he quickened his pace. I didn't think anyone else had noticed, but when his mother chuckled under her breath, I amended that thought.

My dad was smiling nervously. "Nicole, I didn't know you had made any friends yet. That's lovely, honey."

"I wouldn't exactly call him a friend," I mumbled.

"What exactly *would* you call him?" Alexei's dad asked in a shrewd tone.

"Jones, give the poor girl a break." Mrs. Koenig pressed up on her toes to place a kiss on her husband's cheek. "I'm sure it's nothing serious."

I wanted to laugh. Or cry. I *wished* it were nothing serious.

Thank God Alexei had arrived before I felt more pressure to answer.

"Mother." He leaned down to place a kiss on her cheek. "Father."

His dad smacked him on the back. "Alexei, my boy. This is Dr. David Fairweather, the brilliant scientist I told you about!"

Alexei gripped my father's hand in a brief but firm handshake. "Nice to meet you, sir. Welcome to Redwood University."

My father looked between Alexei and his dad, then me. "Thank you. It's nice to meet you as well." Dad pulled me into a side hug. "I understand you've already met my daughter, Nicole."

"I have." Alexei's Adam's apple bobbed as he swallowed, likely trying to figure out why there was so much tension running through our small circle. "Nicole. It's nice to see you again."

"Yeah, you too." I hoped my father couldn't feel how bunched my muscles were.

"Why don't you tell us how you met, son?" his dad encouraged.

Didn't I just cover that? Was he testing the validity of my story? Could he sense I was lying?

Fuck my life.

"Nicole was at a few open rush activities," Alexei replied.

I guess it wasn't technically a lie.

"I see." His father's gaze was icy. Contemplative. "Alexei, Dr. Fairweather is very important to the university and our community. We have high hopes that his research on genetics will help one of our charitable organizations."

"I've been meaning to submit a formal proposal, Mr. Koenig," my dad said. "I've looked over the research your team has already provided, but I'm struggling with some of the terminology and the gene itself. I've never seen anything like it and—"

"You will be given whatever information you require," Mr. Koenig cut him off. "We have certain protocols for sharing our proprietary information and we still have some... paperwork to sign. An NDA and whatnot."

I damn near dropped my mouth open in shock. Were they going to give dad the supernatural mind-fuck, too?

Dad nodded enthusiastically. "Of course. I'm just eager to get started. I don't want to disappoint you, and this is a fantastic opportunity. I truly am thankful to work in such a high-quality lab with your award-winning team. Forgive me for getting ahead of myself."

"Not at all," Mr. Koenig assured him. "I wish more men had your ambition and self-starting attitude." He gave Alexei a side-eye before continuing. "What are you majoring in, Nicole?"

"Fashion design. It's always been a passion of mine."

Mr. Koenig scowled. "I'd assumed you would follow in your father's footsteps and pursue the sciences."

"Oh, honey. Not everyone grows up to be like their parents." Mrs. Koenig chuckled before patting her husband's arm affectionately. I had a feeling she was the peacekeeper in the family.

"Apparently not." He frowned. "I'm sure you're quite disappointed, Dr. Fairweather."

My father squirmed at my side. He wasn't a confrontational man but would defend me. For both our sakes, I hoped he didn't.

"Nicole is being modest," Alexei gritted. "She's double majoring in business and fashion design. She's also a Monet Fellowship award recipient, one of the youngest to accept the honor. Even though she prefers fashion, she's worked in various art mediums and was offered a considerable scholarship to both Parsons School of Design and the Art Institute in Chicago before coming here. She graduated at the top of her class at a private high school in Baltimore."

This time, I couldn't contain my incredulous

expression. How did Alexei know all of this? Was he snooping on me?

Dad beamed before patting my back. "I'm very proud."

Mrs. Koenig looked between Alexei and me. I didn't think it went unnoticed that her son was staring longingly at me, his nose tipped up with confidence as he told his father about my accomplishments.

"I didn't realize the two of you had the time to get to know one another so well." She grinned broadly.

Alexei, seeming to realize his mistake, cleared his throat. "I was helping Mara go over the early applications for Beta Phi."

"Sure you were," his mom noted. "Nicole, I hope you're enjoying yourself. The school is full of handsome young men; it's where I met my husband." She tossed her husband a friendly smile. "I'm sure a beautiful girl like yourself has all the boys in a tizzy."

I blushed. This was supposed to be a professional meet and greet, not a discussion about my dating life. Could she tell how my skin buzzed whenever Alexei was near?

"Nicole isn't dating," Alexei rushed out quickly. *Too quickly.*

His mother clicked her tongue. "Not yet."

His dad scoffed, as if the idea of anyone liking me was humorous.

I tried not to let that offend me. "I'm focused on my studies and getting into Beta Phi right now, Mrs. Koenig."

"You might want to consider finding another house." Mr. Koenig sneered. "Beta Phi is very selective. I'm not sure you would fit in. In fact, I'm *positive* you won't make the cut."

At this, three things happened at once. My father—my perpetually passive father—clenched his fists at his side. Alexei's mother gasped, seemingly horrified by her husband's rudeness, though I suspected this wasn't an isolated incident. Alexei's reaction was possibly the worst of all. I could feel the rage vibrating through him as he struggled to control his wolf. His face reddened. His nostrils flared, and I could swear, his pupils even dilated so much for a split second his eyes looked completely black.

"Father, may I have a word please?" he requested. "*Privately?*"

I knew I needed to get out of here before this escalated any further. I didn't want my dad to say something he'd later regret.

"Actually, if you'll excuse us." I plastered a wide grin on my face. "We still haven't found our table, and the presentations are about to begin soon, so we should probably do that."

Alexei's dad briefly pinned me with the same glare he had aimed toward his son.

"Of course, dear," his mother stepped in, touching my forearm in a soothing gesture. "It was nice meeting you."

The second we were away from them, Dad raged. "Is this what you've been dealing with since we got here, Nicole? I thought you were just nervous about rushing, but that man was downright rude! It's not too late. I can have my lawyer look over my contract, and we can leave tomorrow."

I appreciated my father, and honestly, I couldn't help but toy with the idea of leaving all of this behind. The supernatural world was overwhelming, and my life would be easier at a school for humans where my biggest worry was a final exam.

But I was already in too deep. I was too curious.

And I needed to figure out how I felt about Alexei. Plus, despite Mr. Koenig's rudeness, Dad was so excited to work here.

"It's okay, Dad," I mumbled. "I think the locals run things around here, so it's like this entire school is a club I don't fit into."

"I don't like it," he snapped. "I'm thankful to work here, Nicole. I truly am. But they *need* my research.

They are decades behind me in terms of knowledge, and I'm on the verge of a breakthrough. If they want me, then they'll have to accept my daughter."

I smiled at him. "I am glad you want to protect your baby girl, Dad."

"I just want you to be treated with respect. I doubt that man treats anyone that way. He has an arrogance about him I hadn't noticed before. I feel sorry for his family."

I felt sorry, too. I knew one of the main reasons Alexei would never accept me and our bond was because of his father, and now it made more sense.

"I got it handled, Dad."

We walked around the room until we found our assigned seats. Dad looked relieved as we discovered we were the first ones to arrive at our table. I needed a minute to get my shit together in private though, so instead of taking a seat like he did, I told him I needed to use the ladies' room and promised to be back in a few. I made my way out of the main room, down a long hallway that I had assumed led to the restrooms. The corridor was dark, with dimly lit sconces along the walls. The black and silver damask wallpaper and dark wooden wainscoting added to the ominous vibe. My ears perked up when I heard harsh whispering up ahead. I didn't mean to eavesdrop, but when I realized who was talking, I couldn't seem to help myself.

"What is going on with you and that *human*, Alexei?" his father demanded.

"I told you, *nothing is going on*," Alexei lied.

"Don't lie to me, boy. It's obvious your dick is *quite* interested." Mr. Koenig was keeping his voice low, but I could still hear the venom in his tone. "And normally, I wouldn't waste my time worrying about some girl getting on her knees for you, but *that girl* is off-limits. Do you understand? Her father is too important. He could be the key to unlocking the reason behind the mutation our people are suffering from. I will not allow your hormones to ruin our chances of fixing this! Despite his brilliance, it's clear Dr. Fairweather is a weak man when it comes to his daughter. If she's unhappy, he'll be unhappy. And *that* cannot happen. Are we clear?"

"Crystal," Alexei confirmed.

"And if you've already stuck your prick in her, you'd better do whatever you need to do to ensure she doesn't get her little heart broken. Get Mara involved if you need to."

"I don't *need* to get Mara involved," Alexei insisted. "I said I have it handled, Father."

"You'd better," his dad huffed. "You're already on thin ice, Alexei."

I creeped a bit closer, ducking into an alcove where

I could see them now, but hopefully they couldn't see me.

Alexei gritted his teeth, and I watched as he clenched his fist at his side. "Maybe if you want to keep her happy, you should let her join Beta Phi and not make rude comments about her never getting in."

Mr. Koenig laughed derisively. "A human in Beta Phi? That's never going to happen."

"So you're happy to use humans when it suits your agenda, but not when it doesn't." Alexei scoffed.

His father moved lightning quick, shoving Alexei against the wall before growling at him. I pressed my palm to my mouth and stared in horror as Mr. Koenig wrapped his hand around Alexei's throat and squeezed. "Because that's what we do, *son*. We're apex predators. Humans are just ignorant little toys to help us get the job done. I don't give a fuck about David and his daughter. I just need him to do his job and not get any crazy ideas about leaving. Humans are much more compliant when I don't have to imprison them."

Alexei's face turned a bright shade of red, and I wanted nothing more than to run back to the ballroom, grab Dad, and run like hell away from Redwood University.

"Do you understand me, son?" Mr. Koenig spat. Alexei couldn't speak, but the way his eyes dropped submissively was enough for his father. "I'm glad we're in agreement." His dad released him, looking down on his son in disgust as he straightened his tie.

I flattened my body to the wall, holding my breath as Mr. Koenig stormed down the hall, right past me. I wasn't sure what to do. Part of me was still in flight mode, while the other part desperately wanted to see if Alexei was okay.

"You can stop hiding now, Nicole."

My eyes widened as Alexei stepped into the alcove with me. "You knew I was here?!"

His gaze traveled over my face for a moment. "Yeah, I knew. I can *feel* you when you're nearby."

"Does that mean your dad knew it, too?"

His head shook slowly. "No. He would've confronted you if he had, and then he would've directed Mara to erase your memory of the whole thing. I'd say we got lucky because there are so many people nearby, and his anger preoccupied him, but for future reference, a wolf can smell prey from a great distance. I wouldn't recommend trying to spy on one again."

"I wasn't spying," I insisted, choosing to ignore the prey comment for now. "I needed a moment alone. I was heading to the bathroom, but I stopped when I heard you and your dad talking." I lightly traced the red markings on Alexei's throat but quickly pulled my hand away when he inhaled sharply. "Are you okay?"

His full lips curved into a sad smile. "Nothing I haven't dealt with before."

"Alexei..." I frowned. "Can I do anything?"

He moved closer, pinning me to the wall. I think he sighed as he tucked his face into my neck, breathing me in. "Just... give me a minute."

His hands bracketed my hips, and on instinct, my arms wrapped around his wide torso, squeezing as tightly as I could. Were we... hugging?

Alexei's fingers flexed, digging into the meat of my upper glutes. He lifted his head, our lips a mere hairs-breadth apart.

Was he about to kiss me?

Did I want that? No, that would just make this situation even more complicated. Right?

Right?!

"Alexei..." My voice was breathy. Needy. My spine bowed, straining to get closer, in direct contrast to what my brain knew I should be doing, which was stepping away.

"Nicole..." Alexei's minty warm breath tickled my nose as he spoke. "If you don't want me to kiss you, you need to tell me *right now*."

"We shouldn't." I gasped as he pressed into me, the hard outline of his cock digging into my stomach.

"That wasn't exactly a denial."

I shook my head. "No, I guess it wasn't."

His chocolate gaze bore into mine, so I could see the moment he decided to take action. I knew the kiss was coming, but nothing could've prepared me for the feeling of Alexei Koenig's lips on mine.

"Mine," he growled against my mouth.

There was no longer any hesitancy. Alexei's pillowy soft lips pressed against mine, his tongue licking at the seam, demanding entry. I parted my lips on command, welcoming his velvety tongue into my mouth.

Our chemistry was explosive, an urgency unlike anything I'd ever felt. I reveled in the press of his hard body pushing against mine as his sweeping tongue tasted and savored me. He positioned his muscular thigh between my legs and pinned me in place, as if he was terrified I'd run away. His teeth nipped at my bottom lip, and he swallowed my moans with a grin.

His soft lips moved to my jaw and then the sensitive skin on my neck. He sucked at my thudding pulse while rubbing his hands up and down my sides.

"No one will ever hurt you, Nicole," he murmured before pulling my skin between his teeth and lightly biting.

My breathing was so erratic that every time I

inhaled, I pressed against his chest, my nipples tingling with friction as he moved back to my mouth.

"Look at those pretty lips," he rasped. "I've been dreaming about them for days." He dragged his thumb along my swollen pout, his own mouth parting as he panted. "I just want to suck on them." Leaning forward, he devoured me once more, tugging on my lips with his own while I ground against his thigh.

I was so fucking turned on. It felt *right*.

Until the sound of a throat clearing stopped us both in our tracks.

I shoved at Alexei's chest, and he grumbled, as if the distance I was placing between us personally offended him. "I wasn't done." He reached for my arm to pull me back into him.

I was about to warn him about our audience, but his mother made her presence known before I could.

"Alexei, your mate needs to go sit with her father before people start to get curious. You don't want anyone seeing you or sensing your bond."

Wait a second...

Both my and Alexei's jaws dropped. I couldn't even bother feeling mortified that his mother had just caught me trying to climb him like a tree, because I was too busy focusing on what she said.

Your mate.

"Mother." Alexei shielded me as I straightened my

clothing and did my best to fix my hair. "I don't know what you think you—"

She released the most unladylike snort, which made me smirk. There was nothing funny about this situation, but something about this woman automatically put me at ease.

"Please, Alexei. *Do not* insult my intelligence by trying to deny it. I understand the power of a mating bond *intimately*." I almost laughed at the pinched look on her son's face when she said the last word. I didn't think she was necessarily referring to sex, but I *did* think that's instantly where his mind went. "It doesn't matter how much time has passed. It's not something you can *ever* forget." She smiled when I moved to Alexei's side. "It also means that I can recognize other fated mates much more easily than someone who hasn't met theirs. The pheromones you two are giving off right now are so strong; it's rather cloying, considering you're my offspring. There are certain things a mother does *not* need to know about her son."

"Mom," Alexei tried again, cheeks reddening in embarrassment.

She held her hand up. "Honey, if you care about this girl even a little bit, you'll send her back to sit with her father. This is not the time nor the place for this conversation, and ultimately, you need to protect your mate right now. There are too many wolves who would love to know your weakness."

Alexei turned to me and gave me a determined look. "She's right."

"Goodbye, Alexei. Nice meeting you, Mrs. Koenig," I stammered before putting as much space between us as possible. My mind was reeling as I found my seat. Dad patted my leg, seemingly unaware of the turmoil in my mind.

Was Mrs. Koenig disappointed that her son mated with a human? And would Mr. Koenig allow Dad and me to leave if we wanted to? It sure didn't sound like it. I didn't like the idea of my father being used as a pawn.

And that kiss.

That fucking *kiss*.

It changed everything all at once. I pressed my fingers to my lips while staring at a glass of ice water in front of me. Kissing Alexei was... perfection.

"You okay?" Dad's voice was a low whisper as he leaned over.

"Yeah," I choked out, remembering the heat in Alexei's gaze before I left him back in the hallway.

The look he gave me was loaded with so much more than desire.

It was a promise.

Alexei

"Shit, Mom." I scrubbed my hands down my face. "What the hell am I going to do?"

She looked down the hall, then back at me. "She seems like a lovely girl, honey. In any other circumstance, I'd be so incredibly happy and proud of you. You deserve a mate, Alexei. But..."

"But she's a human," I growled.

For some reason, hearing my mother's reservations made this entire hopeless situation seem worse. Every kid grew up wanting their parents' approval. Mom was always the person who pulled me aside and encouraged me despite my father's aggressive child-rearing. If she thought this was bad, then there was no hope for Nicole and me.

"Exactly." She nodded solemnly. "If your father learns of this, Alexei, it'll be..."

"Disastrous," I finished for her.

"How much does she know?"

I groaned. "*Everything*. This asshole warlock... he slipped a spell into her drink. Nicole knows *everything* about *every* supe. I figured it was pointless to keep our bond from her as well, all things considered."

Her delicate brows lifted. "Are you sure your motives weren't just a tad bit selfish with that revelation?"

I shrugged. "You said it yourself. The bond holds power. *Of course* I wanted her to know. My wolf has been going stir crazy since the moment we met. But my head is *well aware* of all the reasons why Nicole and I could never be together."

Her lips pressed into a firm line. "Your father will always put our people first; that's what makes him such a good alpha, despite how... harsh he can be at times. I think this goes without saying, but I fear if he learned about Nicole being your mate, the risk of keeping her *around* would be too high."

Translation: My father would kill my mate in a heartbeat.

My wolf whined. "I know, Mother. Which is exactly why he can *never* find out."

She gave me a sad smile. "I hate saying this, honey, but you need to put a stop to whatever is blossoming between you two. *Whatever it takes* to make her turn away from you. Be downright cruel if you need to. As painful as it'll be for both of you, it's what's best for both of your futures. Nicole won't even *have* a future if you don't push her away, Alexei."

"But..." I rubbed the back of my neck. "How do I deny the bond? Nicole and I both know this couldn't work, yet we seem to gravitate toward each other, regardless."

She brushed some hair away from my face. "I'm living proof that you can maintain a relationship with someone else, even if you're bonded to another."

"But your mate *died*," I reminded her, though I suspected it was wholly unnecessary to do so. "How am I supposed to deny this pull I have toward her for the rest of my life?"

My mother sighed. "We can discuss the details later, but the last thing I'll say for now is perhaps you should consider pairing with another wolf who'll make a suitable luna? I'm not saying you'd need to get married anytime soon, but you could start the courting process now. I'm sure there are several candidates in Beta Phi you could choose from. If nothing else, being with another woman—a shifter—will show Nicole you intend to move on, which will force her to do the same."

My wolf howled in protest. He didn't *want* any other woman.

When I said nothing, my mother tugged on the sleeve of my suit jacket. "Let's get back in there. Your father's speech will begin at any moment, and he *will* notice if we're not present."

I followed my mother in a mindless haze. How could I possibly go from having one of the greatest moments of my life—kissing Nicole—to the greatest lows? I couldn't keep teasing her. I couldn't keep toying with the idea of a future with Nicole.

My eyes found hers in the crowded room, and it was like getting stabbed in the heart.

She deserved a future. She deserved happiness.

She deserved so much more than I could give her.

It wasn't about me anymore. I could shoulder my father's expectations, and I'd bear the burden of ending us for good, if only to save Nicole's life.

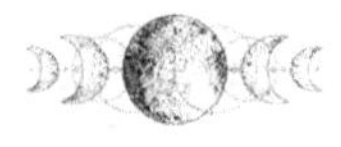

I WAS IN A TERRIBLE MOOD, and Mara's grin was grating on my nerves. We were hosting a sunset pool party, one of the last open rush events. I knew that Nicole would show up. She'd want to talk about what happened last night and make sure I was okay.

She was thoughtful like that. Caring. Compassionate.

So fucking sexy.

I'd lifted the ban on Mara for tonight because, if I was going to end things with Nicole, I had to make sure she never so much as looked at me again. I needed to torch whatever passion was burning between us so she could move on with her life.

"Nice party," Mara purred. "Why do you keep staring at the door?"

I'd picked this particular chair so I could purposefully get this over with as quickly as possible. It was in direct sight of the frat house's front door. The majority of people were partying out back, so there was no way Nicole wouldn't spot me immediately upon stepping inside. Mara sat on my lap, her long legs draped over the side of the chair as she stroked my bare chest. Every touch made me want to vomit. It was all wrong.

"You look cozy and it's creeping me out." Corbin frowned as he approached us.

"I explained why I was doing this." I took a lengthy swig from the bottle of IPA in my hand.

When I returned home from the staff reception last night, I recapped everything that had happened to my best friend. At the time, he agreed pushing Nicole away was the best solution to keep her safe. I had no idea why he was suddenly having a change of heart.

Because he liked her, my brain supplied, making my wolf growl in jealousy.

Logically, I knew Corbin would never cross that line, but even if his feelings toward my mate were purely platonic—which I believed they were—the alpha in me still saw their burgeoning friendship as competition.

"Explain why you're doing *what*?" Mara questioned.

"Haven't you learned not to question my motives yet?" I glared at her. "If you'd like me to find someone else to sit on my lap, say the word, and I'll happily dump your ass on the floor."

Mara bit the inside of her cheek. "That won't be necessary, Alpha. I'll be good."

Doubtful.

But as long as she hung around long enough to make my mate feel as if I betrayed her, Mara would have served her purpose.

Corbin pulled up a seat beside me and his sister. "I know, dude. But maybe there's another way."

"It isn't up for discussion," I snapped. "I've made my decision. This is what's best for everyone."

Mara adjusted the triangles on her bright yellow bikini top, making her tits bounce in front of my face. Her mouth curved into a frown when the action failed to elicit the response she was expecting. Mara was used to using her sexuality to her advantage. And I'd be lying if I said she wasn't hot as hell. But her personality ruined her good looks for me, and always had.

"Tonight is going to be fun," she said, her voice high-pitched and whiny.

No, tonight was going to fucking suck.

I felt my mate the moment she approached the front door. It was like a sixth sense. I let out a shaky breath as she walked into the room. She had on a strappy black dress with bikini strings peeking out from beneath. Her face was bare, and she'd thrown up her hair in a high ponytail. She looked natural and stunning.

It was killing me not to march over to her and kiss her again.

All we'd ever have was one kiss. One moment of passion.

One moment together.

She scanned the room, and the second I felt Nicole's gaze on me, I turned my head to Mara. I wanted to curl my lip in disgust at the sticky gloss on her plump lips. With Nicole's attention locked on me, I grabbed Mara's chin and pulled her close. Mara's eyes popped open in shock.

She moaned when I pressed my lips to hers.

I felt my chest constrict, knowing that this moment would cause my mate pain.

Mara took every drop she could. She pressed her tits against me and roamed her hands over my arms.

Corbin made gagging sounds at my back. "She's gone. Looks like your dumb-ass plan worked."

I pulled away from Mara and wiped my mouth with the back of my hand. Mara hopped off my lap and squealed. "I don't know what that was for, but thank you, Alpha. Every bitch at this party wants to be me right now." She ran off to brag to anyone unlucky enough to be in her path.

Her statement made me feel slightly less of an ass about using her to make Nicole walk away.

I scrubbed a hand down my face and groaned. "You think she bought it, then?"

My best friend nodded. "Oh, yeah. She was broadcasting all kinds of miserable emotions, plain as day. You fucked up real good, man."

"You didn't need to add that last part," I grumbled.

Corbin didn't seem sorry in the least. "I don't like it. And I *really* don't think you thought this through."

"What's that supposed to mean?"

"It means..." I didn't like the snide smirk stretching across his face. "That girl just ran out of here like her ass was on fire. She was also extremely pissed off. Who knows where she's heading now? Who knows *who* she'll run into and what she'll do? I can think of at least one vampire off the top of my head who would *love* to take advantage of her current mental state."

Fuck.

Why didn't I think of that?

"Go after her," I demanded. "I mean it, Corbin. *Find her.* And text me the second you do."

He laughed humorlessly. "Sure, brother. I was planning to anyway. Just wanted to give you something to think about while I'm gone."

I flipped off my supposed best friend as he walked out the door. I had no doubt he would find Nicole, despite the fact that she had a few minutes' head start. Even in human form, our senses were enhanced. Corbin could easily locate and follow my mate's trail. That didn't mean I wasn't on pins and needles the entire time, waiting for his damn text. Every time some asshole tried talking to me, I practically bit their heads off. When Mara made the mistake of coming back for seconds, I told her to get the fuck out and that the ban was reinstated. I didn't give a single shit how rude I was being. I needed to know Corbin had found Nicole, and I wouldn't relax until I had confirmation she was safely back in her dorm.

Then what?

How was I going to stop her from falling into some supe's trap? Or what if someone like that tool, Hunter, got to her? I saw the way Nicole smiled at him. How carefree she seemed while they were floating down the river together. What if he swooped in and charmed his way into her bed? Since Hunter was barely a shifter at all, he wouldn't be held to the same standards as I was.

My wolf stirred, itching to break free.

I thought about my mother's suggestion. How I should try finding an acceptable partner, one who could serve as the next luna of our pack. But I knew I could never go through with it. I would rather lead by myself than be chained to some random woman in a business arrangement. Plus, I knew it wasn't fair for me to be with someone else if Nicole had to spend her life alone. And as selfish as it was, the thought of Nicole being with anyone else was maddening. I knew myself well enough to know I'd do *anything* to prevent that from happening.

I just wished I knew how to fix this. I wished there was some kind of loophole that would allow human and shifter matings. I was frustrated beyond belief. As alpha, I should be able to snap my fingers and make anything happen, but every possible path I could think of was filled with roadblocks.

Keeping my father from knowing Nicole was my mate was imperative. But that was the only clear variable in this entire fucked-up situation.

Maybe the fact that I couldn't solve this problem was a sign I wasn't meant to lead our pack.

Maybe my father's doubts were valid.

Maybe, just maybe, none of this was worth it if I couldn't have Nicole.

TWENTY

Nicole

I wore oversized sunglasses to hide the dark circles under my eyes. I'd spent all night replaying what I'd seen and ruminating in my hurt.

As I made my way to the party last night, thinking about how Alexei was kissing *me* less than twenty-four hours earlier, I found myself wondering if it would happen again. But when I got to the party, he had his tongue shoved so far down *Mara's* throat that I was certain he could taste the ice where her heart should have been.

Regardless of the longing in his gaze at the cock-tail party, I should have expected this. Alexei made it very clear that we could never be together. Multiple times. But it still fucking hurt, and I was pissed at myself for falling for it *again*.

Maybe the mate bond wasn't as special as he'd played it up to be. Maybe he'd gotten a taste and tossed me away.

"I brought bagels!" Corbin's voice was way too chipper for my mood. The damn mutt had followed me home last night, trying to charm me into letting him into my dorm, but I refused. I knew he wouldn't try anything sexual, but I still didn't want to be near anyone who reminded me of Alexei.

"I'm not hungry." I was speed-walking toward the quad for today's tabling event, trying to shake him off, but it was no use.

"Come on, gorgeous." He waved the bag in my face. "You need to eat!"

"Corbin," I sighed. "You don't have to do this."

"Do what? Prevent everyone within a five-mile radius from suffering because you're hangry? I'm doing a public service here, babe." He winked at me, and I rolled my eyes.

I halted mid-step and snatched the bag from his grip, digging through the contents. On cue, my stomach rumbled as I spotted a cinnamon sugar bagel. My sweet tooth wasn't nearly as bad as my dad's, but there was something about sugar and carbs that went well together in the mornings.

I took a giant bite and moaned as I chewed the doughy goodness.

"Shit, Nicky, you're making me hard."

I tore off a piece of bagel and tossed it at Corbin's head. "Shut up."

"Just kidding." He held his hands up in mock surrender, laughing. "Only one lady gives me a boner these days, and her hair's a bit more colorful than yours."

"Have you talked to Juniper?" I asked through a mouthful of food. "About the possibility of dating?"

Corbin made a face when a little piece of soggy dough accompanied my words, hitting his forearm. "Sexy. And no. I haven't talked to June."

I slammed a hand over my mouth, cheeks heating as I finished chewing. "Sorry. I guess I didn't realize how hungry I was until I started eating."

"It's all good." He laughed. "You should see me when there's a bloody slab of meat placed in front of me."

And there went my appetite.

I wiped my mouth with a napkin. "Ew."

Boisterous laughter erupted from his chest. "You should probably get used to it if you're going to be spending time with wolves. We like our red meat, and we like it so rare it's practically mooing."

"Good thing I don't plan on spending inordinate

amounts of time with wolves." My eyes narrowed, the lightness in my chest evaporating entirely. "No offense."

"What do you think is going to happen when you get into Beta Phi, Sugar Pie?"

"You did not just call me Sugar Pie," I deadpanned.

"I'm just testing out nicknames. Trying to find one that fits."

"How about you call me by my actual name?"

"Whatever you say, sweetie honey bum pie snookums. Back to Beta Phi. You *do* realize you'll be spending time with wolves. You've got to get familiar with how we operate."

I sighed. "We both know I'm not getting in, Corbin. I'm only rushing so I can move on, knowing I did everything I could. For my mom, you know?"

Formal rush started this weekend. Today, each one of the Greek houses had tables set up in the quad, trying to recruit last-minute pledges. Even though I came to Redwood U with only one sorority in mind, I figured it wouldn't hurt to check out the other houses to see what they had to offer. Like Jade and Hannah said, it wasn't just about which house would accept me. It was about *me* finding the right house to suit *my* needs.

"Don't give up just yet. I'm researching the bylaws. You wouldn't happen to be related to a wolf down the line, would you? Arctic wolves are endangered, and they'll even accept a dormant wolf if you're a descendent of one. We could fudge your family tree a bit."

I shook my head. "I'm not a wolf. Not even a little bit."

"How would you feel about the furry lifestyle? I think you'd look cute in a wolf costume. You'd have to let people fuck you while wearing it, but—"

"Hard pass." I held my hand up. "And we seriously need to talk boundaries, Corbin. Look. I'm just going to be me. I know I'm good enough, strong enough, smart enough, and ambitious enough. If they can't see that, then I don't want them in my life, anyway."

Corbin gave me a sympathetic look. "Are we talking about Beta Phi or Alexei?"

His question stung. "I'm not going to fight for a man who doesn't see my worth. I deserve more than that, fated mates or not."

Corbin stared at his feet, shuffling from side to side. "What if Alexei is just trying to protect you?"

"Then he's going about it the wrong way. I'm an adult—capable of adult conversations and honesty. If he was worried, he should have talked to me. *Not* sucked Mara's face off."

When I saw Mara and Alexei kissing last night, I was so overwhelmed by the tightness in my chest, logic was the furthest thing from my mind. It felt like someone had literally punched a hole through my rib cage, squeezing my heart in a vise grip. After I gained some distance from the Alpha Nu house, and after Corbin had chased me down, making an obvious effort to lessen my pain, I knew something else was at play. I honestly didn't know why I was so shocked in the first place. Alexei had been fighting this bond from the start. He'd told me in no uncertain terms time and time again that we would never work as a couple. But when *we* kissed, in that brief moment of time, it felt as if nothing mattered but the two of us. That he would raise the dead to overcome any obstacles in our way. That he was *proud* to have me as his mate, and anyone who thought otherwise could fuck the hell off.

After a restless night's sleep and countless hypotheticals running through my brain, I knew without a doubt Alexei had done what he had done to push me away. But like I told Corbin, I wasn't about to excuse his behavior. If Alexei couldn't give me the courtesy of honesty, the chance to work through this problem *together*, fuck him and his fated mates bullshit. I didn't have time for emotional warfare. I was here to get an education, and I refused to let these supernatural assholes take that away from me.

"It's just fucking unfair." Corbin's mouth formed into a pout.

"What?"

"You would be the perfect luna, Nicole. You're confident and strong. Compassionate. I would be *honored* to serve you. I hate that this is happening, but I'm going to support you, okay? We're friends."

I smiled at him. If you had told me a week ago that I'd get along with Corbin, I would have laughed at you. But he was actually a pretty decent guy.

I looked at the long row of tables and noticed Juniper handing out flyers for the witchy sorority. An idea struck me, and I decided to go over there.

"I'm going to talk to your girl." I tipped my chin up and strutted her direction.

Corbin did a little panic jump, then chased after me. "What are you going to say? Are you going to talk me up? Tell her I'm adventurous—no—tell her I love her. Actually, scratch that. Remind her that I have a gigantic cock." Corbin was rambling. "Are you seriously going to be my wingman right now? I didn't think it was possible for me to love you any more."

"I'm just going to talk to her. You can't keep existing in limbo, Corbin. You deserve more than that."

He stopped walking, and I felt his heavy stare at my back.

"But what if she doesn't feel the same way about me as I feel about her?"

I turned toward him, giving him a reassuring smile. "Well, hopefully, it won't come to that."

"But if it *does*?"

"Then..." I paused for a moment, choosing my next words carefully. "At least you know where Juniper stands, and you can decide if you'd like to keep things as they are or... move on. Either way, this uncertainty you're feeling right now will be gone. Don't you want that, Corbin?"

He thought about it for a moment before nodding. "Yes. Yes, I need to know either way." He jerked a thumb over his shoulder. "I'm just gonna... um... find somewhere else to be. Text me later?"

I nodded. "Sure thing."

Corbin pointed at me. "You're a good egg, Nicky."

I smiled. "You're not so bad yourself, Wolf-boy."

Juniper offered me a friendly grin as I approached the table for Kappa Zeta, Redwood U's magical sorority. "Hey, Nicole."

"Hey." I grabbed one of the flyers they had spread out on the table, scanning it for a moment. "So, you're a sorority girl, huh?"

"President," June answered proudly. "Are you rushing?"

"Beta Phi," I told her. "Even though we both know my odds of acceptance are slim to none."

I was careful to speak in code. I knew the rumor

mill was doing its thing, and quite a few supes knew I was in on their little secret, but I wasn't about to flaunt it, either.

Juniper waved a hand around, mumbling something under her breath. When she was done, she said, "You can speak freely, Nicole. I cast an encryption spell over this conversation. Even my fellow supes won't know what we're talking about."

"What?" My brows rose. "That's an actual thing?"

"It is when you know what you're doing." She grinned. "Now... what was I about to say before I did that? Oh, yes! The wolf cult is a little selective, but our guidelines are much looser here at Kappa Zeta, if you'd like to consider us as well."

"Really?" I asked.

"Really. Even if you aren't born with gifts, every creature has energy. We have many humans that take part and contribute to our rituals. It's beautiful. Speaking of, would you be open to selling some hair clippings or saving your period blood? We could use those for spells."

I went from excited to disgusted in exactly zero-point-two seconds.

She watched the horrified expression cross my features. "Oh! Don't worry. The spell Antonio gave you didn't contain any of that. You merely drank a mixture of moondust, water, and the essence of fae."

"Please don't tell me the *essence of fae* is really just a fancy word for fairy jizz."

She nodded. "Okay. I won't tell you."

Holy crap, I was just joking.

I gagged and made a mental note to scrub my tongue with bleach later.

"If you accept humans, how does that even work with the whole containment spell thing? Are they constantly giving directions to the nearest bathroom in the house?"

Juniper chuckled. "No. As far as humans are concerned, we're *wiccans*. They're fully aware of what's going on during rituals and whatnot. Some of them believe in the supernatural—despite the fact that they've probably never seen anything to confirm it—but others want to be involved simply for the spirituality of it. Our oneness with nature. Or they're just using it as an excuse to be naked and bone a lot."

"What?!" I sputtered.

"You know..." The chunky bangles on her wrist clinked together as she waved her hand around. "Witches are all about being free from any bindings— aka clothes—as often as possible, and they like to use sex magic a lot."

"So... are you guys nudists at the house? Or do you have a bunch of... orgies? Is that required to be a sister?"

"No, silly." She laughed. "The nudity is only during rituals, and it's totally optional."

I thought I could handle that. As for the other thing...

"And the orgies?"

"We only have those on days ending in *Y*." When my jaw dropped, she added, "Kidding! Promise. As for the other houses... the vampire sorority is also open to humans, but as you can imagine, it's not a desirable situation. Not unless you want them to feed on you. The fae allow humans as well, but that can be tricky. If you aren't careful, you could end up living beyond the veil." She shivered, as if that was the worst thing that could possibly happen to a person.

"Thanks for the tip," I replied. "Hey, speaking of fae... you wouldn't happen to have any protection charms handy, would you?"

She giggled. "Of course I do. They're one of my biggest sources of income. Those fae are sneaky little bastards."

"I'd need one for me and my dad. He works on campus, but he's not really *in the know*, so if you have something more discreet, that'd be preferred. How much are they?"

"Because my brother so rudely filled your brain without your consent, and because Corbin is so fond of you, I'll give you a steep discount. Let's say... a hundred bucks for both? They regularly sell for two-fifty each."

"Wow. Uh, sure. That would be great. Thank you." I blinked a few times, imagining how much money this woman made at those prices. "Hey, speaking of Corbin... I hope this isn't too intrusive, but can I ask about you two? Do you *like* him?"

"Corbin's great. *Really* great." She winked suggestively. "Insanely talented and blessed, if you catch my drift."

"Um... yeah. That's *great*. But I was referring more to his... personality. Do you think you'd ever want to, like, go on a date with him or something to get to know him in a *different* way?"

She tilted her head to the side in confusion. "I'm engaged."

"I know, but... uh..."

God, awkward much? How did I get myself into these things?

"Did Corbin put you up to this?" Juniper's golden eyes assessed me thoughtfully. "Does *he* want to know if I'd consider dating him?"

Ugh. I was terrible at subterfuge.

"Maybe?" I shrugged.

"I was afraid he was catching feelings." She sighed. "I'm going to have to end things with him."

My eyes widened. "What?! No! Don't do that!"

June placed her hand over mine. "It's okay, Nicole. You didn't tell me anything I didn't already know. I've suspected Corbin's been feeling this way for a while now, but since he's so goddamn amazing in the sack, I selfishly kept things going. But I do truly like him as a person, and the last thing I want to do is hurt him, so it's best to cut our losses before he falls any deeper. I realize not everyone understands what Ivan and I have, but it works for us. And *he* is the *only* man I want anything beyond a physical relationship with. He's my true mate. Corbin will get over me in time."

Dammit, Corbin was going to be so bummed.

Juniper snapped her fingers. "I should do a change of heart spell. It'll make things easier on him. I never intended to upset him."

I tilted my head to the side. "What's that?"

"It's a spell to sever any lingering feelings between two people. It helps someone move on in a healthy way. I do them a lot before summer break so people can enjoy their flings without regret."

My heart started racing. "Would something like that work on fated mates?"

Maybe this was the solution.

"Now what a specific line of questioning. Do you have a mate you want to get rid of?" I could swear she was fighting a laugh.

I nervously looked around. "You know what a

difficult situation I'm in. Don't you think it'd be best if we went our separate ways? I don't know how much longer I can handle his mercurial temperament. It doesn't help that I want to climb him like a tree all the time, no matter how much my head wants to fight it."

Juniper giggled. "Generally speaking, the spell can dull your infatuation with a person, so it's easier to have a clear mind around them, though fated mates are another story. I truly don't think it would work. But how about this..." She grabbed a brochure and handed it to me. "Stop by our house on Saturday. We can discuss setting up a protection spell around your heart. I know you have your hopes set on Beta Phi, but I think you might find a lot of happiness with Kappa Zeta. We value consent, and you never have to participate in rituals you aren't comfortable with. I sense a longing for sisterhood within you, and I can promise you there is no greater bond than what I share with my coven."

I smiled at her. "You kind of scared me with period blood and fae essence."

"You never have to give what you are unwilling, and no one will pressure you. Rush isn't about finding the house you want to be in, it's about finding the house meant for you. It's about finding a home and community that feels right." She patted her heart. "Add Kappa Zeta to your list of contenders. Stop by.

Meet some of my sisters. You are wanted, valued, and worthy. We would be honored to see if you'd be a good fit. Supernatural bullshit aside."

I hadn't realized I was crying until I felt a tear slip down my cheek. I needed to hear this. Feeling wanted was something that warmed my heart.

"Ooh!" Juniper squealed. "Can I please bottle that tear? It goes great in a grief stew, and one of my sisters just lost her grandmother. It'll make her have happy dreams of good memories."

I smiled and tilted my chin up so it didn't fall completely. "Have at it."

She produced a vial and quickly scooped up the tears, humming happily to herself. "See? Not so bad. And you're already supporting your future sisters." She corked the vial before pocketing it.

"Okay." I nodded. "I'll stop by. The first day of rush is about visiting all the houses, anyway."

Juniper gave me a blinding grin. "I do hope you find where you belong, Nicole. But I really hope it's with us."

I'd spent my life dreaming of Beta Phi, but maybe Juniper was right. Maybe I needed to focus on the sisterhood that wanted me back, not the people who kept pushing me away.

I waved goodbye and started making my way to other tables, gathering information about different clubs as I went. It wasn't until I got to the entrepreneurs club that I recognized a handsome man in a suit handing out pencils.

"Hunter!" I waved at him. His face broke into a broad grin, and I felt the faintest flutter in my belly. It wasn't like the roaring inferno of how I felt with Alexei, but it gave me hope.

"Hey! Looks like you're feeling better!" He gave me a one-armed side hug.

"Thanks to you. Sorry we didn't get a chance to talk after all that craziness happened. I wanted to call you, but…"

Hunter looked at his friends sitting at the table. My mind-fuck wasn't going off, so I assumed they were human. "But Alexei is a dominant asshole who wouldn't let me within six feet of you?"

"Sorry about that. I think he was just scared I would ruin his float trip."

"I think he wanted to kiss all your boo-boos." Hunter laughed.

"There's nothing going on with him." I blushed, not sure why I was trying to protect his secret. "So… I was wondering if you'd like to give that date a try?"

He took a step closer and lowered his voice. "I'd love to. How about lunch sometime?"

I tilted my chin up. "That would be nice."

Hunter then did an adorable fist pump. "I'm literally the luckiest guy on campus right now."

Once again, I found myself feeling worthy and desired. It was nice compared to the last week or so.

"Here's my number." I pulled out a card and handed it to him.

Hannah had them custom made so I could pass them out during rush week while making friends. It had a code on the back with all my socials so any friends I made could find me. She said it was all the rage.

He looked down at the card, then back at me. "I'll call you."

"I'll look forward to it."

TWENTY-ONE

Alexei

MARA WAS SERIOUSLY PISSING me off. Beta Phi and Alpha Nu set up their tables right next to each other, and we had the best tent going. My pack mates were dressed up and handing out flyers to every shifter that walked by. A few humans stopped to chat, and I couldn't help but think of Nicole. My eyes scanned the quad every few seconds, hoping to catch a glimpse of her because I was fucking pathetic. Corbin told me that she was really struggling, and my wolf whined every time I thought about how much I was hurting her.

"We look like such a power couple right now," Mara preened while standing beside me. All the other girls wore flowery summer dresses, but she looked like she was ready to go clubbing. Her tight dress and sky-high heels seemed out of place for the event.

"We're *not* a power couple," I growled.

"Whatever you say," she replied. "But if you need to kiss me again, I'm game. Every girl in Beta Phi is jealous. We're like your parents were back in the day. Both of us presidents and the envy of everyone."

Mara was nothing more than a power-hungry she-wolf. I suspected the only reason she was president was because she compelled everyone to vote for her.

I scanned the crowd once more and frowned when I saw Nicole smiling at Hunter.

My knuckles turned white as I gripped the edge of the table so hard I felt the molded poly cracking under the pressure. It took considerable effort to peel my fingers off the table when I saw Nicole handing something to him. *Was that a business card?* My anger grew when I realized what it was. It wasn't uncommon for pledges to have contact cards printed to pass out during rush so anyone they met could easily connect with them on social media. My mate just armed that preppy douchebag with every possible method of reaching her. Corbin even had her old cell phone number transferred to the new provider the other day—which would've been impossible unless you had connections like we did—so I knew that missing wolf motherfucker could now text her anytime he wanted.

Was that what she wanted?

I'd been waiting for Nicole to stop by our tent all morning, but she seemed to make a concerted effort to stop at every tent *but* ours. I knew her first class was in an hour, so I was running out of time. Nicole was adamant about rushing Beta Phi though, out of sheer stubbornness alone, so I knew it was only a matter of time before she made her way over here.

And when she did, she would have to come face-to-face with a smug-as-fuck Mara after witnessing our kiss.

I didn't want Nicole to suffer through that. I needed to get Mara out of here.

"I need you to get more coffee for everyone."

She fluffed her hair and grinned. "Sure. I'll send a sophomore to get it."

"No," I snapped. "I want *you* to get it."

She cocked her brow. "Why? I'm the president of Beta Phi. It's literally my job to stand here. One of the sophomores can get it." She scanned the crowd, her eyes landing on Nicole. "Oh look. Our little human pledge is coming."

"Go get the fucking coffee, Mara."

She turned on her heels to look at me. "Why? Is it because *she's* coming?" Her inquisitive eyes made my stomach churn. Mara would find out soon enough what was happening, and all hell would break loose. "Your fascination with the human is strange."

"Her father is very important. He's working on the missing wolf gene. *My* father said we need to keep her happy." It was only a portion of the truth, but I hoped it threw her off the scent.

"An important human? What an oxymoron," she mused. "Wait. That doesn't mean we have to actually *let* her into Beta Phi, do we?"

A muscle jumped in my jaw. "No."

"Well, at least there's that."

Nicole walked up to us with her head held high, and fuck if it didn't make me fall harder for her. I couldn't see her eyes behind the large sunglasses she wore, but the white sundress clinging to her body showed off every goddamn curve. I internally groaned at the sight.

"Hello," she greeted Mara and me coolly. "I'm looking forward to attending the rush events. I've already submitted my formal application and added another letter of recommendation last night."

Mara sighed. "Yes, I saw. How on earth did you convince Rebecca Graham to write you a letter of recommendation? She's a pretty famous wolf. Married the alpha of the Greenwood pack."

My eyes widened. My parents did trade deals with

the Greenwood pack regularly. It was pretty fucking impressive that their luna was writing Nicole a letter of recommendation. Once again, I hated that she was a human. In every other way, Nicole would be perfect. It was infuriating.

"She's friends with my godmother," Nicole explained. "Hannah Moore? She owns a pretty large subscription company and is a consultant for one of the largest publishers in the country. Another Beta Phi alum, like my mother."

"Your mom died in childbirth, right?" Mara's tone was crass. "But before that, what did she do?"

Nicole's mouth popped open for a brief moment, Mara's question stunning her. "She was a lab assistant with my father."

"Boring," Mara singsonged. "Well, I received your application. Unfortunately, we both know there are some key things you're missing. However, our laws state that everyone is entitled to rush, so, you know, good luck or whatever."

Nicole fixed her expression into a smile as she removed her sunglasses. "I'm excited for the opportunity. Regardless of the outcome, it's important to me that I put my best foot forward."

Mara released a bratty sigh. "Well, we have plenty of worthy applicants waiting to speak with me. I'll see you at the other events. Don't get too comfortable when you visit the Beta Phi house on Saturday. You won't be staying long."

"Mara, knock it off." She was taking things too far.

Finally. *Finally,* Nicole spared me a glance. "I don't need you to defend me, Alexei. I can take whatever the two of you dish out. I know I'm not welcome or wanted. I'm doing this for me, so you can get off on pushing me down, but it won't work. I know my worth."

"I *don't* get off on pushing you down," I insisted.

Mara giggled and raised her hand. "I do."

"Shut the fuck up, Mara." I leveled her with a murderous glare before turning my attention back to the stunning creature in front of me.

Nicole's tongue peeked out to wet her lower lip, making my damn cock stir. This was *not* the time to get an erection, but my body had other ideas when it came to this girl.

My mate straightened her spine, a proud tilt to her chin. "Regardless of your reasons—no matter how noble you think they may be—I do not *want or need* your protection, Alexei." She briefly glanced at the she-devil beside me. "You worry about you, dude. And I'll worry about me."

I had the sudden urge to bend Nicole over my knee and redden her perfectly heart-shaped ass for calling me *dude* again. I didn't think it was wise to reference a previous conversation in front of Mara, though, so I stuffed the thought into the back of my brain to revisit when Nicole and I had privacy.

If she ever gave me the chance to be alone with her again.

Not that I *should* ever be alone with her again. Frankly, I shouldn't be spending *any* time with Nicole if I wanted to save her from my father's wrath. That's why I chose to lock lips with Mara, of all people. I knew that bitch was the one person who'd elicit the strongest level of betrayal in Nicole's eyes, considering their brief but tumultuous history.

I needed to exercise extreme caution. There was no doubt Mara was listening to every word spoken between me and my mate, dissecting every piece, reading the context, and storing that information so she could use it for evil later. Nicole and I would be royally *fucked* if Mara learned we were fated mates. She already knew far more than I was comfortable with, but I knew Mara well enough to know which battles were worth choosing and which were best left to fizzle out on their own when she got bored. Because one guarantee with Mara Sullivan was that she *would* get bored, eventually. Some days, her inner wolf could be vicious, and she would fight to the death for the bone she uncovered. Other days, she had the attention span of a gnat. But today was the former, so I needed to get my mate away from her as fast as possible. Nicole may think she didn't need my protection, but I understood a wolf's nature far better than she ever could, so I knew that wasn't true.

"Well." Nicole gave a single nod. "Thank you for your time and consideration." And with those false pleasantries, she spun around and started heading back down the aisle of tents where she came from.

I knew I shouldn't follow her. I was supposed to be pushing her away. I was supposed to be keeping her safe.

"I'm going to get the coffee," I blurted.

Mara blanched. "What? I told you I'd send a sophomore out for it. You don't have to—"

"I'm going to fucking get coffee, Mara. Worry about yourself!" My booming voice gathered the attention of everyone nearby, but I didn't care. I had too much shit swirling in my brain, and I needed to talk to Nicole. It was selfish of me, but she needed to understand what we were up against.

I quickly walked after her, closing the distance between us as she turned between two buildings, taking a shortcut to her dorm.

Perfect.

Lunging forward, I grabbed her arm and pinned her against the wall. She opened her mouth to scream, but I placed my palm against her lips, muffling the sound.

"We need to talk."

She swatted my hand away. "What the fuck is your problem, Alexei? You keep chasing me down and pushing me away. It's exhausting. Just leave me alone!"

"I just needed to explain myself."

She rolled her eyes. "There is nothing to explain. You're incapable of standing up for yourself. You'll never know what it means to be happy because you've dedicated your life to whatever your father wants. And I get it, I really do. My father isn't cruel, but I know what it means to feel that responsibility. That said, I will *not* be a casualty in your turmoil. You made your decision. Now, please, for the love of God, stick to it."

"My father will kill you, okay?!" My eyes widened to emphasize my point. "If he thinks there's a chance that I'll leave my responsibilities for a human mate, he will *end your life* and think nothing of it. I'm trying to keep you alive."

"He'd *kill* me?" Nicole's voice was soft and timid like a mouse. "Seriously?! Like, he'd actually want me *dead*? He's... *capable* of something like that?"

"Yes." I nodded solemnly. "After talking to my mom, I knew I needed to do something drastic, because clearly, I struggle fighting this need to be with you. I thought if maybe you hated me... then maybe I'd have a chance. Hence... the whole Mara thing. Which, for the record, made me want to vomit."

Her icy blue eyes bounced between mine for a moment. "The Mara thing... I'd be lying if I said it didn't hurt."

I cringed.

"I know, and I'm sorry, okay? For everything. For making you feel like you aren't good enough. For kissing Mara. For pushing you away when it's my job as your mate to make you feel safe. It's all my fucking fault. I'm sorry for dragging you into this mess, for being so fucking confusing all the time. I can't help it, Nicole. Look. I'm trying to do the right thing, but I *have* to have you in my life. I have to protect you. The thought of anything bad happening to you... of being without you... makes me crazy. Me and my wolf."

She sighed, her shoulders slumping at my words. "I get it, okay? I mean... I'm not a wolf, so I can't *fully* understand, but I can imagine well enough knowing what I do about mating bonds."

"I know this is cliche, but you're like a fucking drug to me." I reached up to brush her cheek but pulled away at the last second. "This whole situation is so fucking unfair. Suppressing my instincts like this goes against everything that I am."

"I really need you to try, Alexei. I need you to stay away from me or start thinking of me as a distant friend. We're going to run into one another, and you're going to have to be strong. If your dad is as dangerous as you say he is…"

I looked down at my feet and groaned. "I know. I know. Okay? I get it. I have to do better."

She let out a small huff followed by a half-hearted shrug. "I could use a friend… If it makes your wolf feel better to be around me, then let's be friends. No touching. No flirty banter. No lingering stares. *Just* friends."

I shook my head. "That's impossible."

She gave me a reassuring smile. "You've been training to become an alpha your entire life. You'll figure it out. Because despite everything, I know you at least care for the idea of me, Alexei. I'm your mate, which means you're going to rein in your instincts and figure this out, no matter what it takes. It's the only way to keep me safe, right?"

I blew out a breath. "Right."

"So… friends?" Nicole arched a delicate brow.

I took a moment to think. "Friends talk, right?"

"Yes." Her full lips quirked up in the corner.

"And friends hang out."

Nicole nodded. "In a *friendly* way, yes."

"Friends take care of each other. They look out for one another."

She held up an index finger. "And friends *don't* intentionally hurt one another. I don't care if you... date or whatever. But I don't want to hear about it or *see* it. And I'll extend the same courtesy to you."

I shook my head, my inner wolf raging at the thought of Nicole dating anyone else. "I can't even *think* about touching someone else. No one compares to—"

"A *friend* wouldn't finish that sentence." She gave me a pointed look.

"Fine. Maybe this will work. My father said I need to keep you happy. Your dad's research is really important to the shifter population, you know."

She looked to her left as a group of vampires walked past our hidden alcove. "Friends?"

"Friends," I echoed. The word tasted like ash on my tongue.

Nicole placed a hand on my shoulder, as if she could sense how much I wanted to say *fuck it*, throw her over my shoulder, and run as far away from here as possible.

"Rein it in, Wolf-man."

She then patted my arm and stepped back. Every new inch of distance between us felt like a stab to the heart.

"Friends," I whispered again as she walked away.

Fuck.

How was I going to do this? She was right, though. I *had* to find a way to make it work. If the alternative was not having her in my life at all, I'd take whatever I could get.

TWENTY-TWO

Nicole

I smoothed my hands over my outfit a few times, making sure there wasn't a thread out of place. In my heart, I knew that the next hour would be miserable, but I was determined to get it over with—pride intact.

After speaking with Juniper earlier in the week, I'd decided to look beyond Beta Phi, if only to fuel my own morbid curiosity and meet some new people. The purpose of Letters Day was so potential pledges could tour all the different houses and see who would be a good fit for them. I figured that if I was going to check out two sorority houses, why not check out all four? I had no intention of living with a bunch of fae or vampires—like *ever*—but knowledge was power and all that.

I knocked on the front door to the Beta Phi house, a chill running down my spine as I waited for someone to answer. I knew that this event usually had a lot of fanfare, with current members meeting you with chants or traditions to give you a feel for the house. But as the seconds passed and no one came to the door, my confidence slipped.

Where were they? Was I supposed to just walk in?

I rubbed the back of my neck and looked around, deciding to try the doorknob, but it was locked.

Did I get the date wrong? The time?

A couple of girls walked toward me but paused to laugh when they saw me standing here like an idiot. My cheeks flushed, and I watched them head straight for the backyard like they knew exactly where they were going. It was ridiculous to keep standing here like a dumbass, so I followed them.

Whoa, wasn't expecting that.

The two girls spoke casually to one another as they stripped out of their clothes. "A pack run on the first night was such a great idea! It's the easiest way to weed out all the pathetic humans."

The other girl, who had red hair down to her waist, laughed. "*So* pathetic."

From my hidden spot, I watched as they went from standing buck naked on the side of the house to morphing to all fours. Fur appeared where their smooth skin once was. Their snouts were long, sharp teeth glimmering in the setting sun as they howled. I gasped when one of them turned to look at me, sensing my presence.

They looked terrifying.

At the sound of my shock, they started running for the tree line, leaving me behind.

Shit.

How was I supposed to run after them in wedges? I speed-walked through the grass and tried to catch up, but it was no use.

The night hadn't even begun yet, and I'd already failed.

My eyes watered as I stumbled back to the front yard, feeling defeated. I could dress the part and have the best damn application out there, but it didn't matter. I wasn't capable of getting on all fours and running wild through the forest. My phone pinged, and I checked it with a frown.

Corbin: How's Letters Day going?

I dialed his number while choking back tears.

He answered on the first ring. "Yo! Whatsup, Nicky?"

There was a lot of chatter in the background, and I knew that he was dealing with his own rush activities at Alpha Nu.

"Beta Phi is doing a pack run. I can't just go running through the forest in heels."

Corbin cursed under his breath. "I forgot that Mara was doing that this year. We usually wait until Pref Night. What are you going to do?"

I shrugged. "I guess I'll visit the other houses and cut my losses. I thought I'd at least make it through the house tours, but..."

"No," Corbin snapped. "We aren't gonna give up yet. Give me a few minutes to slip away, okay? I think I have an idea."

What the hell did Corbin have in mind?

"Okay," I mumbled, not feeling confident that this was salvageable in any way.

I waited in the front yard and took my time observing the house. It was much like the others on the street, aside from the large hot pink banner hanging from the windows that said Welcome to Beta Phi. I was so annoyed with Mara. I knew that she was doing this on purpose. If she couldn't compel me anymore, then she was going with the textbook mean girl approach.

Either way, she'd have the opportunity to fuck with me.

A roaring engine barreling down the street caught me off guard, and I turned toward the sound, grinning like an idiot when I saw Alexei and Corbin riding on a four-wheeler. Corbin had his hands wrapped around Alexei and his head resting on his back, cuddling his buddy as they raced toward me.

"This is nice," I noted as they got off.

Alexei killed the ignition, handed me a helmet, and swept his eyes over me.

"Now you can run with the wolves, Nicky!" Corbin patted the seat. "Do you know how to drive it?"

"I'm sure I can figure it out," I mused. "Thanks, guys. This... this means a lot to me."

Alexei gave me a serious look, a million words stalling between the adoration in his eyes and his closed mouth. "Just be... careful."

I frowned. "Should I be concerned for my safety?"

Now that I thought about it, running with a pack of wild animals probably wasn't the smartest idea I'd ever had.

He shook his head. "No. Corbin and I wouldn't be here right now, offering you the quad, if we felt you'd be at risk. Every shifter is perfectly cognizant of their actions, even in their animal form. My pack would *never* attack a human unless threatened."

I nodded in understanding, recalling my wolfy interaction with Alexei. "But won't they think it's weird some rando human fearlessly threw herself into the fray? Could that be perceived as a threat?"

Alexei's throat bobbed as he swallowed. "Mara knows you've been spelled, which means the entire house likely knows by now, so they wouldn't think twice about it. And any pledges participating in tonight's run wouldn't dare question a sister. Mara may be a bitch, but she's not stupid. If you got hurt, she knows she'd have to answer to me, and I promise you, that is *not* something she'd want to do."

I wanted to believe him, but Mara had already proven she was a loose cannon. At the same time, my stubborn pride wanted this more than anything else right now. I needed to show that girl she would not intimidate me, despite her best efforts.

"It'll be fine, Nicky," Corbin assured me. "Like Alexei said, my sister can be an asshole more often than not, but she's not stupid." He jerked his chin toward the four-wheeler. "Now get on and go have fun."

I straddled the machine, adrenaline coursing through my veins as I turned the key and felt the vibrations of the engine beneath me.

I looked over my shoulder before putting on the helmet. "Why are you doing this?"

Alexei cleared his throat. "We're friends, right? Friends help each other."

His words warmed my heart, and I let them comfort me for a moment before tugging on the accelerator and squealing as the machine lurched forward.

I was going to run with some damn wolves.

IT TOOK me a while to find the pack. I was thankful for the helmet because stray tree branches kept running along me as I navigated the lush forest. Howls in the distance helped guide me, and after dodging holes in the ground and fallen trees, I finally found them.

Forty wolves of different sizes and shapes played in a clearing. Of course, the moment my loud ATV came roaring through, they all snapped their attention to me.

Way to make a fucking entrance.

I spotted Mara immediately. While the majority of wolves had silver, white, black, or gray fur, Mara's coat was multi-colored. Her snout was nearly black, the dark color ringing her eyes and running along her spine. The rest of her shiny coat was in various shades of light brown. She was truly beautiful—they all were

—and part of me longed for the camaraderie they obviously shared.

She trotted up to me, her mouth fixed in a snarl. I sat up on my four-wheeler, my pulse thudding in my ears as I did. I refused to let her intimidate me.

She circled the quad, sniffing at the tires and snapping angrily at me. By some miracle, I didn't flinch. I refused to be bullied into not participating just because I wasn't a shifter. Mara glared at me with her haunting eyes, a challenge seeping through her. I knew she was trying to intimidate me, so I met her stare with equal defiance, repeating my new mantra in my head.

I was strong.

I was worthy.

I deserved to fucking be here.

After a full minute, she tilted her head up and howled, the sound cracking through the air like booming thunder.

The wolves took off in a sprint, and with a quick tug on the accelerator, I took chase. The animals clearly had the advantage, their lithe bodies easily able to navigate through the thick copse of trees, whereas I was chained to a machine, but I was determined to make the best of it. I refused to let them shut me out, no matter how hard they tried. The animals yipped and howled in excitement, playfully nipping at each other as they ran.

Before I knew it, the strangest thing happened. I realized I was actually enjoying myself. The wind whipped my hair behind me, my adrenaline spiked as I sped along the narrow trails worn into the dirt. I whooped in excitement, hovering above the bench seat as I rode through the forest. I slowed when we approached a clearing, each wolf gathering along the bank to drink from the clear lake. I killed the engine, silently observing them for a minute. A few wolves' ears perked, telling me they were aware of my presence, but they didn't acknowledge me beyond that.

Screw it.

I was going to *make them* acknowledge me.

Or I would get eaten.

I'd say my odds were probably fifty-fifty.

I climbed off the four-wheeler, trudging toward the pack.

Though feeling cautious, I didn't slump my shoulders or approach them like prey. I forced confidence through every step, throwing off the vibe that I was *meant* to be here. One of them turned to look at me, baring its teeth as I approached.

I bared my teeth back, praying the salad I had earlier wasn't stuck in my gums. But then I reminded myself that vanity had no place here. This was the wild, and I was feeling like an alpha in my own right. My curled lips and wacky expression must have looked extremely amusing, because the wolf backed down and let out a little coughing sound, as if it were laughing.

I reined in my inner badass and sat beside the wolf, bending over to cup some water in my hands and run it over my forehead. I groaned in relief at the refreshing feel of the cool liquid against my sweaty skin, drawing the attention of the others. They watched me as I interacted with their pack mate, suddenly intrigued by my presence rather than loathing it. The wolves and I sat by the lake in companionable silence, and for the first time since coming to Redwood University, I felt a sense of hope that maybe I *could* belong. Maybe Beta Phi *was* still the home for me.

They wanted me to run with the wolves to prove my worth, and with a little modification, I did.

I fucking did.

After thirty minutes or so, the pack started to head back in the direction they came from. As I stood, my new friend ran her long body up against mine and sniffed my skin, somehow seeming pleased by me. I cautiously reached out, asking myself if petting a shifter was some kind of faux pas. When she leaned into my touch, as if accepting me, I smiled.

My fucking heart soared.

She then licked my hand, and I tried to separate the human from the wolf. Hopefully, I wasn't engaging in some damn mating ritual with an eager shifter. I chuckled to myself as I scratched behind her floppy ears, inspecting her. She was jet black all over, even her nose. Her coat shone beneath the light of the full moon reflecting off the lake, giving it an almost glittery effect. Her round eyes were wise and inquisitive, cautious, yet friendly. I laughed as she shuffled on her front paws excitedly. I couldn't help but think she was asking me if she did good, just like a pet dog would to its owner. This shifter really was a breathtaking creature, probably the largest and most striking wolf in the pack. I wondered what she looked like in her human form. I supposed I'd find out soon enough.

Deciding we should probably catch up with the others, I walked back to the four-wheeler, frowning as I reached for the key, but it was nowhere to be found.

I checked my pockets.

I checked the ground.

All of the wolves filtered out but the one that I befriended.

Shit. Where were the damn keys?

I crawled on all fours, sifting through the leaves as my new friend whimpered. Her long nails scratched against the dirt as she dug with her front paws, trying to help me. I was thankful to not be completely alone. I wasn't too proud to admit the forest was creepy at night. The cacophony of nature wasn't helping. Owls hooted in the distance. Crickets and frogs were going haywire. Normally, those sounds would soothe me, but tonight, they only seemed to fuel my anxiety.

"I know the key was right here," I groaned. "Can you shift and help me? I'm freaking out. I don't even know how to get back!"

The wolf simply whined again. I didn't know what that meant, but she obviously didn't want to be naked and searching through the ground with me.

Fucking fuck fuck.

"I bet Mara took it," I guessed. "She was pissed that I was here and..." I turned to look at the wolf. "Do you know how to get back?"

She barked and stomped on the ground with her paw.

"I'm going to slow you down." I already felt bad that I was letting my new friend down. She reached forward and licked the top of my hand, as if soothing me. "I don't want to ruin your chances of getting into Beta Phi. Maybe I should just call for help." I pulled out my cell phone.

No fucking service.

The shifter nudged me, and I sighed in resignation.

This would not be a fun walk in my heels.

I let my new friend lead the way through the shadowed trees. An hour later, my feet were bloodied and blistered. Everything looked the same, and I had to pray that this shifter wasn't leading me deeper into the woods so she could bail on me.

"Thanks for staying with me," I whispered. "I know you could have left, but I'm thankful you didn't."

She whined again, looking over her shoulder. Just when I felt certain we were walking in circles, I heard a deep voice calling my name and nearly cried in relief.

"Nicole!" Alexei yelled. "Where are you?"

My wolfy pal stiffened, a low growl rumbling from deep within her chest.

"Whoa, it's okay. I know him."

It was dark, but I could see the whites of Alexei's eyes round as he spotted us. "Nicole. Don't make any sudden moves. It'll be okay."

The wolf's hackles rose as Alexei came closer. She pressed her gigantic body into me, growling more furiously as he approached. *Wasn't this considered a sign of disrespect? Was she risking her position in the pack by protecting me from her alpha?*

I placed a hand on her head. "It's okay. I know Alexei. We're friends."

That label felt all kinds of wrong, but I didn't want my new friend to get in trouble for insubordination or whatever, so I had to ensure she knew her alpha and I were on good terms.

"Nicole..." Alexei eyed the wolf warily. "I need you to listen to me and follow my instructions to the letter."

"What are you talking about? What's going on?" I made a gimme motion with my hand. "Alexei, give me your hoodie so she has something to wear."

"What?!" he asked. "Why would I do that?"

I gestured to my new friend. "Because it's rude to ask her to shift back and then have to stand here naked while we're fully clothed. I know nudity isn't a big deal to shifters, but it's common courtesy, don't you think?"

His jaw dropped. "You think that's a *shifter*?!"

"What are you talking about?" I threw my hands up but put them back down as the movement agitated my overprotective friend.

I knelt down, wincing as my sore foot snapped a twig. My wolfy friend whimpered, licking my blistered toes. I fought the urge to squirm, reminding myself it was a perfectly natural animal instinct, just like when Alexei cleaned the gash on my leg.

"It's okay. I'll make him turn around and you can shift. He's a friend. He won't hurt me." I smoothed a hand over her head. "And if you don't want to shift, that's perfectly fine, too."

The wolf whined, but as I continued to pet her head, she gradually relaxed, her furry body eventually falling to the ground. I laughed when she rolled onto her back, pink tongue lolling to the side, giant paws up in the air as I scratched her belly.

Alexei also knelt, watching my new friend and me with extreme fascination. "Nicole. That's incredible. *You're* incredible."

"I know, right?" My lips curved into a cocky smile. "Little ol' human me managed to run with the pack tonight. And I even made a new friend." I looked down at said friend. "I hope we can be friends, anyway. Is it going to be totally weird that I'm petting your belly right now? You're just so cute in your wolfy form, I can't help it. God, I don't even know your name. This would be much easier if you shifted so you can talk to me."

Alexei chuckled softly. "Nicole. That's not going to happen."

"Why not?" I frowned in confusion. "What am I missing here?"

"She can't *shift*." He inclined his head toward the black wolf. "Because she's *not a shifter*."

I mulled over his statement for a moment. "That doesn't make sense. If she's not a shifter, then she's..." My eyes widened. "She's..."

"A wild animal," he finished for me. "And evidently, you, my dear mate, are some kind of wolf whisperer." His toothy grin gleamed in the moonlight.

What. The. Actual. Fuck?

CHAPTER

TWENTY-THREE

Alexei

"She's so sweet," Nicole cooed while walking back toward Greek Row. She looked absolutely feral with mud on her cheeks and sticks tangled in her dark hair. When I saw all the Beta Phis come back without her, I went into a frenzy. Every worst-case scenario crossed my mind.

Did Mara hurt her?

Did she get lost?

Did she wreck the four-wheeler?

Was she passed out somewhere?

I sure as shit wasn't expecting to see Nicole hanging out with a fucking wild wolf. It was terrifying and probably shaved ten years off my life. It wasn't

387

until I realized the wolf was protecting Nicole and not attacking her that I calmed down.

Nicole was a wolf whisperer.

"She's sweet when she doesn't want to bite my head off," I joked.

I was a proud mate and couldn't help but puff my chest, even if she could never be mine.

"I need a shower," she grumbled as the wolf pressed against her.

"Come on. You can use mine," I choked out while trying not to imagine her naked and lathering up in my bathroom. It made my cock twitch to think of her wearing my clothes and smelling like me.

"Is that a friendly offer?"

Her wolf huffed.

I gritted my teeth. "Of course."

"Then, thank you. If you have a first aid kit for my blisters, that would be great too. I'm never wearing heels again."

When we got back to the house, I led Nicole up to my room, her new bodyguard hot on our trail. We got more than a few curious looks from my pack brothers, but they were wise enough to keep their mouths shut. I was sure their questions would come in rapid succession the moment Nicole was gone, but if I had my way, that wouldn't be happening for a while.

As alpha, I had the master suite, which fortunately

meant I had an attached bathroom, so we could have some privacy. Nicole followed me into the ensuite, and I directed her to have a seat on the toilet lid while I got her all set up. Her new friend stuck close to her side as I pulled out some fresh towels and sweats, setting them on the countertop.

"Do you want to shower first? It'll probably be easier to assess the damage if we got all the dirt and blood washed off. Do you think you can stand a bit longer?"

"Yeah, that's probably a good idea." Nicole looked down at her muddy, battered feet. "Ugh. I just got your carpet all dirty, didn't I?"

I waved her off. "Nothing that won't come out."

She refused my offer to carry her—not that I was surprised—insisting on completing the trek back to Alpha Nu on her own two feet. I could tell she was in pain, which was causing *me* pain, but I kept my mouth shut. If Nicole could power through, so could I. The wolf was freakishly attuned to Nicole already; it had kept pace with us the entire trip, slowing or stopping each time Nicole appeared to struggle, forcing my mate to take mini breaks along the way. I was grateful for its empathy, but I was also a bit annoyed Nicole had no qualms listening to a wild animal over me. I could've sworn at one point the mutt tried to shoo me away, looking smug as shit, but she figured out real fast I wasn't going anywhere.

My inner wolf did *not* appreciate the canine competition. Nicole already seemed half in love with the damn thing, which made me jealous as hell. But the she-wolf made my mate happy, and Nicole's happiness made *my* wolf happy, so it was a wash.

"Well. I'll just take a shower then."

"Okay."

She gave me a pointed look. "Can I have some privacy?"

The wolf barked, and the look she gave me said, *get the hell out of here!*

Feeling like a dumbshit, I flushed. "Right. Sorry. I'll just be out here."

The wolf followed after me, and when the bathroom door shut, it was just the two of us. I made eye contact with the animal, trying to figure out why she was so attached to my mate.

The more I learned, the more I realized that this wasn't typical. Shifters rarely mated humans, let alone alphas. And now *my* human was a wolf whisperer. It was a possibility that this was just a curious mutt desensitized to humans, but I doubted it. She was protective and loyal.

"I suppose you're not going to tell me what's going on." I frowned at the wolf.

She huffed.

"Just so we're clear, Nicole is mine."

I swear to fucking God, the wolf laughed at me. The barking sound that escaped her snout was full of humor, as if the idea of Nicole belonging to me was hilarious.

"Yo." Corbin strolled into my room. "I just heard some crazy rumor that Nicole walked in looking beat to hell with a wild wolf—oh my God, there's a wild wolf!" My beta dropped the suit coat he had slung over his shoulder before jumping on my bed with his nasty shoes, as if Nicole's new friend was a massive spider and not a wolf.

"You can't be serious right now. You're a wolf!"

"I'm a civilized shifter!" Corbin pointed to the black wolf. "*That's* a wild animal, Alexei!!"

The she-wolf gave Corbin a bored look before sauntering over to his forgotten suit jacket. And then the funniest shit I've ever seen in my life happened.

The wolf crouched over it and pissed.

"No! *Not the Armani!*" Corbin screamed. "Bad dog! Bad, *bad* dog!"

The wolf stared at Corbin and me like we were jokes and continued to soak the expensive wool. My best friend and I both made a face when the unmistakable scent of concentrated urine filled the room, but it was still hilarious she was ruining his suit. My amusement was short-lived, however, when she sauntered over to me, fluffy tail wagging behind her, and squatted on my brand new Jordans.

I jumped back, kicking the soiled shoes off. "What the hell, mutt?"

Of course, Corbin was cracking up now. "Ha! Not so funny when it happens to you, is it?"

The wolf growled, baring her sharp teeth.

"Don't you start with me!" I pointed at her. "You wouldn't be so brave if I brought out *my* wolf and kicked your ass all over the place, would you?"

"Did you really just threaten my new friend?"

Shit.

I was so preoccupied with the piss incident I didn't even hear the water shut off. When I looked up, Nicole was standing in the doorway to my bathroom, a fluffy dark blue towel wrapped around her delectable body. Steam wafted from the room as my eyes fell to her cleavage, little droplets of water beading on her smooth skin.

"I didn't see a thing, swear." My head whipped to the side at the sound of Corbin's voice, his palm covering his eyes as he backed out of the room. "I'm just gonna go so you can, uh... get dressed. Not that I saw you wearing nothing but a towel or anything."

"Corbin," I snapped. "*Get out.*"

Nicole's full lips curved in amusement at the idiot's antics, though I found nothing funny about the fact that my best friend just saw my mate nearly naked. I didn't care if he—and the rest of my goddamned pack—had already seen her in a bikini, which technically covered less. It was the principle of it.

"Are you going to answer my question, Alexei?"

"Why aren't you wearing the clothes I gave you?" I countered. "*The baggy clothes that would fully cover your body.*"

She rolled her pretty blue eyes. "Because I heard you yelling at my new friend, and I wanted to see what all the fuss was about." Her delicate brows lifted. "So... care to explain why you were threatening my pretty dog?"

"She started it," I grumbled.

My mate gave me a wry look. "That's what you're going with, huh? Are you five?"

My eyes narrowed. "In case the delightful aroma wasn't a strong enough clue, that damn dog just deposited a gallon's worth of pee all over my floor! Corbin's designer jacket and my shoes are toast, and I'm probably going to have to have the carpet replaced entirely. Wolf piss is *potent.*"

Nicole scoffed. "I guess you would know, huh?"

"Not funny." I took a seat on the edge of my bed.

"What are you going to do about her, Nicole? She can't exactly stay in your dorm."

The wolf whined, as if she could understand what we were saying. She crossed the room until her nose was nudging against Nicole's hand.

Nicole rewarded the dog's efforts with some scratches behind the ear. "Don't listen to that dumb boy, sweet girl. You wouldn't pee in my room, now would you?"

The wolf's responding howl sounded strangely like, "Never."

"That's a good girl." Nicole combed her hands through the animal's dark fur. "I'm not dumb, Alexei. I know you can't keep a wild animal cooped up in a house, especially not a tiny dorm room. But if my new friend here wants to sleep with me tonight, I'm not going to lie and say she wouldn't give me comfort, knowing someone had my back while I was so vulnerable. Especially after what you told me about your father and the fact that the Beta Phi wolves left me high and dry."

"*I* could have your back while you slept," I argued.

"No. You *couldn't*." The water from Nicole's wet hair dripped down her bare arms as she shook her head. Arms that I'd *love* to see tied to my headboard as I ate her pussy until her voice was hoarse from screaming through a dozen orgasms. "We both know why that would be a monumentally stupid decision on several accounts."

Fuck.

What was she saying?

Dammit.

When the lust-laden fog cleared and Nicole's words registered, I knew that she had a point.

She also *really* needed to put some damn clothes on before I forgot all the reasons why touching her would be a bad idea, and turned my little impromptu fantasy into reality.

A loud bark followed by a growl filled the room.

My gaze shifted to the wolf in annoyance.

What the fuck? Could she read my thoughts just now?

"She needs a name," Nicole mused. "I'm thinking... Macey. Mace for short."

I scrunched my nose up while the wolf jumped excitedly. "Mace?"

Nicole patted her head while speaking in a high-pitched squeal. "Cause she's like my own personal can of Mace! Yes, she is. She's a good girl. She'll keep all the mean bitches away."

Mace. Considering the smell of her piss had my eyes burning, it seemed appropriate.

"Mace isn't a normal wolf, Nicole," I insisted.

"She's very attached to you already, and it's like she can read our thoughts."

Nicole looked at her wolf. "Yeah. This feels… different. Like we connect."

"We should talk to someone about this and get some answers."

Nicole closed the gap between us and sat beside me.

Nearly naked.

I was going to win a fucking award for my self-restraint.

"I can talk to Juniper about it when I see her later." Nicole grabbed my wrist to read my watch. "Speaking of, I'm going to be late. It's kind of cute that their event starts at the *witching hour*. Cool, right? I might be able to squeeze in a visit with the vampire sorority and drop in on the fae, too, if I hurry."

I whipped my head to the side. "What?"

"I can't wear your sweats. Is there a lost and found for hookups around here? All these dudes are bound to have a few ladies leave some clothes behind."

I jumped up to stop her as she started walking toward the door. "First of all, you're *not* going out there in a towel." By some fucking act of God, Mace agreed with me. She blocked the door before Nicole could get there. "Second, I'm not sure how I feel about you going to the vamps and fae. It's dangerous. I'm coming with you."

Nicole shrugged. "I think Mace and I will be just fine, but if you want to be my shadow for the evening, I don't care as long as you don't pull any of your bossy alpha crap. Now, go find some clothes that don't swallow me whole, Alexei."

She walked back to the bathroom, and I groaned as she started humming to herself.

"Are you just going to let her go?" I asked Mace.

The wolf gave me an incredulous look, as if I were an idiot for asking.

"Fine. But we get her out of there at the first sign of trouble."

And with that, Mace barked in agreement.

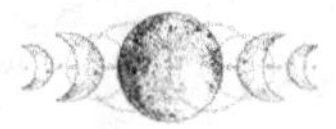

"Man, those vampires sure do know how to spoil a girl." Nicole's tone was annoyingly wistful. "I really wish I could've taken advantage of the pedi station. Stupid jacked-up feet."

I glanced down at her feet as she hobbled along the sidewalk. "Are you sure you don't want me to carry you?"

"Nope." Her toes wiggled in her flip-flops. "Comfy shoes, and these cushy bandages make all the difference."

I wasn't buying that for one minute, but I decided not to press the issue any further. Unsurprisingly, the only women's clothing my frat brothers could produce were random scraps of lingerie, so Nicole conceded to allow Corbin to run to her dorm to grab something from her room. She made him promise he wouldn't rifle through her underwear drawer, which was followed by a threat from me to remove his fingernails if he so much as touched a single piece of fabric in said drawer. Which I later had to admit to my mate when Corbin produced a bag filled with *every* piece of fabric from the damn drawer. He said the only way he could ensure Nicole wouldn't have to go commando without putting his hands on anything was if he dumped the whole thing into a bag.

"You know they only do that whole spa thing to lure you into their trap, right? The bloodsuckers want live-in donors, and pampering humans is the easiest way for them to accomplish that."

"Don't care." Nicole shrugged, showing off her newly painted fingernails. "At least I got a mani out of it. And *an amazing* neck rub. That Rick guy had *really* strong hands. Worked all the knots out."

"Fucking bloodsuckers," I grumbled, thinking

about the overly muscled masseuse touching my girl, soliciting all kinds of sexy noises from her lips as he rubbed her sore muscles.

The worst part was, I just had to stand there with Nicole's adopted pet, watching it all go down. As much as I wanted to rip that guy's limbs off, I was smart enough to know my mate would *not* appreciate the gesture, so I refrained. It was quite possibly the most torturous fifteen minutes of my life.

Nicole laughed. "Aw, don't be such a crab, Alexei. I wasn't really planning to be a Theta Psi girl. I just wanted to check out the vamp's place for the experience."

"You said the same thing about the fae house," I reminded her. "And look how well that turned out."

She shuddered. "I *noped* out of there as fast as I could."

"Smart girl." I laughed.

Our first stop after leaving my place was Lambda Delta, but the moment the woman opened the door, excitedly informing Nicole tonight was *Open Portal Night,* Nicole turned on her heels and hauled ass back to the street as quickly as her bandaged feet would allow. Quite frankly, if she hadn't fled on her own accord, I would've thrown her over my shoulder— witnesses be damned—and gotten her the hell out of there. Time passed differently beyond the veil, and fae had some *seriously fucked-up* rules. Every year, at least a few pledges had disappeared. *If* they somehow made it back to this plane, it was several earth years later, though in their mind, only a few hours had passed. Then there were the ones who fell victim to the whims of a devious fae, returning to earth with so much psychological damage many took their own lives within days. It was a fate I wouldn't wish on my worst enemies.

Fuck.

I needed to hook Nicole up with a protection charm stat. Why hadn't that occurred to me before now?

I had trust issues with virtually every non-shifter faction, but the fae were especially troublesome. Unless you could spend your life avoiding them entirely, securing magical protection was non-negotiable. Thankfully, my beta's overzealous sex life was proving to be useful for once. After asking around, I now knew that Juniper Hale came from a long line of powerful witches. Her coven was one of the most reputable out there, dating back hundreds of years. And according to my lovesick friend, Juniper was also "one hella cool chick."

Speaking of the witchy woman...

Nicole and I—and Mace—were now approaching Kappa Zeta. This sorority along with its fraternity counterpart, Gamma Sigma, were the most diverse on campus. While two-thirds of their residents were magical beings, the remaining third was a mixture of humans and lower-level shifters, like Juniper's fiancé, Ivan.

"Oooh, I like their house." Nicole smiled.

I personally thought it was an eyesore. Instead of building a top of the line home like any normal, respectable organization on Greek Row, they magically transported a legitimate haunted mansion from Spain. The stucco walls and creepy-ass stained glass windows stuck out on our street, but the witches claimed the spirits that lived there gave them a little magical boost.

"Stay close to me, please."

Mace pressed closer to Nicole's side.

"Welcome to Kappa Zeta!" A fit woman with a tight bandanna wrapped around her chest greeted. She had a low, sultry voice and wild green eyes. She wrapped Nicole up in a massive hug, lifting her off the ground and squealing. "I'm so happy you're here. Come on in!"

Nicole beamed at the greeting, and once again, I felt bitter about the way my pack treated her. We needed to be more inclusive and accepting—myself included.

The moment we walked through the door, a

massive group of probably seventy witches started clapping and chanting in the entryway.

"BOOM BOOM!"

clap clap

"KAPPA ZETA, BOOM BOOM!"

clap clap

"THAT BLUE AND WHITE—"

clap clap

"WELCOMES YOU—"

clap clap

"TO THE HOUSE OF NIGHT."

"KAPPA—"

clap

"ZETA!"

clap clap clap clap clap clap clap

"They're putting a spell on us!" I roared before slamming my hands over Nicole's ears. She shrugged me off and gave me an incredulous look.

"It's not a spell!"

Nicole shook her head at me while the witches all said, "Wooooooo! Kappa Zeta!"

She cheered with them and grinned. "It's a door chant. Lots of sororities do them to make potential pledges feel welcome."

I still felt like someone was shoving knives in my ears. It was creepy as fuck. "I feel like this would scare people away instead of making them feel welcome."

Nicole rolled her eyes and scanned the crowd. "Oh! There's Juniper." She shuffled through witches with a big grin on her face and tapped Corbin's fuck buddy on the shoulder. "Hey!"

Juniper spun around and gave Nicole a big hug. "You made it!" She then looked at me and then down at Mace. "And you brought some bodyguards. Wait..." Juniper crouched low and stared at Mace, her eyes locked on the animal as she cocked her head to the side. "You have a familiar."

Nicole grinned. "What does that mean?"

"*A familiar*," Juniper repeated, stroking her hand down the black wolf's long neck. "Where'd you find this pretty girl? Have you given her a name yet?"

"Macey." Nicole chuckled when the wolf licked June's cheek. "I call her Mace for short. She really seems to like you."

"*All* familiars like me," June boasted.

My mate frowned. "That's the third time you've used that term. I know *what* a familiar is, but I'm confused as to *why* you're calling Macey one. My supernatural encyclopedia isn't going off, either."

Holy shit.

Why hadn't I noticed that right away?

Familiars—magical guides who took the form of animals—were fairly common in witchcraft. It was *not* normal for a human to have one, though. But there was no doubt in my mind that was *exactly* what Macey was to Nicole. There was a common misconception that a witch's familiar was simply a bodyguard of sorts, but that wasn't accurate. The animal was capable of many things. They had magical abilities to soothe their person during periods of distress. They could defy the physical limitations of their size, such as with a house cat, if their person were in grave danger. They were known to be healers and magic practitioners in their own right as well. I once met a fortune-teller whose cat assisted her with readings.

The relationship between a familiar and their person ran deep. They were companions in the truest sense of the word. Familiars intuitively understood their person's needs and could sense their emotions. And in time, that psychic connection became reciprocal. I'd even heard of some instances where they could communicate verbally using telepathy. Having a familiar was a great honor.

My *human* mate had a familiar. A *wolf* familiar. My inner wolf preened at the thought. That couldn't possibly be just a coincidence, right?

Why was Nicole given such a remarkable gift?

Because Nicole was remarkable, my brain supplied.

"She's your familiar." Juniper's tone inferred no further explanation was necessary, but she continued anyway. "Your other half. Your magical soul mate.

Usually you have to prove yourself worthy by challenging them before you're blessed with one. If they don't think you're worthy, it could end very badly. And when I say badly... I mean you'd be six feet under. So... did you challenge her somehow?"

All the color drained from Nicole's face. "W-we were at the lake. I kind of bared my teeth at her and pretended to hiss."

I snapped my attention to Nicole. "You did *what*?!"

She winced. "I thought it was another bully shifter trying to make me feel like I didn't belong. I didn't realize it was a wild animal looking to *kill* me if I didn't pass the test. Good thing she thinks I'm worthy, I suppose." Nicole grinned, as if she didn't risk her fucking life earlier.

What good was her magical reference guide if she was going to do stupid shit like that?

"But why did my mind-fuck not recognize her?" my stubborn mate asked.

"Your encyclopedia recognizes entities outside of yourself. It probably didn't pick up on her because she's literally a piece of your soul," Juniper replied.

Nicole dropped her mouth open in shock. "Wow."

"Well, congratulations! Mace will protect you with her life and be a worthy companion." Juniper bent over to scratch behind the wolf's ears. "Such a good girl!"

"Does she have any special skills?" Nicole was practically bouncing in excitement. "Isn't that pretty common with familiars?"

At that question, Mace started jumping up and down, her fat paws landing on my foot.

"Shit!" *Dammit, that hurt.*

"Looks like she wants to show you." Juniper smiled indulgently. "Come on, beautiful. Show us your gift."

Mace sat down and looked at Nicole with a piercing gaze. I waited for her to burst into flames or have fur that turned to needles. Nothing was off-limits for a familiar.

"What's happening?" I whispered.

Juniper shrugged, but Nicole's eyes turned misty.

She pressed the tips of her fingers to her lips. "Oh-oh my God."

Every muscle in my body tensed. "Nicole? Are you okay?"

"She's showing me something," Nicole whispered, a broad grin on her face despite the tears streaming down her cheeks. "It's... it's my mom. She's showing me memories of her. Working at the lab with dad, rubbing her stomach while pregnant with me." Nicole stopped speaking to laugh. "I also see her with Hannah and Jade. They're laughing at the Harvard Beta Phi house."

Juniper gasped and pressed a hand to her chest. "What a precious gift!"

Mace barked, somehow breaking their trance. I watched as Nicole blinked and dropped into a crouching position.

Wrapping her slender arms around Mace, she hugged the wolf while nuzzling her fur. "Thank you, Mace. That was so beautiful."

Juniper was eyeing Nicole now with barely contained curiosity. "Was your mother a witch, Nicole?"

Nicole blanched, standing up to stare at Juniper. "Why would you ask that?"

"Just curious. Familiars can't connect with humans, so obviously you're... more? Maybe not quite a full-blooded witch, because any supe could sense that wasn't the case. You reek of human through and through. No offense. But we definitely need to look into this. There has to be *something* in your bloodline. Maybe some kind of recessive gene."

Nicole played with the necklace around her neck. "I think my father would have told me if that were true..."

"Unless he didn't know," Juniper suggested. "I'll see if I can find anything out. Either way, this is so exciting. We have lots of familiars at Kappa Zeta. Even if you don't join, you should come hang out. It'll be good for Mace to bond with others like her, and maybe you can chat with some of our witches to learn all the ins and outs. Yani, a friend of mine, has a thirty-foot python, and we had to build a big enclosure for the sweet creature. Snakes get really stressed out when they don't have enough room to move around."

I shivered. I was a tough, powerful alpha, but I couldn't deal with snakes. Frankly, they freaked me the fuck out. Having an unfused jaw shouldn't even be a thing. Don't get me started on the thought of some boa wrapping its long scaly body around their prey, squeezing every bit of air out of its lungs while glee shone from their beady eyes. Or the fact that those creepy fuckers have been known to eat *themselves* on occasion. Everything about them was so unnatural.

"Oh!" Juniper stood tall. "I finished those protection charms you asked for."

Nicole held out her hand, palm up, waiting for the witch to pass the charms over. "Thank you so much. What do I need to do to activate them?"

"Wait, when did you ask for protection charms?" I piped in.

Her blue eyes narrowed. "I'm sorry. I wasn't aware I needed to run every aspect of my day by you."

"You don't," I insisted, though I wouldn't deny I

rather enjoyed the thought of knowing what my mate was doing at all times. "I was… curious."

And impressed that Nicole had the foresight to think of it. With every passing hour, my mate was proving there was much more to her than I had originally given her credit for. In my defense, I was raised to believe all humans were inferior. While they certainly served their purpose in society, their humanity made them weak.

"I figured it would be helpful, considering Dad works directly with a fae. Even if she seems pretty cool, I'd rather be safe than sorry."

"You can never be too careful with those guys," Juniper agreed.

"Tell me about it." Nicole groaned. "At least this way, I know he'll be safe."

"But you got one for yourself, too, right?" I asked.

Nicole seemed to have this habit of caring about everyone but herself.

"Of course I did." She turned to Juniper. "So I just wear this and I'm protected?"

June shook her head. "Yes. Oh! And about the heart charm, it'll take a lock of hair from the person you want to protect your heart from." She then looked at me.

"What? What heart charm?" I asked. The witch was eyeing me like I was a prize.

"It'll help Nicole put some much needed distance between the two of you. Help her have a clear head when you're involved, and if she wears it for a few months, her attraction will wane. I did a lot of research, and I think it'll work. We just need some of your hair."

My heart twisted, the agony burning through my soul nearly sending me to my knees. "You can't do that." I turned to look at Nicole, who seemed uncertain. "You want to use magic on our…" I looked around. "Bond?"

Juniper interrupted before she could respond. "Corbin said you were wanting something similar?" she said.

Nicole's eyebrows raised. "Looks like we're on the same page then."

"In the beginning, yes. But things have changed. I thought we were going to try to be friends." I knew I was scrambling for an alternative. I wasn't ready to give her up just yet.

"Alexei," she said, her voice wavering a bit. "This could solve all our problems. Who knows, by the end of it, you might not even *want* to be my friend."

Juniper looked between us, a mischievous smile on her face. Fucking witches. I didn't want Nicole to be ripped away from me. I needed a real solution. "It takes a month to make. Just hand me a couple strands of hair, and I'll get charms made for the both of you."

Nicole watched me as she slowly lifted her hand up and plucked a couple of hairs from her scalp. My heart was practically in my throat as she carefully handed them over to Juniper, who placed them in an envelope. "Your turn," Nicole said to me.

"No."

"Alexei."

"I'm not doing this. I don't consent." I stalked closer to her, lowering my voice. "I want to feel this. All of this. Even if I can't have you, I want to feel our bond, Nicole. I don't care how much it hurts. I don't care if I spend the rest of my life in agony because of it. The world keeps taking you away, but they can't take this." I patted my chest.

Nicole reached up to cup my cheek, her baby blue eyes peering right into my soul. "That's the thing, Alexei. Your feelings could get me killed. At some point, you're going to have to stop thinking about what you want, and start caring about me enough to do right by me." And with those brutal words, she plucked a strand of my hair, her swift fingers moving efficiently.

I didn't know what to say as she handed it over to Juniper. It felt like she was slipping away before I even got the chance to have her. But she was right, I needed to put her safety first.

"Well, that was intense." Juniper cleared her throat. "Let's shift focus back to the protection charms I got you. It'll help protect you against all supernaturals. If you get attacked, it'll shove them off of you. You have to say the magic words, though. Hold it in your palm and repeat after me."

Nicole did as she asked, staring intently at Juniper.

"I, Nicole Fairweather," Juniper began.

"I, Nicole Fairweather."

Juniper grinned. "Love big alpha shifter dicks."

Nicole groaned. "You're impossible."

Juniper tipped her head back and laughed. "The spell is already done. No need to say any magic words or dip it in ogre cum—"

Nicole's eyes widened. "*What?!*"

I was getting tired of this. Witches were too damn quirky for my tastes. I needed time to go home and think about what Nicole had said. I'd been a shitty mate to her from the moment we'd met. I didn't deserve Nicole. "Just put the damn thing on," I snapped.

Nicole stared at me, as if I were a nuisance. But every second she wasn't wearing the protection charm, my anxiety grew. All I wanted was for her to be protected, and I was angry at myself for not thinking of this sooner. Once again, I was failing as her mate. But I refused to fail as her friend.

"Am I supposed to feel anything?" Nicole reached behind her neck to fasten the chain.

I stared at her neck as the silver charm rested next to the necklace she always wore.

Juniper leaned in to inspect her handiwork, a frown crossing her features. "Something is wrong."

Mace tensed up, the hair along her spine standing on edge as she growled.

My gaze zeroed in on Nicole's new jewelry. "What's wrong?"

Juniper reached out to touch the charm. "It's supposed to glow. But the spell is being rejected."

Nicole winced. "Is that supposed to feel so hot? It's getting really warm on my skin." Her fingers trembled as she struggled to unhook the delicate clasp. "Ouch!"

Mace started barking relentlessly.

I reached out to try and remove the charm, determined to break it with my grip, but the moment my hand touched it, I was thrown across the room. My back slammed into the wall, and the tips of my finger burned from where I made contact with it.

Mace lunged for Nicole's neck.

"Nicole!" I roared as she fell to the ground.

Mace grabbed the charm with her teeth and tore it

from Nicole's body before tossing it across the room. Everyone in the room scattered away from it.

"Juniper!" My legs shook from the intensity of the charm as I stood. It felt like I got hit by a bus. Mace was sitting in Nicole's lap, licking at her neck like she was trying to heal her. "What the fuck was that?" I crouched in front of Nicole. "Are you okay?"

"I'm fine," she croaked. "It was just starting to burn me."

Juniper was staring wide-eyed at the scene in front of her, her face twisted in shock. "Who gave you that necklace, Nicole?"

I flashed her an accusatory glare. "You did!"

"Not that one," Juniper corrected. "*That* one. The one around her neck."

Nicole looked down, her brow dipped. "This? It was my mother's. I've worn it for as long as I can remember."

Juniper cleared her throat. "And who gave *her* that necklace?"

"Her friend, Jade. She's been in my life forever. What does this have to do with your faulty protection spell, June?"

"There's a rule. You can't double up on protection spells," Juniper whispered. "They start to fight each other, thinking the other one is a threat. The reason my protection didn't work is because you're already wearing one, Nicole."

"That doesn't make sense." Nicole shook her head. "That would mean…"

"That the people in your life are well aware that supes exist?" Juniper helpfully supplied.

"Yeah." My mate gulped. "*That*."

My wolf stirred. We *really* needed to get to the bottom of this.

"Nicole," I urged. "We need to speak to your mother's friend and find out exactly what she knows. Do you know how to reach her?"

"Oh, yeah," she replied. "And if she knew anything about this and didn't warn me, she's gonna get an earful."

If my mate didn't deliver on that promise, I sure as hell would.

TWENTY-FOUR

Nicole

"HELLO, DARLING!" A grin stretched across Jade's face. "You're calling late. How was Letters Day?"

"It was great." My delivery was drier than the Sahara. "Went on a run with a pack of shifters, found a familiar, and then almost died because my new witch friend tried giving me a protection spell when I already had one hanging from my neck."

Mace sat at my feet, licking her paws while Alexei paced my dorm room. I waited for Jade to respond, perhaps even to call me crazy or ask if I was on drugs. I was taking an enormous risk by laying it all out there. The laws about telling humans were clear, but the spelled necklace around my throat was evidence enough for me.

She responded with a lengthy sigh.

"I knew something like this would happen the moment you agreed to go to that damn school."

"You *knew* this would happen? Why the hell didn't you warn me, Jade?!"

She huffed. "Well, for starters, you'd think I was insane."

"This conversation is insane. You know, Jade. You knew!"

She gave me a guilty look. "Your mother, Hannah, and I managed to escape the supernatural world and certainly never wanted you exposed to it. I tried talking your dad out of accepting the position at Redwood, but without being able to explain why I didn't think it was a good idea, it was a lost cause. Your father needs hard facts to process things. You know this. The giant budget the university promised him didn't help. The man was straight-up giddy, which I don't think I've ever seen before then. He just kept blathering on and on about scientific advance-ments, mutated genes, and micro-something-or-another."

"Wait. Back up." I shook my head. "My mother, you, *and* Hannah are some kind of *supes*?" I didn't know which revelation was the most shocking. "What do you mean, you left the supernatural world behind? How? *Why*?"

Jade groaned into the phone. "When we went to college, we agreed to live like humans. As much as possible anyway. We wanted to know what it was like to blend in for once. To start over. Your mother was... extraordinary, Nicole. You could say one of a kind, which made her incredibly valuable to certain... collectors. As for me, I was... painfully disappointing. My parents wanted to disown me, so I made it easy for them and haven't talked to them since. And Hannah? Well, that's not my story to tell."

"Hold up a sec." I rubbed my temples. "This is a lot to take in. What do you mean my mom was *extraordinary*? What was she? And while you're at it, you can tell me what *you* are."

Alexei stared at me from behind the monitor, his eyes fixed on my mouth as I spoke to Jade.

"I'm a witch. A *terrible* witch born in a family of exceptional magic. After years of training, I was unable to conjure a breeze. I had to pay someone to make that protection spell for you." I could hear the lifetime of hurt in Jade's tone.

My face fell. "Jade."

"It doesn't matter." She waved me off. "As for your mom, I'm sworn to secrecy. Before she died, Hannah and I promised to protect you if anything happened to her, and we take that promise very seriously. We couldn't stop you from attending Redwood University, but we took steps to ensure no one will figure out what you are, what you're capable of. Or what we *suspect* you're capable of, that is."

"Jade, you *have* to tell me. If I'm in some sort of danger... don't you think I should be armed with as much information as possible? You should've fessed up the moment Dad and I told you I was enrolling in this stupid school!"

She combed her hands through her dark hair. "I know, I know. But I couldn't. I *literally* couldn't."

I blew out a breath, grabbing a scrunchie off my wrist and pulling my hair up. "What does that mean? Was anything you've taught me about my mom true? I feel like my entire life is a lie."

"No," Jade insisted, her eyes filling with tears. "*Everything* Hannah or I told you about your mom was one hundred percent accurate. We just... omitted some stuff. Not by choice, I promise."

"Explain."

She sighed. "It's not simple. For starters, there are very intense laws about telling humans about the supernatural world. For all intents and purposes, you're considered a human. If we would have said anything, it could have brought a lot of attention to us. And even if that weren't an issue, it was physically impossible for me to say anything. We did a secrecy spell. It's literally the one thing I'm good at. It was a necessary evil."

"What kind of secrecy spell?" I pressed the heel of my hand against my throbbing eye.

"The kind with magical consequences," she explained. "We couldn't expose your mom's secrets to anyone–not even your dad–because it would've put you at risk. The pact bonded us but made it really freaking difficult after your mother passed. In order to break the spell, all original secret keepers have to consent. When your mom died, she literally took that secret to the grave."

"Fuck."

"I knew Redwood was going to be risky, but my hands were tied. I tried convincing your dad to stay. I pulled so many strings, got him that job offer at NYU so he could be close to y—"

"What?!" I shouted. "He didn't tell me about that."

Her shoulders lifted in a shrug. "Redwood offered way more money and basically promised a Nobel Prize if he joined their team. Quite frankly, I wouldn't be surprised if they used a very powerful persuasion spell to get him there. And even worse, if he'd still declined, they would have brought him in anyway. We hoped that if you went willingly, you'd have a better chance of escaping notice. I knew the university's containment spell wouldn't work on you. You're not human. Or… not entirely, anyway. We've all just been waiting for you to say something so that we'd finally be allowed to talk about things. Everything that's not forbidden by magic to discuss, that is."

I cursed. "This is bad, Jade."

"I know, honey. I was really hoping you'd have a normal college experience."

"Did you know Beta Phi was only for shifters? Why push me to join if you knew it was hopeless?"

Jade gave me a sad look. "You were so excited. I didn't want to break your heart, babe. Your mother would have wanted you to try. She was determined and fearless. I guess part of me hoped that the shifter community had evolved. And maybe a small part of me also wanted you to learn about supes so I could finally discuss it with you. The more you learn without any influence from us, the more I can say. It's one of the few loopholes of a secrecy spell."

"That's a gigantic pain in the ass," I grumbled.

I could tell Alexei was getting impatient. I asked him to stay off screen so I could have the illusion of privacy on this video call, but I could see my time was about to run out if Jade didn't produce answers.

"Tell me what happened. I'm sure you're feeling quite overwhelmed from learning that supernatural beings exist tonight. If I have a clear understanding, maybe I can share something useful."

"Well, for starters, I've known about supernaturals for a while now. Since my second day here, actually."

If I wanted her to be honest and open, I felt like I should extend the same courtesy.

"Excuse me?" Jade blinked rapidly. "Explain, young lady."

I closed my eyes for a moment, gathering the courage to recount the many ways my life had drastically changed over the last few weeks.

"Well, it started when..."

Jade cursed repeatedly when I told her about my magical download from the dude at the coffee shop. She spewed colorful threats when I told her about Mara's attempted brainwashing and how the shifters stranded me at the lake. Smiled when I explained how I met my beautiful familiar, who excitedly yipped in the background as I spoke about her. I didn't know why I was so reluctant to tell Jade about Alexei, but I saved that part for last.

"There is no way in hell I'm letting you date a shifter!" Her anger surprised me.

I looked up at Alexei, who had a look of... embarrassment on his face. Huh. Wasn't so fun when it was *my* family not approving of *him*.

"Why not?" I asked.

"Hannah is way better at explaining this than I am."

"Is Hannah a shifter?"

"Nope. Not going there. Secret forbids it. I *can* tell you that she knows firsthand how terrible shifters can be."

My chest tightened. "They definitely haven't been welcoming."

"That's it. I'd already been debating on coming back. I think Hannah and I need to visit. Bee, too."

"If you tell me my best friend is a supe, I'll probably lose my mind."

Jade grinned. "Nope. One hundred percent human. But... her dad... well... let's just say the military is more involved with the supernatural community than you might think."

I pinched the bridge of my nose. "This is insanity. How could you keep this from me?"

"None of us wanted to, honey. I swear it."

"But you *did*. You let me come here blind. And you can't tell me what my mother was?"

"No," she said solemnly. "I can't. I want to but—" Her voice cut off as if she were choking. "Goddamn spell. It's the equivalent of getting a tattoo of your boyfriend's name at eighteen. Huge mistake that I can't get rid of."

That analogy made me giggle.

"So, what now? Do you think I should tell Dad? I grabbed a protection charm for him, too. He doesn't have anything currently in place that I need to worry about, does he?"

"Not that I know of," Jade answered.

"So, you think I should tell him? He works with a fae, so I need to get the charm in place as soon as possible, but I can't think of a way to accomplish that without explaining myself. He's not exactly a jewelry guy." Dad's charm was set in a simple leather bracelet and was most certainly masculine, but I still couldn't see him wearing it. "He'd understand why he had to keep it on if he knew everything, but like you said before, Dad needs hard facts, which I can't produce. Maybe I should talk to the warlock who spelled me."

Alexei legit growled, even though he wasn't in his wolf form, causing Mace to do the same. "The hell you are. You're not going anywhere near that guy!"

Jade's eyes widened on the screen. "Thanks for the heads-up your supposed mate was eavesdropping, Nic."

I shrugged, not feeling all that guilty considering the massive amount of information she'd hidden from me my entire life. Maybe that wasn't fair of me, but I wasn't in a very forgiving mood at the moment.

"There's nothing *supposed* about it," Alexei

snapped as he took a seat next to me on the bed so Jade could see him. "I *am* her mate."

"Mm-hmm, Shifter-boy," Jade mocked, throwing his surly attitude right back at him. "We'll see about that." Her expression turned pensive as she gave Alexei a good once over. "Well, at least you're pretty, I suppose. I wouldn't exactly kick you out of bed."

"JADE!" My mouth gaped. "What the hell?!"

"What?" Her shoulders lifted. "I'm not blind. If I were twenty years younger, I'd totally bang him."

Alexei coughed into his fist. I suspected he was covering a smile as she stroked his already over-the-top ego.

"No." I made a face. "Just... no."

"Look, sweetie, I know this is all a bit... shocking."

I raised a brow. "You think?"

Jade pointed at me through the computer. "Don't forget, I've changed more than a few of your diapers, young lady."

"Sorry," I mumbled as Alexei placed a reassuring hand on the small of my back.

She waved me off. "Anyway... as I was saying, I know it's a lot, but we'll figure it out. I was being serious earlier. Maybe I can get the girls together for a trip, and we can brainstorm in person. It might even help ease your dad into things if we're there. And I'll talk to Hannah to see if she can think of any way to pry open our magically sealed lips."

"Really?" I asked. "You think you could make it out here? Bee told me she already booked her ticket, but she hasn't sent me the confirmation yet."

With everything going on, I hadn't even realized how badly I was missing them until she brought up the possibility of being together in person. Dad had been so busy since we got here, and I was long overdue for some family bonding.

"I make no promises, Nicole, but I'll try my best. I'll message Bee and see if Han and I can make a trip out at the same time." She held her fingers up in some weird gesture. "Scout's honor."

"Were you even a scout?" I challenged.

"Not even a little," she laughed, making me follow suit. "I love you, honey. I'll call you in the morning, okay? Try to get some rest."

"Okay," I agreed. "Love you, too. Goodnight."

I ended the video call and closed my laptop.

I turned toward Alexei. "What now?"

"Now, we figure out what your mother was and what you are."

I knew he was right, but something about that statement made me pause. "I know why *I'm* interested in learning more about my mother, but why are you?"

He shrugged. "I have a feeling it would explain

why we're mates. I'm an *alpha*, Nicole. Mating a human just doesn't make sense, no matter how hard I try to understand it."

My chest burned from his words. "For the record..." I stood up. "We're *friends*, remember? Secondly, if we *were* mates, you'd be fucking lucky to have someone like me regardless of whether or not I'm a supe. I'm awesome."

He closed the distance between us while looking down at me. "I know you are."

I wasn't expecting him to say that. It made the tension in my shoulders relax some. "How do you figure?"

"You're kind. Selfless. When you walk into a room, you just have this incredible way of looking both confident and welcoming at the same time. You fight for what you want, which I have mad respect for. My best friend trusts you. *I* trust you. Nicole, you're *perfect for me.*"

I gaped at him, shocked that he would so easily admit such things. I thought our mate connection was purely physical, but he didn't mention my looks once in that spiel.

"But it doesn't change a damn thing, does it?"

"The problem isn't how *I* feel. Yes, I initially had an ego about this. I was raised to think shifters were superior to everyone else. But I'm pushing you away,

I'm being your *friend*, because I want to protect you. Because the rest of the shifter world would never accept you, and it's killing me. *It's fucking killing me*, Nicole." He slammed his clenched fist into his chest.

I brushed a hand over my necklace and pondered his words. "We need to figure out what I am."

Alexei nodded. "We need to talk to Juniper. Maybe she knows a way to break that pact and figure out what you are."

I turned to Mace, who was waiting patiently for me on the floor. "Can you give me a hint?"

Mace slowly got up and lazily trotted over to me. I couldn't blame her for being tired. It had been an extremely long day, and I was half ready to crawl into bed. Once again, she sat and peered into my eyes, and once again, a vision fluttered across my mind.

I saw my mom, with her kind blue eyes and jet black hair, running through a field under the bright light of the full moon, laughing with four shifters sprinting beside her.

Holy crap!

There were so many stars in the sky I gasped at the sight. You *never* got to see stars like that in Baltimore. I realized I didn't know where she grew up. Whenever my dad talked about my mom, it was about after they met their freshman year of college. I made a mental note to ask him.

"Hurry up, Celena!" one girl called, pulling her long, flowy dress over her head as she ran, exposing the fact she had nothing on underneath.

My mother chuckled, completely unfazed by her friend's nudity. "You know I can't run as fast as you, Sariah, no matter how hard I try!"

"Fact!" Her friend—presumably Sariah—pumped a fist in the air before leaping forward. One moment, she had rich reddish-brown skin with a thick curtain of black hair falling halfway down her back. In the next, she was a stunning silvery wolf. Her large fangs peeked out as she yipped in that adorably doggy way, beckoning her friends to follow. In the next moment, the remaining shifters, one girl and two boys, stripped out of their clothing and transformed into big, beautiful wolves as well. They took off running, playfully chasing one another.

Was my mom a shifter? Was that what Mace was trying to show me?

"Aw, c'mon, you guys!" My mom threw up her arms. "No fair!"

My mom fell to the ground, limbs splayed. She fingered the chain around her neck, the same chain I wore right now, humming a soft tune.

She tilted her chin up to the sky, smiling at the moon above. "Sometimes I feel like you're the only one who gets me."

"There you are," a deep, sinister voice purred. "I'll admit, you gave me a good run, but I knew I'd find you soon enough."

My mom sat up, gasping as a man walked toward her, completely nude. I knew nudity among shifters was pretty much a non-event, but considering his threatening stance, it put me on edge when he stopped in front of her, my mom's face at eye level with the man's pelvis.

She stood up, walking backward as she held her hand out. "Stay back. I don't want to hurt you. I just want to be left alone."

"*You* don't want to hurt *me*?" The man laughed. "I could snap you in half, little girl." He snapped his fingers to punctuate his statement.

The constellations seemed to shift above their heads, as if the heavens were angry.

Mace whimpered as the vision faded.

"What the fuck?" I shook my head clear of the vision. "What happened to her, Mace? Bring me back!"

My familiar whimpered and sunk her head, quickly easing into a deep slumber, as if the vision wiped her out.

"What did you see?" Alexei gently nudged me.

I looked up at him, feeling hopeless. "She was with a pack of shifters and then..."

"Then *what?*"

"Then... I think someone attacked her. It cut out before I could be sure, but I know he *wanted* to hurt her. I could *feel* it. I think he may have been one of those collectors Jade mentioned."

Alexei's eyes thinned to slits. "I won't let anyone harm you. We may not have all the answers right now, but that's one thing I can guarantee."

I knew he wanted to reassure me, but I wasn't so sure. I had so many questions running through my head my brain hurt. How did my mom get away from that man? To go to college where she'd met my dad and eventually got married? Did any bad guys know she had a child? And if so, have they been looking for *me* this entire time?

TWENTY-FIVE

Alexei

IT WAS a struggle to get through day two of rush, Service Day. I was actually pretty proud of Alpha Nu's philanthropic efforts. We'd been raising money for affordable housing for years, and this year, our charitable organization was projected to raise the most money since my father attended Redwood. But everything that I'd learned about Nicole distracted me. Knowing that she was potentially in danger made me anxious. My wolf was ready to stage a mutiny if we were kept apart for much longer.

I knew in my gut that Nicole was important. That Jade woman mentioned Nicole's mom was one of a kind, which instantly put a target on her back. Rare supernaturals were coveted for their abilities by huntsmen—collectors who either caged them for personal use or sold them off to the highest bidders. My own father had an obsession with a supe that could turn everything it touched to indium, a metal that's vital to the world's economy. If Nicole's mom truly was extraordinary, that meant Nicole had to have something special in her DNA. Even if it was a recessive gene, she could still be considered valuable.

"You seem distracted," Corbin whispered to me while the head of philanthropy spoke about our organization to a crowd of pledges.

"I'm worried about Nicole," I whispered back. "I know she has her familiar, but…"

I'd told him everything I learned, because I knew I could trust him to help keep Nicole safe.

Corbin nodded. "I get it, dude. If it helps, Juniper assured me that she'd keep an eye on Nicole."

"When did she say that?"

"Last night when she broke up with me."

Juniper had broken up with him? Christ, I was an asshole. I'd been so wrapped up in my own shit that I hadn't even realized he was upset. I looked at my best friend's face, trying to find any evidence he had a rough night. Strangely, there wasn't any.

"Are you okay?"

He shrugged. "I think she did some bullshit spell

to make this *easier* on me. I don't feel anything *at all*. Kind of makes it worse, if I'm being honest. Like it was all a joke."

I patted him on the back, feeling sorry for the guy. "That blows, man."

"Tell me about it. I'm glad I know now, though. It would have sucked to get even further involved. It would have never worked anyway. You know as well as I do that I have to find a nice wolf shifter to keep my parents happy." The bitterness in his tone was something I could definitely relate to. It fucking sucked that we were tied to these responsibilities.

I once asked my father why non-wolf shifters could mate with whoever they wanted, but wolves couldn't. He told me it was because wolves were the most superior shifters—the top of the shifter food chain—and it was imperative we protect the purity of our bloodlines. Now, I wouldn't say I disagreed with him about wolves being the best, but there were plenty of other formidable shifters in existence. For example, a grizzly shifter could cause quite a bit of destruction with one swipe of its sharp claws. Any of the big cats had hunting skills so well honed they could rival a pack of wolves any day. A dragon could raze an entire village with one spray of fire from its powerful jaws and swallow a man whole. But the difference between them and us was quantity. As of the most recent census data, there were twenty wolf shifters in this world for every one non-wolf shifter. We gave new meaning to strength in numbers.

The older I got, the more glaringly obvious my father's prejudices became. On the rare occasion someone left our pack because they disagreed with our laws, they were essentially dead in my father's eyes. His own cousin, Malcolm—his childhood best friend—left the pack because he fell in love with a witch. When she got pregnant, my father demanded she either "get rid of it" or Malcolm formally disowned their baby. As alpha, he expected his cousin's compliance. But what he got instead was his cousin's withdrawal from the pack. The last I heard, they had three kids, none of which inherited their father's wolf. To *my* father, those children were abominations. He blamed people like his cousin for the genetic mutation that was now running through our lines. More and more full-blooded wolf shifters were being born without an animal counterpart, and that made my dad *furious*.

Corbin waved me off. "I'll be fine. We need to focus on Nicole right now, anyway. I'm worried about her."

I tried not to feel jealous. In the beginning of all of this, I was practically shoving Corbin at Nicole with the hopes that it would distract me from my own feelings. Now, a small part of me was worried she liked him more. She certainly couldn't deny our physical attraction, but Nicole seemed much more at ease around my beta than she'd ever been with me.

"You don't... you don't have *feelings* for her, right?" God, I felt lame as fuck for even having to ask.

"I *feel* like she's our future luna." The conviction in his tone eased my insecurities. "I want to protect her and support her in the same way I support you."

I breathed a sigh of relief. I'd fucked up so much that I wasn't even sure I deserved Nicole anymore, and I certainly couldn't act on my feelings until I navigated through everything that was threatening us.

I felt stuck and hopeless, and for an alpha tasked with the responsibility of always caring for and protecting his pack, it was a painful situation to be in.

"I can't stand being away from her. I know she's not far, but my wolf needs eyes on her. Physical confirmation she's okay. All these unknown risks on top of the shit with my father are driving me crazy."

"She's okay right now," Corbin murmured. "Beta Phi's philanthropy event was this morning, and she's at Kappa Zeta with Juniper now."

This was news to me. Was Nicole seriously considering joining the witches' house? She must be. A pledge rarely bothered taking part in a house's events past day one unless that house was a contender.

"Oh." For some reason, I was disappointed. I really wanted Nicole to be in Beta Phi. Not only was it her dream, but it would make it easier to watch over her. "I really need to figure out a way to get her into Beta Phi. And why do you know Nicole's whereabouts when I don't?"

"Because clearly, your mate adores me and wants me to be in the know." Corbin smirked when I glared. "Also... June may have mentioned she would be there when we spoke last night. Enough about my shitty love life, let's talk more about getting your mate into the Beta Phi house."

I pinched the bridge of my nose. "It wouldn't be an easy process. Mara would have to petition the council to allow a human. Not only would that take a lot of time, but I doubt any of them would change the rules for her."

Corbin patted me on the shoulder. "Good thing I've already been working on it."

I snapped my attention to him. "What?"

"I might have written a letter to the council a few days ago, posing as my sister. I also may have included Nicole's letter of recommendation from Rebecca Graham. Everyone knows the Greenwood pack is loaded with cash and resources. The council wouldn't want to piss their luna off, and I kind of used that to my advantage."

I could have kissed him. "Are you serious?"

"Yep." My best friend nodded. "Honestly, Nicole did most of the work by getting such a powerful shifter's approval. I just... used a little leverage to expedite things. Got a reply this morning that if Nicole gets voted in, she's golden. Now we just have to convince Mara to let her in."

My spirits dimmed a little at that. Navigating Mara's mood swings was damn near impossible at times. I supposed I could use the angle that Nicole's father was very important to the pack, but my own father would be livid if he found out I went behind his back like this. I couldn't risk doing that, because he would question why I would put my neck on the line for a human. If he looked too closely... Nicole and I would be fucked. My father may not have known first-hand what a mating bond felt like, but he was smart enough to recognize the signs if he paid attention.

"I need to talk to my father. He needs to believe that if Nicole doesn't get into Beta Phi, then her father will want to leave and won't cooperate with his research."

Corbin nodded. "Agreed. And once you have Pack Daddy's approval, you'll be able to order Mara to let her in. It'll be easier since the council has already approved. I don't envy you, though."

"I seriously hate it when you call my father that."

"Which is exactly why I do it," Corbin beamed.

"You're a shithead," I grumbled.

Corbin hooked an arm over my shoulder, pulling me into him. "Ah, but you'd be lost without me."

He was right. As much as I'd like to believe I could handle everyone by myself, my beta had proven the opposite was true since Nicole walked into my life. Corbin's goofy charm softened her. When I had a tendency to behave like an ass because the bond with my mate compelled me to react emotionally, Corbin was there to be the voice of reason. He was so much better with human relations than I'd ever been.

Because until recently, you believed humans weren't worthy, my inner voice reminded me.

Talk about learning a lesson the hard way.

Although... maybe my mate wasn't so human after all. Juniper was right before; everything about Nicole *did* reek of human. But with Nicole's godmother's recent revelations, along with the visions of her birth mother, my gut was telling me something far bigger was at play. Something so far out of the realm of possibility I couldn't even imagine what we were dealing with.

I groaned. "I guess I should schedule a meeting with my father."

"I don't envy you, brother."

"There'll be many more tough conversations in

my future when I'm the official leader of the pack." I shrugged. "Pussying out isn't an option."

"Speaking of pussy…" Corbin waggled his brows. "Maybe I should drop by our not-so-friendly shifter sorority after this and see if anyone wants to console me. What's that saying? *To get over someone, you have to get under someone else?* I wouldn't mind letting a pretty she-wolf ride my cock all night."

I side-eyed him. "I thought you said you *weren't* upset about Juniper?"

"I'm *not* bummed," he insisted. "But I know I *would* be if June hadn't put that spell on me. And in retrospect, I know I wasn't exactly being discreet, following my purple-haired infatuation around like a lovesick puppy. I can use that to my advantage, ya know? Chicks are suckers for brokenhearted dudes."

"So… you're going to *fake* having a broken heart so you can get your dick wet?"

"*Exactly*." He nodded. "Pretty genius, right? I'd ask if you wanted to accompany me, but I'm guessing you have better places to be."

That was for sure. I'd felt like I was crawling out of my skin all day without Nicole. We both had busy days, but I was counting down the minutes until I could show up at her dorm and have some alone time with her. Last night, it went against every instinct I had to leave her, especially after seeing how rocked she was by what she'd learned. I wanted to comfort her. Protect her. But she wanted space to process, and I needed to respect that. But now that I had confirmation Nicole actually had a shot at getting into Beta Phi—provided I could convince my father—I couldn't wait to tell her the news. She needed something to look forward to, and selfishly, I wanted to be the one to make her smile. It drove my wolf insane that my best friend and Nicole's familiar could easily bring her brief moments of joy, yet more often than not, the only emotions I solicited from her were of the pissed off variety.

Or arousal.

I puffed my chest out, smiling to myself at the thought. Whether or not Nicole liked it, attraction was one issue we definitely didn't have.

"Oh shit, you're thinking about her naked right now, aren't you?" Corbin mimicked gagging. "Chill, dude. I don't want your boner anywhere near me."

I turned my head toward my friend in confusion, wondering what the hell he was talking about. "What?"

Corbin snorted. "The look on your face, man. It's pretty obvious where your thoughts just went."

I frowned. Was I being that obvious? I prided myself on my ability to remain stoic in any situation. It was the mark of a great alpha. Yet, ever since I met

Nicole, I seemed to be dropping the ball more and more.

The question was... why wasn't I as bothered about that as I should've been?

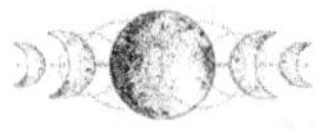

My father was reluctant to meet with me. He had never been a friendly man, always focusing on pack business and his ambitions. He penciled in holidays and forgot plenty of birthdays. My own mother had to send herself flowers on their anniversary.

But there was one thing my father always made time for—looking for an excuse to tell me how pathetic I was. He loved scheduling meetings so he could critique and criticize every aspect of my job. So when I asked if we could discuss rush events, he happily obliged.

When I stepped off the elevator onto the executive level, my dress shoes clacked along the marble flooring. Like most shifters, my father lived an extravagant life. Having the network that we did allowed him such luxuries. This building was in the center of town, and on the top floor, my dad had a bird's-eye view of all the people he controlled down in Ridgeview. Everything about this space was meant to intimidate from its cool monochrome color scheme, oversized leather furnishings, and floor-to-ceiling windows.

Brenda, my dad's secretary, greeted me with dark circles under her eyes. The poor woman looked exhausted, but that was no surprise. My father never kept the same secretary for long. He was demeaning, had unreasonable expectations, and lashed out when people couldn't accomplish the impossible. You could always tell a lot about a man by the way he treated his subordinates, and every direct report my dad ever had was forced to work overtime and do whatever he'd demanded without question.

"He's waiting for you." She was frantically shuffling through papers. "Can you give him this? He wanted the research from the university, but it's not exactly what he's looking for. He's already yelled at me three times today, and I don't think I can handle another round."

I gave her a sympathetic look. This lady was going to need extensive therapy after leaving this job.

"Of course." I grabbed the papers, scanning the first page as I walked to his personal office.

At the top was David Fairweather's name and a list of his past projects. It made me nervous to know my father was so focused on my mate's dad. When Jones

Koenig got an idea in his head, he was happy to bulldoze over anyone who got in his way. I paused midstride when I read a paragraph about mutated genes.

Subject has a genetic defect which makes surviving childbirth impossible. Chromosomal mutation is accelerated.

My stomach clenched. Nicole's mother died in childbirth. Was she the subject? I scanned the document but couldn't find any mention of her name.

"Stop hovering at the door and come in," my father barked.

He could probably hear my erratic breathing. Twisting the knob, I let myself in and took on a false sense of confidence. My father could smell weakness a mile away, and being anything less than perfect was unforgivable to him.

"Thank you for meeting with me." I was careful to maintain an even tone. "Here are the documents you requested from your secretary." I crossed his office, stopping in front of the large desk to hand the papers over.

He ripped them out of my hand. "I'm going to have to fire her. She has no backbone and can't handle criticism."

"You know, Dad, just a thought... but your assistant turnover probably wouldn't be so high if you learned to exercise a bit more patience and a little less aggression."

The tic in my father's square jaw pulsed as his face reddened. An angry vein bisected his forehead, looking like it was about to burst. "If I wanted your advice on how to run *my* company, I'd ask for it, *son*."

Considering I was here to essentially ask him for a favor, challenging him probably wasn't the smartest move; however, if done correctly, challenging the man had the potential to actually earn his respect. And I sure as shit needed that respect if I had any hope of getting him to sign off on this.

"Speaking of your company… I have a proposal for you."

His furious expression instantly morphed into one of curiosity. "Oh? And what proposal is that?"

I threw the envelope that was in my other hand on his desk. "Take a look."

My dad pulled out the folded piece of stationery, taking a few moments to read the letter of recommendation. "Why am I looking at this?"

"Because I want you to sign off on an exception to allow Nicole Fairweather into Beta Phi."

He laughed as if I had just said the funniest thing on the planet. When he finally caught his breath, he continued. "And why on earth would I do that? She's a *human*."

Not necessarily. But I wasn't about to tell him that.

"Because that letter"—I jerked my chin toward the paper now lying on his desk—"is from Rebecca Graham. And Mrs. Graham seems to think Nicole would be an excellent addition to the sorority. Correct me if I'm wrong, but we do a lot of business with the Greenwood pack, yeah? But a majority of those contracts are up for renewal. I heard they were entertaining offers from the Lowell pack; therefore, those contracts may be in jeopardy."

"Yes," my father gritted. "And?"

"*And*, if allowing Nicole into Beta Phi pleased Mrs. Graham, wouldn't that be good for *our* pack? Not to mention how much it would please Dr. Fairweather. You did say he was important to the university, did you not? And that we needed to keep him happy?"

"Get to the point, Alexei," he snapped. "She's a fucking human! Even if I wanted to make an exception —which I don't—a human cannot live in a shifter sorority house! With the glitch in the containment spell, we'd be risking exposure."

Interesting...

I wondered if my father heard about Nicole being spelled. I wouldn't put it past Mara to run right to him, looking for brownie points. Either he genuinely had no idea Nicole knew everything about the supernatural population or he was testing me. Either way, I needed to give him this information if I had any hope of getting him on board with this plan.

"Well, it seems as if you haven't heard yet, but that problem has already been addressed thanks to a meddling warlock who dropped a reveal spell into Nicole's coffee one morning. She knows *all* about supes. And she's handling it impressively well. She even ran with the pack during a rush event. And since we're not allowed to interfere with magic, having Mara wipe her memory wasn't an option."

My father steepled his fingers, absorbing my words. "I was wondering how long it would take you to man up and tell me."

"I didn't feel it was relevant before now. I'm keeping a close eye on the situation, and nothing alarming has happened." I shrugged, acting like I wasn't freaking out on the inside.

Make no mistake, under Jones Koenig's polished exterior lay a complete savage. It was something I *never* forgot.

"Of course it's fucking relevant. What happened to staying away from her? If you fuck this up for me—"

"It's not like she wouldn't have found out. Dr. Fairweather can't work on the missing wolf gene without knowing the full scope of the project. And I can keep a better eye on Nicole if I *don't* stay away from her. I'm surprised you didn't think this through better." I was bullshitting my father, but I learned it was better to "fake it 'til you make it" sometimes. "What exactly is your plan here?"

He scoffed. "I don't answer to you."

I pressed my hands on the top of his desk, challenging him with my stare. "I'm the future alpha, *father*. I have a right to know what's happening at my school. If you want my support, then you should include me in your plans."

Dad's lip curled. "We gave a reveal spell to Dr. Fairweather on his first night here so he could quickly get to work, but his body rejected it. I have a team of witches trying to figure out why. I've flat out *told him* about our people, but that was a giant waste of time. It's like he hadn't heard a word I said, even though I *know* he did. He just stood there with a blank expression. At first, I thought shock was to blame. He is a scientist, after all, and science people like facts. But the moment my supernatural crash course ended, David's awareness returned, and he continued speaking as if the prior ten minutes hadn't happened. I've never seen anything like it before. It's infuriating!" My father swiped his hand across his desk, knocking everything to the ground.

"Maybe this is another glitch in the containment spell," I suggested. "Maybe it's working a little too well with some people, but not well enough with others."

"Impossible." My father shook his head. "Maybe I'd consider that if he tried directing me to the nearest coffee shop, but that wasn't the case. And the fact the good doctor's mental faculties returned *the second* I stopped trying to expose our people tells me there's other magic in play. *Stronger* magic."

I thought about the secrecy spell Nicole's godmother mentioned. Could David be under the influence of something similar?

My eyebrows rose. "So, if you suspect magic is to blame, can't your witches locate the source and reverse it?"

My dad employed some seriously powerful witches. If they couldn't pinpoint the problem, could anyone?

"I said *they're trying!*" His face was turning purple now. "I suspect someone doesn't want us to find a solution to our dormant wolf problem *or* the wacky scientist knows something that he shouldn't. Something that could be extremely damaging if exposed. I want to put *his* brain in a lab, but he's one of the most brilliant fucking scientists in the world! He's the only man I've found who could possibly find the solution to help our people. I'd torture it out of him if I thought it would help, but my witches genuinely believe he's bound somehow. No amount of torture would unlock such a spell if it were powerful enough."

It took all my self-control not to gape at my father. He was unraveling. After learning what I had last night, I thought my father's suspicions were possible. Did Nicole's mother do this? Jade?

"What about Dr. Fairweather's research leading up to this point? What was he working on?"

"He made promising discoveries in genetic mutations, but it's like he's been stuck on the same dead-end theory, never progressing. I thought it was because he didn't have the proper resources, so I brought him here, but since his body rejected the reveal spell, I'm not so sure." My father stood and started pacing the length of his desk. "I have many people counting on his research. I've made promises and—"

"And if his brain is locked, you can't deliver," I interrupted.

I had a bad feeling about this. If my suspicions were correct, then Dr. Fairweather had information that could put those he loved at risk. Why else would someone put such a strong lock on his mind? David and Nicole needed to get far away from here.

"Exactly!" Dad yelled. "Why do you think I'm so angry about this?! I have witches working around the clock. Until we can figure out what he knows, we're giving him pieces of the puzzle, but he's not comprehending all of it."

"Spells that focus on the mind can be dangerous," I countered. "You don't want to damage him for good."

"Obviously," Dad sneered. "But what choice do I have? I've pulled records for every goddamn person he's ever worked with. They're all humans. Who could have possibly done this?"

I swallowed. Dad didn't know about Nicole's mom, and we needed to keep it that way. "Maybe it's best to send them away? It seems like a dead end." The idea of being away from Nicole was tearing me up inside, but I didn't trust my father. He was losing his shit. "I think Nicole would happily encourage the move. She probably couldn't get away from all the supes at this university fast enough."

"Of course you would suggest that," Dad spat. "You're always so quick to give up. But you *do* make a good point." He stroked his jaw and paused his pacing to think.

"About sending them away?"

"No. Nicole's mind wasn't blocked. Whoever blocked Dr. Fairweather didn't bother blocking his daughter. Perhaps they didn't see a need for it. But if I bring Nicole into the fold and perhaps give the illusion that she's helping us and sharing her father's research, the witch that made the spell would come running to save her."

No. This wasn't what I wanted at all. I needed to get my father away from Nicole, not encourage him to bring her closer.

"I'm not sure that would work. You said it yourself, she's a fashion major. She doesn't know anything about her father's research."

My father's eyes narrowed. "Weren't *you* the one recently boasting about her academic accomplishments at the Meet and Greet?"

Shit.

"I was just trying to compensate for your rudeness." I returned his glare. "You were upsetting her father."

"We both know that his worthless, ignorant daughter has no clue what he's working on, but others don't know that. Let her into the fold. Tell Mara I want Nicole to join Beta Phi, and I'll send out a press release in the Wolf Times that the first human is going to be accepted. I'll make sure they discuss her father's research and how she'll be continuing his legacy with a breakthrough revelation on the missing wolf gene. Whoever wants to keep his secrets locked up will come here to stop her, and I'll have them right in my grasp." Dad clenched his fist before pounding the table, making the mahogany crack.

I flinched. We still didn't know what Nicole was, and the last thing she needed was to be broadcasted to the entire supernatural community.

"Dad, I–"

"*Do it.* I'm done discussing this with you."

My dad fell back into his chair, turning his back to me.

I'd been dismissed.

I felt sick to my stomach as I left his office. I achieved what I came here to do—Nicole would be accepted as the first human in Redwood's Beta Phi. But now she was in more danger than ever before.

And it was all my fucking fault

CHAPTER
TWENTY-SIX

Nicole

ACCORDING to my good friend Google, day three of rush was the funnest part of the whole process. It was your opportunity to really get a feel for what being a sister in each house was like. I had been looking forward to it all week. Thankfully, my classes had kept me so busy the weekend was here before I knew it. Since I had no intention of joining the fae or vampire houses, there were only two sororities left to consider. Beta Phi was my first stop of the day, though I couldn't really say I had *fun*, considering hardly anyone spoke to me the entire time. I mostly just stood there in my pretty pink dress and strappy sandals—thank God my blisters had healed in time to wear them—and watched the other girls interact with one another. Mace was by my side the entire time, which seemed to confuse a lot of the shifters. Some of them were downright uneasy, just like Corbin had been, which made me laugh. What kind of wolf shifter was afraid of a wolf? You'd think they had some sort of automatic brotherhood or what not, but there was no mistaking those few shifters' discomfort around my familiar.

I smiled so hard my face hurt as Macey and I approached Kappa Zeta, the remaining contender on my list of possible sororities to join. Let's face it, my odds of getting into Beta Phi were slim to none, but even if I miraculously got in, I didn't think I'd accept. If my visit to the witches' house went anything like the first night, I knew this was the right sorority for me. I'd had my heart set on Beta Phi nearly my entire life, but I had to accept the fact that plans change. Being in a sorority was about building a sense of community. Finding people who accepted you for who you were. Forging lifetime friendships. A true sisterhood, like my mom had.

I rubbed the locket resting in my clavicle as I climbed the steps to the haunted mansion. Mace rubbed against me affectionately and let out an excited bark as Juniper answered the door.

"Nicole!" June held her arms out, pulling me into a brief hug. "Welcome!" She knelt down so she was at eye level with my wolf and seemed to have some sort of silent communication with Mace. "Ah, I see you two are bonding nicely. I'm glad."

I tilted my head to the side in confusion. "Did you just communicate telepathically with my wolf?"

Juniper grinned. "It's my gift. My twin has visions of his future demon spawn, and I can talk to animals. It's why I get along with familiars so well. If you ask me, I got the *much* better end of the stick. Sometimes, when a familiar bond is taking a while to form, I can serve as a bridge between the person and animal. Help it along, so to speak."

"Whoa," I breathed out. "That would be really cool."

"For sure." She stood up, stepping aside to allow us entry. "But I can see that's unnecessary between you and this beautiful girl."

"I think we're getting along quite nicely," I agreed before changing the subject. "I'm excited for my tour of the house."

"Good! I'll give you a private tour and tell you all about Kappa Zeta. I truly think you'll love it here." June looped her arm through mine and pulled me close. She smelled like roses and spice. "Here is the main sitting room. We watch movies and hang out here. We also have quiet study hall hours and game nights." She guided me through a room with dark red walls and black antique furniture. Art work of different flowers and herbs covered the walls, as well as photos of past graduating classes. In the center of the room was a large table with chairs and a pair of witches playing a card game.

"Love the vibe of this place. It's kind of spooky but inviting."

"That's what we're going for. We have a few full-time ghosts that reside in the basement next to the sex dungeon."

I stopped.

Like full-stopped. My feet practically skidded on the ground. "Sex dungeon?" I wasn't a judgmental person, but I didn't want to live somewhere with *any* kind of dungeon, especially a sex one.

Juniper stopped walking and stared at me, her eyes mischievous as she barked out a harsh laugh. "Kidding. It's actually a storage closet, but I've caught so many girls bringing their partners down there for kinky times, I call it that for fun. You're so easy to rattle when it comes to sex, aren't you? It's adorable."

"Right." I blew out a puff of air, suddenly feeling like a blushing virgin, even though I wasn't one. "Sorry... I'm not a prude, I swear. And I would *never* yuck someone else's yum. I'm just not used to people being so open about their sex lives. My time at Redwood so far has been... informative."

"This is college, after all." Juniper winked. "No better time to explore your sexuality, am I right? Lucky for you, you have a virile shifter sniffing around you all the time. I'd bet he'd love to tutor you on Kama Sutra."

My entire body flushed, thinking of sexy tutoring sessions with Alexei.

Nope. Not going there.

I shook off my lusty thoughts as Juniper dragged me to the other end of the house.

"So..." she whispered. "Did you get a hold of your mother's friends? Did you find out who was behind that protection charm?"

I rubbed the locket between my finger and thumb. "Um... I talked to her, but—"

"Bah!" a deep voice shouted, interrupting us. "Out of my kitchen!"

Juniper and I stepped aside as a girl hurried past us, and then into the aforementioned kitchen.

An elf, who was so tall she nearly reached the ceiling, with white hair and a large, bumpy nose stood inside the room. The deep wrinkles in her skin were pale, as if she had never left the house.

"Nicole, meet Mitsy, our house-elf," Juniper said. "She's been here for ages. I've tried telling her she can retire, but the old woman refuses."

"Bah. You'd all starve without me. I like my kitchen. It's MINE. MINE MINE MINE." She waved her hands at Juniper before going back to work. "You get out of my kitchen, too!"

My mouth watered as I spotted five different pies spread out on the counter. I'd never seen an elf before, but my mind-fuck told me that they were loyal creatures who were very territorial of their home and work. Once they picked a place to be, they happily stayed there for the entirety of their life.

Juniper smiled indulgently. "Mitsy is lovely. Just don't try kicking her out of the kitchen, and say you like whatever she cooks. Of course, you're welcome to make your own food and store groceries in one of the refrigerators, but just know she will hover and take over if she doesn't think you're doing it right. I've been making ramen my entire life, but apparently I'm not very good at it, because she steals the ingredients out of my hands before I can even plop it in the microwave. Oh! And she thinks microwaves are portals for demons, so she purposefully breaks the one we have from time to time." Juniper whispered the next part. "I keep one in my room."

"I heard that," Mitsy roared as we walked toward the enormous staircase, but June ignored her.

"On the top floor is our ritual room. It's where we perform group spells. You won't be allowed to even step foot in that room until you've completed a spell safety course. Spells are tricky, and sometimes even the wrong perfume can throw it off."

I was hoping to see the ritual room but didn't want to mess anything up. "Why?"

"We once had a freshman that liked to spritz lavender on her pillow to help her sleep. She forgot to shower before a ritual, and the scent messed with the spell. Instead of acing our finals, we all forgot everything we'd learned that semester. It was a mess. The smallest thing can throw the magic off, so we have to be extra careful."

I nodded. "A spell safety course sounds fun."

"It's not," Juniper replied honestly. "It's worse than drivers ed."

"Noted."

We traveled up the stairs, and she pointed out photos of important alumnae. I was surprised how many CEOs Kappa Zeta had produced. I supposed running a business was easier when you had magic on your side.

"Here are the bedrooms. We will complete a compatibility spell to pair you with someone who will best suit your personality. We also take into consideration your familiars and make sure you both have accommodations. Since Mace will need room, we'd make sure to give you a suite with a balcony so she can sit outside. Open air is so important to her."

I scratched Mace behind the ears and smiled. Everything about Kappa Zeta seemed perfect. Not only would I fit in, but there was room for Mace, too.

A girl with silver hair and sleeves tattooed down each of her arms stepped out of one of the rooms, smiling when she spotted us. "Hey! I'm Aurora! You're pledging, right?"

"I am," I confirmed. "It's nice to meet you. I'm Nicole."

"Aurora is a sophomore this year," Juniper stated. "She also recently met her familiar, an adorable kitty named Ralph."

"Ralph?" I laughed. "I don't know if I've ever met a cat named Ralph before."

Aurora brushed her pixie bangs to the side. "At first, I named him Toby, but he didn't hesitate to express his displeasure."

As if he sensed us talking about him, a striped ginger cat came padding out of the bedroom, weaving between her legs.

I instantly placed a hand on Mace, preparing to hold her back, but she stood there calmly like the sweet girl she is.

"Uh... if I lived here, my familiar wouldn't be a problem for your familiar, would she?"

"No way," Aurora assured me. "They all get along just fine. Ralph's bestie, Lynx, is a parrot."

Mace leaned down, nostrils flaring as she sniffed the newcomer. When Ralph the cat gave Macey face nuzzles, all three of us said, "Awwww."

Juniper pressed a hand to her heart. "See, Nicole. You and Macey will fit in at Kappa Zeta just fine."

Yeah. I think we will.

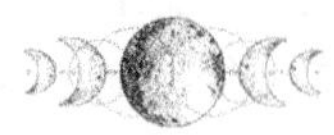

"ALEXEI? WHAT ARE YOU DOING HERE?"

"I needed to see you." He walked into my dorm room while running his hands through his hair nervously.

Mace sat up from her position by her food bowls and glared at him. I was about to shut the door, but Corbin placed his hand out, stopping me.

"Hey there, hot stuff. Can I come in?"

"Knock it off, Corbin," Alexei snapped. "I'm already on edge as it is."

Corbin's grin tightened as he eased himself inside. "I'm just here to see if Macey wants to go out with me for a bit? We need to get to know one another better, and wolves need to run. I was hoping if we hung out while I was in my wolf form, she'd warm up to me."

My lips twitched. "Are you asking my friend out on a date, Corbin? Won't Juniper mind?"

"What?!" he balked. "*No!* That's... I don't even have words for how wrong that is on *so* many levels."

"What's the big deal?" I teased. "She's a wolf... *you're* a wolf."

"I'm a *wolf shifter*!" The apples of Corbin's cheeks reddened. "Big, *big* difference! You know we *never* have sex in our animal forms, right? It's humanoid pussy for me or *no* pussy. The same applies for any oral or backdoor action. *No exceptions.*"

I was pretty sure Macey just snorted in amusement at the same time I did. And I *did* know shifters never banged while they were animals, but I couldn't resist riling him up.

"Also..." he added. "June dumped my ass because I caught feelings, so..."

My face fell. "Oh, Corbin. I'm sorry. I didn't know."

His shoulders lifted in a shrug. "It's okay. She slipped me a spell so I wouldn't get sad or whatever."

Ouch.

Sensing the poor boy desperately wanted me to change the subject, I looked over at my familiar. She still was giving Alexei the stink eye, but her tail was wagging. "What do you say, Mace? Want to go with Corbin?"

She tilted her nose up, the haughty expression on

her face making me giggle. She then growled at Alexei in warning before waltzing over to the door.

"I'll take that as a yes." Corbin scratched the back of his neck. "We'll be back in a couple of hours. If she decides to eat me or something equally brutal, please delete my internet search history."

I laughed. "Not it!"

Alexei rolled his eyes at his friend. "Go. I'll text you when we're done."

"Sounds good, boss." Corbin nodded, patting his thigh. "C'mon, pretty doggy. Let's go have some fun under the moon."

Mace howled excitedly when Corbin said the last word, scaring the crap out of a girl coming out of the room across from mine.

I watched the pair as they walked down the hall, my familiar stopping in front of the door leading to the staircase, nudging her snout at the handle. Cypress Hall had an elevator, but Macey seemed to prefer the stairs, and Corbin went with it. Once they were out of sight, I walked back into my room, closing the door behind me.

"What's going on?" I asked Alexei. "Why do you seem so agitated?"

"I needed to see you. You've been blowing me off all week, and I couldn't wait any longer."

"You said that already," I reminded him, refusing

to feel guilty for needing space. The longer we were apart, the more I ached to be near him. If this *just friends* thing was going to work, I needed to condition myself to not reach out to him every time I wanted to. "But you didn't say *why* you needed to see me so badly."

"Can we sit?" Alexei brushed his dark hair out of his eyes as he dropped onto the edge of my full-size bed. When I first moved in, there was your standard lumpy twin bed, but a new pillow top mattress magically appeared one day while I was eating lunch in the dining hall. I suspected it was one of Alexei's anonymous gifts, but he refused to take credit for it.

I eyed the mattress warily. "Is that code for something dirty?"

His brown eyes widened, as if it hadn't even occurred to him before now, but in the next moment, Alexei's gaze was hooded. "Do you *want* it to be code for something dirty?"

His words conjured an image of Alexei's muscular body stretched over mine, his full lips sucking gently on the delicate skin along my neck.

Yes?

Wait... most definitely *no*. Friends. *We were supposed to be friends,* I reminded myself.

Then I imagined him working his way down my torso...

Maybe?

Crap. Stupid pheromones.

I blew out a breath, shaking it off, but I was pretty sure he saw me shiver. "Alexei. You looked upset when you first arrived. Why?"

That seemed to make him snap out of his lusty haze. "I have news."

"What kind of news?"

He sighed. "I wanted it to be good news, but now... now I'm not so sure."

"Can we not talk in code?" I requested. "It's late. I've had a long day, and I want to get a good night's rest for the last day of rush tomorrow."

"They gave your father the reveal spell," Alexei forced out.

"Why didn't you start with that?!" I shot across my room to pull on my sweater and tuck my feet into my slides. "He's probably freaking out right now. I need to—"

"It didn't work, Nicole." Alexei frowned. "The spell didn't work, and when they told him about it, he tuned it out. Went total *space case*, then acted like he couldn't hear a thing. My father is working with witches who think your dad has a block on his mind."

"Why would he have a block?" My throat suddenly felt clogged.

"I don't know. It could be related to his research?"

Alexei theorized. "Someone doesn't want us to know what he's working on..." Alexei pinched the bridge of his nose. "And my father wants to use *you* to draw them out."

My heart started racing. Was my mother somehow responsible for the block? If Mr. Koenig wanted to talk to the person responsible, then he'd be sorely disappointed. More and more, I felt like we weren't meant to be here.

"How does he plan on doing that?" I choked out.

"He's letting you into Beta Phi. I just got back from talking to Mara, and she was pissed. Threw a fucking Louis Vuitton shoe at my head and told me I'd rue the day."

"What does Beta Phi have to do with this?" I knew I was supposed to be excited about getting in, but I'd accepted that I didn't feel *welcome* there. After going through rush, I didn't think that house was the right fit for me.

"He wants to use it to get some publicity. Let everyone know you're here and you're helping the university with your father's research. He wants to fucking put *you* in the spotlight so the person who blocked your father's mind comes out of hiding."

I blew out a puff of air. "Shit."

Alexei gave me a guilty look. "It's my fault. All of this is my fucking fault."

"I think my father and I should leave."

I didn't want to become a pawn in Alexei's father's game. The more I learned, the more I realized that we seriously needed to get away from here as quickly as possible. I wrapped my arms around myself and looked down at the ground. It had only been a few weeks since we met, but I already felt close to Alexei. I was confused about our mate bond and what the differences between us meant for our future, but I still hated knowing that we'd never get the chance to figure our shit out.

If I left, did that mean I'd never see him again? Would he forget me? Move on?

"My father won't allow that," Alexei murmured.

"I have to try."

Alexei got up and placed both hands on my shoulders, his espresso eyes peering into mine with determination. "If you try, he *will* stop you. Once my father becomes interested in something, he won't stop. He has investors funding your father's research and witches working around the clock to figure out the block."

"We should have never come here." My eyes filled with tears.

"It wouldn't have mattered. My father would have dragged you here kicking and screaming if you refused. Nothing stops him when he puts his mind to something."

"So what do I do, Alexei?" I choked out.

"What do *we* do? We're in this together, Nicole. I will not abandon you when you need me more than ever."

I scoffed. "I appreciate the sentiment, but forgive me if I don't want to put much faith in... this." I gestured between us. "We're barely friends, and that was just a last ditch effort to stop us from fighting or fuck—"

Alexei closed the distance between us and grabbed me by the collar. His knuckles grazed my skin, and he jerked me forward. His lips hovered over mine, his eyes locked on me. "We're not fucking *friends*, Nicole. You're my *mate*. Which means I'll take care of you."

"Then take care of me, Alexei," I challenged him. "I'm so fucking lost. All of this is just driving me insane. I don't know what I am. I don't feel safe. I—"

"Know this," he whispered before slamming his lips to mine.

His caressing tongue was both demanding and tender. He swallowed my moans. He devoured my fears. Alexei kissed me like I was precious, like every atom, every cell, was worth chasing and cherishing. He pressed his forehead to mine. "I'll protect you, Nicole."

I kissed him again. Deeper. Hungrier. I sunk my teeth into his bottom lip and let my hands roam his chest, shoulders and back. Wrapping his hand around my thigh, he helped me hike my leg up, aligning us so perfectly that I gasped.

"You're so fucking perfect." He kneaded my ass as I sucked on his neck. And when I moved my body like a wave against his hard muscles, he broke away from me and guided me back to the mattress, laying me down with his strong arms before kissing me once more.

How did we even get to this point? One minute, we were discussing our parents, and the next, we were making out, frantically tearing at each other's clothes. The sweater I just put on was the first thing to go.

"Alexei," I panted as he broke our kiss, raising my arms up so he could remove my sleep tank. "Maybe this isn't such a good idea."

"Don't care." He pulled his own shirt over his head in that stupidly sexy one-armed way guys do. His mocha-colored eyes fell to my naked chest, pupils dilating. "So fucking beautiful."

I lifted my butt as his fingertips slipped under the waistband of my pajama pants, pulling them down my legs in one fell swoop. Now I was dressed in nothing but a bright pink thong. "Are we moving on to friends with benefits?"

I moaned as Alexei kissed his way across my breasts, pulling a peaked tip into his mouth. His light stubble scraped my sensitive skin as he pulled away with a pop and sat back on folded knees.

God, speaking of beauty...

"We can pretend to be friends all we want, Nicole. But we both know that's not true. I told you, you're my *mate*. And after tonight, there's going to be no question about it."

Alexei was still wearing jeans, but there was plenty of bare skin on display to admire. His bronzed chest was wide with a small scattering of hair. Defined pecs were tipped in perfectly proportionate light brown nipples. I'd never really given any thought to that part of a man's anatomy before, but Alexei's were perfect.

Every physical part of him attracted me in the most primal way.

I bit my lip. "What exactly do you think is happening tonight that'll be so convincing?"

He gave me a sexy smile. "I think it'd be better if I *showed* you what I'm talking about."

I surreptitiously checked for drool as my gaze roamed his abdomen. The boy had a legit eight-pack, with a thick trail of dark hair disappearing beneath the denim he wore. There was no mistaking the bulge behind the zipper of those jeans, creating a gap between the material and Alexei's skin.

"What if I said I don't want you to show me?"

"The eye-fucking you've been doing for the last few minutes says otherwise," Alexei quipped. "But... if you actually wanted me to stop—at any time—just say the word. You know that, right? Contrary to popular belief, I'm not a fucking Neanderthal."

I nodded. "I know you'd never intentionally hurt me."

It was strange, because we met such a short time ago, but I had no doubt my statement was true. I was a firm believer that actions spoke louder than words, and while I didn't necessarily agree with the methods he employed all the time, I *did* believe Alexei was always acting in my best interest. I decided at that moment to see this through. I didn't know what the future held, but I knew if I had to walk away tomorrow, never being able to see Alexei again, I wanted the memory of his hands on me. I wanted to know what it felt like when our bodies were fused together.

Alexei's gaze roamed from my head to my toe with equal parts arousal and intrigue. Maybe I should've felt some sort of awkwardness being so exposed, but oddly enough, I was perfectly at ease.

"Please don't kick me in the balls when I ask you this, but I need to know."

Well, now *I* was intrigued. "I make no promises, but ask away."

I suppressed a laugh when Alexei scooted off the bed, standing at the foot of it.

"Just in case." He gave me a lopsided smile. "Have you done this before, Nicole?"

"Done *what*?" I lifted a brow.

I knew what he was alluding to, but if he was going to ask me something so personal, I was going to make him work for it.

Alexei groaned, looking to the ceiling for some divine guidance. "Are you a virgin?"

"No." My head slowly sliced from left to right.

"I don't know whether or not to be pissed off or relieved about that." He blew out a breath. "On one hand, the thought of anyone seeing you like this— touching you—drives me mad."

Ha! So much for not being a Neanderthal.

"But on the other hand?" I prompted.

"I'm sorta relieved because I don't know if I have it in me to be gentle right now. At least not the first time."

I lost my virginity to a guy named Xander, my boyfriend for a few months during senior year. Unsurprisingly, we broke up soon thereafter. I supposed since the thrill of the chase was no longer there, Xander lost interest. But quite frankly, I didn't care. I was underwhelmed at best as far as sex went. My trusty vibe gave me more pleasure than Xander ever could've, and I was in no hurry to hook up with another fumbling boy.

Until I met the man in front of me.

Something told me sex with Alexei Koenig would be *over*whelming, but in all the best ways. No blind fumbling with this alpha male.

Only one way to know for sure.

I curled my finger in a *come hither* gesture. "I'm not made of glass, Alexei. Show me what you've got."

A sultry grin stretched across his face. "Oh, I'm gonna show you, so hard, baby, you're gonna forget any other guy exists."

I could hardly wait.

TWENTY-SEVEN

Alexei

NICOLE SQUEALED AS I POUNCED. The mattress bounced as I landed on top of her, being careful not to crush her small frame with my weight. She spread her toned thighs on instinct, welcoming me into that heavenly space between her hips. The only thing separating me from officially claiming my mate was a tiny scrap of satin.

I propped myself up, looking into her eyes. "You sure? Because there's no turning back after this, Nicole. Resisting you has been nearly impossible from day one, but it'll be *literally* impossible. I mean it. There'll be no more of this *just friends* bullshit. If you tried to run, I'd find you. I would move fucking mountains to get to you. If you have any doubts, you need to tell me now. Because once I make you mine, you're *mine*. And I'm yours. No more back and forth."

She gasped as I pressed into her, the head of my dick teasing her entrance through her panties. "What about your father?"

"Fuck my father. Fuck *everyone* else. I'm not saying we should announce it to the world—the consequences are too great. Believe me, I'd love to shout it from every rooftop, but we need to remember who we're dealing with here. I won't risk your safety. But thankfully, I have an excuse to spend time with you in public now. And when it's just you and me, we will behave as mates in every sense of the word."

Nicole reached up and traced her finger along the edge of my jaw. "What about your pack? What about being alpha? You can't do that with me by your side. Regardless of whether I'm human... or something *else*, we know I'm not a *wolf*."

"If my pack won't accept you as their luna, I will walk away."

Her delicate brows crinkled. "Alexei... no. I don't want you to do that. This is something you've been working toward your whole life."

"It means *nothing* if I can't have you." I felt relieved as I said it out loud. "No matter what happens... with my pack, my dad, I will do everything in my power to be a man worthy of you, Nicole."

"This is crazy." Her blue eyes filled with tears. "We barely know each other."

"It doesn't matter." I shook my head. "It never does. We have time to learn the details. But the fates wouldn't have given us this gift if we weren't perfect for each other in every way. Set aside your human logic, Nicole. It has no place here." I pressed my palm over her left breast, feeling the steady beat of her heart. "Listen to this." I leaned down, pressing my lips against hers. "And this." She moaned as I dipped my tongue into her mouth, infusing our kiss with as much sincerity as I could muster.

I pulled away from her mouth, nibbling along her jaw and nipping at her neck, while I kneaded her tits, rubbing her pointed nipples between my forefingers and thumbs.

"*God, Alexei.*" Nicole writhed under my touch as I continued my journey south.

"I will worship you until the day I die." I placed an open-mouthed kiss on her hip bone. "But first and foremost, I need to taste you."

"You don't have to do that," Nicole panted. "I don't need you to..."

I scooted down a little more, nudging her thighs apart, hooking her knees over my shoulders as I focused on my target. Nicole groaned deep in her throat as I gave her one long lick down the center of her panties before pulling back, blowing warm air over the wet spot. "If you're about to tell me I don't have to eat your delicious pussy until your throat is raw from screaming my name, shut the fuck up, Nicole. With all due respect."

I teased the silky seam before grabbing the flimsy string over her hip with both hands and ripping it in half.

"What the hell?!" Nicole shrieked. "Was that necessary, you caveman?"

"Absolutely." I smirked, pulling the torn material away from her body and tossing it to the side. "Because it prevented me from doing this." I moaned as I got my first real taste of her cunt and growled, "Mine."

"Oh-praise-Jesus-Gucci-Prada-and-Versace!" Nicole screamed as I swiped my tongue over her slick flesh.

This woman was intoxicating. Infuriating. Intrinsically a part of my soul. I had no doubt she was as essential to my future happiness as I was to hers.

Determined to show her pleasure unlike any she'd ever known, I ate Nicole's pretty pussy like a starving man on death row. I licked and sucked and swirled my tongue as she squirmed beneath me, telling me how good it felt. Begging for it to never end. We groaned in unison as I inserted a finger, her walls gripping me tight. When I added a second digit, Nicole fisted the comforter, muttering unintelligibly. My patience had worn thin, so I pumped my fingers in and out while my tongue zeroed in on her swollen clit. I needed her climax like I needed fucking air. The compulsion to please my mate was overriding everything else.

And when Nicole came apart for the first time, it was glorious. I had never seen a more stunning sight, watching my mate throwing her head back in rapture, chest rising and falling with labored breaths as her silky thighs squeezed my head like a vise. It was better than I'd ever imagined—and my imagination had been pretty damn vivid.

After eating her through two more orgasms, I couldn't wait any longer. I *needed* to feel her riding me. To know firsthand how her pussy felt wrapped around my cock. As difficult as it was, I pulled away from Nicole to dig through the pocket of my jeans, retrieving a condom from my wallet before discarding my pants and boxers in one go. Nicole's periwinkle gaze was locked on me the entire time I ripped the foil open and slid the rubber down my shaft.

"Last chance to back out, baby."

She sat up on her elbows, spreading her thighs invitingly. Her sweet cunt glistened with arousal, making my dick jerk in my hand. "I'm not going to back out, Alexei. I want this. I want *you*."

I climbed on top of her, lining myself up against her entrance. I captured her mouth in a kiss at the same time I pushed forward, burying myself to the hilt in one long stroke.

"God," she gasped against my lips.

I moved slowly in short, shallow thrusts, giving Nicole time to adjust to my girth. "You're killing me, Nicole. So. Fucking. Tight."

Her nails scored my back as she wet her lips. "*Move*, Alexei. I won't break."

Nicole's spine arched in the most seductive way as I heeded her command and increased my pace. I drove myself in deeper, her breath catching each time as my hips pistoned with a little extra punch. We kissed as we found a rhythm together, the heat between us blazing with its intensity. My fingers dropped to her clit, rubbing circles around the sensitive bundle of nerves, the pressure in her body building and building until her muscles were so tight she imploded.

Her pussy squeezed my shaft, pulsing through the remnants of her release. Sweat slicked our skin as I hitched her leg up higher, hooking it over my elbow as I went impossibly deep. The smell of sex filled the air. The sounds of our bodies slapping against each other was the sweetest symphony I'd ever heard. Nicole cried out as I hit the perfect spot inside of her, rubbing up against it until she exploded once again. Lightning barreled down my spine as I followed immediately after, groaning with my forehead pressed against my mate's shoulder.

I held her tightly as we lay there waiting for our breaths to slow. And in that moment, I knew I would never get enough of this. Of her.

Nicole Fairweather wasn't just my mate.

She was my motherfucking queen.

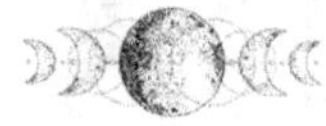

WE WOKE up to the sound of loud knocking.

"C'mon, Nicky," Corbin whined. "Macey and I had a great night and all, but I can't hold her off any longer. She wants you." There was a commotion out in the hall, followed by a slam against the door. "Calm down, puppy! She's coming!" More knocking. "C'mon!"

Nicole groaned as I rolled out of bed, pulling my jeans on. "Hold your tits. I'll be right there."

I unlocked the door and opened it just enough for the black wolf to come barreling through the door. I swear the thing gave me the pissiest look I've ever seen. She jumped onto the bed and started licking Nicole's face.

"Mace!" Nicole giggled, turning her face away from the slobber. "I'm fine! Down, girl!"

The familiar whimpered as she climbed off the bed and went straight for her water bowl.

"Have a good night, brother?" Corbin wagged his brows from his position on the other side of the door.

I started closing the door. "Goodbye, Corbin."

"Wait!" He stuck his foot in the crack. "C'mon, dude. We need to get going before the masses wake up and catch you doing your walk of shame."

Shit. He was right.

I didn't like the term he used, because there was *nothing* shameful about my night with Nicole. But we *did* need to be more careful.

I cleared my throat. "Give me a minute."

Corbin nodded and stepped back so I could shut the door.

"Time to go?" Nicole rolled onto her side, pulling the comforter over her chest.

Fuck, what a sight to wake up to.

"I don't want to."

What I *wanted was* to crawl back into bed with her and go for round four. Sadly, I was out of condoms and Nicole wasn't on birth control. As much as I loved the idea of watching her belly swell with my child, the timing wasn't right. Sure, people our age had kids all the time, but until I knew I could keep my mate safe, I sure as hell wasn't going to bring a new pup into this world and put them at risk as well.

But damn. The thought of her being pregnant with my child took my breath away.

"What are you thinking about right now?" Nicole's luscious lips curved into a sleepy smile. "You have a goofy grin on your face."

"You probably don't want me to answer that." After last night, I think it was safe to say Nicole was warming up to our mating bond, but she still clung to her human ideals like a lifeline. It was probably a little too soon to start trying to convince her to have my babies.

She pouted when I grabbed my shirt off the floor and pulled it over my head. "More wolfy caveman thoughts?"

I laughed. "You could say that."

Her pretty blue eyes danced with humor. "Come here and kiss me goodbye, Alexei."

She didn't need to tell me twice.

I jumped on the bed, careful not to crush her, much to the familiar's dismay. Macey growled as I kissed the shit out of my mate. She even resorted to nipping at my feet until I pulled away with a curse.

Nicole thought the whole thing was hilarious, but I didn't find Mace's tantrum nearly as amusing.

I pointed at Macey. "Get used to it, dog."

The wolf whimpered, making Nicole laugh again.

"Aw, be nice to my baby, Alexei. She's just trying to protect me."

I planted one more quick kiss on her swollen lips as I slid my foot into my shoes. "You don't need protection from me. You're *my mate*, and that bond trumps a familiar bond any day."

More growling.

"I think Mace would agree to disagree."

"Don't care." Okay, maybe just one more kiss. I groaned as Nicole clung to me, not wanting this moment to end any more than I did. The blanket slipped down in the process, revealing her more-than-a-handful breasts. Pure male satisfaction coursed through me as I spotted the stubble burn across her skin. "I really need to go before I say *fuck it* and climb back into bed with you."

She gave me a little shove. "Go. I'll text you later."

I turned the doorknob, hesitating for a moment. "Good luck at Pref Night."

"Thank you."

I hated that we both had another busy day ahead of us. But this was the last rush event, so hopefully things would slow down a bit afterward. As president,

I needed to meet with my pack to complete the list of who'd be getting a formal invitation tonight, which was always cumbersome, no matter how quickly we tried to move it along. Nicole wanted to spend the day with her dad meal prepping before she had to get ready for her first house visit.

With one more glance, I stepped into the hall where Corbin was waiting. He waited until we were in the elevator before speaking.

"So... how was it?"

I folded my arms across my chest. "How was *what*?"

"Oh, c'mon, man. Don't be like that. How was your night with Nicole? Specifically, the bow chicka wow wow? Was it everything you ever dreamed of and more? And don't even try lying to me, because you *reek* like you've been dining on and drilling pussy all night."

"You're ridiculous." I laughed, telling my cock to stand down at the thought of doing just that. "And I am *not* discussing this with you."

"All the answer I need, brother!" He held his arms up in a touchdown pose. "I do have one serious question, though."

Oh, this oughta be good. "What's that?"

Corbin seemed to be choosing his words carefully. "With your bond... was there a noticeable difference? I heard screwing your mate is like upper echelon shit. No matter how great sex has been for you in the past, it doesn't even come close to being with your mate. Is that true?"

I didn't answer him, because, best friend or not, I would not discuss my sex life with my mate. I was sure the giant grin plastered across my face said it all, though. Was sex with Nicole the best I'd ever had? Did every other encounter I'd had pale in comparison?

Abso-fucking-lutely.

TWENTY-EIGHT

Nicole

I woke up feeling warm from the inside out. My limbs were languid, and my heart was swollen with emotions. Last night was so intense. It felt like Alexei and I were finally on the same page. Our bodies moved perfectly together, like intricate choreography. All this time, I knew that we had chemistry—that we were connected in a way that made little sense—but last night really solidified that for me. It was strange to vibe so well with him, but also a relief.

But no matter how wonderful it was, I still had this inkling sense of doubt. I couldn't help thinking it all seemed too good to be true. Sure, we had these intense connections, but they were always eclipsed by life and shifter politics. It seemed as if there was always something waiting in the wings to ruin our chance at happiness.

I thought I would feel excited when I got dressed for Pref Night. The champagne-colored jeweled dress I wore was the very gown my mother had on the night she pledged all those years ago. My father had saved it, and although we had to have it altered, wearing it felt like such a beautiful tribute to the woman who I never got to meet.

The floor-length chiffon had a slit up the thigh and a tight bodice that pushed my breasts up. It dipped low at the back, exposing a lot of skin while still feeling classy.

I'd hoped to feel accomplished and beautiful while staring at myself in the mirror, but I felt conflicted. A few weeks ago, I would have been thrilled to know that Beta Phi was accepting me. But now that I'd seen how much I didn't fit in, I couldn't conjure up any excitement. Not to mention, the fact that Alexei's father wanted to use me didn't sit right.

I felt like a pawn nobody wanted.

That was a lie. *Alexei wanted me.* I just had to trust that he would protect me during all of this.

I turned in my official application to Kappa Zeta, which according to Juniper, she and her sisters were excited about. Thankfully, each sorority scheduled the start of their Pref Night events at different times in case someone was pledging more than one house like I was, so I didn't need to worry about missing out. Even though my heart wasn't in Beta Phi anymore, I still felt like I needed to see this through. And okay, maybe a part of me wanted to see the look on Mara's face when I declined their invitation.

If what Alexei said was true, that is.

It wasn't that I doubted him, but I wondered whether Mara would comply with an order she clearly disagreed with. As president of the sorority, she would have ultimate control tonight, and as she'd already proven, she wasn't afraid to defy her alpha.

I supposed we would see shortly.

I grabbed my small rainbow-sequined clutch and headed out of my dorm toward Greek Row with Macey at my side. My wolf seemed alert and on edge, her eyes scanning the road with the intensity of a bodyguard as we walked. There was a hint of fall in the air, but my heart was pumping wildly enough with anticipation to ward off the slight chill. As I approached the Beta Phi house, a sense of unease washed over me. I shook it off, telling myself it was just nerves as I climbed the front steps and rang the bell.

Mara swung open the door, a cruel smile fixed upon her face. "Ah, the guest of honor is here.

Welcome, Nicole. We are *so* glad you came." There was definitely a hint of sarcasm in her tone. It didn't sit right with me, but my doubts were put on hold when she wrapped her manicured hand around my wrist and pulled me inside the house. Macey growled at her tight hold on me, and she released me. "I see you brought your pet."

"I don't go anywhere without my familiar." I didn't like that Mara was diminishing Macey's role in my life by calling her a pet.

"Familiar. Sure," Mara replied with a wink, like she was placating me.

Fucking bitch.

They decorated every inch of the Beta Phi house with balloons, streamers, and flowers. Shifter girls fluttered around in their dresses, giggling with others and hugging. Aside from Mara's greeting, no one seemed to notice me.

I was an outsider. I didn't belong here.

I knew in my heart that I was making the right decision by turning them down.

"Make yourself at home," Mara said. "I'm sure you have *so* many friends you'd like to catch up with. The festivities start soon. I invited Alexei and Corbin to be our guests of honor. They're so excited about all I have planned."

A twinge of insecurity hit me for a brief moment. I

saw how all these she-wolves looked at Alexei. I was positive he'd taken more than a few of them to bed. As I observed the women around me interacting with one another as if they were family, I thought about how much easier Alexei's life would be if I stepped back. If I took myself out of the running so he could find a fellow shifter to be with. I would never be accepted like literally any other woman in this house would. His pack wouldn't question his leadership abilities. They wouldn't challenge his position as their alpha.

But Alexei said there was no turning back after last night. He said he wouldn't be able to stay away from me.

But that wasn't entirely accurate, though, was it?

I knew from my information download that there were two stages of solidifying a mate bond. The first was physical intimacy, which obviously had been covered multiple times last night. The second was a bonding ceremony under the light of the full moon. Supposedly, an ancient magic washed over both of you once certain vows were made and the lunar goddess gave you her blessing. The magic was so powerful any other shifter could easily recognize it, and the goddess's blessing demanded the utmost respect within the shifter community. Once both rituals had been completed, the bond was unbreakable.

In theory, anyway.

What if the goddess rejected our bond?

Would Alexei drop me like a bad habit?

I shook off the thought. I knew Alexei had potent feelings for me. You couldn't fake what we'd shared last night. I had felt nothing like it before.

I was lost in my thoughts and hadn't noticed Mara leaning closer to me. I'd thought she'd walked off to mingle with the other shifters. My spine stiffened as her nose brushed against my neck. She inhaled deeply, a look of fury crossing her features.

"You smell," she noted.

I arched my brow. "I'm sorry? What did you say?"

She breathed me in again, her eyes practically rolling back. "You smell like *him*."

I swallowed. Could the shifters smell Alexei on me? I knew they had superior senses, but I thought my shower was enough to throw them off. Apparently not.

I'd opened my mouth to say something—anything—but a heavy hand on my shoulder stopped me in my tracks.

"Hello, Nicole," Alexei's voice purred.

Mara glared at the two of us, and I reluctantly relaxed under his touch. I wasn't sure where we stood or how I was supposed to act now that we had stopped fighting our attraction for one another.

Turning, I looked at Alexei and nearly melted. He looked damn good in a suit. His hair was gelled to the side, and the slight scruff on his jaw made me lick my lips.

"Thank you for the invite, Mara." He gave her a pointed look before removing his hand from my shoulder. "I heard my father called this morning."

Mara's face twisted up, as if she'd swallowed a tart lemon. "Yes. Your father called and made his expectations very clear. I'm nothing but a dutiful member of the pack." She gave a slight bow. "In fact, I need to make sure everything is ready. If you'll excuse me."

Mara sauntered off, swaying her hips and smiling at the other shifters in the room. I released the breath I was holding and took a step away from Alexei.

"You shouldn't stand so close," I whispered. "Mara said she could smell you on me."

Alexei had the audacity to look proud of himself. "I guess I marked you last night," he growled.

"And you're not worried?"

"I probably should be, but I'm not. I've got a plan, Nicole. Everything is going to work out. You'll see." He leaned closer, brushing a wisp of hair away from my face.

"Alexei..." Jeez, I was practically panting. "This is dangerous."

"I know," he whispered against my ear. "But I

can't seem to help myself. I can't stop thinking about last night." I shivered as the bridge of his nose brushed against my lobe. "And how badly I want to do it again. Fuck, Nicole, this hunger inside of me feels like it'll never be sated. But I'm willing to try as many times as we need to."

"I can't stop thinking about it either." I fought a smile and forced myself to take a step back. "And I feel just as starved."

My nipples hardened against the inside of my bra. Thank God the material was thick enough to hide the evidence of my arousal.

Alexei's gaze briefly scanned the room before training his dark eyes back on me. "I think we have time before the ceremony starts. Wanna go find a closet?"

I laughed, thinking he was joking, but when I saw the unmistakable lust in his expression, my eyes rounded as I whisper-shouted, "Are you crazy?!"

"Crazy for *you*. C'mon, they won't even notice. I bet I could make you come in under a minute, and we'll be back before you know it." He winked.

I damn near gave in, despite the fact that something like that would be incredibly stupid under the circumstances. If the cocky smile stretched across Alexei's handsome face was any indication, he knew it, too.

"Nuh-uh." I took another step back and shook my head. "Don't you have some alpha things you should be doing right now?" I made a shooing motion. "Go on, do 'em."

He laughed. "It can wait."

Before I could reply, a round of applause scattered throughout the room as Mara started walking toward the makeshift stage.

I nodded to her. "Looks like time's up."

"We'll pick this up later," Alexei promised before striding away, giving me an excellent view of his muscular butt in those dark slacks.

Mara stood on stage, a smirk on her face as she adjusted the microphone. "Thank you all for coming tonight. As you might have noticed, we have some special guests in attendance. Future alpha, Alexei Koenig, and his beta, Corbin Sullivan, are joining us tonight. The three of us have been working on a project for a few weeks, a bit of entertainment for all of you."

My breath caught in my chest. Alexei walked on stage, a proud smile on his face. *What was she talking about?*

Mara turned to the projector screen behind her and grinned as a video popped up. The screen was black, which confused me even more, but when I heard Mara's voice, I realized a voice recording had been dubbed over it.

"Come on, bro. Tell me what's really going on. Alexei is acting strange around Nicole."

After clearing his throat, Corbin's voice rang through the speakers. "Look, it's nothing you need to worry about."

"Tell me," Mara whined, the tone of her compulsion laced in the command.

"Don't worry about who he sticks his dick into, Mara. It's none of your business."

"So he *is* sticking his dick in her?" Mara pressed. "I thought *you* were dating her."

"Nah. After Antonio slipped her the reveal spell, she was immune to my charms." Corbin laughed. "But it was obvious she *was* attracted to Alexei, so we altered our plan."

"*What* plan?" Mara asked.

"You know her dad is important to Alpha Jones. He wanted her to feel at home so her dad would cooperate. We decided what better way to make her comfortable than to loosen her up with a few orgasms? It's harmless. Truly. And she may be human, but she's hot as fuck, so it's not exactly a hardship for whoever had to bang her."

"You're telling me Alpha Jones wanted you to *fuck* her?" Mara's tone was accusatory.

"No, I'm saying he told us to make sure she didn't do something stupid like decide to drop out and take her father with her." Corbin let loose another playful laugh. "We made an executive decision. We figured Nicole would want to stick around if Alexei licked her clit every so often. Chicks love riding his face. Among other things. You should know. You've been practically begging for his cock since we were sixteen. You have to admit, it's a brilliant strategy. If Nicole is too busy being stuffed by Alexei's cock, then she's—"

Mara's response was stiff and full of anger. "I don't need any more disgusting visuals, thanks. I get the point."

My mouth dropped open in shock. I looked at Corbin, my eyes watering as he held his hands up. "Nicole. No, I um..." Instead of finishing his sentence, he ran for the back of the room where someone was controlling the video.

Mara laughed when she saw how mortified I was, a look of pure, evil glee painted across her face as the pledges joined in.

Her green eyes bore into mine as she said, "Just wait, sweetheart. The best is yet to come."

Macey paced in front of me, whimpering as she sensed the tension in the room. All eyes were on me, and I wanted to cower and hide. Alexei was breathing heavily as he stood by Mara's side, but he said nothing.

Why wasn't he saying something?

I gasped as an image popped up on the screen and the footage started playing. I was frozen in place, my stomach clenching as I watched Alexei on top of me, his ass flexing as he pumped in and out. My cheeks reddened as my guttural groans and the sound of skin smacking against skin blared through the speakers.

Some of the shifter girls squealed and giggled. Some of them booed when I moaned Alexei's name.

I felt a heavy sense of dread. I glared at Alexei as a fresh wave of tears fell down my cheeks. He wasn't even looking at the screen. He was watching me carefully, waiting for my reaction.

"You filmed us?! How could you?"

I didn't care how many witnesses we had. I wanted answers. No one else was in my room last night, just Corbin and Alexei. One of them had to have set up a camera, and now the entire house was witnessing a very private moment.

Excited murmuring caught Alexei's attention. He looked around, his expression locked on the corner of the room. I didn't follow his gaze, I was too consumed with my need for answers. I didn't want to miss a thing. I needed him to find a way to explain what was happening that didn't make everything we shared over the last month seem like one big joke. But when Alexei's shoulders relaxed and an easygoing expression slipped across his features, I knew I wouldn't like what was about to come out of his mouth.

"Come on, babe. It was fun while it lasted." He smirked, as if he didn't give one flying fuck that I was being humiliated right now. In fact, he seemed to revel in it. I also noticed that he didn't deny filming us.

What was the purpose of all of this?

I stalked closer to the stage. "Was I a joke to you? Are we even really fated mates?"

Someone gasped loudly. Others started voicing their shock, making me realize I'd just admitted our secret in front of his entire pack.

Fuck.

"Mates?" Mara repeated. "That's impossible. You're not *worthy* of a mate like Alexei. Tell her, babe!"

Alexei's nostrils flared. He scanned the room once more, and then to my horror, he scoffed. "Shifters can't mate with humans, Nicole. That was a little white lie to get you to spread your legs. What's the problem? We had some fun. You got off more than a few times. If anything, you should be thanking me. Do you even know how lucky you are to have me as a notch on your bedpost?"

Lucky?

I raced through every interaction we'd ever had,

doubt tainting my mind and making me second-guess everything. "I can't believe this."

Mara interrupted as the video was abruptly shut off. I spun around and saw Corbin arguing with the girl in charge of the presentation in the back.

"You were just screwing me—*manipulating me*—so... what? My father would continue his research here?"

Something about this story wasn't adding up. I was willing to stay long before I met Alexei. I didn't care about dating him. In fact, I was happy walking away from this insanity when he claimed we were mates. I *tried* walking away.

He shrugged. "I wasn't sure if we could get you into Beta Phi, so I gave you another reason to stay. But now that you're in, there's no point for us to continue fucking, unless you want to, of course. You weren't bad in bed. Maybe even top twenty." He gave me a smarmy wink that made me want to puke all over the polished hardwoods.

No. I refused to believe this was happening. There had to be a reasonable explanation.

"Alexei, can we talk about this in private?" Tears blurred my vision.

This wasn't him. It couldn't be true. Maybe Mara was somehow pulling the strings with her compulsion. Maybe she found a way to compel an alpha.

Alexei looked around the room and laughed. "She wants my dick again already! What do you say? Should I throw the human a bone?"

More laughter boomed in my ears, and I practically cowered at the cruel sounds. Macey touched her cold nose to my hand, prodding me to move.

Alexei looked off to the side once more before turning his attention back to me. "Look, Nicole. I think you need to chill out. No need to go all Stage-Five Clinger on me. You wanted to know what it's like to be a shifter, so I gave you a taste. You wanted to join Beta Phi, and I made it happen. Welcome to the pack, human. Now you know how amazing it could be and that you'll *never actually* be one of us."

A roar of approval erupted, cheers echoing off the walls as his voice washed over me. It felt like I'd been punched in the gut.

So I did what any sensible person would do if they were publicly humiliated by the man they were falling for.

I ran.

CHAPTER

TWENTY-NINE

Nicole

FAT TEARS blinded me as my familiar and I ran from Beta Phi. Thank God for Mace. I don't think I would've gotten out of there without her. It felt like the house was closing in on me the moment I started to flee. The crowd seemed to thicken as I waded through jeering bodies. But one warning growl from my familiar had them parting like the Red Sea so I could make my exit.

The dark campus welcomed me and my gloomy mood as I made my way toward Dad's lab. Mace kept scanning the road, making sure none of the cruel pledges were following us. I couldn't believe what had just happened. Alexei's harsh words were ringing on repeat in my mind.

"You should consider yourself lucky..."

I started walking faster and faster, my feet practically flying across the pavement as tears streamed down my cheeks. I asked myself question after question.

Was any of it real?

Did Alexei ever like me?

Was Corbin ever my friend?

Why was I even fucking here anymore?

Though devastated by what all had happened, by the time I got to my father's lab, a fresh wave of anger was coursing through my veins. My life had gone to complete shit ever since I'd gotten to Redwood University. I never asked for any of this. I didn't want to know about the monsters under my bed or the potential legacy my mother was truly leaving behind. None of it made sense, and I wanted to run away from all of it before it destroyed me.

"Dad!" I bellowed once through the doors. He was hunched over a table, tinkering with a microscope when he jumped on his stool from the sound of my frantic voice.

"Nicole? Are you okay?" He braced his hands on my shoulders. "What's wrong, honey? Why are you crying?"

I sniffled. "I can't do it anymore, Dad. I can't stay here."

He frowned, handing me a tissue from the box on one of the counters. "What? What do you mean? What happened?" He pulled a stool out from under the table and patted it. "Sit down and tell me everything."

I shook my head. "I don't have time. Just please, I need you to trust me. This university, the people who run it, they're not what they seem. They're horrible people, Dad, and we need to get as far away from them as soon as possible."

The crease between his brows deepened. "Nicole. Slow down. Is this about a boy?"

I laughed humorlessly. "I wish it were that simple."

This may have started because of *a boy*, but we were so beyond that at this point. An entire world I never knew existed had been laid before me. And it was a cruel, cutthroat society I had no interest in being a part of.

I tugged on the sleeve of his white lab coat. "Please, Dad. I can explain in the car. But we can't stay here."

"What do you mean we can't stay here? I have a job, honey. You have school. We can't just leave."

"We *need* to." I choked back a sob. "These people are dangerous, Dad. They don't care about anyone but themselves. I know this is your dream job, and I would never blindly ask you to give that up. You know me.

You know that. I just need a little faith from you right now."

"Sweetheart, I'm on the verge of a monumental breakthrough. If I left... I don't know if I can make as much progress as I'd need to without access to all of the equipment and funding I have at Redwood. When Mr. Koenig offered me—"

"*Mr. Koenig* threatened my life." I didn't mean to just blurt that out, but the look on my dad's face told me it got his attention.

"What?!"

I tugged on his arm again. "I'll explain in the car. You're parked out front right?"

"Yes," he confirmed, reluctantly following me across the lab. "But I can't just leave, Nicole. At the very least, I need to grab the boxes from my house. I never got around to unpacking, so it wouldn't take long. My research is there... memories of your mom. I can't leave that."

I sighed. "Okay. Let's go back to your place and grab your stuff. I swear I'll explain everything once we're away from this godforsaken university."

I supposed I could stop by my room as well and throw all my things in my suitcases. I didn't bring much, so it would be quick and easy. Sure, I might have been humiliated and heartbroken beyond belief right now, but I didn't feel like there was an immediate threat to our safety. Anyone who witnessed what happened to me tonight likely thought I was back in my dorm by now, throwing myself a pity party. Or they were too busy partying it up back at the sorority, laughing at my expense.

Alexei and Mara were probably having their own special little celebration up in her room.

I choked back bile at the thought.

"You know, if you weren't so mature for your age, I wouldn't be agreeing to anything without a full set of facts laid out before me. I'm talking a PowerPoint presentation listing the pros and cons of leaving versus staying and at least thirty possible alternatives, along with projected possible outcomes based on historical human behavior."

I offered the most genuine smile I could manage at my dad's attempt to inject some levity into this conversation using his nerdy humor. Unfortunately, I didn't think data on human behavior would help in this situation, considering we weren't dealing with humans at all.

Dad shrugged off his lab coat and looked around. "Are you sure we have to leave tonight? Maybe you should sleep on it? If he threatened you, we need to call the police."

I pinched the bridge of my nose. Dad was analytical and reasonable. I knew that I had to find a way to appeal to his morals.

"Dad." He stopped fidgeting with his collar to look at me. "Mr. Koenig has the police in his pocket. He's powerful—more powerful than you can imagine."

He straightened. "I'm not doubting you, Nicole. I'm just trying to make sense of this. You're here out of the blue and not giving me much to go off of. If he's threatening you, then we need to go to the police."

"I'll go to the police. I'll tell you everything. I promise. But not in this town. Hell, not until we're a thousand miles away from this place. We don't have the resources to go against him on his turf. Please. *Please* believe me, Dad."

He made his way over to me and grabbed my hand. "Sweetheart, you're my daughter. I'm always on your team. If you say we're in danger here, I believe you. Okay? I *believe* you. Let's get our things and leave."

I hugged him tightly, thankful that in this crazy world of shifters, vampires, witches, and fae, I could still count on him. My father had always been in my corner, and right now I needed him more than ever.

He wrapped his arm around me, on alert as we walked back outside. "Did anyone see you come here

—holy mother of Jesus Christ fucking hell." He jumped back and nearly fell on his ass, his face pale as a sheet of paper as he pointed at Mace, who was sitting guard on the front steps. "Nicole, don't make any sudden movements, but we need to get back inside."

It took me a moment to figure out what was making him freak out. "Oh, don't worry about Macey. She's my fa—my new pet."

My father's eyebrows shot toward his hairline. "Your pet?! First of all, since when do they allow pets in dormitories? Secondly, that's a full-grown wolf, Nicole. Not a pet!"

I held my hand out. "Mace, come here, girl."

Macey eyed my dad warily as she approached before nudging me with her snout, leaning into my touch as I scratched behind her ear. "See? Hold your hand out. Let her sniff you."

My dad looked at me like I'd grown three heads, but he slowly extended his hand, allowing my familiar to take in his scent. I stroked her back as she sniffed him before her giant pink tongue reached out to slather his palm with kisses. My father laughed nervously, looking half intrigued and half ready to piss himself.

I smiled. "I think she likes you."

"I'm so confused." There was awe in his tone as she nuzzled him. "Where did you find her? How long have you had her?"

I jerked my head toward his Civic parked a few spots down. "C'mon, I'll answer all your questions along the way."

I opened the rear passenger door after my dad unlocked his car, telling Mace to hop in before I slid into the front seat and buckled up. My dad took his place behind the wheel, glancing in the rearview at my beautiful black wolf as he started the ignition.

"Has she been in a car before?"

I looked back at her, waiting for some telepathy to conveniently kick in. Man, I wished Juniper were here. I frowned as I retracted that thought, wondering if the purple-haired witch's kindness was all a front, too. Was anything I'd experienced since coming to Redwood U real?

I cleared my throat, overcome with sadness again. "That's a good question. I'm not sure. I found her in the woods on campus. I was lost... she helped me find my way. She's barely left my side since."

My dad offered me a small smile. "How long ago was that?"

"Not long." I shrugged. "But I feel like she's been with me for years."

Dad drove slowly to his apartment, as if tonight was just a leisurely ride through campus and not us fleeing. I wanted him to put his foot on the gas, but he kept his hands at ten and two, leaning forward with his eyes squinted on the dark road.

"Don't let me forget to pack my cell phone charger. Do you think we have time to grab that new cookware set I bought?"

I calmed my breathing, trying not to be frustrated with him. "Just the essentials, Dad."

"Fine, fine," he replied grumpily.

When we pulled up to the apartment, I told Mace to stay in the car, and we walked up to the front door. Dad clutched his keys and kept listing things we needed to grab. "My laptop is in my bedroom. Your mother's box is in the storage closet. I've got some research I need to organize on the kitchen table."

He slowly unlocked the door, and I started running through the house, shoving items in boxes and duffel bags while Dad slowly sifted through the documents on his kitchen table.

"I suppose I should leave the research Mr. Koenig brought over?" He picked up a graph and peered at it.

I was about two seconds from shaking his shoulders and forcing him to move with purpose. "Take whatever you want, Dad. We have to go!"

I ran a box of mom's belongings and Dad's laptop out to the car, popping the trunk and carefully setting it inside. The small space didn't hold much, but we'd manage.

"What about my new plants, Nicole?" Dad called from inside. "I just bought them!"

I took a steadying breath. "Sure, Dad. Hurry up, we still need to stop by my dorm."

I was about to go back inside, but Macey started barking furiously and scratching at the window, drawing my attention.

"What is it, girl?" I glanced out into the darkness, but my eyes couldn't make out anything. Why didn't they have street lamps here? The small bulbs adorning each porch hardly gave out much light. Macey continued to bark, and just as I put my hand on the door handle to let her out, I saw why. I froze as a group of shadows moved toward me in perfect synchrony.

"Oh, fuck."

"Nicole?" my dad called as he stepped outside. "What's all the ruckus about?"

A chorus of menacing growls rang through the air as the group of at least a dozen giant wolves approached us. Alexei's father stood in the middle of the pack in his human form, the promise of violence radiating off of him in waves, along with two burly men who screamed *bodyguard.*

The alpha somehow knew we were trying to leave. And now he was here to stop us.

I glanced back at my father and found him staring off into space.

"What the hell?" I rushed up to him, waving a hand in front of his face. "Dad. Get in the car. We need to go now!" I shook him. "Dad!"

"Heading somewhere, Miss Fairweather? Or may I call you Nicole... considering how well acquainted you and my son are?" Mr. Koenig stepped forward, brushing a piece of imaginary lint off his suit.

"Dad!" I pulled on his arm, but I couldn't make him snap out of whatever trance he was in. I turned my gaze on the alpha. "What did you do to him?"

"Watch how you speak to me, girl," Mr. Koenig sneered. "And *I* didn't do anything to him. But I would like to know *who* did so I can get them to fix it."

"Dad," I tried again, fighting back tears.

What the hell was wrong with him?

"Don't bother." Alexei's father laughed mockingly. "If my team of witches can't remove the block on his mind, a sniveling human certainly can't."

Shit. This was the block Alexei was talking about.

"We don't want any trouble." I held my palms out. "We just want to leave."

"Oh, you pathetic girl." Mr. Koenig tsked. "If you

think there's any chance of that happening, you're not nearly as smart as my son tried giving you credit for. Your father is my *asset*. He is not going *anywhere* until he figures out how to reverse the genetic mutation my people are suffering from."

"What are you talking about?"

"Aw, did my son not fill you in on our plans during pillow talk?"

I glared at him. "I am *not* talking to you about Alexei."

The wolves growled until he put a hand up to silence them. "Watch how you're speaking to me. I don't enjoy repeating myself, so this will be your final warning." Mr. Koenig took a threatening step closer to me. "I don't particularly care who you fuck. My son obviously has his priorities mixed up, and if he wants to use your body in his spare time to release some stress, who am I to stop him? I personally think humans are lackluster lovers, but they're good enough when you're bored." He laughed at his own joke.

I nearly vomited.

"Stop." My voice was weak, though I wanted to sound more authoritative. I didn't like the way this man made my skin crawl.

"My point is... you'll be staying here until I no longer find you useful. You're definitely not going to leave without my permission."

I turned to Dad, willing him to wake up and snap out of his trance. "Dad. Please. I need you."

At that moment, I felt like I had no one. I couldn't trust Alexei. Everyone at this damn campus was the enemy. Dad mumbled something to himself, and I shook him harder. The charm on my neck started to burn as I turned all my attention on him. I just wanted my dad to be okay. I wanted someone to believe me.

"Dad!"

I was at my breaking point, my nerves shot, my mind full of all the betrayal and insanity of my time here at Redwood University.

"Someone please shut her up," Mr. Koenig demanded with a bored roll of his eyes.

Heat from my charm necklace started to travel through my limbs. It was a fiery inferno igniting all my cells as I clung to my father. Two wolves stalked closer to me, making my panic rise more and more. The burning sensation swirled around my chest, making every thudding pound of my pulse ignite and spread the warmth from the top of my hair to the bottom of my feet. I could feel the hot energy burning the soles of my shoes, grounding me to the pavement and connecting me with something bigger, something dangerous.

"Dad!" I screamed once more, my words more ethereal, deadly almost. "Wake up!"

A burst of energy seemed to pass through me in a moment, knocking the two wolves that were closing in on me back a few feet. Mr. Koenig took a step back, his eyes wide as I hugged my father.

Dad's stiff posture slowly released. His shaky arms tentatively wrapped around me. His whispers danced along my ear, and I gasped at the words that escaped his lips.

"I remember..."

I pulled away from him, my eyes squinting in the dark at his shocked expression. He looked around at the wolves with terror. "Shifters... Nicole... Nicole we have to..."

Mr. Koenig took large strides toward us, gripping my small wrist with his large hand. He pulled me aside as he motioned for the two men on either side of him to close in on my father. Mace barked and howled wildly as she bounced around the interior of the car.

"No!" I struggled as the two meatheads grabbed my father, but the alpha's hold on me was so tight it felt like he was one breath away from snapping my bones.

I cried out when he fisted my long hair, yanking it until my neck bent back at an awkward angle.

"Nicole!" my dad yelled right before one of the beefy guys put him in a headlock, choking off his protest.

"Dad!" I screamed again, scrambling as much as I could while being restrained.

"Gentlemen, please take Dr. Fairweather to his new *accommodations*. And be careful. I need his brain intact, especially now that that pesky block seems to have magically gone away. I'll be in touch after I take care of this problem."

Meathead Number One nodded. "Yes, Alpha."

"Wait!" I begged as the two men bound my father's hands behind his back and started hauling him away. My dad was fighting the best he could, but his wiry frame was really no match for them. He grunted in pain as they tossed him into the back of a waiting SUV. "Where are you taking him?"

Alexei's father tightened his grasp on me, pulling me against his hard chest. He groaned as I tried wriggling out of his hold, and I stopped moving entirely when I felt his dick harden against my back.

So gross.

"Listen here, you little slut." His warm breath wafted over my cheek as he spoke into my ear. "This is how it's going to go. First of all, you're going to tell me how you just removed the block from the wacky scientist's head. And if you value your miserable life at all, you will not even *think* about bullshitting me."

"I don't know!" I whimpered as he pulled my hair

even harder, practically bending me in half backwards.

He considered that for a moment. "You'll be sorry if I find out you're lying."

"I'm not lying!" I swore. "Please don't hurt my father. I'll do whatever you want."

"Oh, you'll be doing that regardless." He released a dark chuckle. "But your father's days will be infinitely more enjoyable if you cooperate."

"What are you going to do with him? Where did those men take him?"

"Don't you worry your pretty little head about that. For now, you're going to go back to your dorm room and pretend this whole thing never happened. Before you get any stupid ideas, if you say a word to anyone about this, I *will* know, and you *will* pay. I'll be watching you, Nicole. *Never* forget that. I'll have one of my representatives reach out to you in the morning with your next set of instructions. If you know what's good for you, you'll follow them to the letter. Are we clear?"

Every instinct in my body told me to rebel, to stand up to the cruel alpha taking my father hostage. But I had to be smart about it. I had to obey if I wanted to get us out of here alive.

"Yes, sir," I gritted, though I was certain there was defiance in my icy gaze.

He preened. "Look at that. Seems you aren't completely useless after all. The hallmark of a good woman is knowing when to heel, Nicole. You just might survive if you keep your sense of self-preservation."

I imagined clawing his eyes out and told myself that the fantasy would have to do for now. I needed to put my father's safety first. But if this man—or his son for that matter—thought I would be a submissive little human they could crush in their fists, they were both in for a big surprise. A powerful buzz coursed through my veins, demanding action. I felt more alive and self-assured than I ever had. These vicious, vile people had awakened something within me, and there was no turning back now. I was going to save my father, and we were going to get the hell away from here no matter what it took.

I'd burn this entire university to the ground if I had to.

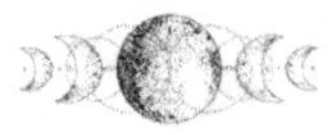

TO BE CONTINUED in To Save A Mate...

DO YOU NEED emotional support after that giant

cliff we left you hanging on? Do you want to simply yell at us, demanding book two immediately? Maybe you are just super stoked for all things Poppy and want access to exclusive previews? Join others like you in our Facebook reader's group, **Poppy Ireland's Little Witchlings**

About the Author

Poppy Ireland writes paranormal and fantasy romance. She is the brainchild of two longtime friends and *USA Today* Bestselling Authors who like to use their freaky mind melding powers to write spicy romantasy stories that will keep you on the edge of your seat.

If you're wondering who we are, well, that's a secret we'll never tell.

Xoxo,
Poppy

To stay up to date on all the latest news, sign up for Poppy's newsletter at: https://www.subscribepage. com/poppyirelandbooks

You can also find her on social media:

Facebook: @poppyirelandbooks
Instagram: @poppyirelandbooks
TikTok: @poppyirelandbooks
Goodreads: @poppyirelandbooks
BookBub: @poppyirelandbooks